Something from

MELISSA HILL

sourcebooks
landmark

Published by Sourcebooks Landmark, an imprint of Sourcebooks
P.O. Box 4410, Naperville, Illinois 60567-4410
(630) 961-3900
sourcebooks.com

Originally published as *A Gift from Tiffany's* in 2011 in the United Kingdom by
Hodder & Stoughton, an imprint of Hachette UK. This edition issued based on the
paperback edition published in 2012 in the United States by St. Martin's Press.

Printed and bound in the United States of America.
LSC 10 9 8 7 6 5 4 3 2 1

Dedicated again to my lovely Carrie,
the greatest gift of all.

Chapter 1

THE SIGNIFICANCE OF WHAT HE WAS ABOUT TO DO WASN'T LOST ON Ethan Greene. It was a big moment in his life, would be in any man's, he guessed.

But as he battled through the Manhattan crowds on possibly the busiest shopping day of the year, he now wished he'd chosen a better time.

Christmas Eve on Fifth Avenue? He must be mad.

Taking a deep breath of the cold air, which was refreshing and not as damp as it usually was in London, he couldn't help but think how little had changed since the last time he was in this city and, at the same time, how much had.

Arriving in New York only two days before, he'd surprised himself by how well he remembered the landmarks and how easily he found his way around. The jostle of the subway ride from Midtown to downtown and back again, the scent of well-worn vinyl taxi seats, and the endless hum of a billion voices—human or inanimate—buoyed him. The unmistakable buzz of the place put a new spring in his step, something he hadn't felt in years.

But now Ethan was in a hurry and acutely aware that the

minutes were ticking by, and the crowds seemed to be growing thicker. There wasn't much time left.

Alongside him, Daisy squeezed his hand briefly as if sensing what he was thinking, yet she really had no idea what he'd planned. All he'd said was that he needed to make one more stop before they returned to the warmth of their hotel.

Mindful of how much he hated crowds (and shopping for that matter), she was probably just trying to put him at ease.

How would she react? Okay, so the idea had been in the cards for a while and had been mentioned more than once recently, so by rights, today shouldn't really be too much of a surprise.

While she seemed keen, Ethan realized now that he really should have spoken to her about it in more detail. It was unlike him not to discuss such matters, but the truth was he was nervous. What if her reaction wasn't as positive as he'd anticipated? An anxious lump appeared in his throat. Well, he'd find out soon enough, especially when they reached their destination.

She looked especially pretty today, he thought, wrapped up in a multitude of layers to keep out the teeth-chattering cold, her blond curls creeping out under a dark woolen hat, and wearing a black embroidered cape. Despite the cold, she was loving New York just as he'd known she would, and everyone knew there was no better time than Christmas to visit the city. Yes, this was a good idea, Ethan reassured himself. Everything would work out fine.

Finally, having negotiated through the multitude of last-minute shoppers, they reached the corner of Fifth Avenue and Fifty-Seventh Street. He looked at Daisy, and her eyes widened in surprise as he took her hand and steered them both toward the entrance.

"What's going on?" she squealed, gazing at the familiar name-plate beside the doorway, its typically clean-line wording on polished granite, today surrounded by verdant pine branches especially for the Christmas season. "What do we need *here*?"

"I told you, I need to pick something up," Ethan replied, lead-ing the way and giving her a brief wink as the glass revolving doors deposited them into the hallowed halls of Tiffany & Co.

Daisy was immediately captivated by the vast, high-ceilinged shop floor and its column-free design, and she gazed in amazement at the long rows of glass-fronted cases, their precious wares twinkling alluringly under the spotlights.

"Oh wow, it's all so beautiful," she gasped, standing in awe in the middle of the aisle as crowds of equally captivated shoppers and tourists milled around, each one fascinated by the breathtaking jewelry displays. The store was one of the few in Manhattan that didn't utilize lavish festive decoration, its twinkling wares requir-ing little embellishment, and this combined with the unmistak-ably romantic Tiffany's allure was more than enough to create that magical Christmas feeling.

"It is, isn't it?" Ethan agreed, his nervousness dissipating some-what now they were here. He took her arm and guided her through the various display cases and down the back toward the elevators, his tired feet temporarily soothed by the soft-carpeted floor.

"Where are you going?" she asked, following him reluctantly. "Slow down a bit. Can't we take a look around? I've never been here before and… Where are we going?" she continued, bemused as the elevator doors opened.

"The second floor please," Ethan requested from the suited lift attendant.

"Certainly, sir," the man said and complied, bowing graciously beneath his top hat. He smiled at Daisy. "Madam."

"But why would be we going there?" she asked, her voice hushed, and he deduced she'd read from the directory display overhead what was on this particular floor.

Ethan's heart began to hammer in his chest as the elevator doors closed. Would she be okay with this? Again, he probably should have just come right out and asked, but he figured that she'd enjoy the surprise, and he also thought it was important that she felt very much a part of it. She was certainly taken with the place, but he knew she would really be impressed by the second floor.

His voice was light. "Like I said, I need to pick something up."

Now Daisy gazed at him with wide blue eyes. "You're not…" She gasped, immediately understanding, but from her expression, Ethan still couldn't quite gauge her reaction, and he guessed the presence of the attendant was intimidating her into not asking further questions.

Within seconds, the elevator doors reopened and he and Daisy stepped out into the wood-paneled room of Tiffany's famed Diamond Floor, where he had come to collect his purchase.

"I can't believe this," she said as they approached one of the hexagon-shaped wood-and-glass display cases, her head swiveling from left to right as she watched various happy couples around the room being served champagne while they made what would arguably be the most important purchase of their lives. "I really can't believe it! *This* is what you're picking up?"

Ethan smiled nervously. "I know I should have said something but—"

"Ah, Mr. Greene." An elderly, distinguished sales assistant addressed Ethan before either had a chance to say anything more. "Pleasure seeing you again. Everything is in order and ready to go. We weren't sure, and I forgot to ask on the phone if you preferred your purchase already gift wrapped or if you wanted to show the lady first." He smiled at Daisy, who beamed back at him, wide-eyed.

"Course I want to see it!" she exclaimed and then put a guilty hand to her mouth, evidently conscious that she really should be using a little more decorum—especially in a place like this.

Ethan hid a smile.

"Well, here we are," the older man said, his voice low and gentle as he presented them with the world-renowned little blue box. Placing it ceremoniously on the glass display in front of Daisy, he pulled back the lid to reveal the platinum marquise solitaire Ethan had chosen a couple of days before.

The ring had needed to be sized correctly, which was why he was picking it up today, and now considering it afresh, he was pretty sure he'd made a good choice. It was a classic Tiffany setting: the diamond lifted slightly above the band and held in place by six platinum prongs in order to maximize the stone's brilliance.

"So what do you think?" he asked Daisy, but it was pretty obvious from the expression on her face that she was captivated by the beautiful ring, although that wasn't really the question Ethan was asking.

But when she turned to look at him, her delighted expression told him everything he needed to know.

"It's the perfect choice, Daddy," Ethan's eight-year-old daughter assured him, "and Vanessa is going to absolutely *love* it!"

Chapter 2

THANK GOODNESS HER REACTION HAD BEEN POSITIVE.

All day—no, strike that—all *month*, Ethan had worried about how Daisy would feel about this. Especially when this New York trip held a special significance for both of them.

Earlier that day, over a couple of hot chocolates in a Midtown café, he had watched his daughter pick at an iced lemon cupcake and had known that something was on her mind. Just as her mother had always done, Daisy got that squinty look in her eyes and offset her jaw ever so slightly when deep in thought.

"Did you like Times Square?" he asked, fishing. "With all the lights and everything?"

She nodded. "Everything's just so beautiful," she replied and then paused, looking out the window at the bustling street. "Mum said Manhattan was like one big Christmas tree at this time of year. She was right."

"You really remember how much your mother talked about it, don't you?" he asked.

She gave a little smile. "I know I was only small, but I loved hearing about it."

Ethan nodded. "Of course, she was right about it being like a big Christmas tree. Your mum was right about lot of things."

Suddenly, the significance of sitting here with his daughter in the city that her mother had adored so much washed over Ethan and almost took his breath away. Swallowing hard, he tried to gather his thoughts.

"You know what else she was right about?"

Daisy looked intently at him as she always did whenever he had something about her mother to relate. It wasn't lost on him that his daughter was seldom more attentive than when he offered some piece of the puzzle whose parts probably seemed quite scattered to her. To him, it was as if she were an archivist of some sort, gathering and assembling the pieces of a great legacy and putting them in order.

Ethan continued with a smile, "She was right that you would grow into a bright and beautiful girl."

Daisy grinned and turned back to the window to watch the goings-on of a very busy Park Avenue on Christmas Eve.

It had been nine years since his last and only other trip here. Jane, Daisy's mum, had persuaded him to see the city, and making the trip from their home in London, see it they did.

Jane was a born-and-bred New Yorker and just couldn't bear to spend another springtime "without a stroll through Central Park as the flowers begin to bloom." She said dramatic things out of the blue like that now and then, to which Ethan usually responded by asking if it was actually her and not he who was the English language lecturer. "No, Professor," she would say with a wink. "You're the brainy, creative one around here, whereas I'm just a born romantic."

Jane's parents had retired to Florida in the meantime, so she rarely got to visit the city of her birth as often as she'd like.

Daisy had been conceived in the Big Apple during that visit nine years before. The running joke between them—one that Jane had no problem sharing with their friends and family—was that Daisy existed because they'd taken the expression "the city that never sleeps" quite literally.

As a personal trainer and nutritionist, Jane did her best to keep Ethan in tip-top shape, a fact that was all the more ironic when she'd developed ovarian cancer and discovered she had mere months to live.

Daisy was five at the time, and while Jane and Ethan were head over heels in love but had never gotten around to getting married, he'd wanted to change that, especially once they heard the news.

"Don't be ridiculous, sweetheart. We've been happy so far. Why change now?" Jane insisted. "Besides," she added jokingly, "soon I won't have enough hair left to hold a veil."

By then, Ethan would have gone along with anything she wished, and Jane had several last wishes.

One of them was that he take their daughter to visit New York at Christmas when she was old enough to appreciate and enjoy it. She had spent hours weaving for Daisy tales of the magic of Manhattan and her own childhood Christmases there.

When a few months back, Daisy herself started talking about making the trip, Ethan knew it was time.

One evening over dinner, he mentioned the idea to his girlfriend, Vanessa, hoping she might be keen to join them. Although he knew the trip to the city would hold particular significance for him and Daisy because of its association with her mum, he also felt it was important that Vanessa be part of it.

Their relationship had taken a serious turn over the last six months, and maybe, just maybe, it was meant to be that the three of them should go to New York together.

Perhaps this trip would be a kind of rite of passage into the next stage of his and Daisy's life? It had been three years since Jane's death, and Ethan was pretty certain they had her blessing to move on; another of her last wishes before she died was that he shouldn't remain alone.

"Go and find a woman who'll bake you bread," she'd teased in what he knew was a reference to a long-standing joke about their dietary habits.

Jane's healthy-eating preference meant they rarely ate refined starchy foods like bread or potatoes, something a carb fan like Ethan had always found difficult.

And in the end, it didn't matter what any of them ate; the cancer had taken her from them anyway.

But he knew there was a metaphorical element to the remark too, and although at the time, he couldn't bear the thought of moving on with someone else, as the years went by, the feeling lessened. A woman to bake him bread? Ethan wasn't sure if this described Vanessa exactly, but he did know he loved her and felt she would be the perfect role model for his rapidly maturing daughter.

When Ethan had suggested the three of them spend Christmas in New York together, Vanessa was all for it. She knew the city well, often traveling to Manhattan on business or to visit friends.

"Do you think Mum would be proud of me?" Daisy had asked, and when he looked at her and cocked his head inquisitively, she continued. "She always said she was proud of me every time I trusted myself and tried something new," his daughter said. "And here I am in her favorite place, trying something new."

"I can guarantee it, buttercup," Ethan told her softly, his blue eyes watering slightly. "Do you know who else is proud of you?"

"Yes," she replied without hesitation before finishing the last of her hot chocolate. "You are. And Vanessa is too. She told me on the plane."

Ethan smiled. That was all he needed to hear.

Now, as he and Daisy waited together for the Tiffany's assistant to gift wrap his purchase, he was relieved that everything seemed to be working out. Of course, there was still the small matter of Vanessa's reaction to all this, but he was pretty certain he knew what that would be.

To the ring if nothing else.

He'd learned from Jane, who used to wax lyrical about Tiffany's, that the famous little blue box was a true symbol of classic New York romance. According to her, there wasn't a woman in the world who could resist it, and the store and its wares enchanted the dreams of millions.

Something from Tiffany's had certainly always made Jane go weak at the knees, and Ethan's one big regret was that he'd never had the chance to present her with one of their famed diamond rings.

He hoped Vanessa would appreciate it just as much, although he was pretty confident she would, given her appreciation for the finer things in life. Her dedicated work ethic ensured she was able to afford the best, and as far as Ethan was concerned, the best was exactly what she deserved.

Thinking about the cost of the ring, he gulped, once again thankful for those stock options that he'd cashed in a few months before. The shareholding had been a gift from his father, and it was only because of that windfall that Ethan had been able to spend so much on the diamond or indeed a suite at the Plaza Hotel.

"Would you prefer our classic white ribbon for the box or something a little more festive for the holidays?" the assistant asked him. "A red bow, perhaps?"

"Daisy?" Ethan urged, letting her decide.

She seemed to think for a moment. "Definitely the white."

"Ah, classic Tiffany's style," the assistant agreed with a smile. "Good instincts, young lady."

Daisy grinned again and looked from the assistant to her father. "My mum used to tell me about here," she said shyly. "She told me that Tiffany's was a magical place filled with fantasy and romance."

The assistant looked to Ethan, and he smiled, silently acknowledging that Daisy was at the age where this kind of fanciful stuff was important.

"Daisy's mum is no longer with us, but she was very much a Tiffany's devotee," he told the man. Ethan knew that Jane would no doubt have waxed lyrical to Daisy about the store in the course of her many tales about New York. The love of his life had been a romantic old soul, the type who believed in whimsical things like fate and the mysteries of the universe.

For all the good it did her, he thought, but lately some of that seemed to be coming through in Daisy. Then again, she was an eight-year-old girl who had posters of princesses and unicorns all over her bedroom walls, so he supposed this was normal enough, given her age.

In any case, Ethan would much rather see this more imaginative side of his daughter than the solemn, fretful little girl who, since her mother's untimely loss, was prone to worrying about the slightest thing.

"Ah." The man nodded as if understanding. He hunkered down to Daisy's height. "Well, as you can see, there's lots of romance happening right here at this very moment," he whispered, indicating the other customers, all enclosed in their own starry-eyed bubbles, "and I must admit, I myself have experienced a few magical moments throughout my time here. Like meeting you today for instance, young lady," he added with a wink, and she blushed happily.

Ethan looked on, his heart soaring at the sight of his little girl's smile.

Then, when the all-important package was nestled safely in the small robin's-egg-blue bag and the assistant handed Ethan his purchase, Daisy beat him to the punch and grabbed the soft handles herself. "Can I carry it?" she asked, staring at the bag as if it contained something rare and precious.

Which indeed it did.

"Of course you can." Ethan was beaming as he put the receipt and accompanying documentation into his jacket pocket.

He couldn't have hoped for a better reaction, and he felt more certain than ever that he, Vanessa, and Daisy being together in New York was the first step in the wonderful journey they all had ahead of them.

Chapter 3

"Hey, gorgeous, what's up?" Gary Knowles said, answering his phone from inside the changing room at Bergdorf Goodman.

He placed the device between his cheek and shoulder so he could have both hands free.

Turning sideways, he threw back his shoulders to size himself up in the dressing room mirror and smiled, catching sight of himself in the Ralph Lauren shirt he was trying on.

"Yep, glad you're enjoying it," he continued absently, turning his head to get a better look at the way the tapering shirt fit his torso and back from behind. "Hmm? Yeah, just finishing up now."

Nodding approvingly, Gary brushed aside some strands of sandy blond hair (tinged with just enough peroxide to give him a certain edge) and figured that this shirt was another definite.

"Shouldn't be too much longer. Why don't you go ahead and get yourself ready?" he said. "I'll meet you back at the hotel later. Can't say for sure…around seven, maybe? I still have a couple of things to do here." He raised an eyebrow. "What, you've got all yours done already? Not bad, and for a girl too." Laughing at his joke, he slipped out of the shirt and now studied his bare chest. His six-pack looked especially impressive in this light. Shame nobody else could see it. "Grand. I'll see you back there, then? Yup, me too."

With that, Gary ended the call and put the phone back in his pocket. Then he slipped his own clothes back on, grabbed the pile of bags at his feet, and headed in the direction of the checkout counter.

He was soaking up every minute in the Big Apple. It was a trip he had wanted to take for years but for some reason had never gotten around to it. And since business was so slack these days, he couldn't really justify laying out the cash for such a jaunt.

Back in the glory days of the Irish house-building boom, Gary's one-man construction company was charging telephone-number prices for sticking up telephone *box*-size extensions, but unfortunately those days were long gone.

He had a few quid tucked away, of course, and wasn't destitute quite yet, but trips to New York were a good bit down the pecking order when you had four rental property regrets (two of which were currently without tenants) and an expensive motorbike hobby to maintain.

Luckily for him, along came Rachel who, nine months into their relationship, gifted him the trip for his thirty-fifth birthday. His girlfriend had been to New York a few times before and assured him that Christmas in the city was really something special and definitely the best time to go.

His head held high, Gary navigated his way through the crowds of other shoppers toward the nearest checkout queue. However, a display of Tag Heuer watches nearby caught his eye, and before he knew it, the small "Christmas Eve Price Reduction" sign forced him into a bit of a dilemma. Eventually deciding he had enough watches, he made his way along the jewelry case to see what other bargains he might encounter.

Now they weren't on sale, but the Paul Smith cuff links certainly would look good—especially for meeting the bank manager. Stuff like that was always worthwhile, he told himself. In his line of business and especially in these tough times, a fella had to look the part. The cuff links were a bit pricey, but wouldn't they be an investment in his future?

At his request, the assistant took the box out of the display case so he could take a better look. "And perhaps something for the lady in your life?" the man suggested, and Gary's heart nearly stopped.

Rachel...

He had checked out some nice underwear for her earlier, but it had just dawned on him that he hadn't actually *bought* his girlfriend anything yet.

"Uh, no...no. Just the cuff links, thanks," he muttered, his mind racing.

He couldn't get her perfume or the like again—he'd bought that for her birthday—but what other options were there at this hour on Christmas Eve?

It was almost six thirty, and he'd told Rachel to be ready around seven. They both knew he was always late, so in reality that actually gave him an hour or so of leeway, but he was getting hungry, and the shops would be closing soon.

Paying for his shirt and cuff links, he decided to head back out onto Fifth Avenue and try the next place that caught his eye.

After all, she was having a great time and clearly happy just to be here in New York with him. Any gift at all as a token of their trip would do, wouldn't it?

When just ahead he spied Tiffany & Co., Gary breathed a sigh of relief.

Some famous jewelry shop or something, wasn't it? Perfect. Somebody somewhere was obviously looking out for him, and this might be less hassle than he'd thought.

He pushed open yet another of those blasted twirly doors that seemed to be everywhere in Manhattan but that made Gary dizzy.

Going inside, a glass display counter on his right immediately caught his eye, not so much for what was inside but rather what was behind it. The beautiful buxom blond smiled in his direction and automatically drew him in.

"Happy holidays," she greeted as he approached.

"Hello. Same to you." Gary ran a quick gaze over the display of swanky-looking necklaces and promptly broke out in a cold sweat. *Christ alive, look at those prices!*

"Welcome to Tiffany's. What can I help you with? Are you looking for anything specific?"

"Well, no, not really. Just something nice for…I need something for…my sister." If Gary told her it was for his girlfriend, the woman would think he was a right tightwad if he didn't spend big. "Nice but not too…well, you know yourself." He felt like a right fool for thinking he could just randomly pick something out in a place like this.

"Ah, I've got just the thing. Follow me," she said, walking ahead of him to another counter. "Now charm bracelets are always a popular choice, especially for the season," she said, pointing out a row of silver bracelets. "People just love these. The perfect gift for a sister, I would think. Thoughtful, yet not too intimate."

"Ah, can I have a look?" he asked nervously.

"Of course."

Studying the bracelet, Gary quickly sought out the price tag and breathed an inward sigh of relief.

Yep, this would do nicely. Thoughtful, not too intimate, and more importantly, not too pricey. "Right so. That'll be perfect... Amanda," he added, reading her name tag.

"You'll take it?" She chuckled, her blue eyes wide with surprise. "That was fast."

"Yep," Gary said with a little wink. "I don't hang around."

"You know, I just love your accent," she said, looking closely at him. "Are you English?"

"Christ, don't insult me!" he quipped, feigning horror, then seeing her dismayed expression, he shook his head. "Ah, don't worry about it. Bit of an old joke. I'm Irish. From Dublin. Ever been?"

"Afraid not. Maybe one of these days," Amanda said, laying the bracelet inside a soft felt pouch before putting it into a square blue box. Then she tied the entire package together with a white satin bow. "Here you go. I just know your sister is going to *love* this little blue box. Every woman does."

"Yeah, yeah, I'm sure she will. I'll be the favorite brother this year," Gary muttered, whipping out his Visa.

After ringing up his purchase, Amanda handed him back the

card along with a small Tiffany's carrier bag. Gary had to admit, he felt a bit of pride picking it up.

Tiffany's no less. Rachel would be thrilled.

"Thank you, sir," the assistant finished with a smile. "Enjoy your visit to New York. I hope you have a fabulous time here."

"That I will. And you, gorgeous, have a lovely Christmas," he said, winking.

"Why, thank you!" Amanda giggled, and Gary gave her one last appreciative glance before picking up the rest of his bags and heading back out onto the street.

Mission accomplished, he thought, a grin on his face. His arms weighed down with bags almost made him feel like a victorious hunter, home afresh from the field.

But now, he needed to find a quick way back to the hotel in SoHo.

Where was his motorbike when he really needed it? He groaned, frustrated. Even with all these bags hanging off him, having his Ducati just then would be a hell of a lot easier than trying to hail a cab amid the surrounding crowds already attempting the same feat.

Oh well. Gary decided, lifting his hand and stepping out onto the road like they were always doing in the movies. *When in Rome…*

Chapter 4

COMPLETELY SHOPPED OUT, ETHAN AND DAISY HAD ALSO JUST exited Tiffany's.

"So how about it, buttercup? Do you want to head for the Disney Store now?" he suggested, although truthfully he hoped she was as tired as he was. It had been a long day, and he wasn't sure he could handle much more of these crowds.

"No, I think we should head back."

"I think you're right." He took her hand and was just about to say something else when a loud shout interrupted him.

"Thanks for nothing, gobshite!" came a yell to his left that rang out above the cacophony. The unmistakable accent was familiar to him, since Vanessa was Irish by birth.

They both turned to look. "Don't worry about that, honey. Just some guy trying to hail a cab. Good luck to him in this crowd. So what do you—"

Again, a sound interrupted, but this time it was the blare of a horn followed by the piercing screech of braking tires. Ethan turned back to see the Irish guy now lying on the side of the road, shopping bags scattered on the street all around him.

"Freakin' idiot!" a cab driver yelled from his window.

Holding his daughter's hand tightly, Ethan pushed his and Daisy's way through the quickly gathering crowd. As a university lecturer, he was certified in CPR and as such felt obligated to step in when any such emergency presented itself.

"Someone call an ambulance, quickly," he ordered as he made his way out onto the road.

Kneeling at the injured man's side, Ethan could immediately see the man was still breathing, and with some relief, he took to clearing a space around him.

"Is he okay?" the driver of the taxi said, a shell-shocked expression on his face. "Man, he just came out of nowhere. I couldn't have avoided him, seriously."

"I can't honestly say." Ethan gently wiped the blood from the injured man's brow and ensured nobody else tried to move him while they waited for help.

"I swear to God, he just came out of nowhere. My fare will back me up on that and…oh man!" Ethan followed the driver's gaze back to the cab, which was now empty of passengers. Typical, he thought wryly, some people in so much of a hurry they couldn't wait around long enough even to see if the guy their own cab struck was dead or alive.

"Try not to worry. I'm sure he'll be fine," he reassured the driver, who seemed even more distraught now that he'd lost his witness. Worried about a lawsuit, perhaps?

There was a large crowd gathered, and while the man's health was foremost on Ethan's mind, he was also rather mindful of his belongings. The last thing the poor guy needed was for some quick-thinking thief to steal his stuff, especially on Christmas Eve.

"Can you gather up his things?" he asked Daisy, who was standing there looking very worried indeed. "It's okay, poppet. He'll be okay," he reassured her quickly, almost sorry now that they'd gotten involved in something that could potentially be quite traumatic for her. "We just need to make sure no one steals his shopping bags." That seemed to make sense to Daisy, and she quickly leaped into action, much to Ethan's relief.

Eventually, a blare of sirens could be heard in the background, although it seemed to take forever for the ambulance to navigate its way through the sea of Fifth Avenue traffic in order to reach them.

Once the medics were on scene and had taken charge, Ethan's next priority was simply getting his little girl back to the warmth and safety of their hotel.

Telling the medical staff what little he knew about the incident, he soon was free to go as they loaded the still-unconscious man—and his plethora of packages—into the ambulance.

"Hey, mister," a gruff voice called to Ethan. It was another yellow cab driver who must have been watching the scene from nearby. "That was mighty nice of ya. Howza 'bout I give you and your girl a lift to wherever you're headed? It's on me."

"Thanks, that's really very kind of you," Ethan answered, thinking that perhaps New Yorkers weren't nearly as brash as people made them out to be. "But we're only up the block, and I think we need to walk this off anyway. But thank you. And Merry Christmas. I mean, happy holidays."

"No problem. Same to you." The driver tipped his baseball cap, and Ethan and Daisy continued on toward the Plaza, just a short walk away.

Back in their hotel room, Ethan helped Daisy unbutton her winter jacket and warm up her hands.

Vanessa was still out, and in truth, he was glad to have some more time alone with Daisy after what had happened. Since losing her mother, she was prone to worrying about every little thing, especially (and perhaps understandably) about losing him too.

Sometimes she was like a mini version of Jane, scolding him about his diet and how he shouldn't eat too much junk food. Ethan also blamed advertisements continually peddling cures for heart disease and diabetes for scaremongering his eight-year-old into worrying about health problems, when at her age, she should be concerned with little more than the outcome of the books she read.

Following the taxi accident, it seemed the old worrywart Daisy was back, and he needed to nip that in the bud.

"You okay?" he asked, and she nodded uncertainly. "You were a big help back there. Sad to say, but there really are people who would have stolen that man's shopping. You helped him just as much as I did, you know. We're a good team, you and me." At this, Daisy smiled proudly, and his heart lifted a little. "Why don't we order room service while we wait for Vanessa, and then we can tell her all about it. Fancy another hot chocolate?"

"I don't know," she said hesitantly. "We had a big mug already today and—"

"Well, as your mum used to say, you can never have too much hot chocolate in New York at Christmas."

Daisy grinned. "Really? Well, okay then."

"Great. While we're waiting, why don't you go wash up, change into your pajamas, and meet me back here when you're ready?"

"Okay."

Fifteen minutes later, Daisy was relaxing in the chaise longue with a cup of hot chocolate topped with marshmallows, just the way she liked it, Ethan seated in a cozy armchair across from her. It was a strange day, he thought, and sensed that she was feeling it too.

Well, a lot of things had happened today.

"You're very quiet," he said, moving across to sit on the end of the lounge. "I hope you know that the doctors will do all they can to help that man."

"I know. I've seen stuff like that on TV, Dad."

"Good. Then you know he's in good hands."

So it wasn't just the accident she was thinking about. Ethan wasn't entirely sure if this was a good or a bad thing.

"How are you feeling about the ring…about me asking Vanessa to…to be your stepmother, I mean," he continued, reaching for her hand. "She's been in our lives for a while now, and you know she really loves you, loves reading with you and taking you to dance class and everything. It would be nice to be a family again, don't you think?"

Daisy took a long sip of her chocolate and stirred the marshmallows with her finger. "Yeah. Being a family would be nice."

"Of course, you and me have always been a family too," he said, and suddenly overcome with emotion, he had to pause before he could go on. "I remember," he said, turning over her hand in his and opening her palm, "I used to hold your tiny hand in mine and marvel at how much the same and yet how different the lines in our palms were." He traced his index finger over the lines while Daisy listened attentively.

He knew she adored hearing stories about what she was like as a baby. All children did, but perhaps Daisy even more so because all those stories tended to feature both of her parents together.

"You and I share so much, inside and out. You'll always be my baby girl, but I can see you growing and changing every day— becoming more and more of the person you are. It's been…it's been so wonderful and yet…hard sometimes without your mum," he said, his voice faltering a little. "But I love being here for you, buttercup, and I want you to know that I wouldn't change a thing. I just… Look, I'm probably not making any sense." He ran a hand through his dark hair, wondering why all this felt so surreal now, when back at Tiffany's, it had seemed so right. Covering her little hand with his big one, he continued, "Just know how much I love you. You will always be my number one girl. But maybe now, as your mum used to say, we *both* need to trust ourselves and try something new."

Chapter 5

Rachel Conti loved New York at Christmas.

Although a visit to the city was always a treat, at this time of year, Manhattan was truly at its finest—all decked out in sparkle and full of holiday cheer.

As she sat drinking hot chocolate and looking out the window at the lights of the skyscraper opposite her SoHo hotel, she was mildly sorry she hadn't gone whole hog and booked somewhere farther uptown like the Plaza—or at least a place with views over Central Park.

It would have been so much more romantic, especially as it was forecast to snow tomorrow. But when making the reservation, Midtown was all Rachel had been able to afford.

She and Gary were merely two of the hordes of NYC visitors at Christmastime, and most of the better hotels were either fully booked up or way too expensive.

She wished her boyfriend would finish up his shopping and come back soon. He'd spent a lot of time out and about today—even longer than she had. But since they were only here for a few days, she supposed she could hardly blame him for wanting to prolong the New York experience for as long as possible.

Rachel couldn't help but wonder about what he might have chosen as a gift for her this time. Since they'd only been together a couple of months at the time, she had given him the benefit of the doubt the previous Valentine's Day when she'd gotten one of those gift-shop single chocolate roses wrapped in colored foil. Then, on her birthday a few months later, she'd been disappointed again when he'd presented her with a bottle of perfume and a gift certificate for a well-known discount clothing store.

Useful, certainly, but hardly thoughtful, considering, though she'd figured Gary just wasn't the type who went for grand gestures or over-the-top sentiment.

Still, maybe this time he would really step it up? After all, she had gotten him this magnificent trip as a birthday gift; surely he would rise to the occasion now in return.

Not that she'd had ulterior motives, despite what Justin, the head chef at Gillini, the bistro Rachel co-owned back in Dublin, seemed to think.

"Ooh, that's quite an investment," he'd teased. "You hoping he makes a big one too?"

As well as an employee, Justin was a friend, and while Rachel was used to his direct, sardonic manner, even she was taken aback by this.

"Don't mind him," soothed Terri, her best friend and business partner. "Just because *he* needs an ulterior motive to do something nice, doesn't mean everyone does."

Rachel sensed that her friend too had been somewhat taken aback by her generosity, particularly when she and Gary hadn't been seeing each other that long. But despite his best attempts at hiding it, Rachel knew that Gary's business was going through a tricky time, and since hers was booming, she'd wanted to do something to help cheer him up. There was nothing more to it.

They'd had a wonderful trip so far. Last night, they'd gone to see *The Lion King* on Broadway, and tonight they planned to go out to a steakhouse nearby for a relaxing Christmas Eve dinner and a couple of drinks before coming back here and… Rachel smiled.

She supposed she'd better start getting ready. Gary had said he'd be back around seven, though knowing his timekeeping, she still had a half hour or so to spare.

Stepping out of a quick shower and into a suitably festive red dress, Rachel looked herself up and down in the full-length mirror.

She smiled, remembering how, as a teenager, she had hated her petite frame and not being supermodel tall, but now she loved the way her just-curvy-enough hips offset her distinct waist and more-than-a-handful breasts, as Gary called them. A direct result of her Sicilian heritage, as was the relatively uncommon combination of dark hair, blue eyes, and sallow skin.

Her boyfriend had something wonderful up his sleeve; she could feel it. She didn't want something grand or expensive, just something thoughtful, something carefully chosen especially for her.

Fastening her strappy, four-inch silver heels and intentionally bending over to make sure her breasts were secured inside the plunging neckline of the dress, Rachel decided to lay out Gary's gifts on his pillow for him to find when they returned from dinner later.

An hour later, she had rearranged the packages several times, ordered wine from room service, eaten three cookies from the hotel minibar, and touched and retouched her lip gloss over and over.

But that was Gary, chronically late and always pushing the limits. And while it was mostly endearing, this time it was kind of irritating.

Reaching for one last cookie, Rachel was both relieved and startled when the hotel room phone rang. Odd that he wasn't calling her cell though.

"Good evening, I'm calling from Mount Sinai Hospital," a stranger's voice intoned, and instantly, Rachel blanched. *A hospital?* "Do you happen to know a Mr. Gary Knowles?"

"Yes, of course," she replied, her heart hammering. "Why? What's happened?"

"I apologize for the nature of the call, but I'm afraid there's been an accident," the woman continued, her tone steady. "Mr. Knowles is in stable condition but hasn't yet regained consciousness. We found his hotel key and called the front desk hoping to find next of kin."

Next of kin? But that could only mean... "Oh my God." Rachel could hardly speak. "Is he okay? I'm his girlfriend and—"

"He was hit by a cab, ma'am, but his injuries aren't severe at this time," the woman confirmed, and Rachel quickly exhaled the breath she'd be holding. "We expect him to regain consciousness soon, so feel free to come down and see him whenever you like. Your name, please?"

"Rachel, Rachel Conti. Yes, yes, of course, I'll be right there."

Changing her shoes to a pair of flats so she could get around faster and wrapping up in a warm coat, Rachel managed to make it to the hospital in under forty-five minutes—not bad for a cab ride on Christmas Eve.

It didn't take her long to find directions to Gary's room after she wrangled a nearby nurse to get all the details.

"He suffered a couple bruised ribs from the collision, plus a laceration to the head and subsequent concussion from the fall," said the woman, reading from the chart. "Apparently some Good Samaritan stepped in and moved the crowd back, kept the wolves from carrying off his shopping too. Stuff's right there," she said, pointing to a pile of colored shopping bags on the chair beside the bed.

"Will he be okay?" Rachel asked nervously.

"He'll be fine, but don't expect him to come around till morning. He woke about half an hour before you got here, but we sedated him to keep him still and resting. Feel free to stay for a while, but you might as well take his stuff and head back to get some rest yourself. He's not going anywhere for at least a couple of days, maybe three. Oh, and happy holidays," the nurse finished, poking her head back around the curtain. Rachel barely raised a hand to acknowledge it as she leaned over Gary to gently kiss his forehead and stroke his arm.

"Bloody gobshite…" he mumbled almost imperceptibly.

The nurse poked her head around the curtain again. "He's been mumbling stuff like that all evening. Any idea what it means?"

Rachel actually felt the hint of an unexpected smile. "Just an Irish expression."

"Ah, I see," the nurse said, nodding quickly as if this explained everything. "I guess I don't blame the poor guy. Have a great evening."

"Thanks. You too."

Then Rachel turned back to Gary. She lifted his hand and held it in her own. "Poor baby, look at you…always pushing it," she whispered, holding back tears as she moved to caress his forehead.

She sat there with him for an hour or so, trying to discern the extent of his injuries and wondering if there was anything the nurse hadn't told her. Apart from the bruises and head wound, he seemed okay, though she would have much preferred him awake and able to speak to her.

Eventually, when there were no further signs of him stirring, Rachel decided to take the woman's advice and head back to the hotel.

It was late, visiting hours were long over, and there wasn't a whole lot she could do here, not when he was so heavily sedated. She gathered up his bags, deciding it was safer to take them back with her rather than leave them out in the open.

Just as she was leaving, an orderly met her with yet another bag, this one containing Gary's clothes and other personal effects.

Heavily laden, Rachel turned to look at her injured beloved one more time. "Love you honey. Merry Christmas," she whispered, pausing for a moment before leaving the hospital mere minutes before Christmas Eve gave way to Christmas Day.

"A little late to be finishing Christmas shopping, ain't it, lady?" the cab driver joked as outside, Rachel piled in with all Gary's bags and boxes.

"I wish," she replied, her tone short, before giving him the hotel address. "If you could just take me to my hotel. Please," she added then, somewhat gentler.

After all, it wasn't *this* cab driver's fault that poor Gary's Christmas was ruined.

Chapter 6

BACK AT THE HOTEL, RACHEL PLOPPED DOWN ON THE COUCH, LETting the packages fall around her feet. She felt tired and defeated, and while she was sure Gary was in good hands, she couldn't help but worry.

In addition, the twinkling Christmas lights from the streets glowing faintly through the window seemed to be mocking her now, and all Rachel could think about was the poor guy lying there in the hospital.

Should she call his mother? She bit her lip. Perhaps it was better to wait until morning when she'd spoken to the doctors and knew more. If she phoned Mrs. Knowles now, the woman's Christmas would also be ruined with worry, and she didn't want that.

Getting up to pour another glass of wine seemed like a much better idea, so that was exactly what she did.

Then, tossing her red dress on the bed and slipping into the hotel's fluffy robe (instead of the sexy little negligee placed neatly on Gary's pillow), she remembered the bag of clothes from the hospital and decided she should check his stuff was in order.

She didn't like the way everything was bundled away in a bag on the floor; it almost made it seem like he was dead or something. No, much better to tidy it up and have all his clothes washed and ready for him when he got back.

Rachel picked up the plastic hospital bag and settled back on the bed. Taking everything out, she set his wallet on a nearby bureau, then hung up his leather jacket, which looked clean and undamaged, putting it neatly into the wardrobe.

His shirt was dirty and bloodstained from the head wound, as were his jeans, so they needed to go into the laundry. Rachel checked the pocket for anything that might be ruined in the wash. From his jeans, she pulled out a list, which, judging by what was scribbled on it, looked to be a Christmas shopping list.

In true Gary fashion, she thought, smiling as she read through it, there was one column for names and one column for corresponding stores, presumably where he'd either bought or intended to buy gifts.

Hmm…where was he planning to buy hers? Then, suddenly conscious that she was prying, Rachel set the list down on the nightstand beside her.

She switched on the TV, turned off the bedside lamp, and took another taste of wine, this one more akin to a gulp than a sip.

She glanced toward the list again, her interest well and truly piqued about what Gary had in mind for her. Oh, what the hell, she reasoned, reaching for it again; it was just a list of stores. So what could it hurt?

Before Rachel knew it, the list was in her hands, and she had clicked the lamp back on to have a better look. At first glance, she didn't see her name written down. At a second more careful look, she still didn't see it. Frowning, she set it down.

Then it hit her. Of *course* her name wasn't on the list. Gary would no doubt have known exactly what he wanted to get her for Christmas, so why would he need to write it down? Silly.

With that, Rachel poured herself a second glass and a more generous serving. It was essential, really, since she was alone and worried in a New York hotel room on Christmas Eve.

Going back to the bed, she climbed under the covers, gently plopping the gifts she'd bought for Gary one by one onto the floor next to the bed.

First went the negligee, next the heavy box with the leather motorbike trousers in it, and third went the handcrafted wallet monogrammed with his initials.

Her gaze moved then to the pile of bags not more than twenty-five feet away from her. Inside one of those was presumably her unwrapped Christmas gift.

"No, I'm not going to look," she said out loud, grabbing the television remote and starting to click through channels. Some of the show titles looked rather intriguing, and others not so much. "Yikes, glorified porn on Christmas Eve?" she muttered and kept clicking until she came upon *It's a Wonderful Life* about halfway through.

Perfect.

By the time George was hearing bells ringing and believing, Rachel had the empty wine bottle in one hand and Gary's list in the other. With tears streaming down her face (as they did every time she watched that film), she headed back to the couch, whereupon she promptly started matching gift bags with the names and stores on the list.

With each matching set she found, she moved the corresponding bag to a pile.

When she reached the end of the list, there was still a bag from Bergdorf Goodman with men's clothes and some expensive-looking cuff links in it.

And then, more conspicuously, one small but gloriously familiar blue gift bag…

"Oh my goodness!" Rachel cried aloud. Her heart pounding in her chest, she checked the list again, turning the paper over and over in her hand.

Could this be hers? Had Gary *really* bought her something from Tiffany's?

He must have.

Rachel's eyes sparkled even brighter than the festive lights outside. Checking her watch, she swallowed hard. Well, it *was* now officially Christmas, wasn't it? She peeked expectantly inside the bag.

Only to spy the world-famous little blue box.

Chapter 7

UNABLE TO SLEEP, ETHAN GOT UP AT DAWN AND WAS STANDING AT the window watching the sun come up over Central Park and the surrounding buildings.

In fact, he was up before Daisy on Christmas morning for the first time since she'd been old enough to be excited about it. Snow was gently falling, and he was sipping coffee, thanks to the Plaza's in-room coffee maker. It was a picture-perfect New York Christmas morning, even if he was yawning after tossing and turning all night.

Ethan thought again about Daisy's mother and smiled a little as the aroma took him back in time. Jane wasn't enamored of his habit and had always insisted that if he *had* to drink coffee, it should be organic beans or nothing. In turn, all the baby food for Daisy had been homemade and, yes, organic too. Jane had been an amazing mum, and he had a healthy, happy daughter because of her.

Happy? His train of thought halted at the word. Sure, Daisy was generally content, but it still seemed to him that there was so much missing, so much he wasn't giving her. Ethan ran a hand through his thick brown hair and felt his eyes fall gently shut as he thought about the three years he had spent alone and how many nights he had cuddled and sat with her until she could fall asleep, her last words always about missing her mummy. Those instances had lessened, but still there was nothing he wanted more than to be a family again.

It was best for Daisy. Not to mention that he really did love Vanessa. Yes, he had been cautious in the early days, but over the course of the last year, they had grown especially close, and he was certain she was the perfect addition to their family.

He'd met her at a book fair of all places. His good friend Brian, a former colleague at the university where Ethan lectured, was now a highly successful and well-respected novelist. Just over a year before, he had, after much coaxing and cajoling, convinced Ethan that leaving Daisy with her grandparents for three days while they made the trip to Frankfurt did not make him a neglectful parent.

"After all, mate, it's basically a business trip," Brian reassured. "We're going to talk about my book this time, but we'll be going for yours next. Maybe this'll inspire you to get your arse in gear and start writing that great British novel," he teased, referring to Ethan's own latent ambitions. "Not as great as mine, mind, but I'm sure there's room for us both on the Booker short list."

Ethan couldn't really argue with this (the reason for the trip—he had no illusions about getting anywhere near any list, Booker or otherwise), so in the end, he decided to go along.

And then on day two of the fair, he saw her: the poised and immaculately groomed blond who was heading their way.

Ethan had caught her eye a couple of times as he and Brian browsed through the stands and found him himself intrigued by her calm self-possession. When she first approached, Ethan suspected she might be one of Brian's many literary "groupies" but gathered from the polite but familiar conversation that ensued that she and Brian's paths had crossed before at publishing events. It turned out that she too worked in publishing and was senior editor of a literary imprint at a major London house. The next thing Ethan knew, the three of them were having lunch, and he discovered that Vanessa lived in the vicinity of Teddington, not far from his home in Richmond.

Not long after that, just the two of them were having dinner—first there in Frankfurt and then back in London. He enjoyed her company and lively conversation, they had a shared appreciation of literature and the arts, and he also admired the single-minded determination with which she ran her professional life, having worked her way to the top in a highly competitive field.

Still, her ambition didn't end there. Vanessa wanted the most respected and accomplished literary authors for her list, and she laughingly informed Ethan that her original intentions in approaching them at the fair was to see about poaching Brian from his current publishing house.

She was so different from Jane, focused and driven as opposed to Jane's relaxed approach to life, that Ethan surprised himself by first becoming intrigued by her before eventually falling for her completely. Sometimes she made his head spin with her broad and intricate knowledge of travel, food, and wine, as well as the seemingly effortless confidence she exuded in everything she did. This self-assurance was one of the first things that had captivated him, but there was also a somewhat enigmatic side to her that made him want to get closer.

Still, he had waited almost six months to introduce her to Daisy. Just because he was moving on, there was no reason to force his daughter to do the same, he reasoned.

When the big meeting did finally occur, Ethan arranged for Vanessa to meet the two of them after Daisy's weekly Saturday dance class. He had done his best to ensure it was light and informal and to keep the focus on Daisy, but he wasn't fooling his wise and perceptive daughter. As the three of them walked along the Thames, eating ice cream, Daisy kept giving her father the same look her mother always had. Ethan called it the "sideways-squinty-eyed" look, one that often appeared from his daughter during poorly disguised homework bribes and early-to-bed coaxing.

Over time, though, Daisy came around. She loved it when Vanessa read to her; storytelling was one of her favorite things. She especially loved Vanessa's accent, a rich combination of a decade and a half spent in cultured London coupled with the lilt of her Irish roots. It was something that at the beginning had greatly appealed to Ethan too, although she liked to insist that fifteen years living in England had eradicated most of her native brogue.

He always wished that Vanessa would read more than just one bedtime story at a time, but he reminded himself that it was different for people who'd never had children of their own, and no doubt she would get a feel for that kind of thing with time.

He should know; he had never considered himself the doting-father type but had fallen completely in love with his baby daughter when she wrapped her tiny newborn hand around his index finger in the delivery room. And when afterward he'd cuddled her fragile little body close to his bare chest, skin to skin, Ethan had there and then given her his heart.

Given time, it would be the same, he thought; Vanessa and Daisy would share a moment that would cement them. It couldn't be forced. It would probably happen once they all lived together, when they spent time together like a real family. Sadly, due to Vanessa's inability to conceive (something she'd disclosed frankly to Ethan early in the relationship), there would be no additions to that family, but he was fine with that too.

As daylight gradually crept across the park, Ethan lifted his head, wondering how long he had actually been standing there daydreaming. The sun was peeking through the clouds, and despite the brief flurry of snow, a clear sky was visible in the distance. He reckoned that this was a good omen since it had been overcast and gray in the city since they arrived. Today was different for a reason; the powers that be must be smiling on him and his intentions...

"Merry Christmas, darling."

At the sound of the voice nearby, Ethan jumped, and coffee splashed on his bare chest through the opening of his bathrobe.

"Oops." Vanessa laughed, coming up alongside him. "Sorry, I didn't mean to startle you..." Her voice trailed off as she rushed to the bathroom, and in a flash, she was back with a cool washcloth and a fresh robe.

"It's my own fault. I was miles away," he replied, smiling. "Anyway, it's cold by now."

"Why so jumpy? Still thinking about that accident yesterday? I'm sure the guy is fine."

Holding the cloth to his chest, he stood there in his boxers, assuring her she had just caught him in a daydream. "Honestly, I didn't expect anyone else to be up so early." He handed her back the cloth and put on the fresh robe. "Join me in a fresh one?"

She smiled. "Love to."

Ethan moved to the side table and poured a steaming cup of coffee for the woman he was about to propose to. Coffeepot in hand, he noticed he wasn't nervous as such but not quite his usual calm, collected self.

Evidently so did Vanessa. Taking the cup from him, she put her other hand on his before he had the chance to let go. Ethan looked up to see a kind of knowing look in her eyes, as if she could guess exactly what he was thinking.

It shot right through him. Resisting a step backward, he knew he must have looked startled again, because she seemed to quell the slightest smile as she looked away.

She knows, he thought. Maybe she'd noticed that one of her rings had gone missing? A little while back, he had purloined one of Vanessa's costume rings from her jewelry box so that he could establish the correct size.

"So as I was saying, Merry Christmas," she repeated, reaching forward to kiss him. "It's wonderful being here on Christmas morning with you and Daisy. It means a lot, especially when I know how important the city is to you two. Because of Jane, I mean."

She was so perceptive and always so generous and understanding about Jane's memory that Ethan felt himself fall in love with her all over again.

Living in another woman's shadow would undoubtedly be a challenge for some, but thankfully this didn't seem to be the case with Vanessa. Even if she did have any qualms—hidden or otherwise—those would surely be erased once he produced that little blue box.

"Thank you for asking me to come with you," she went on, her voice slightly hoarse. "You were right. New York at Christmastime really is something special."

Ah, that was it, Ethan realized with some relief. Vanessa had no idea what was coming. It was just the Christmas thing she was emotional about.

"Me too, and I'm so glad you're here. This is a really special time...for all of us." He paused. The light through the window caught the hazel in her eyes, and the weight of what he was about to do took his breath away for a moment. "I love you too, Vanessa. I do. I mean, I..." he stammered. "I mean, I do love you."

She smiled and gently rested her hand on the side of his face.

"Merry Christmas!" Daisy squealed from the doorway connecting to her bedroom, as if poised for a grand entrance. She raced toward them, leaping and landing on the big double bed with a flourish. "Let's open our presents!"

"How about good-morning greetings and some breakfast first?" Ethan replied, his tone half-scolding.

"Yes, you'll need to get your strength up for all the presents you'll be opening," Vanessa chimed in.

"So do you," the little girl replied with a coy smile, and Ethan gave her a warning look, which made her giggle.

"Okay, let's get some room service organized," he said, practically diving for the menu in order to change the subject.

"Hot chocolate. I suppose that's our first priority?" Vanessa teased, sitting down alongside Daisy.

"That's not very healthy, you know," she replied solemnly, and Ethan and Vanessa shared a smile. He hoped that once they were all together as a family, Daisy would feel more secure and her anxieties would start to wear off.

"But it's Christmas morning!" Vanessa insisted with a grin. "I'm sure one day of indulgence won't kill us."

He couldn't help but wince at her unfortunate choice of phrase, but luckily Daisy didn't seem to notice.

"You're right. Can I have a cinnamon roll too, Dad? I love cinnamon rolls."

"You can have whatever you want, poppet. Any requests, Vanessa?"

She shook her head. "What Daisy's having sounds good to me."

"Okay then, hot chocolate and cinnamon rolls all around," he agreed, picking up the phone to order.

Half an hour later, the three were sipping hot drinks and sitting around the little tree they'd bought and decorated especially for the occasion.

Daisy tucked her legs up beneath her on the floor and licked icing from the pastries off her fingers.

"All right then, let's see what have we here," Ethan began, handing a brightly wrapped package to his daughter.

"No, Vanessa first," she insisted, grinning coyly.

"You're in an excitable mood today, even for Christmas morning," he said, giving her his own, more subtle version of the sideways-squinty-eyed look. "Go ahead and open yours first, okay?"

She gave a big, exaggerated sigh. "Okay, Dad."

"Yes please." Vanessa laughed. "I think you're going to like that one, or at least I hope you will. It's from me."

"Great." Daisy sat cross-legged as she tore open the wrapping. A collection of softcover books landed in her lap. "Animal stories?" she said, looking at the covers of a Thornton Burgess story collection.

"Yes. I had those when I was a little girl. They're just at your reading level, so you can read them to yourself at bedtime."

"Oh," Daisy said flatly, twirling one of her curls with her index finger. "Thanks."

"But one of us will still read them to you too, honey," Ethan put in quickly, picking up on her obvious disappointment.

"Vanessa's turn now," she insisted.

He smiled. At least she was still excited about the proposal, more so than he could have hoped for. Giving her a surreptitious wink, he said, "Agreed," and she giggled with delight and clapped her hands.

Vanessa raised an eyebrow. "Daisy, you've got me intrigued now. This must be a pretty good gift."

"I certainly hope so," Ethan murmured, handing her the Tiffany's gift. The distinctive blue box and ribbon combination was so unmistakably elegant, it was a travesty to even consider wrapping them further. "This is from me, and Daisy helped me pick it out.

She has great taste," he added, giving his daughter a smile, which she giddily returned.

Vanessa seemed duly taken aback. "Oh my…something from Tiffany's?" she gasped, her face lighting up as Ethan had hoped.

Jane was right; there really was something about the packaging alone that turned even the most sophisticated of women to mush.

Letting the little blue box rest in her hand for a moment, Vanessa went to untie the white bow, but then paused and looked up.

"Daisy, I've already told your dad this, but I just wanted to let you know how happy I am to be here, to be sharing Christmas with both of you. It means a lot, darling." She reached over and patted Daisy's hand, who in return gave her a huge Cheshire Cat grin.

"Go on, open it!" the little girl urged, and Ethan smiled, enjoying the moment.

He moved closer to Vanessa and reached out to take Daisy's hand.

Smiling, Vanessa pulled slowly on the soft satin ribbon as if savoring every second. When it gave way and fell into her lap, she took a deep breath before finally lifting off the lid of the box.

As she did, her eyes grew wide. "Well, what have we got here," she murmured happily, opening the little felt pouch and reaching inside. "A bracelet. How lovely."

What the…?

Ethan stared at the box, unable to believe what he was hearing. He glanced sideways at Daisy, who was just as wide-eyed.

If he didn't know better, he could have sworn that Vanessa was joking, but it wasn't really the kind of thing to joke about.

Moving closer to get a better look, he checked to see what she was holding in her hand. Yes, there was no mistake—it was indeed a bracelet, a charm bracelet.

Cute, but no diamond solitaire.

What the hell is going on?

"Yes, we...um...picked it out together, didn't we?" he said, catching Daisy's eye. She sat there looking just as shocked as he. "It seemed like a nice keepsake of our trip—our special time here, just the three of us."

Ethan's mind was racing. Lecturing had its advantages in that it helped him think on his feet.

"Yes, we got it at Tiffany's," Daisy said rather unnecessarily. She looked at him as if trying to gauge what they should do next.

"It's beautiful. Thank you," Vanessa said, but he barely heard her.

For a moment, he wasn't sure how to react, but he knew deep down that he had to try and rescue the situation before she noticed something was amiss.

Eventually he reached for the box. "Here, let me. I want to see how it looks on," he said, lifting the bracelet out of the pouch. He took Vanessa's arm and fastened it around her wrist. "Beautiful, though not as much as the woman wearing it." He smiled but was certain she would be able to see through it. He'd always been dreadful at deception.

"Thank you, both of you." Vanessa twirled the bracelet around on her wrist. "It's just...beautiful and the perfect memento." Sitting up straighter, she took a deep breath and smiled conspiratorially at Daisy. "So I think it's your dad's turn now."

"Oh no, we should really let Daisy open the rest of her things first," Ethan interjected quickly, running a hand through his hair and making a great show of looking around for his coffee cup.

Any excuse to extricate himself from this uncomfortable and truly mystifying situation while he tried to get a grip on what he should do or say. What in God's name had just happened?

He could hardly come right out and tell Vanessa that, instead of a bracelet, she should now be sporting a sparkling diamond ring. By rights, all three of them should be celebrating their engagement! So much for a romantic Christmas surprise.

No, first and foremost, he needed to sort this out so as to deliver the proposal she truly deserved.

"No, I insist. Really. We should take turns."

Daisy gave him a look. "No, Dad. Your turn now. It's only fair."

"Okay, I defer to the ladies," he replied, feigning a grin in an attempt to break the discomfort and retain some of the Christmas cheer.

But his nerves were in tatters, and given what had just happened, Daisy was edgy too. And while he could very well be imagining it, he was certain that Vanessa also knew something was off.

He sat back on the floor and leaned against the end of the chaise longue as he tried to stop his mind racing and focus on what came next.

"Here it is," his girlfriend said, reaching under the tree, and he sensed a slight affectation in her voice as he took the long rectangular box from her hand. Perhaps it wasn't intentional, but sure enough it was there, beneath the surface of her tone and the facade of her smile.

She picked her now-cold coffee off a side table and looked away while taking a long sip.

Ethan felt the urge to say something enthusiastic again, but as he opened his mouth to speak, he realized that it seemed pointless now. How could he rescue this?

"Were you going to say something?"

"Ah, no," he replied, peeling back the pieces of sticky tape with uncharacteristic deliberation.

"Hurry up, Dad," Daisy urged, moving closer.

"Okay, okay." Opening the box, a relieved smile (this one genuine) came over Ethan's face. "Well, would you look at this? See, great minds really do think alike."

With some relief, he held aloft a silver bracelet. It looked to be antique and very masculine, a series of rectangular pieces joined together. What were the chances?

"There's an inscription," Vanessa pointed out.

"Oh." His immediate thought was to wonder whether the Tiffany's bracelet she'd gotten by mistake was inscribed with anything. If so, maybe that would be a clue as to where the hell it had come from.

Then he read the inscribed words on Vanessa's gift for him, and his heart fell into his stomach. *She loved him with too clear a vision to fear his cloudiness*, it said, the words delicately etched into the individual pieces.

"Vanessa…" He could hardly meet her gaze. "I don't know what to say. Thank you." He reached across to kiss her gently at the corner of her mouth and lingered there for a second.

The quote came from *Howards End*, a story she knew he loved.

During one of their arguments earlier in the relationship, she had told him that this particular line always reminded her of him, in that he always seemed to hover in haze within her reach.

It had become sort of a running joke since, one of those poignant references between two people that reminds them of how far they've come and unwittingly breathes life into the demons of their past.

They had both quoted it off and on, over dinner, wine, and conversations about the future and over the still-unresolved issue of living together. Regardless, the reference had always been intended as a loving and intimate exchange, but this morning, it felt more like an unintentional kick in the teeth.

Poor Vanessa. If only she knew that today was the day that his "cloudiness" should have been lifted.

"What does it say?" Daisy asked.

"Um, it says that I'm just about ready to open a gift from my beautiful daughter now!" he teased, tickling the sole of her bare foot. She laughed out loud and pulled it back.

"Okay, here it is," she said, extending her arm proudly. "I wrapped it up all by myself at school."

"At school?"

"Yeah, I bought it at the Christmas gift sale. People donate stuff so we can buy gifts for our parents without them knowing."

Vanessa stroked Daisy's arm. "I would have taken you shopping, darling."

The little girl shook her head. "That's okay. I wanted to do it this way."

"But thank you, Vanessa," Ethan said, reminding his daughter of her manners.

"Yes, thank you, Vanessa," she echoed cheekily.

He unwrapped the gift with considerably more speed and grace than he had the previous package.

"It's a book with nothing in it," Daisy announced.

"Yes, I can see that," he said, faintly puzzled.

"So you can fill it yourself, silly—write your own book. You know, like you talk about," she clarified.

"What a very clever daughter you have, Ethan," Vanessa said, cocking her head and smiling. According to Vanessa, another element of his "cloudiness" was his all-talk-and-no-action approach to writing a book of his own. She was always encouraging him to put pen to paper.

He'd made a start and cobbled together some sort of outline, but finding the time to write and be a single father was like trying to count the number of raindrops that fell in London any given year.

"Thank you, honey. I promise I will carry this with me everywhere and write longhand whenever the muse strikes me."

Finally, when Vanessa left the room to shower and get dressed, Ethan snatched some much-anticipated time alone with his daughter.

"Can you believe it?" he gasped, running a hand through his hair. "What on earth happened to our lovely ring?" Not to mention pretty damn *expensive* ring, but Ethan guessed Daisy wouldn't truly understand his concerns about that aspect.

She put her bare feet up next to his on the coffee table and frowned. "I know. It's so weird, isn't it? I don't understand it. I remember that happened to me at school once though. I went to eat my lunch and got someone else's lunch box, which only had ham and yuck plastic cheese on white bread with no yogurt. I was so annoyed."

Despite himself, Ethan had to chuckle at the comparison. "Erm...yes, I suppose it is a bit like that."

"Well, of course I know this is different, but you know what I mean." She paused and looked down, scraping something from beneath one of her fingernails. "But what do you think happened, Dad, and what are we going to do now?"

"Well, there's nothing we can do now, is there? Today, I mean. I suspect Vanessa was disappointed, though. Perhaps she might have known something or maybe expected...oh, I just don't know." He sat forward. "Okay, you and I are going back to Tiffany's in the morning to get this straightened out. There must've been some kind of a mix-up while they were wrapping it up or something. Remember that nice man sent it away while we waited?" That was about the only explanation he could think of.

She nodded. "Yeah, that has to be it. Um, Dad?"

"Yes?" he replied, expecting some helpful insight into his predicament.

"Am I going to have hair on my toes like you do?"

Ethan burst out laughing. "Yes, definitely." He moved his feet closer so that the outside of his right foot was touching the outside of her left one. "In another five years or so, your feet will look exactly like mine. And I hear that touching our feet together actually speeds up the process."

Daisy squealed and ran back toward her bedroom. "Stay away

then!" she cried, and while normally, Ethan would have taken the cue and followed to tickle her, instead, he didn't have the energy.

He could only assume the staff at Tiffany & Co. would be able to shed some light on everything tomorrow, but what if they couldn't? What then?

Should he confess all to Vanessa? No, that would be way too anticlimactic, considering. But what next?

He checked his watch. It wasn't even close to noon yet. This would be the longest Christmas Day he had ever spent. Where *on earth* was the ring?

Chapter 8

Rachel rolled over in bed, habitually running her hand through her hair.

One thing she loved about hotel stays were the thick curtains—so thick that if you closed them well enough, you could scarcely tell it was daytime if it weren't for a seam of light at the bottom.

Leisurely mornings had always been a luxury for her. For someone who was usually in the kitchen by 6:00 a.m., staying in bed until eight was quite a treat.

Although she'd woken earlier, full of concern about Gary and wanting to rush to the hospital to see him, but then she realized that it was far too early for visiting hours, even on Christmas Day.

So instead, she had cozied up with his pillow, then dozed and half dreamed about their soon-to-be engagement.

Relishing one last vision of herself in white, Rachel opened her eyes. Stretching her arms out in front of her, she gazed at her left hand and pictured that stunning solitaire on her ring finger.

She'd really wanted to go to sleep wearing it last night but felt so guilty about finding it in the first place that she'd returned it to its box.

Now leaping out of bed, she realized her excitement was indeed tainted by morning-after guilt. She really shouldn't have rummaged through Gary's bags, and she certainly shouldn't have opened the Tiffany's one.

Still, to think that if she hadn't...

It was a wonderful surprise, particularly after the shock and worry of his accident. It was also quite romantic, considering—her all alone on Christmas Eve, discovering by chance that he was about to propose...fairy-tale stuff and more than Rachel could have dreamed of.

She had almost gotten used to life on her own, having lost both her parents in her teens, and a fresh bubble of happiness developed when she realized that after all this time, Gary would be her family.

But perhaps the biggest surprise of all was the discovery that he cared about her way more than she'd realized.

Yes, they had fun together and she adored him too, but she honestly hadn't expected anything like this. She certainly hadn't expected anything like that ring. The beautifully cut diamond was stunning and, from Tiffany's, had clearly cost him a fortune. Who would have thought it?

Everything happened for a reason though, she told herself, so perhaps finding the box was exactly what she needed to allay any misgivings she might have had about their relationship.

This man was unpredictable in more ways than one.

She eyed the shopping bags in the corner of the room, thinking that she just had to have another look. To think that this was actually going to be hers for the rest of her life!

Rachel was giddy. Opening the box once again, she was startled afresh by what she saw. The ring was utterly stunning and the diamond itself looked so much bigger in daylight and indeed even without the cozy filter of a wine buzz.

Again, she was faintly shocked that Gary had spent so much on a blingtastic ring when he had never even alluded to marriage. Or that he loved her even.

Strange too when, on the flight over, he'd been complaining about how much he was going to have to spend on fixing something wrong with his bike. While he could never have been described as generous, she'd noticed he'd been particularly careful with money over the last while, and now she understood why.

Clearly the bike thing had been just a ruse and merely went to prove how much he really cared. Her ring was even more important than the Ducati. She shook her head fondly.

One thing you could say about Gary was that he was *always* full of surprises. But this had to be the biggest, *best* surprise of all.

It then occurred to Rachel that she really should rewrap the box at some stage so that he wouldn't notice anything untoward when he got back, but then she decided it could wait.

Her first priority was getting to the hospital to spend at least part of Christmas morning with her future husband, so stashing the box back in the bag, she showered and put on some makeup, jeans, and a sweater before bundling up and heading out to hail a cab. She could pick up something for breakfast at the hospital.

During the cab ride to the hospital this time, she was only too happy to ramble away to the driver, a chatty man whose passenger seat was littered with gyro wrappers.

A little while later, she reached the hospital, and going up to Gary's floor, she approached the nurse's station.

"Hi there, Merry Christmas," she greeted happily. "I'm here to see Gary Knowles in room 303. How is he?"

"Merry Christmas to you too. Go ahead on in. He's fine and resting well," the nurse on duty said in what Rachel recognized as a thick New Jersey accent. "He's a fidgety one, though. I'm guessing it's the meds, but he's been talking in his sleep off and on all morning. Something about a Ducati?"

Rachel smiled apologetically. "Yes, he's a bit of a motorbike enthusiast. Sorry, I'm sure there are things you'd rather be doing this morning than listening to his ramblings."

"Oh, don't worry about it." The nurse chuckled, waving an arm. "It's kind of ironic you know. My husband has a Ducati too, and if I didn't know better, I'd ask if your guy's injuries were from riding. Al, my husband, slipped on black ice two weeks ago and had rib problems similar to your husband's."

"Oh, he's not my—" Rachel caught herself before she uttered the word *husband*. But the very mention of the word sent fresh flutters through her stomach. "I mean, we're engaged but no, he got hurt in an accident. His first time in New York and he gets hit by a yellow cab," she added with an ironic half smile. "I'm sorry to hear about yours though."

"Oh no, he's fine. Couldn't keep him off the bike if I tried. Honestly, I think if he had to choose between me and that, I'd probably be a single woman by now." The nurse laughed good-naturedly. "Well, I won't hold you up. You have a nice visit."

"Thank you…Kim," Rachel said, reading her name tag. "I'm Rachel, and maybe I'll see you on my way out."

"Sure."

Then catching sight of Gary in his room, her joy suddenly gave way to a potent dose of reality.

He looked even worse than he had the night before. One side of his face was swollen, scraped, and black-and-blue, and he was hooked up to an IV. He looked so still and pitiful that she felt her stomach lurch, and she swallowed hard as she sat in the chair next to his bed.

Racked with guilt, she berated herself for being so carefree when her poor fiancé was lying here in agony. Then, telling herself he probably looked much worse than the extent of his injuries, she leaned over and kissed him tenderly on the forehead.

As Gary batted his eyes open, her vision blurred a bit through her tears. This was all so strange, she thought.

Did this man who spent most weekends riding with his bike club and who was getting ready for a three-week European tour next spring really want to marry her?

What if his injuries *had* been from riding? How would she feel then? Or what if—

She stopped thinking and rebuked herself for being negative, especially when she was usually so good at focusing on the positive.

"Morning, honey," she whispered when Gary moaned again. "Merry Christmas."

It took a good ninety seconds for him to respond. "Hey…in a feckin' accident," he slurred. "Some asshole hit me."

"I know, I know, a taxi. But you're okay. I mean, it's nothing serious and… Gary, I'm so sorry." Rachel couldn't help but feel responsible. "This was supposed to be the trip of a lifetime. I can't believe this happened."

"Yeah, stupid gobshite," he groaned, barely perceptible before his eyes fell shut once again. Hoping he was referring to the taxi driver and not her, it made Rachel smile. He was obviously high on the medication.

"Hey, sorry for being nosy," Kim whispered from the doorway, "but what does *that* mean? He's been saying it off and on all morning too."

Rachel was grinning. "It's sort of an Irish swear word?"

"Ah, I see. Well, pardon me for saying so, but I always thought that accent was kinda sexy." The nurse chuckled, going to the top of the bed and doing something with the saline drip bag. "Even with that bruised face, I can see why you fell for this one."

Rachel smiled proudly. "Yes, I really did fall, hard and fast," she replied. "I just wish I could let him know that I…" Her voice trailed off, and when Kim looked at her questioningly, Rachel shook her head. "Never mind. I'm rambling." She didn't know if it was a combination of being basically alone in a strange city at Christmas or just the excitement of bearing a big secret, but for some reason, she felt very much at ease with this nurse. Maybe it was the fact that Kim had also fallen for a motorbike enthusiast?

"Christmas," Gary mumbled suddenly. "You're gonna love what I got you. Wait till you see it." He seemed to be talking to himself, and Rachel wondered if he was even aware that she was there. "And you should see my cuff links." That was the last thing he managed before the drugs got the best of him yet again.

"Well, now I'm intrigued," Kim said, smiling at Rachel. "Wonder what he got you that's s'posed to be so great?"

"Actually, I kind of already know," she confessed, unable to hold it in. She winced, hoping that telling someone else might help absolve some of the guilt. "I already opened up the package."

"You're kidding me! And what did you get?"

When Rachel didn't answer but instead looked guiltily at a sleeping Gary, Kim raised an eyebrow. "Something tells me you could use a cup of coffee and a chat right now, sweetheart," she said, grinning. "I'm due to take a little break soon. Wanna join me? Trust me, he'll never know you left."

Rachel looked from Kim to Gary. He certainly wasn't going anywhere. "Thanks, I'd love to," she said.

"I can't go far, but let me grab us something from the machine and you can join me in the lounge," the nurse said, already moving in that direction.

"Thank you. This is so nice of you." Rachel was delighted to have someone to talk to. She hadn't wanted to unload such troubling news on anyone back home just yet, especially given the time of year.

"So I take it you two had big plans for Christmas?" Kim asked as they picked up two cups of coffee with creamers, sugar packets, and stir sticks.

"Well, *someone* obviously had big plans." Rachel paused as she stirred her sugar. "But I knew nothing about them."

Kim nodded in the direction of Gary's room. "You mean that good-lookin' Irishman back there."

"Exactly. Problem is, it was supposed to be a surprise. A big surprise. You see…" She told Kim all about the Tiffany's bag that had been with Gary's shopping. "I'm sure you're a good nurse, but I think you'd be an even better detective."

"Well, don't be so sure about that. And don't feel so guilty either. See, typical guy—didn't have his shopping done or gifts wrapped by Christmas Eve. Then when he's rushing back to try and make up for lost time, he goes and gets himself hit by a cab." Kim shook her head in mock exasperation. "If you ask me, it's his own damn fault you found that ring and probably his own fault he got mowed down in New York traffic too."

Rachel laughed out loud. "Oh, I really shouldn't be laughing, but thank you. Telling someone is such a load off my mind."

Fifteen minutes after the start of Kim's "ten-minute break," the two of them were still chatting away.

"It's funny," Rachel was saying. "I suppose you just never know who you'll end up with. I don't know…there's just something about Gary. This is so like him, hitting me out of the blue like this, catching me completely off guard. It's exciting. *He's* exciting."

"Exciting is good. Hell, so are big rocks on your finger. Not that I would know, mind you," Kim said, looking at her own hands with some sarcasm. "Just be sure you've got the lasting friendship stuff going on too. That's one thing Al and I have. I was only kidding before about him choosing the Ducati over me. At least I think I was," she said, smiling at her own joke. "We're really pretty crazy about each other, you know. Got married young and have been together a long time."

"I want to be like that," Rachel said dreamily. "Gary believes in me, and that means a lot. He's a builder, you know, and last year, he helped my best friend and I turn our dreams of opening a restaurant into reality. He gave us the cheapest construction quote by far and later admitted it was only because he wanted to ask me out," she said. "He worked day and night to get the refurbishments finished on time, and then the day before we opened, he pulled up to the bistro." She smiled at the memory. "We were just having the equipment hauled in, and I was covered in dust and paint. I was exhausted and looked a complete mess, and I looked up to hear someone revving a bike. It was Gary. He insisted on helping us out…as a favor." She shook her head. "Looks like he's surprising me for the second time, and again it worked."

"It *almost* worked," Kim clarified. "You make sure he gives you a proper proposal too. Don't let on for a minute that you know about that ring."

"Of course I won't. I'm just dying to have it on my finger though. Oh, you should see the size of it," Rachel cried excitedly. "It's absolutely breathtaking. Must be worth a fortune."

Rachel noticed Kim twisting the wedding ring on her own finger. It was a simple gold band.

"I would say one thing, and don't get me wrong now. This is just the standard advice I give to all my friends who have gotten engaged, mostly 'cause marriage is such a huge leap."

"What?" Rachel sat forward, only too happy to get the benefit of this lovely woman's experience.

"Just make sure that he thinks *you're* worth more than that ring is. There. And I don't just mean the way you look with that body and that hair and those huge eyes... Uh, you can stop me anytime." Kim paused, laughing. "But seriously. You know what I mean. Make sure he really...you know...knows you, loves you, cares about what makes you happy."

Rachel didn't answer for several seconds. She took a long sip of her coffee.

Kim reminded her of Terri in a way. Her friend was a real rock of sense, naturally cautious, and unlike Rachel, Terri wasn't prone to mad bouts of reckless enthusiasm.

Just as well she was the business brain in the partnership.

"Being impetuous can only get you into trouble," her friend routinely teased, but Rachel guessed that her own impulsive nature had come from her roots since her dad was Sicilian and second-generation Irish.

"I know what you mean," Rachel said to Kim, standing up. "I suppose I'd better go see if he's awake."

"And I," Kim said, checking her watch, "better head back to work, half an hour too late. Ah well, it's Christmas."

"Thanks for this. Will I catch you later? Or if not, will you be on duty over the next couple of days? Maybe we can do this again."

"Course. I'm not going anywhere. Believe me, I can't wait to hear how this love story plays out."

Chapter 9

THE FOLLOWING DAY, FIFTH AVENUE WAS ONCE AGAIN SWARMING. While Ethan knew there would of course be crowds, this morning the surrounding buzz of activity merely exacerbated his worries and confusion.

All he could think about was Vanessa. Fortunately, she had wanted to take advantage of the post-Christmas sales and had set off on her own for the better part of the day. That gave him the chance to try to do something about the missing ring besides stressing about it.

As it was, Vanessa wasn't much of a shopper by nature, didn't usually care about sales, and hadn't made any mention of shopping throughout the trip. Not until a particularly awkward moment the night before.

By all accounts, yesterday had been a disaster, and it seemed that her newfound interest in retail would be a welcome break from the unspoken tension between them for the last twenty-four hours.

Just then, a passerby stepped on his foot with no regard, and stifling an expletive, he tugged at Daisy's hand, pulling her out of the crowd and into a nearby café.

"Time for more hot chocolate, I think," he muttered darkly.

"Really, Dad," she replied, giving him a disapproving look. "I think you need to lay off the sugar a bit."

"Well, I'm sorry, but it's absolutely necessary just now," he said as they each took a stool at the counter. "Hot chocolate and a coffee, please," he said to the barista. He winked at Daisy. "Is that better?"

She nodded, mollified. "Much better."

Stirring milk into the paper cup, he tried to take a moment to gather his wits. Last night, after Daisy had gone to bed and to help make up for his ill-fated proposal plans, he'd hoped for a romantic night with Vanessa and ordered a nice bordeaux from room service and had it delivered with a red rose.

When he wheeled the cart into the bedroom where she was already cozy in bed, she looked up and gave him a wan smile that made him feel kind of foolish, as if he were trying too hard.

He'd poured them each a glass and then sat facing her on the bed.

"To us," he toasted, looking into her eyes. She nodded and looked back at him somewhat quizzically, then raised hers to toast him too. He thought she looked particularly beautiful and always loved it when she wore no makeup and was just fresh and natural.

Still, despite the cushion of red wine, the conversation between them remained stilted at best. It was then that she mentioned something about spending the following day apart.

"Well, of course, whatever you like," he said, surprised but wanting to be nothing but supportive. "It is New York after all, and you deserve to treat yourself."

This seemed like a good opener as any to set aside the wineglass and then turn back to slowly kiss her neck. When she responded, he paused to turn on his phone docked on the nightstand. Roberta Flack's "The First Time Ever I Saw Your Face," a favorite of hers, filled the room.

Ethan expected the mood between them to be transformed and hoped to supersede the events (or non-events) of the day. Even with the wine and the music, though, the whole thing felt tense and detached, as if they were both just going through the motions.

"Okay," he said to Daisy now, trying to refocus his attentions on tracking down the ring, "let's get going on our treasure hunt."

"What? Dad, you didn't take even a sip of your coffee, and I'm already finished with my hot chocolate."

"Yes, but I'm thinking we really shouldn't delay too long either."

Ethan plopped a couple of dollars in the tip jar, and the two headed back out onto the street in the direction of 727 Fifth Avenue.

"Sir, hello." The same elderly Tiffany's assistant who'd sold them the ring greeted Ethan and Daisy effusively upon arrival. He smiled benevolently. "So how did the lucky lady like her Christmas surprise?"

"Well, perhaps there is a lucky lady somewhere who is enjoying it very much," Ethan replied, his tone sounding edgier than he'd intended, and the man raised an eyebrow. Then Ethan sighed. "I'm sorry, but it seems there's been some kind of mistake."

"A mistake? Please, take a seat," the assistant urged, looking concerned as he led them aside.

Ethan and Daisy both sat in front of one of the octagonal service areas while he tried his best to explain.

"I don't know how this could have happened. When my

fiancée…or should I say my intended fiancée…opened the box yesterday morning, there was just a charm bracelet inside." His palms sweated even thinking about it. Ethan rubbed them on his jeans. "No ring, no diamond solitaire—just a silver charm bracelet."

"A *charm* bracelet?" the assistant repeated in bewilderment.

"Yes. I was thinking that maybe there was some kind of mix-up with the wrapping or that I'd been given the wrong bag." This was the most likely scenario, yet the one Ethan half hoped wasn't the case, because it meant that his purchase was surely in the possession of one very happy stranger.

"But this is unheard of," the man blustered. "As it is, we sell only diamonds on this floor. Gift items are available on the ground level or up on three, the Silver Floor." He looked thoughtful. "Just a moment. Let me call my supervisor."

Ethan's jaw began to work and his heart sped up afresh. This didn't look good. And worse, he hadn't even had the chance to insure it yet. "Of course, thank you."

While the assistant made the call, Daisy rested a hand on his knee. "Dad, it's okay. I'm sure everything will be fine," she said, sounding anxious.

Ethan looked at her and immediately felt bad for having to drag her through all this rigmarole.

"I know, and I'm sorry for getting so flustered. Just…"

The next thing he knew, he and Daisy were being greeted very graciously by the Tiffany & Co. general manager and whisked away by him and a couple of other suits to take a look at the Christmas Eve security tape footage.

It seemed to Ethan, sitting there in the dim room, that there must be nearly as many security cameras as diamonds on the premises. Luckily, this meant they could watch his and Daisy's visit to the store and their activity on the Diamond Floor from multiple angles, but disappointingly, nothing seemed untoward.

There was certainly no confusion with another purchase, and from what he himself could tell, definitely no mix-up.

He figured that the security guys were probably just as suspicious—if not more so—of him than he was of them, as no doubt it wouldn't have been the first time that someone had tried to claim a missing item.

Yet the bottom line was that there was nothing at all revealed in the tapes. He and Daisy absolutely looked to have left the store with the diamond.

End of story.

His mouth dry with anxiety, Ethan thanked the manager and the security team for their assistance, and they in turn promised to offer any support and he should keep them apprised of any progress.

"Thanks, and likewise," he said, shaking hands all around, while inwardly his blood pressure was spiraling so high he thought he might combust.

Back on the street outside, he was even more flustered.

"What now, Dad?" Daisy asked.

"I really don't know," he replied, racking his brain to try and come up with his next move. If there was no mix-up, no oversight in Tiffany's, then what on earth could have happened?

They'd gone straight back to the hotel after being there, hadn't they? Or had they stopped off somewhere else? Damn, he was almost certain he was forgetting something, but by now, his nerves were shredded and he couldn't think straight.

"Do you think we could maybe get something to eat now?" Daisy piped up. "Sorry, but I'm really hungry."

He looked at his watch—it was almost lunchtime, and they'd been in the store much longer than he'd anticipated. "Okay, I suppose we—"

A sudden screeching of tires in the background cut off the rest of his sentence.

"Of course!" he exclaimed then, looking in the direction of the offending car. The accident... That *had* to be it. He turned to her, eyes wide. "Remember that man who got hit by the cab, the one we helped on Christmas Eve? He had all those packages, remember?"

"Yes." Daisy nodded.

"Don't you remember? When I asked you to gather his things up and keep an eye on them...is there a chance that there was some confusion, that the man's and our things might have gotten mixed up?"

All of a sudden, she looked scared. "No, no, Dad, I really don't think so." She bit her lip, the notion that she could have been the cause of all this obviously troubling her greatly.

"Honey, it's okay. It's really okay if it did, and it isn't your fault," he was quick to reassure her as his heart raced, this time in panic. "But it makes perfect sense, doesn't it? Yes, that has to be it. Right," Ethan announced, the weight on his shoulders suddenly feeling a hell of a lot lighter as he began to figure things out. "Let's go find a restaurant. Might as well make the most of that New York pizza while we're here, yes? You can eat as much as you like, okay? Me, I've got some calls to make."

Chapter 10

"Sir, it's like I said. I'm sorry, but we can't just give out that kind of information. It's against hospital policy. I wish I could help. I really do."

"You don't understand," Ethan said, stepping closer to the nurses' station and growing more impatient by the second. He wasn't usually one to play on his charm (not since his Cambridge days, anyway), but it was apparent that this young nurse, Molly, might be a bit smitten.

And the accent probably didn't hurt either.

After hours of dead-end phone calls and one fruitless hospital mission after another, Ethan finally had a solid lead on the guy who had been hit by the cab on Christmas Eve and was less willing to take no for an answer.

He moved closer to the desk, cocked his head, and gave her his most winning smile.

"Sir." Another obviously more senior nurse stepped in and positioned her large frame between him and the desk. "I sympathize with you and your situation, but you and those big blue eyes can just take it elsewhere. And you," she said, turning to the younger woman, "should get back to work."

"But…"

She stopped Ethan in his tracks with a disapproving look. "I overheard most of it, and let me tell you, you have no cause for disturbing this patient and no claim to his identity. You don't even know his name, for goodness' sake. Now I don't care where you're from, what your schedule is, or when you have to fly home. And I don't know what you want from this guy, but I suspect that whoever he is, he's already been through enough. You simply may not see him. Period."

At this, Ethan felt a prickling sensation at the back of his neck. He knew people generally considered him passive, something that actually irked him to no end, as he was far from it, just very choosy about where he expended his energy. However, when he did commit himself to an idea, a cause, or a person, he could not be swayed, and in this case, there was a (very expensive) diamond—not to mention an entire relationship—at stake. Ethan was not backing down.

Taking a deep breath, he rounded on the nurse. "Well, since you're defending this man's privacy and seem to know precisely who I'm talking about, then I can only conclude that he must be here at this hospital."

"I said no such thing," she protested darkly. "Besides, if he's not a family member as you say, why does finding this guy mean so much to you?"

Following a phone call to the first hospital, during which he'd spilled all the details, Ethan had quickly realized that his story sounded implausible and he came off as a madman, so in all subsequent searches, he'd decided to leave out the part about the missing ring.

"Look," he told the nurse now, hoping to appeal to her better nature. "I lost something in all the mayhem, something important. And the thing everybody seems to be overlooking here is that if it weren't for me and my daughter, the guy might not have made it. We most likely saved his life."

"Saved his life?"

"Yes. I gave him first aid while we waited for the ambulance to arrive, and my daughter here made sure to protect his belongings."

"Wait, *you're* the one who helped him?" the younger nurse piped up again. "The paramedics were talking about you."

"Yes." With some satisfaction, Ethan crossed his arms and spread his feet in a solid stance as he continued to stare down the older nurse, who still didn't look convinced.

"Nice going, Employee of the Month," she said, rolling her eyes at her colleague. She turned back to him. "Okay, perhaps this changes things a little. I mean, no one does that sort of thing in Manhattan," she said, shaking her head in bewilderment, and Ethan's shoulders relaxed a little as she paused, seemingly deep in thought. "Well, seeing as you extended yourself to help, there's possibly a gray area, and I suppose we *could* allow you to see him, as long as you were supervised, of course."

Ethan was ecstatic at the prospect but did his best to contain himself. "I'd really appreciate that."

"And no, I'm not looking for volunteer chaperones," she said sharply to her younger colleague, who had risen hopefully from her station. "In fact, why don't you keep an eye on the little lady here while I get someone to take Mr. Greene to the room."

"Sure," the other nurse replied. "Is it okay if I get her a soda and a snack?" she asked Ethan.

"Yes, whatever she likes," he said. "Is that all right with you, buttercup?"

Daisy nodded, and soon after, Ethan was led by an aide to the room of who he hoped was their guy.

Poking his head around the door, he was instantly relieved to see that the patient in the bed was indeed the man he had helped in the street two days before. And he released the breath he'd pretty much been holding since the day before.

Finally…

"Can I speak to him?" he asked the aide.

"Afraid not. He's in and out of consciousness since he came in. It's mostly the meds, but he's pretty banged up too."

Damn, Ethan hadn't anticipated that. Still, at least it was the right guy, which meant that his own Tiffany's bag must still be among his packages, and given that the guy had been so out of it, chances were he still didn't have the foggiest idea about the mix-up.

So really, all Ethan could do now was wait for him to wake up, which he sorely hoped would be soon. They would talk, sort it all out, and quick as you like, Ethan and his girls would be on their way back to London. But first, he'd ensure they'd once again gather around the Christmas tree in their hotel room, and Ethan would drop to one knee and propose to Vanessa just as he'd originally intended.

It would be wonderful.

Then, over one last dinner in New York, the three of them would chat about the new life they would build back home together.

As if nothing had ever happened.

Ethan had it all worked out in his head and almost had to restrain himself from nudging the injured man awake.

But ten minutes later, he still wasn't conscious, and Vanessa was calling. She was finished with her shopping and wondering where Ethan and Daisy were.

Waiting in the hallway outside the man's room—whom he'd since learned was called Gary Knowles—Ethan had seen her number come up but had let it go to voicemail while he tried to concoct a reasonable story. "Hi, darling," he said now, trying to sound casual.

"Hi. Where are you two?"

"Oh, down by Battery Park," he lied. "I took Daisy on the Staten Island ferry for a waterside look at the skyline." He winced, disgusted with himself for blatantly deceiving her. But there was nothing to gain from trying to explain this convoluted mess, especially now. Not when he was so close to getting it back. "But we're almost finished and should be back in an hour or so, depending on traffic."

"Okay, great. See you back at the hotel, then?" She sounded tense and he supposed he couldn't blame her. He'd been so distracted and secretive, it would have been impossible for her not to pick up on it. He supposed he'd better head back soon all the same. If Knowles remained unconscious, there was little point in hanging around here much longer, and Daisy would be growing restless.

But what to do in the meantime?

Pushing his luck a little further, he decided to inquire at the desk some more. He headed back toward the nurses' station and immediately saw Daisy jump up to greet him. "Is it him, Dad?" she asked eagerly.

"Yes, it is him."

"Yay! Does he have the—" Seeing his sharp look, she caught herself just in time. "Does he have our shopping bag?"

Ethan glanced toward the young nurse Molly who was watching the scene with renewed interest. He took a deep, frustrated breath. "I'm sure he does, but unfortunately, I can't ask because he's unconscious."

"Oh no." Daisy's face fell.

"Excuse me?" Molly, who had heard the exchange, piped up. "Did you say something about a shopping bag?"

"Yes, why?"

"Well…" She looked around edgily as if terrified her overbearing supervisor would hear. "It's just that I was here when he was brought in, and he did have a lot of shopping with him. Some really nice stuff too," she added.

"Yes, Daisy here looked after it while we waited for the paramedics. You know how people can be," he continued, pressing home the point that they'd been looking out for Knowles's best interests at all times. "I wonder… It's just that the bag we lost was very important—"

"So *you're* the guy who helped the schmuck in room 303."

Ethan looked around to see yet another nurse approach from behind.

Damn. He cursed the interruption, certain he was the on the verge of getting Molly to let him know where Knowles's stuff was currently.

"That's right," he said, forcing a smile.

"Very kind thing you did, helping out some guy in the middle of the street like that."

Ethan was getting tired of everyone telling him how wonderful he was, yet he still didn't seem to be getting anywhere! "I'm sure anyone else would have done the same."

"In this town? Don't count on it, honey." She smiled at Daisy and winked.

"Yes, well. I'm certified in CPR and everything, so it's really second nature. By the way, I'm Ethan Greene, and this is my daughter, Daisy." He figured he might as well try to get as many people on his side as possible.

"Nice to meet you both," she said, shaking Daisy's hand too. "I'm Kim, and Mr. Knowles is one of my patients. Must say, it's good to see that kind of spirit alive and well, on Christmas Eve too." She laughed. "You know, his girlfriend will be here soon. She'll want to thank you in person, I'm sure. So if you want to hang out a little longer…"

A girlfriend? This was something he hadn't anticipated. So chances were *she* was the one in possession of the man's packages.

He wasn't sure if this was a good or a bad thing. On the one hand, it could be good, because he wouldn't have to wait around for Knowles to wake up, but on the other, what if the girlfriend didn't believe his sorry story?

But surely if he explained everything as it had happened, she would understand. It was a desperate situation, that was for sure, but Ethan was very rapidly becoming a desperate man.

Still, now that he knew the bags were no longer being kept at the hospital, he figured there was little point in sweet-talking the nurses. Instead, he needed to see this girlfriend.

"She's coming here…today?"

"Of course. She was here earlier but just popped out. I'm sure she'll be back soon."

"I see." Ethan thought quickly. "Well, why don't we grab a quick coffee ourselves while we wait," he said to Daisy, who nodded easily. She was clearly becoming quite distraught about her part in all this—another good reason, Ethan realized, for getting it sorted out as soon as possible.

Feeling like a heel for lying to her yet again, he called Vanessa to tell her that they were stuck in downtown traffic and might be a little later getting back to the hotel. But time was of the essence, and this needed to be resolved.

In the hospital café, seated over two bowls of chicken noodle soup, Daisy was quiet and Ethan was restless.

"Do you really think we're going to get it back, Dad?"

"Of course," he replied. "Now that we've finally found our man. And when his girlfriend gets here and we explain everything, I'm sure there won't be a problem."

The only snag was, he no longer had Knowles's purchase, as he couldn't very well take the bracelet back from Vanessa to make an exchange, could he?

Still, he could also explain this to the other woman and let her know that he'd arrange a replacement. Which meant of course that he'd have to shell out yet more money at Tiffany's, but if it ensured he got his ring back, by then, Ethan didn't care.

He realized Daisy was idly picking up noodles and plopping them back in the bowl. "Not hungry?"

"Not really."

"Why? You didn't eat much at breakfast either. Is everything okay?"

She hesitated for a minute, as if about to say something, but then shook her head. "I'm just worried about the ring, that's all."

"Try not to be," he said, feeling doubly guilty for giving her an excuse to fret. "And remember, it wasn't your fault," he assured her again. "Just a mix-up, that's all. We'll get it back. Let's finish up here and see if we can get to the bottom of it once and for all, okay?"

"Okay, Dad," she said, but he could tell this was really troubling her.

They returned to the nurses' station to find the two they'd spoken to earlier sitting behind the desk.

"Is Mr. Knowles's girlfriend here?" Ethan asked the older one, Kim.

"I'm sorry, no, she hasn't arrived yet, and he's still sleeping."

His face fell. "That's a shame. We really were hoping to speak to her today. We're heading home to London soon."

"I wish I could help you," Kim said, looking at the chart she held in her hand. "Like I said, she should be back by now—"

"Probably out shopping for wedding dresses already." Molly giggled conspiratorially.

Ethan felt like he had just been sucker punched. "I'm sorry, what did you say?"

His mind raced. No, this couldn't be happening. The girlfriend... she couldn't possibly have found...

No, but of course not, he reasoned, mentally kicking himself for letting his imagination run wild. This couple were probably already engaged. The guy was unconscious, so how on earth could he have proposed? Especially when he didn't even know he had a ring...

Still, as he tried to figure out the various permutations, Ethan's brain was moving faster than he could keep up.

"Mr. Greene? Are you all right?" Kim asked then.

"Daddy, maybe we should tell them," Daisy said, tugging at his sleeve, and the nurses exchanged a glance.

"Tell us what?"

"It's nothing," Ethan said quickly. The last thing he needed was these two busybodies involved. Though they seemed to know quite a lot about Knowles's personal life.

"Wedding dresses...isn't that nice," he said, trying to gather his wits about him. He looked at Daisy, then turned again to the nurses, at a complete loss as to what to say or do next. Vanessa was waiting for them, so he couldn't very well hang around here all day. "Tell you what. When Mr. Knowles's girlfriend gets here, can you give her my number and ask her to call me? I'd really like to speak with her. And of course, I'll want to follow up with Mr. Knowles, see how his recovery goes."

"No problem."

Ethan duly wrote his details on the piece of paper Kim handed to him. "Well, thanks again for your help—both of you," he continued awkwardly.

"Pleasure," Kim replied, and Molly grinned. "I'll be sure to pass on the message, and it was nice to meet you. You too, Daisy."

"Yeah, thanks for helping," his daughter replied with a smile.

With that, they were off to catch a cab.

On the journey back to the hotel, Ethan continued to mull over the situation.

All this talk of the other couple's engagement worried him. There was no way his ring could have had any hand or part in that, was there? Not when the guy hadn't been able to open his eyes, let alone muster up the strength for a proposal.

And the girlfriend couldn't possibly have known what was in his shopping, unless they'd planned to get engaged on Christmas Eve? In which case, his ring really couldn't be involved in any of it, he reassured himself.

"Dad, are you okay?" Daisy asked again, and he made a conscious effort to try and set aside his worries so as not to concern her further. Still, given the importance—to say nothing of the expense—it was downright impossible.

"I'm fine, buttercup. Just thinking about our flight home. I wonder if we should maybe stay on a little longer, just in case this takes more time than we thought to sort out."

Her expression brightened. "We could do that?"

"Sure." He couldn't realistically leave the city without doing so, and while an extended stay would cost extra, it would hardly be grievous, considering. "Would that be okay with you? A day or two more wouldn't kill us, and as long as we get the ring back and are home in time for New Year…"

"Yay! Can we go to the M&M's store again? We didn't really get to see much of it last time."

"Of course, whatever you like," Ethan replied absently.

He wondered what Vanessa would think or how he would explain this sudden decision to take more time in the Big Apple. "Let's have a nice afternoon with Vanessa for the moment. I'll wait for this girlfriend's call, but I might have to come up with some other...erm...reason to slip away again. Do you follow me?"

Daisy nodded. "Of course. We still can't let Vanessa know anything's going on or tell her what happened with the ring. It'll ruin the surprise."

"Good girl," he said, putting up his hand for a high five while at the same time feeling desperately guilty for having his eight-year-old collude in such trickery. She raised her hand and smacked his palm.

"But put some gloves on, Dad. Your hands are freezing."

❧

"Well, well, well, don't you have gorgeous hunks just crawling out of the woodwork?" Kim announced when, not two minutes after Ethan had left the hospital, Rachel returned.

"What?"

"Well, you've got one in the room down the hall, and now a McDreamy look-alike just left you his number. I'd call him too if I were you."

"What are you talking about?" Rachel said, bewildered.

The nurse laughed out loud. "Sorry, I couldn't resist. Seriously, you won't believe this, but the guy who helped Gary after the accident came here today with his little girl. He's the one who waited with him until the ambulance got there."

"Really?" Rachel had heard about this Good Samaritan and was doubly impressed that he'd followed up and inquired after Gary's health. "I wonder how he found us?"

"No idea. All I know is that he's drop-dead gorgeous, and she's cute as a button."

"And he left his number? Why? I'm sure you told him Gary was going to be fine."

"Of course I did, but apparently he lost something at the time and wanted to see if you knew anything about it. As well as checking on Gary, of course. Honestly, you should call him."

Rachel was confused. "Okay, I suppose I'd better thank him in any case. But if there's something he's lost, I don't see how *I* can help him find it."

"Oh well," Kim said with a shrug. "Only in New York, I guess."

Chapter 11

LATER THAT EVENING ETHAN, VANESSA, AND DAISY WERE TAKING IN the sights around Times Square when the call came. Taking his vibrating phone out of his pocket, Ethan didn't recognize the number on-screen and figured it had to be the girlfriend.

Thank goodness.

He stepped outside the M&M's store, relieved to escape the place and leave the girls to the frantic, multicolored world of grinning candy.

"Hello," he answered, trying not to sound too urgent, but his hands were shaking.

"Hi there. Is this Ethan Greene?" asked a feminine voice in an Irish accent similar to Knowles's, and he exhaled with some relief. "I'm Rachel. The nurses at Mount Sinai gave me your number."

"Hello. Yes, thank you so much for calling," he replied. He looked up to see Vanessa watching him through the window and waved nervously as she and Daisy waited in line to pay for something. Soon they'd join him outside, and he deduced he had about thirty seconds of privacy before then. "Yes, I wanted to inquire after your…erm…Mr. Knowles, but—"

"Gary's fine. Thank you so much for helping him," she continued warmly.

"Oh, that's good to know. Has he regained consciousness?"

"Not yet I'm afraid. But since you were there, it would be great to find out more about what actually happened. As you can imagine, it was all a bit of a shock for me, since I wasn't with him at the time."

Ethan exhaled in relief, pleased that she had given him an opening.

"Of course, I'd be more than happy to. Are you free to meet for coffee—tomorrow, perhaps? I'd also hoped to speak to you about something else, as it happens."

"Well, yes, the nurse did mention something."

"It seems there was a mix-up at the scene and… Well, it's a long story and is rather delicate, actually." Ethan tried to choose his words carefully as Vanessa and Daisy rounded the corner and came up alongside him. "But I've got some free time tomorrow morning, and it would be nice to speak to you in person in any case. Would that suit?" He smiled at his girlfriend, who was watching him closely.

Rachel seemed hesitant. "Okay, but I'm at the hospital mostly."

"Why don't I meet you there? Say eleven?" he said, hoping he wouldn't scare her off by sounding too pushy, yet at the same time, he had little choice but to press the issue. And if he could get this done and dusted without having to change their flight home, even better.

"Yes, I suppose that would be okay."

"Fantastic. See you then."

"What was all that about?" Vanessa asked when he hung up

the phone. "You're meeting someone in the morning?" She looked puzzled. "But tomorrow's our last day."

Fortunately for him, Ethan had a cover story already worked out in his head. "Believe it or not, that was an agent I submitted my proposal to a while back," he said with forced enthusiasm. "I emailed her before Christmas to let her know I'd be here in New York around now and, lo and behold, she wants to meet with me!"

He knew Vanessa would only be too happy to go along with this; after all, she was the one always encouraging him to dedicate more time and energy to his writing.

He smiled as if unable to believe his luck. "I can't really pass up the opportunity, can I?"

"That's amazing news!" she gushed, obviously not pausing to dwell on the likelihood of such a thing happening. Clearly she thought his ideas were considerably better than he did. "Of course you must go. What agency is she from? Perhaps I know her?" Before Ethan had a chance to reply, she smiled at Daisy. "Wow, looks like we've got a girls-only day ahead of us tomorrow!"

"But I want to come with you, Dad," his daughter protested, looking hurt. "Please?"

Ethan ran a hand through his hair, not at all sure how to handle this. While he could understand Daisy's concerns about wanting to be there when he got the ring back, surely she understood that he needed to be careful about it all in front of Vanessa? But of course, subtlety wasn't exactly a strong point among eight-year-olds.

"Well, I suppose that would be okay. That way, you can have some time to yourself, darling," he said, turning again to Vanessa.

"What? But I've had lots of time to myself. In any case, Ethan, do you really want to bring your child to a business meeting?" she questioned dubiously.

"Ah, no, it'll only be an informal chat. Anyway, I mentioned in my submission how much of an inspiration Daisy is, so I'm sure she'd love to meet her too," he insisted, but it sounded incredibly feeble, and he knew it.

"Really?" Vanessa looked from him to Daisy, and something changed in her expression, as if she'd figured out that this so-called meeting was some kind of cover story, but for what, she couldn't tell. "Well, all right then. I suppose I could find something to pass the time, perhaps visit the Guggenheim again, and meet you two later."

"Great idea," Ethan enthused, trying to get through the awkwardness of the situation by focusing solely on the reward at the end of it all.

It was because of his grand plans for their future that he was being forced into this situation at all, so surely the little white lie couldn't really hurt?

Yes, by this time tomorrow, all would be fine. Ethan was sure of it.

Chapter 12

REACHING THE HOSPITAL THE FOLLOWING DAY, ETHAN REALIZED HE had no idea what this Rachel looked like, but he supposed he could ask the nurses when he got there.

Assuming they would tell him, of course. As he'd already discovered, the Swiss Guard had nothing on the medical staff.

Going up in the elevator, Daisy held his hand tightly. He looked down at her and smiled. "Come on then, poppet. Let's go get our ring back once and for all."

Arriving at the nurses' station just a little before eleven, he immediately spied a curvy, well-dressed woman with long, dark hair standing in front of it. This couldn't be her surely; he hadn't expected someone so poised and…elegant to be with a guy like Knowles.

While of course he'd been happy to help anyone in trouble, Ethan's overall impression of the man, judging by the yelling and cursing at the traffic they'd heard beforehand, was that he was rather obnoxious.

He walked up alongside the woman, suddenly hesitant now, and when she turned to look at him, his breath caught a little. She was stunning.

"Hello," she ventured with an uncertain smile. "Are you Ethan?"

He nodded. "Rachel?"

"Yes. I figured it had to be you," she continued, smiling at them both. "The nurses mentioned you had a cute little lady with you. Hello there, honey."

"That's right," he said, swallowing hard while surreptitiously checking her left hand, but nope, no ring. "Thanks so much for taking the time to meet with us. This is Daisy."

"Very nice to meet you," Rachel said, shaking hands and then bending down to greet Daisy, who smiled shyly, on her level. "Thanks for coming in, but I should warn you, I really can't talk long. The doctor will be coming around to check on Gary soon, and I need to be there."

"Of course, we won't keep you." *Damn*, Ethan thought. This wasn't exactly the kind of thing that could be rushed. "But you have time for a quick coffee, I hope?"

"Well…" She seemed torn. "I suppose that would be okay."

They walked to the hospital cafeteria, Rachel having asked the nurse on duty to call her when the doctor was on the ward.

Taking the seat across from her, Ethan distributed a plate of cookies and fresh coffee he'd bought at the counter, his palms sweaty at the thought of having to explain it all.

"So listen, I can't thank you enough for helping Gary that night. Both of you," Rachel began, turning to Daisy, who looked bashful. "I hear you were quite the little heroine too. Gary's never been to New York before, you see, and I can't imagine why he thought he could just barge his way through the rush-hour traffic."

She smiled indulgently. "I'm assuming that's what he was trying to do?"

"Well, we didn't see it happen, but I understand he was trying to hail a cab."

She nodded as if this explained everything. "It was really good of you to intervene. Thank you. He can be such a handful at times." She shook her head indulgently.

"No problem." Ethan was eager to move the conversation along. "But actually—"

"How did you find him?" Rachel continued. "Here at Mount Sinai, I mean?"

"Ah, just a few phone calls. It didn't take too much," he said quickly.

"Well, regardless, I am eternally grateful. We're just here for a few days over Christmas. We're not locals as you can probably guess." She laughed lightly. "And while the trip didn't turn out quite as I planned, it seems there's a silver lining to everything," she said with the hint of a smile on her face.

"Silver lining?" Ethan asked suspiciously.

"Well, realizing that there are genuinely thoughtful people in the world—like you and your and lovely daughter. What a gorgeous dress you have on," she said to Daisy, who grinned delightedly.

"Thanks. I like yours too," she replied, and Ethan sat forward, keen to move past the mutual appreciation and get to the real reason they were here.

"Yes, we're just in the city for a few days ourselves," he said. "Our flight home is later this evening actually."

"Ours would have been too…if this hadn't happened. But the airline was great about changing, especially given the circumstances."

"Of course. So—"

"You said you live in London? That's one of my favorite cities, and I love spending time there. Granted, I haven't been over for a while, what with the restaurant and everything," she continued. "My friend and I run a bistro and bakery back home in Dublin. We cater too, on occasion."

"Ooh, do you make cookies?" Daisy asked.

Ethan smiled fondly at his daughter. "Daisy's become quite the cookie connoisseur on this trip."

"Yes, although I don't like to eat too many of course. Too much saturated fat," his daughter pronounced solemnly, and Rachel smiled, briefly meeting Ethan's amused gaze.

"Well, I do make cookies as it happens—*much* better than these, if I do say so myself," she joked conspiratorially. "We only use fresh ingredients too," she added, and Daisy grinned. "Yep, cookies and pastries and bread and…all kinds of yummy stuff—you'd love it! In fact, tell you what. Why don't you give me your address in London, and when I get home, I'll send you a box of goodies for being so helpful to Gary. You don't have to eat them all at once. How's that?" she suggested, winking at Daisy.

"Yes, well, thank you very much, but on another note," Ethan said. "I'm not sure if that nurse mentioned this to you, but actually it seems there was some confusion that day, and in all the melee—"

"Oops, sorry, that's my phone," Rachel interjected, taking a ringing device out of her handbag. "Might be the nurse. Hello? Is the doctor there now? I'll just be…what?" Ethan watched her previously animated expression go dark. "Oh my goodness, is he okay? But what about…? Okay, yes, yes, I'm on my way." Her brow furrowed, she disconnected the call. "I'm so sorry, but I have to go," she said, jumping to her feet. "They changed Gary's pain medication because they were afraid he was sleeping too much, but now it seems he's had some kind of reaction… I'm not sure exactly what's going on. I'm so sorry, but I really have to go."

"No, no, of course. Shall we go back up with you?" Ethan asked, completely appreciating her panic but also not wanting to let the possibility of getting the ring back slip through his fingers.

"No, thank you, though. You're so kind. Um…you have my number, don't you?" she added, flustered. "Text me your address, and I'll send those cookies over as soon as I get home, okay?"

Standing up too, Ethan ran a hand through his hair. "Yes, well, good luck with everything. Hope he's okay," he mumbled, feeling foolish and also completely clueless as to what to do. He couldn't very well say anything now, could he? Not with the poor girl in such a state. Stupidly, he held out his hand to shake hers.

"I hope so too," she replied, suddenly throwing her arms around him in a hug that caught him completely off guard. "Thank you so much again for all you've done—it was wonderful. Bye, Daisy!" she added, waving, and in a flash, she was gone.

For a long moment, Ethan stared after her, not sure what to think.

"I really like her, Dad," Daisy said, completely unperturbed by the fact that after all that, they'd got absolutely *no*where. "She makes cookies. *And* she smells so nice."

Ethan smiled distractedly. "Yes, yes, she's lovely."

Christ. What on earth was he going to do now?

Suddenly he felt completely exhausted. He was all out of ideas. It was too late to change this evening's flight, and even if the airline was amenable, they'd no doubt charge him a fortune to do so. In any case, even if they did stay on longer, it wasn't as if he could camp out here at the hospital until Knowles got better.

At this point, it was becoming embarrassing. Far from being blown away by Tiffany's magic, Vanessa would surely just think he was a complete numbskull.

He was starting to feel that way himself and was now kicking himself for wasting all that time on small talk when he should've just come right out and said something. But he'd also been a little caught off guard by Rachel's sunny personality and how effortless she was with Daisy so it felt wrong to be rude.

Damn him and his bloody manners…

He picked up his coffee and drank from it, although it might as well have been ditchwater. In fact, he hadn't tasted anything or indeed eaten properly since Christmas morning, when all this started.

"What are we going to do now, Dad?" Daisy asked. "Should we just go back to Tiffany's and get Vanessa another ring?"

Oh, the innocence of eight-year-olds! As if Ethan had another small fortune tucked away somewhere.

He picked up the cookie she'd been eating, hoping that the sugar rush might help sort out his nausea at least. "Give me a bite of that."

"But, Dad, you're not supposed to eat too many."

"Who says?" he teased. "There's no such thing as too many

cookies." He shoved a handful of them into his mouth in a weak imitation of the Cookie Monster from *Sesame Street* in a desperate attempt to cheer her, and indeed himself, up.

She giggled, a sound that always made his heart lift. "Dad, you're silly."

"No, you are."

"No, *you* are."

And as Ethan continued to banter with his beloved daughter, he remembered that no matter what, there was always at least one woman in his life who made everything seem better.

Chapter 13

"I KNOW, ISN'T IT JUST *WONDERFUL*?" RACHEL SANG GIDDILY INTO the phone. She and her best friend, Terri, had been playing phone tag over the last day or so, and this was the first time they had connected.

Despite that very scary turn he'd taken at the hospital earlier, Gary was once again in a stable condition but barely lucid, which meant that Rachel was still waiting for her grand proposal.

As there was little point in her hanging around the ward, Kim had advised her to head back to the hotel and get some rest, and she had promised to call if his condition changed. In the meantime, Rachel had taken the opportunity to call her friend back and tell her the big news.

"All I can say is when he does ask you, he'd better get down on one knee, or the next time he comes in here, the only beer he'll get served will be right over his head," Terri muttered.

Rachel had to smile. The two typically shared this sort of good-natured banter about Gary, but beneath it all was an undercurrent of mutual love and support. They had met in catering school many years before, and right from the time they were partnered up during a bakery class, their connection had been instantaneous.

That day, as they were braiding dough, Rachel broke off a piece, cupped it beneath her nose, and breathed in the aroma and warmth of it. "God, what is it about the smell of fresh dough?" she'd asked, moaning softly and closing her eyes.

"I don't know, but maybe save your enthusiasm for my sourdough," Terri quipped. "It'll make your mouth water and your legs quiver."

Rachel laughed out loud. "Nah, just wait till a warm piece of my Sicilian olive bread passes your lips and melts on your tongue. Then you'll know all about it."

"Bring it on."

And so it went. At the time, Rachel was new to Dublin and without many friends, whereas Terri was Dublin born and bred. The next day after lectures, the two got together at a nearby greasy spoon for dinner, and from then on, they were inseparable.

Weekends were spent in St. Stephen's Green over baskets of their own freshly baked bread as well as cheeses, fruit, and lots of wine. In the course of the next few months, they bonded over shared recipes—a blend of tastes, textures, and fragrances—and respective life stories.

Their mutual love of food and cooking, especially baking, made the friendship seem fated, and after graduation, the two spent a whirlwind summer traveling throughout Europe. Afterward, they both spent the intervening years in various different catering jobs but remained firm friends and strongly entwined in each other's lives.

Then, a year before, Terri's father—who ran a small café/bar in Dublin city center—became ill, and the friends decided to look into buying him out and refurbishing the café, turning it into a more high-end Mediterranean-style bistro, which they called Gillini.

One thing could be said for certain: there was nothing like it in all of Dublin.

An eclectic blend of art, furniture, fragrances, and Mediterranean food, the bistro drew people from miles around. The artisan bakery section was practically becoming a tourist destination in itself, following write-ups first in local newspapers, the *Irish Times*, and then a special mention in the *Dublin Food Guide*. Within a few months of opening, she and Terri had to post a "Reservations Recommended" sign in the window.

Their focus on creating an authentic palette of individual dishes and blending flavors and textures from various countries had paid off in greater ways than either had imagined. Although they originally intended to keep the off-site catering aspect to small and intimate gatherings, their services were increasingly in demand.

When it came to their shared enterprise, Terri's business sense and Rachel's creativity worked well together. Although their arguments were vehement at times, the laughs generally trumped the quarrels. While Rachel loved her friend's pragmatism and wit, Terri in turn admired Rachel's passion and impulsiveness.

"You're the looker, I'm the leaper," Rachel would tease whenever their roles blurred at work, and while ordinarily Terri would have been the one organizing the café's renovations, on the day in question, her dad had taken a turn, and Rachel had agreed to meet with the builder instead.

Who just happened to be Gary Knowles.

Now, sitting with her feet up on the windowsill of her hotel, she couldn't believe the strange twist of fate that day had ultimately led to her meeting the man she was going to marry.

It could just as easily have been Terri here in New York now bringing her up to speed on what had happened, but at the same time, she couldn't see it. The two people Rachel loved most in the world didn't always see eye to eye (if ever), and as such, she definitely couldn't see those two engaged and planning the rest of their lives together.

Not that she and Gary had managed to do that yet either…

"Never mind getting down on one knee," she said to Terri now. "I couldn't care less if he stands on his head, just as long as I get to reopen that little blue box."

"Tiffany's—who'd have thought it?" her friend mused. "Not that you don't deserve it, of course, but I must admit I didn't think Gary had that kind of…taste."

"Really, and what kind of taste did you think he had?" Rachel tried to sound petulant, but there was a smile in her voice. In fact, she knew exactly what Terri meant; she'd thought the very same thing.

"Oh, don't give me that wounded-kitten act. You know what I mean."

Rachel popped a piece of cheese into her mouth. "I suppose it was a bit…unexpected," she replied with her mouth full. "But that's Gary all over."

"What are you eating?"

"Just some feta I picked up earlier."

"Ah, feeling a bit homesick, are we?"

"If you're implying that I'm missing you, guess again. Any occasion for cheese, that's what I say. I passed a lovely little Greek deli on the way back from the hospital and picked up this cheese plate. Not as good as *our* cheese plate, mind you, but it'll do."

Besides that, Rachel hadn't been eating properly for the last few days. As it was, the last thing she'd managed until now was a cookie with that guy Ethan and his daughter earlier that morning.

For as far back as she could recall, food and cooking had been an extension of her very self and the life she experienced all around.

It was really only in the kitchen—her hands covered in sticky dough, her senses filled with the rich sweetness of the egg and sugar-laden mass, and her arms tired from kneading—that Rachel felt secure and confident. It represented a link not just to her past but to her zest for the present and her identity in the future.

Thus came her passion for baking bread. Bread—like real love—took time; cultivation; strong, loving hands; and patience. It lived, rising and growing to fruition only under the most perfect circumstances. If the water was too warm, it killed the yeast; too cool, and the yeast was not inspired to grow the bread. Without enough sugar, the yeast would starve, leaving the bread flat and lifeless, and if the air was humid enough, the yeast could not spur the bread to reach its full potential.

Hard and simple all at once, depending on how you looked at it.

Rachel heard another call coming through on her phone, interrupting her musing. "Yikes, it's the hospital again," she said to Terri. "I'd better go."

"No problem. Let me know when lover boy is back on his feet, and don't worry about this place. Justin and I can hold down the fort till you get back."

"Thanks. I promise I'll make it up to you. Say hi to Justin for me. Talk soon." She hung up and clicked through to the other line. "Hello?"

It was Kim. "Did you manage to get some rest?" the nurse asked. "Because chances are you won't be getting much of it from now on."

"What do you mean?"

"Well, I'm very happy to report that your man is on the mend."

Her heart soared. "He's awake?"

"Yep," Kim confirmed, a smile in her voice. "Looks like you'll finally get a chance to put that great big rock on your finger for keeps."

Chapter 14

RACHEL FELT A THRILL BUBBLE UP IN HER THROAT AS SHE ENTERED the hospital and took the elevator to the relevant floor. She could hardly contain herself and did a little skip as she rounded the corner to the hallway that led to Gary's room.

She was about to burst straight through the door but instead opened it softly and peeked around the edge of it. He was sitting up in bed with the TV remote in his hand, flipping through the channels.

Seeing him look so normal and well, a burst of emotion shot right through her.

"I can't believe you're really awake!" she cried, swooping in to give him a big hug.

"Whoa, whoa! I'm still sore, babe," he replied, holding up a hand to warn her.

"Oops, sorry." Rachel stroked his forehead and the side of his face, which was stubbly with almost three days of beard growth. "So tell me, how are you feeling? Do you remember what happened?"

Gary grimaced. "I suppose I'll survive. Bloody taxi driver… mowing me down in the middle of the road like that." He shook his head in disgust. "I hope the cops got him afterward, stupid gobshite."

"You poor thing. It must have been awful."

"Hey, was my stuff okay?" he asked. "The hospital said you'd taken my bags. I hope nothing got lost or stolen even. Some people would take the eye out of your head," he added, gasping a bit as he tried to sit up straighter.

She smiled fondly. He was barely conscious and his mind was already on the engagement ring. "No, nothing missing as far as I know, thanks to a very nice man and his daughter. They came to your rescue, waited with you, and looked after your stuff till the ambulance came. Anyway, I'll tell you more about that later. I'm just so glad you're okay. I called your mum, of course, but reassured her that you were fine and she shouldn't worry."

Gary bristled. "Not that fine. I'm still very sore, you know."

"Oh, I know," Rachel soothed. "It's just I didn't want her to worry, what with us being on the other side of the Atlantic and given the time of year and everything. It's a pity you missed Christmas, but don't worry. We can celebrate properly as soon as you're out of here." She grinned. "And exchange gifts too."

"Yeah, I suppose," Gary replied nonchalantly. "I can't believe I was out of it for so long though. We'll need to get back home soon. I've got a job on first thing Wednesday. What date is it today—the twenty-seventh, is it? I think that's what the doc told me."

Rachel's expression dropped. "But I got our flights extended because I didn't know how long you'd be here." Then she smiled softly. "Gary, you can't start a construction job so soon after leaving the hospital. You said yourself you're still not a hundred percent, so you need to take it easy for another while at least."

He seemed to be thinking it over. "I suppose I could always ring the guy and tell him I'll be there first thing after the New Year."

"That's more like it. Anyway, I thought that once you got out of here, maybe we could stay on in the city until then?" Rachel figured he might be up for it under the circumstances, especially with his grand plans for a proposal going astray. New Year's in New York would no doubt be amazing. They could go to Times Square and take in the atmosphere while waiting for the ball drop; it would help make up for missing Christmas.

Gary looked at her as if she was mad. "Not a hope! You'll have to change them back, babe—the cheapest ones you can get. To be honest, after all I've gone through, I can't see the back of this place fast enough."

"Oh."

"And I'll need to get out there and start getting a few more jobs in. Money doesn't make itself, you know."

"Oh, I see." Rachel hadn't expected him to be quite so…negative.

"Don't get me wrong. I appreciate this trip and all that. And I had a great time the first few days. It's just…you know…work and then the big New Year's bike ride, which I'm still doing despite these blasted ribs, I swear."

"No, no, I understand that," she said, raising a smile. After all, he was right. Money *didn't* make itself, and she reminded herself that he had already laid down a good chunk of that for the ring. Chances were he was also thinking ahead and budgeting for their wedding and honeymoon too, so thinking about it, an extended stay would indeed be too much of an extravagance.

Not to mention that Rachel had her own responsibilities with the bistro.

No, it was probably better in the end, she decided. Gary would no doubt have already thought this through and was likely waiting until they got back home to propose now.

Oh well, Rachel thought. It seemed she'd just have to wait that little bit longer to get that ring on her finger.

"That's my girl. Come here," he said, motioning to embrace her, and she duly leaned in and kissed him tenderly. "Now let's get the doc to write me a prescription so I can get the hell out of here."

He seemed unusually keen to leave the hospital. Or maybe he wanted to propose imminently. Even better! To Rachel, an engagement in New York—be it on Christmas Day or otherwise—seemed much more romantic.

But definitely not in these clinical and decidedly *un*romantic surrounds.

"Hello there" came a voice from the doorway, and they turned to look.

"Kim, hi!" Rachel greeted warmly. "Oh, I'm glad you're here. I... *we* wanted to say thank you and goodbye. You've been so kind, and I loved talking with you."

"I wouldn't have missed it. I think he's being discharged tomorrow, but just in case I'm not here when you leave, I wanted to pop in and say hi. Hey there, Irishman," she said, turning her attention to Gary. "How does it feel to be back in the land of the living?"

"It'd be a lot bloody better if I had some painkillers," he replied rudely, and Rachel looked at him, mortified. "And why can't I get out today?"

"Gary, have some manners," Rachel chided. "Kim has been looking after you very well while you were here, and me too."

"Well, someone had to keep your lovely lady company," Kim replied, evidently unperturbed. "I'm glad you'll be back on your feet soon. Quite a knock you had. She's been like an angel watching over you," she told him, putting her hand on Rachel's shoulder. "Anyway, I'll leave you two to your catching up. Just wanted to wish you well in case I don't see you. I'll find out from the doc about your discharge and come back and let you guys know."

"Thanks, Kim. We really appreciate it."

"No problem." The nurse turned to go but then paused and looked back over her shoulder. "And you, sweetheart…you remember what I told you before, okay?"

Rachel flushed, and her eyes darted toward Gary for reaction. Of course, he had no idea as to the reference Kim was making, but still she felt a little caught off guard. She hadn't noticed the clock on the wall before, but all of a sudden, the ticking from it could be heard clear as day. "Of course, of course I will," she replied quickly. "And thanks again."

"What was all that about?" Gary asked after Kim had closed the door.

"Oh, nothing. Just some insider secrets on helping you get better," she said, stroking his arm and trying to sound carefree. "Anyway, I can't wait to have you out of here either. We've got a belated Christmas to celebrate."

"Yeah, I hope you got me something nice. After all this, I think I deserve it," he said, and Rachel had to smile at his ironic sense of humor.

Clever diversion, honey, she thought happily.

Chapter 15

As it turned out, much to Gary's annoyance, the doctors refused to discharge him until the following afternoon.

In the meantime, Rachel once again contacted the airline and arranged to rebook (at considerable expense) their flights back to Ireland on the twenty-ninth, which meant that once he got out, they would be spending one last night in New York.

Back at the hotel, she'd gone out of her way to ensure that their final night in the city would be extra special. All things being equal, she was sure that Gary would have had his own elaborate proposal plans in place, and the least she could do now was try and make it easy for him.

So when at 6:00 p.m. sharp, the knock on the hotel room door came, Rachel leaped up from where they sat on the couch to answer it.

Tipping the room service waiter, she wheeled in a cart with two prime rib dinners, two lit candles, and a freshly chilled bottle of champagne.

"Wow, pulling out all the stops, aren't you, babe?" Gary grinned as she put everything on the table within reach to make it easier for him. He was getting around pretty well on crutches but still seemed a bit crotchety, despite the Vicodin haze.

"Well, we did miss Christmas," she said, giving him a wink and biting the inside of her cheek as she tried to hold back a giddy smile.

Earlier, he'd again brought up the subject of exchanging Christmas gifts, so it looked as though she didn't have too much longer to wait.

She managed to make it most of the way through dinner without her hands shaking too much. On the contrary, he seemed considerably more relaxed, and for this, Rachel was grateful. Part of her was afraid that if he hadn't been seeing her through the rose-colored glasses of pain medication, he might have been suspicious that she was onto his plans.

"Ugh, I can barely move after that," she said, scraping the plate with her knife and fork. "I think I've overdone it. More champagne?"

"Perfect," Gary said. "I'd pour it myself if I could, but I don't think my ribs could handle the strain."

"Don't worry. I've got it." Rachel glanced at the bottle, which was worryingly almost empty. They'd have to order another one to celebrate their engagement, if Gary ever got around to proposing, that was. Sometimes he could be so laid-back it was funny, but not this time. "So," she went on, trying to sound lighthearted, "I suppose now might be a good time to break out the presents. I'll just get yours, and we'll open them together, okay?"

"Great. I could do with some cheering up. While you're at it, can you grab what I got you from my stuff?"

Rachel's heart raced. This was it. "Sure, but how will I know which one is mine?" she asked, grateful that her strengths lay in cooking and she hadn't instead tried to pursue an acting career.

"Well," Gary replied, raising his eyebrows playfully. "That would be the one in the little blue gift bag." He sounded uncommonly pleased with himself, and she grinned.

"Sounds nice," she said, feigning ignorance about the significance.

A couple of minutes later, she returned to the table with the Tiffany's bag and several gift-wrapped packages meant for him.

"Tell you what. Why don't we move onto the sofa for this? It'll be more comfortable for you," she said. That way, there was less risk of Gary injuring himself when he got down on one knee.

"Okay. Give us a hand though, would you?" He stood up, and Rachel gently guided him the few steps across the room. "Grand, and don't forget my top-up," he added, indicating the champagne.

"Hold on. I'll bring my glass too."

Once they were both seated side by side on the sofa, Rachel handed Gary his carefully wrapped presents.

"You first," he said.

"No, you go ahead," she insisted. She appreciated his manners but figured the engagement ring deserved to be the grand finale. He didn't seem nervous at all, but then again, she supposed he was lucky; most men didn't have the cushion of Vicodin to help them through.

Gary complied and several minutes later had his motorbike-riding trousers, leather wallet, and a nice Hugo Boss shirt next to him on the couch. Rachel had picked the shirt up in the meantime, realizing that the gifts she already had seemed miserly compared to the amount he would have spent on her. "Thanks, babe. I can't believe how much you've spoiled me. I'm so lucky to have you. Now, your turn."

She looked at him nervously, waiting for something more ceremonious but realizing that in his current state, she should just be happy that she'd soon be wearing his ring.

She reached for the bag and held it up. "Oh wow, Tiffany's!" she exclaimed, playing her part to perfection.

Gary grinned. "Yep. Nothing too shabby for my girl."

Taking out the box, she smiled, hoping she had done a good enough job of retying the ribbon so that he wouldn't notice it had been tampered with.

But it seemed he hadn't spotted anything amiss. "Can't wait to see it on you," he said, and she swallowed hard.

Here we go…

Rachel pulled at the delicate white ribbon, and as it fell away, she gently lifted the lid off the box. "Oh my goodness," she gasped, wide-eyed, slowly opening the velvet ring box inside. By now though, she was no longer acting; the sheer beauty of the ring was more than enough to send her swooning all over again. "Gary…"

"I knew you'd like it. I saw it, and straightaway, I thought, yep, perfect for Rach. She'll be able to wear that with just about anything."

His sense of humor certainly kept her on her toes, that was for sure. This wasn't exactly the right time for joking, although Gary was such a devil that she wouldn't put it past him to keep her on tenterhooks just for the fun of it.

Despite his best attempts at levity, Rachel still couldn't help but be overcome by emotion. From now on, she had someone to share her future with—someone who'd be there throughout all of life's ups and downs.

And right then, she sorely wished her parents were still around so she could share this momentous milestone and reassure her beloved mum and dad that she was doing okay without them.

She smiled, tears pricking at the corner of her eyes. "Well, yes, of course I will. I'll never take it off."

She looked at Gary, still waiting for him to make some sort of romantic gesture, even if he wasn't able to get down on one knee just yet.

"Let's have a look then," he said. "Put it on."

"Well." She turned the box toward him. "I was kind of hoping you'd help me with that."

Suddenly, his eyes grew even bigger than hers, and for a long moment, he couldn't seem to meet her gaze. The silence was beginning to make her uncomfortable when finally he spoke. "So you...erm...like it then?"

Rachel's eyes shone, and all of a sudden, she understood. He was nervous; in spite of all his jokey bluster, the poor guy was terrified. "Gary, I *love* it! And I love you. I will be so proud to wear it."

"I...yeah...me too...I mean, proud to have you wear it," he fumbled, trying to sit up a little straighter.

She nodded at him encouragingly, still holding the box.

"Oh, right," he said, reaching to take the ring out.

She set the box down and held out her left hand.

"So...do you want to...will you marry me?" Gary asked, his jaw quivering a little.

"Yes, yes, I will. Of course I will!" Rachel replied, overcome, a tear streaming down her cheek. She could never have imagined this would be so emotional, considering. What would it have been like if she *hadn't* known in advance? Leaning over to hug him, she then sat back to see that he was still wide-eyed. "You poor thing, I can't believe you pulled this off in your condition. We really could have waited till you were feeling better." Then she paused. "Oh, who am I kidding?" she continued, laughing and wiping another tear from her face. "I'm so glad you didn't. It's so gorgeous. I love it. And I love you!" She beamed, holding the ring up so the diamond sparkled magnificently in the light.

"Yeah, me too. Ah…how about some more of that champagne?" he said, sounding weak too—from the emotional strain, no doubt.

"Yes, of course. A toast." Her heart singing, Rachel picked up their glasses and topped up each one with what little champagne was left. She handed him his glass, waiting for him to say something meaningful, but before she knew it, he'd knocked it all back in one go. "To us," she said, faintly disappointed that he hadn't waited, but still, what did it matter?

Taking a sip of champagne, she relished anew the lovely sensation of bubbles on her tongue. Here she was, in New York, engaged to be married! And not only that, but she now owned the most stupendous, amazing, *magnificent* Tiffany's diamond ring.

It was every girl's dream come true.

Chapter 16

Later that night, well after Rachel had fallen asleep, Gary lay wide-awake in bed alongside her in the darkness for a very long time.

What the hell? he kept asking himself, the light from the digital clock on the nightstand reflecting off the side of his face. Even after popping an extra Vicodin an hour before, he just couldn't quiet his mind long enough to nod off.

Over and over again, he replayed the scenarios in his head: shopping for the bracelet, seeing the cashier wrap up and place the *bracelet* in the bag, going outside, waking up in the hospital…then tonight, Rachel beaming at him as he placed this colossal diamond ring on her finger.

Eventually, he drifted off, but in his dreams, he was back in Tiffany's arguing with the blond over how much his credit card had been dinged for. Was there some kind of girlie conspiracy thing going on or something?

Then minutes later, he was once again wide-awake, the images from his dream still clear in his head. Tiptoeing out of the room, he slunk off into the sitting area and fired up his laptop to check his credit card statement.

Well, well, well.

Gary took a deep breath. There it was in digital black-and-white: he had indeed only been charged a couple of hundred dollars for the charm bracelet.

Well, okay then.

Granted, he hadn't planned on getting engaged, but there was no denying that he'd done well out of this particular deal.

But now, through no fault or effort of his own, he was an engaged man. Gary's jaw tightened. The timing wasn't the best, that was for sure, not when there were a few loose ends at play, and now he'd be under pressure to tie them up.

He sat back on the sofa, thinking about Rachel. Did he want to marry her? He certainly could do worse for a wife, he reasoned, thinking of some of the girls he'd been involved with over the years. She was great fun, easygoing for the most part, and while she could be a bit overemotional at times, all women were a bit like that, weren't they? No, if he thought it about it properly, Rachel was a good catch: she had her own business, was scorching between the sheets, and most importantly wasn't constantly in his ear about the time he spent off with the lads on their bikes.

Anyway, a ring didn't necessarily mean they had to get married in the morning, did it? Rachel certainly seemed happy enough with just a ring on her finger, and if she was happy, maybe he should be too.

One thing was for sure. He might as well make the most of being in the good books for as long as possible.

So all things considered, maybe he shouldn't look a gift horse in the mouth.

Powering off the laptop, Gary shrugged.

Like the man said, sometimes you just had to roll with the punches and take the hand life deals you.

Chapter 17

Ethan took Vanessa's gloved hand in his and felt buoyed about being back in London. Daisy was catching up today with her grandparents, and he was looking forward to spending some time alone with Vanessa.

His parents had been so supportive and helpful since Jane's death. Having themselves been married for almost fifty years, they had become more than just a stable bedrock for him. They were a touchstone, a sort of third-eye perspective for his own life, and it was something that had comforted and cushioned him over the last few years.

But since he and Vanessa had dropped Daisy off at their house yesterday, something had been different.

He couldn't put his finger on it. He knew that the feeling didn't really have anything to do with his parents per se, but he couldn't shake the annoyance he felt at his mother's doting, lingering tendencies. His parents' black Lab Bailey had barreled in from outside as they were saying goodbye to Daisy, and as the dog shook off the dampness—a long, controlled, full-body, rhythmic motion—Ethan felt almost envious.

He wished he could just shake things off like that too, get a grip on what was bothering him, and then play happily or lounge by the fireplace without a care in the world.

Whatever it was, it was reminiscent of a feeling he had had while shopping on Christmas Eve, only this time he wasn't invigorated and feeling one step ahead of things. The opposite, actually.

Since their return from New York, he'd furiously argued back and forth with himself the merits of telling Vanessa about what had happened with the ring, but it was almost too far past the point of explanation now.

Especially given the additional complication concerning Rachel Conti.

What woman would want to hear that a complete stranger was going around giddy with happiness with the very ring meant for her?

So many times, he'd wrestled with himself about coming clean once and for all, but since he seemed even further away from getting it back, he figured it would merely make him look even more of an idiot and an altogether disastrous choice as a prospective fiancé. Especially when Vanessa herself was so no-nonsense about these things.

No, instead he'd finesse it all into coming good so that he could finally deliver the proposal she deserved.

He just had to figure out how.

Now, unaware of his own pace until he heard the snow crunching beneath his feet in closer intervals, Ethan tugged on Vanessa's hand and told her the quicker they walked, the sooner they would be stopping for lunch.

"I'm not that cold though. I'm actually enjoying the pace. It's such a lovely day. Let's make the most of it."

He forced a sigh and watched his breath turn to vapor before his eyes. She was right. Since coming home, he was too wrapped up in his own head, too fixated on nothing else but losing that ring. He needed to relax.

"I'm sorry, darling. Just getting back into things after the break has me a bit stressed, I think." He squeezed her hand and shot her a smile. "Yes, let's enjoy it. In fact, let's give that place over there a shot for lunch today. What do you think?"

"The Snug?" Vanessa said, stopping in her tracks. "Why on earth would you want to go to an Irish pub?"

Despite her heritage, he didn't think he and Vanessa had ever been in such a pub in London together. She tended to avoid them in favor of more traditional English establishments, but he supposed that to her, they weren't remotely like home and were actually rather kitsch and fake. Still, he'd always liked this particular one. It was cozy and welcoming.

"I don't know. I suppose I just feel like trying somewhere different for a change."

"Really? On the plane, you were saying how much you were looking forward to getting back into our routine. You even mentioned our café."

By "our café," Ethan knew she meant the one they often went to for lunch on the weekends. "Right, and I am—we are. But why not bring some new flavor into the routine? I haven't been to the Snug in ages. Besides, the gastropub food got four out of five stars in the

Times recently, and we might even see a celeb or two," he added, offering a little background color that he figured might appeal to her.

She laughed, looking incredulous. "You researched this place?"

"Well, I wouldn't say I did any full-blown research, but I just came across a review, only yesterday actually," he said, muddling his way through an explanation. "Don't be fooled by the outside. I know it seems a bit shabby, but the menu really does look impressive." The look on her face wasn't communicating much, and Ethan wasn't sure if she was impressed with his thinking or suspicious of it.

"You've just never struck me as the Irish-pub type," she finally said.

The observation set him off-kilter. Just what type *did* she consider him? In fact, what type did he consider himself? As they stood there on the path across from the pub, the cold breeze suddenly became a wind.

"Okay then, I must admit I'm slightly intrigued," she conceded. "As long as you don't ask me to guzzle back Guinness and start singing rebel songs, I suppose we could try it." She smiled and brushed the snow out of her fair hair.

Ethan threw his head back, catching snowflakes on his tongue. "Great. You'll love it."

"You seem pretty sure of yourself."

Did he? This was something she had never said to him before. He quite liked the sound of it, as in truth, since Jane's death, he didn't think it was possible to be sure of anything. He grabbed her hand and led her across the street.

Seated inside the pub dining section at a white-linen-topped table, Vanessa voiced her approval. "Well, I have to admit…it's not exactly what I expected. No neon shamrocks in sight. Actually, it's rather nice."

"Good." Ethan smiled, feeling almost as if he'd won a battle of wills of sorts. "Seems I was right then."

Lunch passed pleasantly. Vanessa enjoyed brown bread and homemade potato and leek soup while Ethan devoured a platter of fresh oysters. Halfway through, he decided that a Guinness would complement the meal perfectly, and since the glass was only halfway empty by the time his plate was clean, he then decided he needed something else to finish things off. Apple crumble with custard did the job nicely.

"Good God, Ethan. Did you bring this appetite back with you from New York?" Vanessa laughed. "I don't think I've ever seen you eat like this before."

He chuckled. "I know. Pretty good, eh?" But the mention of what he might have brought back from New York merely reminded him of what he *hadn't*.

He grew quiet for a while, and Vanessa said little in return. It was as if the mention of New York had brought into focus the weight of unspoken questions hanging between them. They hadn't talked all that much about the trip since their return, and while Vanessa had insisted she'd enjoyed it, he knew that she sensed, however vaguely, that something had shifted in their relationship while there. He could only imagine how his seemingly out-of-the-blue distraction and evasiveness since Christmas Day had come across to her since.

When she'd asked how the "meeting" with the New York literary agent had gone, he'd been deliberately ambiguous, telling her that it wasn't really a meeting at all, more of a brief chat over coffee until the agent was called away.

"So what did she say about the proposal you sent? Will she be offering representation?"

"I'm not sure. She needs to read more of the story before she decides."

"Well, you'd better get cracking on that then, hadn't you?" she'd teased, and Ethan had tried to divert it off topic by presenting her with yet another gift, a little silver apple charm for her bracelet.

He'd picked it up in Tiffany's on the way back from meeting Rachel at the hospital and had hoped it would act as a peace offering of sorts and a memento of their time in the city together.

Or more likely, Ethan admitted, a weak attempt to salve his own conscience for lying to her.

Now, two days back in London, he was still no way further down the line to retrieving his engagement ring and wasn't sure what his next move should be. Since his return, he'd called Rachel Conti's number again under the guise of inquiring about Gary Knowles but only got voicemail, upon which he'd left his own contact details.

He had to trust that the situation would automatically be resolved once the man recovered from his injuries and subsequently examined his bags and became aware of the mix-up. Then, he and Rachel would put two and two together, and Ethan would have the ring back in no time.

"Shall we?" he asked, reaching for the bill.

"Absolutely. It's nearly time for you to pick up Daisy, and I need to go home tonight as I haven't quite unpacked yet. But I can still take her to her ballet class tomorrow afternoon if you like. And then dinner?"

"Sounds good."

Later that evening as the sun went down, Ethan came in from the balcony of the two-story town house he shared with Daisy in Richmond.

He sat in the leather chair adjacent to the dancing flames of the fireplace, and with his elbows on his knees, he leaned forward and bit softly on the thumbnail of his left hand.

He stopped and smiled at the unbidden memory that arose on doing so.

Jane had always loved secretly watching him bite on that nail while he was lost in thought. She said the way his hair fell part of the way across his right eye made him look sexy. She loved his blue eyes anyway, but she admitted she found them most irresistible "when they were reflecting mysterious thoughts." What she loved even more, though, were his hands. She used to say they were strong and masculine yet sensitive and artistic. She loved the way they held a coffee cup and the way they held her—especially the way they looked on her bare skin.

Hearing Daisy stir in the other room, Ethan shook off the memory and sighed as he sat back, the leather chair exhaling beneath his weight. He loved the earthy scent of that leather. It made that particular chair his favorite place to sit in the entire house. Rubbing a hand over his torso, he smiled, thinking about the lunch he had devoured earlier, and before he knew it, his mind began replaying eating chocolate chip cookies that day he and Daisy had met Rachel.

He wondered where she was now, the woman with his ring. Was she still in New York, tending to her injured boyfriend, or back in Ireland? The day after tomorrow was New Year's Eve, and she'd mentioned she ran some kind of restaurant, so surely she would have to return to that soon?

Ethan checked his watch. It was late but not that late if she was still in New York. Should he try her number again and just come out and explain everything this time? Then again, he couldn't imagine upsetting her in such a way, particularly with all the strain she was under. She'd seemed like an especially lovely person, kind...warm... with such an infectious laugh and eyes that sparkled.

Immediately, he shook the feeling off. It was almost Daisy's bedtime, so really there wasn't enough time for telephone calls and explanations now. He stood up and went to check in on his daughter.

"Almost ready for bed?" he asked from her bedroom doorway. If there was one thing he had learned about raising an eight-year-old girl, it was to never enter without announcing himself or asking permission.

"Come in, Dad. Just drawing," she said, sitting on the bed in her nightgown.

"What are you drawing?" he asked.

"Just my favorite memories from our trip," she answered without looking up. There, scattered around her, were page after page of scenes from their time in New York. "I want to show them to my friends when I go back to school."

Ethan sat carefully on the edge of the bed so as not to disturb his little artist at work. He surveyed the pictures of the moments that were apparently special to her. There was one of her sitting on the plane next to him, another of the Statue of Liberty, one of the two of them walking down what he suspected was Fifth Avenue, their view of Central Park from the hotel, and the Christmas lights on Park Avenue. Then, oddly, one of him tending to Knowles after the accident.

"You picked this as a good memory?" he asked, holding up the picture.

She nodded. "Yes, Dad, because everyone says you and me were heroes that day."

He smiled weakly. "I suppose we were." Then he spotted another drawing, this one of a trio at a table eating chocolate chip cookies and smiling. At first, he'd thought it was a representation of the two of them and Vanessa, but it quickly struck him that the hair color was wrong.

He raised an eyebrow.

"What?" Daisy asked, looking up. "Don't you like them?"

"They're beautiful. So is Vanessa in any?"

"Yes, here," she said, pointing to a picture of three people sitting around a Christmas tree. Sure enough, there was Vanessa, but sort of tucked halfway behind the tree.

"Ah, yes. I see her now," he said. It wasn't lost on him that what had to be Rachel's depiction was smiling, front and center in the picture, whereas Vanessa pretty much blended into the background. "Did you have a good time, poppet?"

"Yes, very much." She sighed and shook her head. "You already asked me that so many times, Dad."

"I know. I suppose it just didn't turn out exactly as we expected, did it? I still have to get the ring back and ask Vanessa to marry me. Are you still okay with that? You know, do you still think that's a good idea?"

She nodded. "Of course. I don't think she had a very good time in New York, though, but I suppose that could change."

Ethan grimaced. He'd half hoped that Vanessa's distant behavior had almost been a figment of his imagination, but it seemed not. "It was a bit topsy-turvy, our trip, wasn't it?"

"Yes." Daisy paused and looked at him. "Dad, did *you* have a good time? I mean, if you drew a picture of your favorite memory, what would it be?"

"Well…" Ethan was stumped. For a moment, he honestly couldn't think. Then he chuckled. "I suppose it would have to be the one of me force-feeding you M&M's on our last night. Here, give me a piece of paper and one of those crayons."

Daisy giggled with delight. Then, when Ethan was done with his own rendition of their chocolate feast, she raced into the kitchen to place it prominently on the fridge door along with her own, where Ethan had every intention of letting each one stay until the edges were yellowed and cracked.

Chapter 18

"I'M TELLING YOU, I DON'T KNOW HOW IT HAPPENED," GARY SAID, crouching down as he tightened the last bolt on a new fuel line he was installing on his motorbike.

He was glad to be back home, a wrench in his hand and a beer on the concrete garage floor. It had been a long flight across the Atlantic with his broken ribs, but at least not as long as the bloody hospital stay. He shrugged and looked at his best mate, Sean. "Sometimes, when you see the cards you're dealt, you've just got to bluff and keep your poker face on."

"Well, you could have knocked me under a bus when you told me you were getting hitched, but with the way things panned out, I suppose you couldn't do much about it." Sean guffawed. "Anyway, you could do worse than Rachel, you know. You'll never go hungry, *and* you get to have those curves in your bed every night." He grinned and raised the beer can to his mouth. "I suppose one of us had to take the plunge soon enough. Hate to admit it, you bastard, but you're looking at a win-win."

Gary and Sean had been close buddies for over thirty years. They'd grown up together in the same area of Dublin and had always shared a fascination for things that went fast...from homemade go-carts to BMX bicycles, then eventually on to street bikes. Somewhere along the line between those came fast girls and then fast women. While Rachel didn't exactly fit the "fast" category, she'd certainly been lusty and spontaneous enough to catch Gary's eye and, more importantly, meet the approval of his mates.

He stood up, wiped his hands on a greasy rag, and tossed it onto the workbench. "Throw me another one of those," he said to Sean, who reached into a half-empty twelve-pack of Heineken and obliged. "Well," Gary said, opening it with a loud hiss, "in fairness, marriage is never a win-win, but if I have to take the plunge, I suppose the odds are in my favor this time."

"Yeah, well, just as long as it doesn't change you," Sean said, waving the can in his hand dismissively. "Although at least Rachel never tries to come between you and your mates. Hell, she even keeps the brew flowing every weekend after the rides. How many birds would give us the thumbs-up on that?"

"Cheers," Gary said, not entirely comfortable with this line of conversation—about weddings and being changed and all that. He'd just wanted to hear Sean's take on what he should do about the ring if it all went south with Rachel. "One more thing, you can't breathe a word of this. As far as the rest of the lads are concerned, I bought the ring and I proposed. I got it under control. Okay?"

"Say no more. You have my word," Sean said solemnly.

Gary laughed. "I'd better. All right, throw us over yours now. Mine's good to go." It was almost an unspoken pact between them to meet at Sean's house on Sundays after their Saturday rides to keep their bikes in tip-top shape. Because of his injuries, Gary wasn't up to riding just yet, but today was a good excuse to catch up with his friend.

"And speaking of coming up trumps, I suppose you'll have a big payout coming soon—from the cab company, I mean," Sean said.

Gary frowned. He hadn't thought of that.

Sean saw the hesitation in his face and laughed. "You do know you can take 'em to the cleaners, don't you? They'll expect that kind of thing. Aren't the Yanks themselves always suing one another left, right, and center?"

Sean was right. The cab company was probably waiting for a summons to come through the mail, and here Gary was sitting around like a fool and doing nothing about it. "You know, you could be onto something there."

Sean shrugged. "You'd be stone mad not to. From what you told me, it's all cut and dried."

That was true. There he was in the middle of Manhattan, minding his own business, when this gobshite comes out of nowhere and mows him down. Of *course* he should get recompense for that. And for all the money he'd had to pay out for the hospital bills too, although in fairness, his health insurance covered most of it. But thinking about it now, wouldn't the cab companies have insurance for that kind of thing? So really, he was stupid not to at least inquire about it.

"You're right." He'd phone a solicitor first thing after the New Year. In these troubled economic times, nobody could afford to let opportunities like that go astray. And wasn't he entitled to it after all? As it was, he was still suffering, and if not for the fact that the lads were willing to wait for him, he'd have missed the New Year's bike ride. In fairness, because of the hospital stay, he'd been forced to postpone one construction job, and who knew how many others his injuries would put a stop to?

Not to mention a few quid would come in handy right now.

"Listen, thanks a mill again for holding off on the big ride until I'm up for it," he said to Sean. "These bloody ribs will take a while."

"No problem. Sure we'll do it as a team, same as always," Sean assured him. "The rest of the lads are fine about it. They're all on for the party too."

"The party…yeah," Gary replied, grabbing a fresh cloth while Sean applied the engine cleaner. On the way back from New York, Rachel had come up with the bright idea of throwing a big do to celebrate their engagement.

"We can have it at the bistro on New Year's Eve, when everything's already set up for a party," she'd gushed, her mind already racing with the possibilities, and he could do nothing else but agree.

"One thing I am learning about all this engagement stuff…" He grinned. "Lots of booze and partying. Can't balk at that, I suppose."

"Too right," Sean agreed, taking one last swig and tossing his empty can across the garage and into the recycle bin. "I'll make sure you'll have the stag night to end all stag nights too. Rachel didn't waste any time pulling this one together, did she? A New Year's Eve engagement party." He pulled his towel back and gave it a stinging flick that landed on Gary's arm. "Very fancy."

"Dickhead. You'll regret that when I'm back in fighting form," Gary said, grabbing another beer from the box and tossing it to Sean.

"Sure, are you ever any other way?" his mate replied with a wink.

Chapter 19

"WAIT A SECOND," BRIAN SAID, PAUSING TO TAKE A SIP FROM HIS wineglass and then setting it on the bar. He looked at Ethan in disbelief. "You bought a two-carat Tiffany's rock for Vanessa?"

Ethan looked at his friend, wondering why he sounded so surprised. "Yes, it's been in the cards for a while. I thought you knew that."

"Well, I knew you two were close, but I didn't think it was that serious actually. But more to the point, then you went and *lost* the bloody thing?"

"In a word, yes," Ethan muttered. "And thank you for summing it up in a way that makes me sound like an absolute plonker. I know I can always count on you for that," he added, raising his own glass for a toast, which Brian gladly accommodated.

"Glad to be of service," Brian quipped, finishing off the last of his Montrachet with one swig. He motioned to the barman for another.

Ethan shook his head. "I thought we agreed to meet for *a* glass, not three."

"No such thing as one. What's the point?" Brian retorted. "Besides, you haven't told me how Vanessa reacted when you told her what happened."

"I didn't actually tell her. How could I?" Ethan quickly polished off his own glass, then habitually raised his hand to his mouth to chew on his nail.

His friend gave him a sideways glance. "So you haven't proposed yet?"

"No, how could I? What woman wants a proposal that ends in the man telling her he's bloody gone and lost the ring?"

"Unbelievable." Brian shook his head. "I know I wouldn't have let it out of my sight for a second, let alone drop the bag on the street to help some stranger. You're way too nice for your own good sometimes, my man."

"Well, that's the thing," Ethan replied, explaining that the bag had actually been in Daisy's care. "She's blaming herself of course. But I reassured her that it wasn't her fault. It's not as though the stuff got mixed up intentionally."

Brian looked sideways at him. "I take it she knew about the grand Christmas proposal plan then. How'd she take it?"

"Brilliantly actually. She didn't know when it was happening until I picked up the ring in New York, but she was fine, really enthusiastic."

"That's great, Ethan. I'm glad Daisy's okay with it. That kind of thing could have been a big milestone, especially when she's so attached to you."

And why wouldn't she be, Ethan thought, when it had been just the two of them for so long?

"Is she still just as gung ho on the health stuff?"

He smiled sadly. "Afraid so. The other day, she brought home this leaflet she'd picked up somewhere about superfoods." It broke Ethan's heart to see that most of the items listed were being lauded for their cancer-fighting abilities. "And she's doing her utmost to try and make me take up jogging as a New Year's resolution," he told Brian. "Says it'll help keep my stress levels down."

Another reason why he was still at pains to reassure his daughter that the mix-up with the bags wasn't her fault and that he'd be able to get the ring back with minimum hassle.

The problem was he didn't yet know if that was true.

"She's a great kid. And you're a great father, Ethan, better than I could ever hope to be. Not that *that's* in the cards," Brian added sardonically. "Or if it is, I know nothing about it nor want to."

"Thanks." Ethan smiled, thinking that with Brian's reputation, it was very likely that he might indeed have offspring somewhere that he didn't know about. Although he didn't know if what his friend had said about him being a good father was true. He'd muddled his way along so far, but there was so much he didn't know about bringing up a little girl in today's world. Which was why he was so happy to have found Vanessa. There was no replacing Daisy's mum of course, but it was plain to see that his beloved daughter needed a strong woman in her life.

"So what's your plan for getting it back then?" Brian asked. "I take it you're still going ahead with the big proposal."

Ethan looked at him. "Well, of course. Why wouldn't I be? Seems like I might need to take a trip to Dublin soon." He explained how the numerous messages he'd left for the other party were so far unreturned.

Brian looked incredulous. "And how exactly do you plan to get this mysterious trip past your lovely bride-to-be without telling her what's going on? Hell, mate." He paused, shaking his head. "Call me old-fashioned, but if you're going to marry the woman, then shouldn't you be able to actually *talk* to her?"

Ethan pushed aside his empty glass and set his elbows on the bar. "That's funny coming from someone who hasn't stayed with one woman longer than six months."

"Point taken." Brian grinned, unable to deny he was a player, his esteemed profession helping a lot in this regard.

"Anyway, as it turns out, things aren't that simple. The woman who has the ring now... I met her in New York. Knowles's girlfriend," Ethan continued, stumbling over the words. "We had coffee and exchanged phone numbers. So I suppose I'll just have to try and—"

"Hold on...*woman*? What woman? You didn't mention a woman. I thought some bloke had the ring."

"He did. At least I think he did, but he didn't...*doesn't* realize it." Ethan glanced across at Brian and felt the weight of his perplexed look, something he'd last seen when his car had a flat and he'd admitted he didn't know how to change a tire.

"Look, I'm not trying to say the way you're handling this is wrong," his friend said, his tone suddenly serious. "I just think you need to grab the bull by the horns. Anyway, what's happening here? You're usually the advice man, and now you've got me being the touchy-feely-thinky one. I don't do this. I save it for the writing. So just get all this sorted so we can get back to our normal roles here, yes?"

Ethan raised his glass with fresh determination. "You're right. No more waiting around. I should indeed do just that and get the ring back and propose to Vanessa as planned." It all sounded so easy and far more straightforward hearing himself say it out loud.

Brian said nothing but raised his drink in return and gave Ethan a look that said he wasn't quite convinced.

They sat in silence for another couple of minutes before his friend spoke again. "Actually, I'm not even saying that's the right thing to do. Get the ring back, yes. Hell, if I'd spent that much on a piece of jewelry, I'd be *swimming* to Dublin to get it back, let me tell you. But in terms of proposing to Vanessa...just make sure it truly is what you want. I know you're anxious about Daisy, but don't sell yourself short as a parent either. Fool yourself into thinking you're on some sort of timeline—there should be no race to the finish when it comes to something like this." Brian paused for a moment. "I suppose what I'm saying is don't be afraid to take your time so as to make sure it's what you *both* want."

"Thanks for the advice, but speaking of time..." Ethan gulped down about half of the newly poured wine and set the glass purposefully on the bar. "I'd better go. Vanessa's coming over this evening. She's picking Daisy up from ballet class and then we're having dinner." He checked the time on his watch—it was after six thirty. "They're probably there by now."

Brian in turn set his glass on the varnished wooden bar top and gave the barman a nod for the bill.

"Hoofing it or cabbing it?" his friend asked when they got outside.

"I'll walk actually." The two men stood on the path for a moment in the glow of red and green neon. "Thanks, mate," Ethan said. "Happy New Year."

"Same to you. Have a good one. And if you need any help sorting out your conundrum," Brian said, referring to what Ethan suspected was the ring, "give me a bell."

"Will do."

As Ethan turned to go, he felt something at the edge of his brain. It was that feeling again, but now it was highlighted by Brian's comment about taking his time. Time was exactly what he *didn't* have. If he could just make a decision, some sort of decision, and act on it…

Yes, that was what he needed. And Daisy needed it too. Action.

Pulling on his gloves, Ethan noticed on his wrist the bracelet Vanessa had given him. He remembered the quote and mumbled it to himself. "*She loved him with too clear a vision to fear his cloudiness.*"

"Nothing to fear here," he said, trudging toward home in the melting snow with a warm cushion of alcohol to buoy his determination. He was going to make a lovely dinner for his two girls. They would have a great evening, cozy up by the fireplace, and watch some TV. Vanessa would stay the night, and Ethan would make sure she knew *exactly* how he felt about her. Maybe he would even bring up the subject of the future. He still wanted the ring to be a surprise, but if they broached the subject as to where the relationship was headed, surely the tension that had existed between them since Christmas would soon dissipate?

A few minutes later, he arrived back at the town house and, opening the door, immediately smelled garlic. The place was strangely quiet considering that Daisy and Vanessa were both there.

At least Ethan assumed they were, because Vanessa's Volvo was parked outside. "Where are my lovely ladies?" he called out.

"Hi, Dad," Daisy cried, coming straight from her room. She was still dressed in her leotard and pink tutu and looked adorable.

"Hi, buttercup. How was dance class?"

"It was fine. Vanessa was a little late to pick me up, so I just practiced for a few more minutes. Come on. She's in the kitchen. We've been looking at my drawings—and yours too," she continued chirpily, leading to where Vanessa sat on one of the three barstools in front of the small kitchen island.

"Hi, there," he said, kissing her cheek. Then he noticed she was just finishing up some Milanese chicken. "Oh, you've already eaten?"

"Yes, we couldn't wait. Dinner was ready for six, like we agreed."

"Oh." Instantly he felt wrong-footed.

"I called to check how much longer you'd be but there was no reply."

Sure enough, there was a missed call notice on the screen of his phone. "I mustn't have heard it vibrating. I just met Brian for a glass and a catch-up."

"*A* glass? Smells like quite a bit more to me," she replied with a smile that he knew belied her annoyance.

"Sorry. I was sure we'd said seven."

"It's okay, Dad. We saved some for you." But Ethan didn't really hear her. Instead, he was surveying the pictures Daisy had drawn of the trip, which were sprawled across the island unit. Just as she'd said, the two had been looking through them. "I showed Vanessa where she is in this one," his daughter continued.

"Yes, nice to see I *am* in one." Vanessa laughed but he could hear the edge in her tone. She rinsed her plate and put it in the dishwasher. "All your favorite memories of our trip. You should put those in a scrapbook, Daisy. Yours too, Ethan." Her voice had enough sincerity in it to appease Daisy, but Ethan knew well that she was irritable. "That one of you and Daisy eating cookies is lovely," she said, idly picking up the picture of their meeting with Rachel. "And this must be the agent you met?"

"Yes." He nodded noncommittally.

"It really was the best trip ever, wasn't it?" Daisy mused, smiling, and he grasped at the opportunity to change the subject.

"Definitely. Especially because it was your first real trip, honey. But there will be more. The three of us will take many more jaunts together," he said pointedly. "Maybe next time, Vanessa can choose the destination." He paused, waiting for her to agree.

"Maybe," she finally replied. "Are you finished with this already, Daisy? You didn't eat much."

"No, I'll have some more now. I just wanted to wait for Dad."

Ethan helped her up on the stool and shrugged awkwardly at Vanessa. He grabbed the plate and put it in the microwave to warm it up. Then he warmed his own and took a seat while she kept moving about, cleaning the counter and adding more dishes to the washer.

"Leave those. I'll get them later," he told her. "Come sit with us." He reached out and gently rubbed her arm. "There's some chocolate ice cream in the freezer for all of us when we're finished. I'm so sorry I was late."

"No, you two carry on. I think I'm going to call it a night actually. I've got an early start tomorrow. Big meeting first thing."

"Ah, please stay. I was really looking forward to us having a nice evening, just the three of us," Ethan said, dropping his fork and taking both of her hands in his.

"Ethan…" Vanessa looked straight into his eyes, the barstool putting them at eye level. "Not this time. Sorry." She pulled away and grabbed her purse off the countertop. "Good night, Daisy," she said, rubbing the top of the little girl's head and planting a kiss on her wavy locks.

"Night," his daughter replied, her focus squarely on the food in front of her.

Ethan jumped up to walk Vanessa to the door, and she stayed ahead of him the whole time, taking her coat off the back of the couch without a misstep. He managed to slip in front of her by the door.

"I'm sorry. I know you're annoyed with me, and I also know I've been a little…off lately. It's not you, honestly. I love you, and Daisy loves you too. We're…we're a team, the three of us, aren't we?"

"Dad, *Sing* is on! Can we watch it?" came Daisy's shout from the kitchen.

Vanessa closed her eyes for a couple of seconds and pressed her lips together.

"Just a second, hon," Ethan called back, exasperated. He turned back to Vanessa. "Hey, I'll phone you in the morning. Let's meet for lunch tomorrow? I'll come and pick you up from the office."

She hesitated, then nodded. "Okay, that would be nice." Vanessa turned to leave, and Ethan listened to her footsteps move away from him down the hallway just as Daisy's came toward him from the kitchen.

Chapter 20

At 7:00 p.m. on New Year's Eve, Terri was running around the bistro making last-minute preparations before everyone started arriving for Rachel and Gary's engagement party.

They'd closed the place early today, after lunch, as originally intended, Rachel suggesting they should use the night off as an opportunity to celebrate the big event.

Terri was cognizant that tonight would also mark a huge shift in the friends' shared history, a separation of paths as such, and while she was thrilled to see Rachel so happy, she also couldn't help but feel a little trepidation too.

Still, despite her misgivings about Gary, she really had to hand it to him for surprising her out of the blue in New York with that whopper of a ring.

Her eyes had nearly popped out of her head when she'd seen the size of it, and she felt bad for having clearly misjudged the guy. So in preparation for tonight's celebrations, she had spent the morning in a corner of the kitchen baking various breads and pastries to accompany savory canapés for the New Year's Eve—cum—engagement party.

Just then, Justin walked through the swinging kitchen door, closely followed by an excited Rachel.

"Still here?" he jibed. "Everything's ready to go, so you two should just go off and get changed and, more importantly, get out from under my feet."

The older chef had been with them since the beginning and was practically a part of the furniture at Gillini now. Besides his talent in the kitchen, they also appreciated his rapid-fire wit and good humor, a plus for keeping the waiting staff smiling when the place was filled to capacity.

"Terri!" Rachel gasped, and Terri could tell that despite her buoyant mood, her friend was a little flustered. "Why aren't you changed yet?"

"I know, I know. I'm going now." Terri wiped her hands and put some fresh blinis in the fridge. "Just wanted to make sure we have enough of everything." Rachel paused then, and by the look on her face, Terri suspected she was about to go all emotional on them, as she was prone to do.

"Hey, just in case I don't get to say it tonight," her friend began, tears shining in her eyes, "thanks for helping me pull this party together so quickly. I know it was a lot, asking you to give up your night off, and I want you to know how much I appreciate not just your efforts tonight but the two of you as friends." Rachel took a deep breath and waved her hand in the air as if this would somehow stop her from blubbering. "This is such a huge and truly unexpected step in my life, and thanks for helping me celebrate it."

The sincerity in her voice merely made Terri feel even worse for thinking so badly of Gary before.

"Have you been on the vino again?" she joked, by now well used to such emotional outpourings. Rachel was an unbelievable softie and had this unyielding ability to see the good in everything that Terri envied. "You silly goose. Of course we're going to help you celebrate! It's not as though we need much of an excuse, and anyway, we're thrilled for you. Aren't we, Justin?"

"Yep. You deserve every happiness, honey, and this is going to be a great party."

Rachel beamed. "Thanks, guys."

After Rachel exited the kitchen, Terri met Justin's eye. "Nice dodge," she said sardonically.

He shrugged. "Unlike some people, I'm not going to lie and say I'm *happy* about it."

"What do you mean? Of course I'm happy for her."

"You're happy that she's marrying a Neanderthal? Some best friend you are."

There had never been any love lost between Justin and Gary, who were pretty much chalk and cheese.

Terri shrugged and leaned against the kitchen worktop. "What do you want me to say? If she's happy, that's all that matters. Isn't it?"

"Hmm, remains to be seen," the chef replied. "But from where I'm standing, this fairy-tale engagement has horror show written all over it."

❧

In the small back office of the bistro where she'd left a change of clothes, Rachel picked up her handbag and rummaged inside it for the gorgeous, sparkling Tiffany diamond that she still couldn't believe was hers.

Since New York, she couldn't stop looking at the ring and hated not being able to wear it all the time. Not that she was complaining or would ever say anything to Gary, but it was so big it was actually a bit awkward for someone who worked with her hands so much. Something she hadn't thought about until she was back in the kitchen and it had promptly gotten caught up in some mushy cookie dough.

Still, it was a teensy inconvenience that Rachel could happily overlook for the privilege of owning such a perfect expression of love and devotion. Then suddenly she put a hand to her forehead. Cookie dough! She'd completely forgotten about Ethan Greene and her promise to send some to London for his little girl.

She had missed a call from him the day she and Gary had gotten home from New York, and what with jet lag and organizing the party, she had neglected to call him back. She made a mental note to remind Gary to phone him soon; her fiancé would no doubt want to thank him too, and they could make arrangements to have the cookies sent over.

Rachel slipped out of her chef's whites, jeans, and T-shirt and into her red dress, the same one she had worn on Christmas Eve. After all, Gary hadn't gotten to see it that night, so it seemed fitting that she should wear it now.

She pulled on her thigh-high stockings and fished a pair of

dangly, antique earrings that had belonged to her mother out of a pouch tucked safely inside her handbag. Then, pulling her hair back with matching diamanté clips on either side, she left some light tendrils hanging down past her cheekbones to fall just below her jaw.

Having applied just enough makeup to accent her wide eyes and redden her lips, she finally smiled at herself in the mirror of the small adjoining bathroom. The lighting wasn't great, but she knew she looked the part. How could she not? She had never been so happy.

"Knock, knock," she heard a voice say from outside the office door.

"Come in. I'm almost ready."

"I don't know why you wouldn't just go upstairs to mine to get changed and—" Terri raised both hands to the sides of her face. "Wow, you look amazing! I love the dress." Then her friend paused and shook her head. "Look at the two of us and how far we've come since traipsing around as a couple of students barely able to make ends meet. We could hardly afford bus tickets back then, and now… With this business and your wedding, suddenly I feel all grown up. Where does the time go?"

Rachel smiled, a lump in her throat. Unlike herself, who got emotional at the drop of a hat, it was very rare for Terri to show her softer side. Rachel hugged her, her own eyes welling up afresh. "Oh, stop with the fuzzy stuff. You'll ruin my makeup!"

"Actually, I don't know where the hell that came from," Terri muttered, sounding much more like herself again. "We both know you're the sappy one on the team. I dunno. I think maybe the engagement just caught me by surprise and I'm still trying to get my head around the fact that we're not going to be the terrible twosome anymore."

"I know exactly what you mean." As it was, Rachel felt as though her brain was still trying to catch up with her heart, or vice versa. "Are you sure you're happy to be my bridesmaid?"

Terri's eyes widened. "Are you joking? Wild horses couldn't stop me, although I don't envy you having to find a dress to match this rug," she added wryly, indicating her riot of red hair. With her pale Irish skin, which contrasted wildly with Rachel's Mediterranean complexion, the two women couldn't have looked more different. "So what did Gary's mum say. Was she thrilled?"

Rachel shrugged. "I think she had pretty much the same reaction as everyone else to be honest—a bit taken aback. Although she's delighted too of course, and she's coming along tonight."

"Great," Terri said. "Well, I suppose I'd better go home and get changed myself." She didn't have far to go, "home" being the little flat above the bistro. "We're pretty much good to go outside, so you take your time getting ready." She turned for the door but then paused.

Rachel looked up. "What?"

Her friend shook her head. "It's nothing. I was just thinking what a brilliant way to end the year. And next year will be even better what with the big day itself, won't it?"

Well, she and Gary hadn't actually set a date yet, and in all honesty, they hadn't really had a chance to discuss it since their return from New York, but yes, like Terri, Rachel automatically presumed the wedding would be in the coming year.

Personally, she hated long, drawn-out engagements—what was the point? And since the proposal had more or less come out of the blue, she was certain Gary felt the same.

"Should be, but lots to sort out yet."

"And plenty of celebrating to be done too!" her friend said with a wink before going back out to the restaurant.

"You can say that again." Rachel smiled through happy tears, wondering what she'd ever done to deserve such joy.

Chapter 21

ETHAN WAS SITTING IN THE KITCHEN OF THE TOWN HOUSE DRINK-ing a glass of wine, waiting for Vanessa to arrive. It was New Year's Eve, and he had arranged for Daisy to spend the night at her friend Tanya's house as he really felt that he and his girlfriend needed some time alone.

He hoped he could make tonight special. He had champagne on ice and had spent the day preparing a lavish meal in the hope of showing her a good time and making her realize just how committed he was to her.

But he couldn't help wishing that things could be different and that instead of him secretly fretting about how he was supposed to get the ring back, they could be discussing their impending nuptials tonight. He'd thought yet again about coming straight out and telling Vanessa everything in the hope of clearing up the tension that was rapidly forming between the two of them, but he just couldn't do it.

The ongoing mess would be a million miles from the proposal he'd intended or indeed how he'd always pictured it. He wanted the moment to be something special, something romantic she would remember forever, rather than a long and confusing story about some bizarre mix-up.

Until he got the ring back, he could at least try to show her how committed he was, that their relationship meant a lot more than a simple silver charm bracelet—that *she* meant much more than that.

Then a sudden thought popped into his mind and his pulse quickened. Of course.

Before Ethan had time to ponder his revelation further, the doorbell rang, and he went to answer it.

Vanessa stood at the door looking exquisite. She always looked beautiful, but tonight she was dressed in a well-cut black cocktail dress that fitted her slim frame to perfection. Her blond hair was piled elegantly on top of her head, and a simple pear-shaped diamond pendant adorned her throat. *My future bride*, he thought. If only she knew it.

"Hello, darling. You look beautiful." Ethan wondered why he sounded so wooden, so stilted all of a sudden.

She smiled and stepped into the hallway. "Thank you." Placing a light kiss on his cheek as she passed, she moved into the living room, taking off her coat.

"Why did you ring the doorbell? Did you forget your key?" he asked, trying to make light of the situation.

She blushed a little. "I don't know really." Again, an uneasy formality appeared between them. She looked around. "Where's Daisy?"

"She's staying over with one of her friends. I thought it might be good to make tonight just about you and me."

"Oh, that's nice." Vanessa smiled again, but it didn't reach her eyes, and Ethan felt his heart deflate. *This is so awkward.* It was as if all their shared history had somehow been erased and they were starting over from scratch.

"Would you like a glass of wine?"

"Yes, if you're having some."

Ethan moved to the kitchen and picked up the bottle of red that he had already opened. When he turned around, the openly tense expression on her face took him aback. He needed to change the mood here—and quickly.

"Here you go." He handed her a glass and held out his own for a toast. But she didn't wait, instead bringing the glass to her mouth and drinking deeply. "Er, cheers then," he joked lamely.

"Oops, sorry." Laughing a little, she belatedly clinked his.

Ethan perched on one of the high stools at the edge of the kitchen island. "You know, I heard that you should always try and end a year the way you started it."

"Is that so?"

"Yes. And this time last year, you and I were very happy, remember?"

"Ethan..."

"No, please, just let me finish. I know there's been some tension between us lately, especially since New York, and...well, frankly, I'm not sure why that is. I love you, Vanessa. Daisy loves you. I need you in my life, and I want you to be happy."

Vanessa lowered her gaze. Whether it was because of the emotion of the moment or the strain in the room, he didn't know.

"Ethan, I am happy. I just… You're right, there is some tension, and I thought…" She trailed off, shaking her head.

He stood up and went to her, taking both of her hands in his. "Regardless, none of that matters now. Well, it does, but…" He shook his head, aware that he was babbling a little. "I wanted to talk to you about something, a serious subject."

She brought her gaze up to meet his. "Serious?"

"Yes," he said, swallowing hard. He hoped this idea would go over well, a temporary diversion of sorts, at least until he had the ring back.

"What is it?" A strained smile played at the corners of her mouth, and he wondered what she was thinking or expecting him to say.

He cleared his throat. "Well, I thought that maybe we should take our relationship to the next level. Start acting more like a family." She smiled hopefully at him, and he felt his heart begin to lighten. "I was thinking that maybe we should think about moving in together… I mean you…move in with us."

There was silence for a moment, and his hands started to sweat. He couldn't believe he was this nervous. After all, if everything had gone according to plan, by rights they should already be engaged, so he felt almost silly for worrying about her answer to this. What if she said no?

Finally, she spoke. "Move in…here with you and Daisy, you mean?" she asked, her face brightening.

Ethan smiled. "Yes," he replied and immediately noticed her eyes get teary. "I love you, and so does Daisy. You must know that."

A tear crept down her cheek, and she threw her arms around his neck.

"Oh, I feel so silly. You have no idea what I've been thinking this past while. I thought that my being in New York with you might have been a mistake, that it brought back too many painful memories of…" She shook her head. "Of course. Of *course* I'll move in with you. I'd love to!"

Ethan exhaled with relief. He felt fantastic. He wasn't sure where the idea had come from, but clearly it had been the right move.

Now, all was back on track, and even though she didn't admit it fully, he knew *exactly* what Vanessa had been thinking since New York. She was obviously concerned that his sudden withdrawal was due to the fact that he was still pining for Jane.

All because of that stupid bag switch. And until he got that sorted, this was the perfect interim solution really.

He recalled Brian's comment about taking his time and not rushing into anything. Well, this at least gave him the opportunity to buy some time, didn't it?

Time to get that ring back from Knowles so he could move on with his life once and for all.

Chapter 22

RACHEL WAS TALKING ON HER PHONE, AND IT WAS CLEAR BY HER sparkling eyes that she was talking to Gary. Her eyes always looked like that when she spoke to him, and Terri could never quite figure out why.

Then, Rachel ended the call and practically danced toward her, impulsively embracing her. "Ah, life is good when you're in love," she gushed.

"As it should be." But Terri's tone must have lacked conviction, because her friend pulled away to look at her.

"What's up? You sound…weird."

"Ah, you know me. All this happiness and joy just pulls at my heart," Terri said lightly, trying to inject her usual, more sardonic tone into her voice. She couldn't help thinking about what Justin had said before.

Was Gary the right man for Rachel? Yes, the engagement seemed to have come out of nowhere, but it was an engagement nonetheless. And any fool could see that Rachel was blissfully happy, so surely that counted for something?

"Oh, give over. We both know that deep down you're a real softie."

"Yep, that's me." Terri looked at her watch. "Bloody hell, it's almost eight. The masses will be arriving soon. Tell us, where's your knight in shining armor?"

"That was him I was just talking to. He was on his bike so I could barely hear him, but it sounded like he was asking about us having enough beer." Rachel rolled her eyes. "You know the way those lads won't be caught dead drinking wine."

Terri did. Gary's mates were as infantile as he and should be grateful enough about being fed and watered for free at this party, let alone start making demands. But Rachel didn't seem to mind, so perhaps Terri shouldn't let it bother her either.

Then as if on cue, five bikes zoomed past on the street outside. Rachel gave a little jump and clapped her hands together. "Here we go—party time! I'd better freshen up," she said, scampering toward the ladies' room.

Terri headed farther down, to where Justin was already handing out canapés to the first of their guests.

"Lover boy and his posse have just arrived," the head chef muttered wryly.

"Yes, I witnessed the caravan."

As if on cue, Gary and his leathered-up biker crew came through the door just as Rachel reappeared. He tossed his helmet onto a nearby chair and grabbed her around the waist, spinning her around. The handful of onlookers already present applauded, and Gary grinned while his fiancée smiled demurely. Then she handed out beers to each of his mates before pouring a glass of champagne for herself.

Terri saw Justin suspiciously eyeing the spectacle. "How come His Highness is only rolling in now? Wouldn't you think he'd have been here earlier to lend a hand?"

"To be fair, this is our specialty, not his. Unless you wanted the kitchen extended or something." Now that he and her friend were betrothed, Terri felt somewhat duty bound to defend Gary.

"Oh my God," the chef continued, open-mouthed, motioning in the direction of the happy couple. "Did I just hear her ask him if he liked the dress? She had to *ask* if he liked that dress? Now *I* need a drink."

An hour later, thirty or so people were grazing their way through tray after tray of quiches, cheese plates, blinis, and a plethora of other Gillini specials. The DJ arrived, a friend of Justin's who promised to play the perfect party mix through the bistro's sound system.

Some people were dancing, but Terri was nursing her second glass of champagne when she looked over to see a woman standing tentatively in the doorway. There was something vaguely familiar about her, and when someone else came in behind her and a gust of wind caught her strawberry-blond hair, revealing more of her face, Terri knew in an instant who she was.

"Hello," she said, greeting the woman warmly. "You must be Gary's mother."

"Yes," the petite woman replied, looking pleased to be noticed. "I feel terrible for being so late, but I got a bit delayed." Mary Knowles's diminutive stature initially made her seem too young to be Gary's mother, but on closer look, Terri noted the lines in her face.

"Not at all. Everything's just getting started really. Come inside and get something to eat. Can I get you something to drink? A glass of champagne maybe? Isn't it great news about the engagement? You must be so proud of your son."

Mary took a deep breath and cocked her head to one side as if trying to buy time while constructing an answer. "Very proud, yes. And a bit surprised too, I have to say," she replied, taking a sip of champagne. "That son of mine has been in love with those bikes for so long, I never thought a woman would be able to hold his attention."

Rachel happened to look up then too and waved at Mary. She tugged on Gary's arm and motioned him toward her. Quickly finishing his conversation, he excused himself and went over.

"Mam," he greeted. "I didn't think you were going to come."

"Why wouldn't I?" Mary reached across and hugged Rachel and then her son. "Congratulations, love."

"Thanks, Mary," Rachel said, beaming and extending her hand, and Terri watched with interest as Gary's mum did an actual double take on catching sight of the ring.

"Stunning, isn't it?" Terri gushed.

Mary just nodded, apparently dumbstruck. She looked curiously at her son, as if trying to work out when Gary had become Mr. Generous all of a sudden. "I'd say you spent a fair few quid on that."

He didn't meet his mum's gaze, and Terri sensed that something unspoken was hanging between them. Did Mary seem…annoyed?

"Ah well, you know yourself…"

Then Mary smiled at Rachel. "It's beautiful. Congratulations."

"Thanks. I must admit it was a surprise but a lovely one. Your lovely son really is an old romantic at heart," she added, looking lovingly at Gary. Then she clapped her hands together. "So now that everyone's here…"

Terri watched her dash up to the DJ, and seconds later, the music dropped to background volume while Rachel stood by the buffet tables and asked for everyone's attention.

"Thanks." She smiled as people hushed their conversations. "First of all, Gary and I both want to thank you for spending your New Year's Eve with us and helping us celebrate our engagement." She looked at her fiancé, who just shrugged and looked back at her.

Out of sight of Mrs. Knowles, Justin rolled his eyes at Gary's offhand response while Terri bit her lip and stifled a smile.

"Second," Rachel went on, and her voice caught a little, "as you know, my family is part Sicilian, and I'd like to continue a tradition we Sicilians have in honor of my parents, who I know would be so proud to see this. And also in honor of you all, who've practically become family to me too." Eyes shining, she leaned down and took out a basket of bread from beneath the linen-covered table. "Many of you will have already tried my olive bread or some variation of it. Well, this," she said with a sway of her hips and dramatic wave of her hand, "is the authentic Sicilian recipe. For those of you who don't know, it comes from my great-great-grandmother's recipe. In Sicilian tradition, this particular recipe is made only for special celebrations and is symbolic of sharing wholeheartedly in the occasion and its fruition. So if I could ask my husband-to-be to come up and join me in taking a piece," she said, entreating Gary with a smile. "And then we'll pass around some for you all."

Everyone clapped as Gary sauntered up to Rachel. She took one piece of bread in her own hand and gave another to him, entwining their arms together in the traditional wedding pose used for a toast. She took a bite and then continued to eat the entire slice, smiling as she did so.

Gary nibbled a little on his before setting it back down on the table.

"One of the downsides of marrying a chef—bad for the old waistline," he joked, laughing and patting his chest, and his mates joined in the joke, jeering and raising their glasses.

"Oh…dear…God," Justin said, coming up alongside Terri. "And I thought gay people were vain."

"But there is something I would like to do," Gary continued then, and Rachel's face brightened. "As you probably heard, I was in a terrible accident recently, and believe me, if there's any justice in life, the gobshite responsible will get what's coming to him," he said, jaw tightening. "Anyway, I was pretty battered and beaten by the time I got out of the hospital, but that didn't stop me." He winked at his fiancée. "If anything, it made the surprise even better. Poor Rachel probably felt a bit like I did when that cab hit me, although of course, she didn't have to suffer a few torn ribs." Everyone laughed as he paused and made a great show of rubbing his midsection. "So," he said, turning to her, "since I didn't get the chance to do this properly the first time…" He cocked his head toward her, and after a beat, she figured out his train of thought and took off the ring, handing it to him. With that and first ensuring everyone managed to get a good look at the diamond, Gary dropped to one knee. "Rachel, wanna get hitched?" he asked, and all the guests cheered.

"Of course I do." There were tears in her eyes as Gary slipped the ring back into place.

"How romantic." Justin tut-tutted.

Terri was trying her utmost to be devil's advocate. "Look, I know we've always thought that Gary was a prat of the highest order, but maybe we should give him a break? Seems like he's really into this."

The chef sighed. "Well, think what you like, but if you ask me, there's something very wrong with this picture. The guy has the emotional development of a sea urchin, and I for one can't believe he'd planned a big New York proposal, let alone shell out for a rock that size."

Terri's gaze returned to the happy couple, and she looked sideways at Justin. "You're not jealous, are you?" she teased, nudging him. "That Rachel is going to be first to do the big white wedding thing?"

He snorted. "Nah. I suppose I just can't believe that our Rachel is actually going to marry this amoeba. Why? What the hell does she see in him? I know she says he makes her laugh, but is it intentional?"

Terri shrugged. "Each to their own, I suppose. Just because you and I are hopeless with relationships doesn't mean we should be cynical about everyone else."

"Speak for yourself, sunshine. Bernard's planning something special for our day off tomorrow, and while I think of it..." Justin's sentence trailed off. He reached into his pocket. "These two messages came in while you two were getting ready earlier. One from the accountant—he was rambling something about an end-of-year VAT return." He shook his head. "Don't ask. You know all that business stuff is gobbledygook to me. And another call from a guy that I forgot to give to Rachel. Phoning from London, *very* sexy accent, and seemed a bit frantic actually…something about a mix-up in New York with Gary." He made a face. "Said he got this number from her voicemail. Can you pass it on?"

"Of course." Terri read the piece of paper with the caller's name inscribed on it.

She looked again at her best friend's betrothed, who having played the part of the dutiful fiancé was now right back in the middle of his mates, handing out beer as if it were going out of style, while Rachel did the polite thing and circulated among the guests.

"What?" Justin asked, shrewd as always. "I think I know that look."

Terri shook her head. "Nothing."

But for some reason, her Spidey sense was tingling. What kind of "mix-up" could have happened in New York? Something to do with the accident maybe? Why else would some English guy be phoning here frantically looking for Rachel?

She bit her lip. Darn it. Maybe Justin was right; maybe there *was* something wrong with this picture.

What else had Gary been up to in New York?

Chapter 23

"DAD, YOU SHOULD PHONE THE RESTAURANT AGAIN," DAISY URGED Ethan, sounding much older than her eight years. Despite his previous attempts to get in touch with Rachel Conti over the holiday period via her personal and business details, the Irishwoman hadn't returned his calls.

He was loath to be too much of a pest, especially when she'd been so nice before, but nice or not, he needed to get his ring back. At this point, he was starting to feel like a chump.

"I know, I know." He picked up the phone. "So you really are okay with Vanessa moving in?"

She sighed heavily. "Dad, why do you keep asking that? If you'd asked her to marry you, she would have moved in eventually, wouldn't she? So since I was okay with that..."

"All right, all right." It wasn't exactly what he wanted to hear, but she was correct—there was little point in persisting with unnecessary questions. "Okay. Let's get this sorted out once and for all."

This time, there would be no pussyfooting around. The other woman's discomfort aside, he would explain the situation to Rachel and outline in full what had happened. Though chances were she and Knowles would have worked it all out by now and he wouldn't have to explain anything.

Then why haven't they been in touch? his subconscious mind asked, but Ethan chose to ignore it.

Dialing Rachel's number, he waited as the line connected in Ireland. He really hoped she would answer the call this time rather than have to explain himself again to a staff member who obviously hadn't bothered to pass on his last message. Finally, on the fourth ring, the line was picked up.

"Gillini bistro, how can I help?"

"Hi, Rachel? This is Ethan," he greeted smoothly, but when there was no immediate reply, he added, "We met in New York recently?"

"Ethan, of course!" she exclaimed. "Goodness, I'm so sorry. Don't mind me. My mind is just all over the place these days. Yes, I got your message from before and passed your number on to Gary. He hasn't called you back yet?"

"Ah, no, he hasn't."

There was a brief silence. "Really? I was sure he would've by now, so let me apologize on his behalf. I know he's been up to his eyes since we got back, and with so much going on too... But I also know he really wants to talk to you and to thank you of course for that wonderful thing you did for him."

"Actually, about that..."

"And we've just gotten engaged, which is possibly the reason he simply hasn't had time to contact you yet," she went on blithely, and Ethan went white. "We've been so busy since we came back. So much to plan, and we've just had a big engagement party and..."

Ethan's brain thudded with anxiety. He wasn't sure what to think. There wasn't a chance that… No, surely not?

Gary Knowles wouldn't have been stupid enough to swipe the ring—*his* ring—and use it to propose, would he? What right-minded person would do such a thing?

Then a thought struck him. What if Knowles *wasn't* actually in his right mind? Perhaps his brain had been injured in the accident, and he had a touch of amnesia or some such, which meant that he didn't know anything about a mistake and may even believe the ring was his! Trying to work it out, Ethan's mind raced, and he saw Daisy look at him curiously.

"You two got engaged?" he mumbled. "When?"

Rachel laughed. "Gary proposed right after he got out of the hospital. I couldn't believe it to be honest. Apparently he had it all planned for Christmas Eve, even just bought the ring at Tiffany's and everything, but of course the accident put the kibosh on that."

Ethan's insides dropped, and his fists automatically clenched. What the hell? "And how is he? After the accident, I mean?" he asked through gritted teeth. "Did he suffer any lasting injuries?"

"Nothing major, thank goodness. Just some bruising to his ribs," she sang. "Really, you're so good to be concerned, thank you, but luckily all worked out okay."

"No head damage?" Ethan persisted. "Memory problems? Anything like that?"

"No, nothing at all like that." Now she sounded a little taken aback. "I mean, according to the doctors, he's fine. Why do you ask?"

"I just wasn't sure. I thought at the time he might have suffered a concussion, but maybe I was mistaken," he replied, thinking fast.

Christ, was this for real? Was the guy that much of a crook that he would seriously try to pass off that ring as his own?

It was certainly obvious that despite what Rachel thought, Knowles had no such proposal in mind before the accident, seeing as his Tiffany's purchase was a mere charm bracelet.

Big proposal my ass.

Ethan's heart hammered. But what on earth should he do now? Or more pertinently, what should he say?

Then a flash of anger flared up. Damn it, the time for talking was well and truly over. Enough tiptoeing around. He would go straight to Dublin and pay Gary Knowles a visit—sort out this entire situation face-to-face, man-to-man.

But to think that anyone would be so bald-faced... Ethan couldn't believe the nerve of the guy.

Furthermore, how could he himself now burst the poor girl's bubble by saying anything? Rachel seemed way too nice to be marrying someone so immoral and devious.

No, Ethan decided determinedly, this was definitely something that needed to be tackled in person with the man responsible.

Realizing that the line had gone quiet, he snapped back to reality. "Well, it seems congratulations are in order." Given what she had just told him, it was the obvious response, although his mouth tasted like bile as he forced himself to say it.

"Thank you. Everything's happening just so fast, and of course, there's so much to do and plan and... Oh, listen to me. I'm a bridezilla already! You don't want to hear about all this."

You can say that again, Ethan thought wryly.

"Actually, now that I have you," she continued cheerfully, "can you let me know your address so I can send your lovely daughter those cookies I promised her? I would have sorted it before now, but as I said, things have been so crazy since Christmas. I'll bake a fresh batch and pop them over by courier."

At this, Ethan had a sudden flash of inspiration. "No, it's fine. I'll come and collect them actually."

"Collect them?"

"Yes, you're in Dublin, aren't you? Well, as it happens, I actually have some business there next weekend. So if you let me know where your café's based, I could call in and pick them up. Perhaps catch up with your...fiancé while I'm there."

He knew it was a weak story, but in all honesty, he didn't care. What business would he—an English language lecturer—have in Dublin? He held his breath, almost waiting for Rachel to call his bluff or at least question his motives. However, if anything seemed amiss, she didn't seem to notice.

"Oh. Well, it's a bistro, not a café. We're just on the quays, not far from the Ha'penny Bridge, do you know it? It's called Gillini. The building is painted deep purple, and our sign is bright orange, so you really shouldn't have any trouble finding us. We're hard to miss." She laughed. "But yes, it would be lovely to see you, and I'll let Gary know you'll be in town."

"Actually, probably best not to arrange anything too concrete for the moment—just in case I'm caught for time." Ethan didn't want to give Knowles too much of a heads-up about his arrival, just in case he decided to do a runner. With a rogue like that, who knew? "If I do have some free time, I'll pop in for lunch or something. Would that be all right?" He just hoped he could get a last-minute weekend reservation at a centrally located hotel.

"Yes, absolutely. But are you sure you don't just want me to send over those cookies just in case? I really wanted to do something, however small, to thank you and Daisy. And it goes without saying that if you do have the time to call while you're in Dublin, then lunch is on us!"

"Really, no thanks necessary. Perhaps I'll see you on the weekend."

"Looking forward to it. Oh, and tell Daisy I said hi, won't you?"

"I certainly will. Goodbye, Rachel."

His brain still hammering wildly in his head, Ethan hung up the phone and exhaled.

Daisy was looking up at him, frowning. "Why didn't you tell her about the mix-up with the bags, Dad?" she asked.

He felt his mouth go dry. Yes, why the hell didn't he? After all, he didn't know this woman, and it wasn't up to him to protect her feelings, so really he should have just said something there and then. He looked at his daughter. "Her boyfriend seems to have used our ring to propose," he told her, and her eyes widened.

"What? Oh no!"

"So I thought it might be better to say nothing just then so as not to hurt Rachel's feelings."

"That is really kind of you, Dad," his daughter said, patting his hand. "So that's why you're going to Dublin?" she asked. "To sort everything out with that man?"

Ethan nodded tiredly. "Yes."

Yes, that was him, he thought grimly, too bloody nice for his own good. Brian would have an absolute field day with this. He knew his friend would have no compunction about telling it straight on the phone, given the circumstances.

But Rachel was such a sweet person and sounded so deliriously happy about her supposed fairy-tale engagement just then that he just couldn't bring himself to break the poor girl's heart by coming clean.

Though come next weekend, Ethan decided grimly, it remained to be seen how nice he would be when Gary Knowles's thieving mug was in front of him.

Chapter 24

"WHO WAS THAT?" TERRI INQUIRED WHEN RACHEL HUNG UP THE phone. They were in the kitchen prepping for the bistro's evening sitting, and she was up to her elbows in chopped peppers and red onions. "Did I hear you say something about cookie dough? I checked earlier. We've still got loads for today."

Rachel was rolling out pasta. "No, it's fine. I was going to send some to Ethan Greene's daughter, but there's no need."

"Who?" Terri asked. The name sounded familiar, but she didn't know why.

"The nice Englishman who helped Gary after the accident in New York. Remember I told you about him?"

"Of course." Terri had forgotten about this Good Samaritan until Rachel mentioned him again when she'd passed on the New Year's Eve phone message. "Didn't Gary phone him back afterward?"

Her friend colored a little. "Seems not. It was a bit embarrassing actually. I thought he would've gotten in touch to thank him in the meantime, considering. Still, I suppose he's been so busy with work and everything."

Some stranger saves Gary's life, and he doesn't have the courtesy to pick up the phone and thank him? Terri thought uncharitably. Even worse since the do-gooder was clearly eager to hear about his condition and make sure he was okay. Not only that, but poor Rachel was being saddled as go-between. Romantic proposal aside, this sounded very much like the Gary of old.

"You shouldn't feel bad. It's not your fault that Gary hasn't bothered to call him back."

"I'm sure it just slipped his mind. Anyway, turns out he might be here on business this weekend, so hopefully the two of them will get a chance to have a good catch-up chat then."

"Wait. Who might be here this weekend?"

"Didn't you hear me on the phone just now? Ethan Greene, of course."

Terri frowned. Hadn't Rachel told her before that this guy was a professor or something? If so, what kind of business would he have here, and over the weekend too?

"Wonder what a university lecturer could be doing in Dublin?" she queried dubiously.

Rachel shrugged, her body language indicating that she, on the other hand, was completely uncurious about it. "Who knows? And besides, what does it matter? If it weren't for him, Gary could have died or been robbed even. I'm happy to get the opportunity to thank Ethan again in person."

"And he said he's coming here to the bistro—to see Gary?"

It seemed strange and not entirely coincidental to Terri that this Ethan Greene, whom Gary had met in New York but who lived in

London and had been so persistent on the phone, was now about to appear in Dublin.

"Yes, if he has the time." Rachel paused and looked at her. "Why all the questions?"

Terri stopped what she was doing and put one hand on her hip. "Well, it just seems a bit strange, doesn't it? This guy seems very interested in Gary's condition for someone who doesn't even know him. You said yourself he called the hospital in New York, and he's been phoning here too."

Rachel laughed lightly. "I don't see how someone being interested in Gary's well-being is such a big deal. You weren't there. You didn't see how banged up he was."

"I know, but if Greene is a stranger, why would he care?"

"Of course he's a stranger. What else would he be? Actually, he's a lovely guy. You should have seen all the nurses mooning over him," Rachel said.

Terri cocked an interested eyebrow. "Oh, so he's good-looking too?"

"I'll say." Rachel winked at her. "Actually, if he does appear this weekend, maybe I should introduce you," she joked knowingly. "He has a daughter, but for some reason, I get the impression that he's single."

"Cripes, just because you're Miss Loved-up Bride-to-Be, stop trying to foist me onto every man in sight. I'm grand as I am, thanks very much."

"Okay, okay, you're right. I'm sorry." Rachel laughed. "But honestly, he's lovely—very English, all manners. He even offered congratulations on our engagement just now, which I thought was nice of him."

Terri looked again at her friend, who'd continued calmly rolling out pasta, and couldn't believe she wasn't more curious about this apparent stranger's impromptu visit.

But that was Rachel, happy to take everything at face value, irrespective of the circumstances. Maybe she was right too; perhaps Terri herself was far too suspicious and skeptical about things for her own good.

But since Justin had suggested on New Year's Eve that there was something "off" about the engagement—as well as their long-held mutual misgivings about Gary—how could she be blamed?

The two settled back into their work, making idle small talk about this and that, when the door leading from the dining area burst open and in strode the man himself.

Dressed head to toe in his biking gear, Terri wrinkled her nose at the smell of leather and exhaust fumes drifting off Gary. She hoped Rachel would shoo him out, as she didn't like him stinking up the prep area.

But now, as soon as he walked in, Rachel's face lit up. "Hey there! What are you doing here? Shouldn't you be at work?"

He shrugged laconically. "Nothing much doing, to be honest. Only a few jobs to price and I've done that, so I took the rest of the day off." He stepped back a little as she reached to embrace him. "Babe, watch that flour on my jacket," he chided.

"Oh, of course," Rachel said, pulling back. She grabbed a dish towel and began to wipe off the flour spots she'd made on his precious leathers.

Terri sighed inwardly. Yep, the dashing Romeo from New Year's Eve had now well and truly vanished, only to be replaced by the Gary they all knew and...yeah.

Really, what on earth does Rachel see in him? she wondered, watching Gary just stand there and let her fuss over him. Then suddenly, a thought popped into Terri's head, and she bit her lip, deciding to see if this particular cat might upset any pigeons.

"So Rachel just got another call from Ethan Greene," she said casually.

"Who's Ethan Greene?" His face was blank, and Terri could almost picture the wheels grinding slowly in his mind.

"The nice man who helped you, silly. After the accident?" Rachel reminded him. "He and his daughter made sure you got to the hospital safely."

A strange look flitted across Gary's face then, Terri was sure of it, and instinctively, she felt the hairs on the back of her neck stand to attention.

Something *was* going on there. Hooray for Spidey senses.

"He called here?" Gary asked, his voice catching just a tad on the word *here*.

Terri nodded. "Yup, just a couple of minutes ago." She kept her eyes glued to his face; he was like an open book. Probably because he wasn't smart enough to hide anything that might betray him.

"What did he want?" he asked, looking at Rachel.

She shrugged easily. "Just wanted to check up on you, see if you were okay. It was a bit embarrassing actually, love. I thought you would have phoned him by now."

"Yeah, I was going to but I…I lost the number."

Yeah and I'm Gordon Ramsay, Terri thought sardonically. There was *definitely* something amiss here. But what?

"I thought it must have been something like that," Rachel replied, glancing pointedly at Terri. "Anyway, I told him you were fine. He's so nice, and to be honest, I think he was more worried about you than was strictly necessary." She laughed. "Then again, I suppose I wasn't the one who picked you up off the street, was I? But thinking about it again, it really was a wonderful thing he did that day, and you, a complete stranger too. We should both be very grateful to him."

"Right," Gary grunted, not having the look of a grateful man.

"Anyway, doesn't matter that you lost his number," Terri added, studying him closely. "You might be able to thank the guy in person soon anyway."

"What?" His head snapped up.

"Oh yes, I almost forgot." Rachel smiled. "Ethan said he might be in town this weekend and was thinking of popping in for a visit."

"Here in Dublin?"

Was it Terri's imagination, or had Gary's face turned green?

"Yes. Strange how it goes, isn't it? I'm glad though. It means we might get the chance to repay him a little with lunch, or maybe even dinner depending on how much time he has."

"You mean he's coming here—to the bistro?" Gary blustered, his eyes shifting back and forth at a very quick rate.

Now Rachel looked up, finally noticing the edge in his voice. "If he has the time. Why? Don't you want to thank him in person?"

"Well, of course I do but… Did he actually say he was coming here?"

"Not exactly. He just said he might be in town and that if he had any free time, he'd give us a call to see if we were available. Sounded like a very loose arrangement really. It's not as though he expects us to get the welcome wagons out or anything. Why so touchy?"

"I'm not touchy," Gary grunted, sounding decidedly so. "Just… surprised, that's all."

"Like I said, we might see him, we might not. But either way, it would be good for you to give him a call. It's been me he's been getting ever since, and I hate having to keep making excuses."

"Okay, okay. Stop nagging me, Rachel."

Terri harrumphed. *Nagging* him? The cheek of it!

But Rachel didn't seem the slightest bit perturbed. "So tell us, what brings you all the way over here? Missing me already?" she teased.

"Yeah. I was going to ask if you wanted to grab a bite? I haven't had lunch yet so…"

"Sounds lovely. Where would you like to go?"

"Oh. Well, I thought we could just stay here," he added lamely, and again, Terri felt like throttling him. Of course, yet another freebie.

"Makes sense," Rachel agreed, turning to Terri. "Okay if I take off now?"

"No problem," she replied through gritted teeth. "Justin's in at two, so I'll take lunch myself then."

"Great. Let me just wash my hands, and I'll be right with you," Rachel told Gary.

"Hey, where's the rock?" he asked, frowning at her hand.

"Oh, I have to take it off when I'm working usually," she explained, sounding a little guilty. "It's so big, it tends to get caught up in everything, and I wouldn't want to damage it, you know?"

The two went through to the dining area, and Terri watched them go, wondering yet again why her friend stood for Gary's nonsense. And the way he was going on about the ring—like some kind of over-protective dad or something. Granted he'd spent a fortune on it, so perhaps he was entitled to wonder, but at the end of the day, it was Rachel's now, wasn't it?

Something was tugging at the back of Terri's brain, pulling at the edges, and telling her to pay attention to some important detail, but she just couldn't put her finger on it.

Moving the tray of vegetables aside, she set about making puff pastry and thought a little more about Gary's reaction to the mention of Ethan Greene. He seemed thrown by his upcoming visit to Dublin, that was for sure, but seemed happier when Rachel admitted that a meeting wasn't set in stone.

For her part, she was certainly interested in finding out if this so-called hero would be putting in an appearance over the weekend, because from where she was standing, all this couldn't merely be about simple consideration for Gary's well-being.

There was indeed more to this than met the eye, and Terri sorely hoped it didn't mean trouble for Rachel.

Chapter 25

"So exactly how long are you going to be in Dublin?" Vanessa asked Ethan from where she sat on the bed, watching him pack.

He smiled easily at her. "Just over the weekend."

It was early Saturday morning, and she had not let up on the questioning ever since he'd mentioned his travel plans earlier in the week, asking if she would mind looking after Daisy while he did so.

Following their conversation about moving in together, Vanessa seemed much happier and had since stayed over a couple of nights at the town house, but it would take some arranging before she packed up her own flat and came to live with him and Daisy permanently.

"Remind me again why you're going? All this seems to have just come out of the blue."

"Well, not particularly," he replied, trying to sound casual. "You know how excited I was to meet that agent in New York. Well, I've simply decided that I'm going to get cracking on this book once and for all."

"I see." Her eyes widened slightly, as if the opposite were the case and she didn't see at all. "And going to Ireland will help... how exactly?"

Good grief, she was persistent. "Well, for research of course."

"Oh, so there's an Irish aspect to the novel now?"

He smiled tightly, distinctly uncomfortable with this incessant questioning. "There always was. I just didn't do anything about the research side, because as you know, I was procrastinating about it all. But now, with it being the start of a brand-new year and Daisy's not-so-subtle hinting," he added, holding up his daughter's Christmas present to him, "I've decided the time is right to jump straight in. New Year's resolution and all that."

"Well, I'm pleased to hear that certainly," Vanessa said, smiling, and Ethan exhaled, realizing that this cover story was actually proving to be a bit of a lifesaver. "And goodness knows the critics do love an Irish element—all that good old reliable Catholic repression," she joked lightly. "So that New York agent must have been very positive about what you've written so far. What was her name again?"

"Erm, Rachel with some Italian-sounding surname. She was at one of the bigger agencies but has just set up on her own," he said, thinking quickly. Damn, he hated this bald-faced lying, but wasn't it still necessary, given the circumstances? A few more days and this would all be over and done with, and everything could get back on track. "You probably wouldn't have heard of her," he continued, smiling nervously, and at that moment, Daisy walked into the room, and Ethan wanted to hug her.

Saved…

"Hello, darling," Vanessa cooed as his daughter sat on the bed next to her. "I'm just trying to get your dad to explain why he has to run off to Dublin this weekend and leave us."

She gave him a conspiratorial smile. "For his book, silly."

"I know but…" Vanessa looked from Ethan to Daisy. "Actually, here's a thought," she suggested suddenly. "Why don't we all go—all three of us?"

Ethan's head snapped up. "To Dublin?" He gulped. The last thing he needed was a repeat of the scenario in New York where he had to keep making excuses to sneak away.

"Yes, why not?" she said, smiling. "I can sort the tickets online in a jiffy. It would be a good excuse, actually. I haven't been home to see Mum and Dad for a while, and of course I didn't get to see them at Christmas, what with being in New York." Her parents lived in one of the Dublin suburbs, but her visits home were infrequent, and Ethan had only visited there on one occasion to meet them.

"But what about my ballet class tomorrow?" Daisy whined somewhat dramatically, and Ethan gave her a grateful look. His girl knew exactly what was going on, having in the meantime been fully briefed on his cover story. "And my piano lesson too. I can't miss another one. I'm already behind after being in New York." She gave them her best petulant look. "I don't want to go away again."

He met Vanessa's eye and shrugged helplessly. "It's a good idea, but Daisy's right. We've only just come back from a trip, so perhaps it's just too soon to take another. Not to mention that I'll be mostly working anyway." He turned back to his packing. "Probably best to wait for a better opportunity. Midterm maybe? We could tie it with a proper visit to your mum and dad's then, spend some quality time with them rather than just a quick flying visit."

"Perhaps you're right." Vanessa seemed to be thinking it over, and Ethan knew that she still wasn't altogether convinced about this so-called research trip.

He sighed inwardly. Well, there was really nothing he could do about that just now. This entire charade was ultimately for her benefit, so really, he should stop feeling so guilty. He took a deep breath. Christ, all this fibbing and ducking and diving questions was really taking its toll. Clearly he would never have been cut out for MI5.

"We'll be so proud of you when the book comes out, Daddy," Daisy said, smiling at him.

"Well, I'll try my best, but of course there are no guarantees," he muttered, not wanting to add even more pressure to all this by having to produce a decent manuscript at the end of it.

Vanessa stood up. "Yes, that is true. The trip will be well worth it. Go and do your research, darling, and enjoy every minute. Daisy and I will be sure to have lots of fun while you're gone. I think I'll make some tea. Anyone like some?"

Ethan nodded, eager for her to leave the room so he could have a moment alone with his daughter. "That would be lovely, thanks."

"Daisy?"

"Yes, please."

Vanessa went to do the honors, and as soon as she was gone, he turned to Daisy. "Good thinking, buttercup. For a moment there, I really thought we'd all have to go."

"That's okay, Dad. I knew you wouldn't want us tagging along."

"Well, it's not so much that. More that I'll probably need all my time there to try and get the ring back from Rachel."

Daisy shook her head. "I just can't believe she's wearing your ring." She looked up, her expression thoughtful. "Does it fit, I wonder?"

"Sorry, what?"

"The ring. Does it fit Rachel, or did she have to get it made smaller or bigger or anything?"

"I have no idea, sweetheart. I was so taken aback to hear that she was wearing it at all that it really wasn't something I thought to ask."

Daisy nodded as if thinking something over. "Well, you should really check."

"Yes, yes I will," Ethan replied absently, although in truth, he couldn't care less. What mattered was that the ring was *his*—made to fit Vanessa—and for the sake of his relationship (and indeed his sanity), he needed to get it back.

Pronto.

Chapter 26

Up in the Wicklow Mountains, Gary was in his element. He and Sean zoomed along the rough terrain on their bikes, bouncing the tires along the granite trails and landing heavily on the surrounding bog. Hard on the old ribs, but Gary didn't mind. He'd had enough of sitting around on his backside for the last two weeks and was itching to get back in the saddle.

It was bad enough having to delay the gang's usual New Year's ride until he was 100 percent recovered, so a little bit of soft scrambling was just the tonic. Anyway, there was also a side of him that was anxious to get away and out in the open by himself for a while. Since this whole engagement thing, Rachel had been coming on hot and heavy with the wedding talk, and it was making him uncomfortable.

Gary couldn't understand the big deal about how many different layers of cake they should have or what color the bridesmaid dresses should be. While all this engagement stuff had sounded fine from the outset, already he was getting the distinct impression that he was in way over his head.

Just then, Sean pulled up alongside him. "Bloody fantastic, but I'm feeling thirsty," his mate said. "Fancy a pint?"

By rights, Gary didn't like drinking when riding the bike, but one would be okay as it was under the limit. And although he didn't like to admit any weakness to Sean, he could do with a bit of a breather too. He followed his mate across the bog trail and through the fields out onto the main road, which led to a small village not far from picturesque Glendalough. It was a bit of a touristy spot, but the pints were good, and there was always a roaring fire going in the lounge.

"So how's yer missus these days?" Sean asked as they both hunkered down at the bar. "Wrecking your head with all the wedding talk still?"

Gary grimaced. "Ah, you know yourself." He felt a small bit guilty for moaning to Sean about that actually and figured he should start showing a bit more loyalty to Rachel, since they were supposed to be together for good now. "I suppose she's just excited."

"Ah, they all get like that," Sean replied knowledgeably, and Gary wasn't sure how his friend would know when he'd never gone out with a woman longer than a couple of weeks. "She give you any grief about going out on the bike today?"

"Not too much." Actually, Rachel had been okay about that, considering. Gary had expected her to nag him about his injuries, but instead, she'd just urged him to try and take things easy.

"For your own sake," she'd said. "You don't want to miss out on the big ride when it does happen, do you?" Which was a good point in fairness.

"So have you thought any more about suing that tool who knocked you down in New York?" Sean asked, referring to the taxi driver.

Gary had done a lot more than that. First thing after the New Year's break, he'd phoned his solicitor to ask him about it, and like Sean, Frank Donnelly was confident he had a very good case. "Yep, it's all in hand. My solicitor's setting the wheels in motion."

"Proper order. I'd say you could be looking forward to a nice little payout from that."

"Hopefully there's nothing little about it," Gary joked. "Would be nice to get some new wheels out of it at least."

"Assuming the missus doesn't get her hands on it first, of course. You know how demented they can get with all this wedding business." Sean laughed. "Good party last week though. Herself sure knows how to put on a proper spread."

Gary nodded and sipped his Guinness. "Yeah, all things considered, she's not a bad catch, is she?"

Sean looked at him curiously. "Sounds like you're still weighing it up. Bit late to be doing that now, isn't it?"

"Nah. Was just saying is all."

Although the decision had been more or less foisted upon him, Gary found he was increasingly okay with the idea of settling down with Rachel.

What was bothering him, though, was that call she'd gotten recently from that English fella Greene, the one who'd helped him in New York. The notion that the guy was inquiring after his health didn't sit right with him for some reason, and the fact that he'd supposedly phoned a couple of times since seemed a bit too suspect for Gary's liking. He looked at Sean, wondering if he should just throw the idea out there and get his take on it.

"Remember I told you about that do-gooder in New York?"

Sean looked at him. "The fella that called the ambulance for you?"

"Yeah."

"What about him?"

"Well, it's a bit weird, but he followed me to the hospital afterward and has been sort of sniffing around ever since."

"What do you mean 'sniffing around'?"

"I don't know. That's what I'm wondering. He met Rachel at the hospital when I was out of it, and I don't know if maybe he took a fancy to her or something."

"Why would you think that?"

"Just a notion. He rang her a couple of times since we came back, and the other day, he said something about calling in to the bistro next time he's in Dublin."

Sean raised an eyebrow. "I get you. You're wondering why he's been ringing your missus, not you."

"Well, he doesn't have my number to start with, and I've never met him. Rachel's been going on at me to ring him to say thanks and all that bullshit, but I just couldn't be arsed." Gary took another sip. "The way I see it, any fool would call a bloody ambulance."

"Too right. But I get what you're saying. It does seem a bit weird." Sean looked thoughtful. "And there's no denying that Rachel is hot as hell, so who could blame him?"

Gary nodded, a strange combination of pride and protectiveness running through him.

So he wasn't imagining things. Clearly Sean thought there was something off too.

"Maybe you should give this fella a buzz all the same, suss out exactly what he's up to," Sean went on.

Gary looked into the fire. "Maybe I will."

Chapter 27

ETHAN'S FLIGHT ARRIVED IN DUBLIN EXACTLY ON SCHEDULE, AND now he stood in the taxi queue at the airport, waiting for an available car, checking the directions to the bistro for what seemed like the hundredth time.

Finally getting into the cab, he explained to the driver where he was going, and the man grunted in agreement and pulled away from the curb.

Despite himself, Ethan was full of anxiety. Why, he didn't know; after all, the ring was his property. He just hoped that he'd be able to get everything sorted with the minimum of unpleasantness.

Thinking of Knowles, he felt another jolt of anger. What kind of man would do such a thing? Take a piece of jewelry, a very expensive piece of jewelry, and blithely pass it off as his own?

Even worse, what kind of man would give a stolen ring to the woman he supposedly loved?

A thief would, Ethan thought. What a nasty piece of work this Gary Knowles must be. He thought again about Rachel and their meeting in New York. She seemed like an incredibly sincere and lovely woman. How could she be remotely attracted to such a rogue?

Then he sighed. Perhaps he shouldn't make assumptions. For all he knew, Rachel could be in on the whole thing, and all those offers of cookies for Daisy were merely a smoke screen to throw him off the scent.

No, he decided then. She *was* lovely, an absolutely genuine person, he knew it. Why else would she have been so open about her engagement or so willing for him to visit them at the restaurant?

He was sure that by now, Rachel would've mentioned to her fiancé that he would be in the city, and he wondered what Knowles would have made of that.

Maybe the man couldn't care less; goodness knows he'd been bald-faced about everything else so far. Notwithstanding the ring, he hadn't had the decency to even bother picking up the phone to thank Ethan for helping him out at the accident, so why should he expect him to feel ashamed about nicking his ring?

Because Knowles *must* have realized what had happened.

Rachel seemed adamant that he hadn't suffered a brain injury or anything that might cause him to believe that he had somehow, unbeknownst to himself, spent a five-figure sum on a ring.

Ethan couldn't help but wonder about that too. If Knowles had intended on proposing to Rachel, then surely he (and ergo Vanessa) would have ended up with a diamond ring, albeit a different one, instead of the silver charm bracelet.

So what on earth was this guy's game?

Ethan looked out the window as the cab approached central Dublin. It had been a while since he'd visited the city, and he'd forgotten how much he liked it. Maybe it would make a good location for his "novel" after all. He felt a pit in the bottom of his stomach as he thought again about his lies to Vanessa and sorely regretted having to bring Daisy in on the ruse too.

But of course, it would all be worth it in the end, and with regard to the novel, Ethan could always pretend afterward that he'd had second thoughts and that Dublin didn't suit the story line after all.

Or even better, that "the New York agent" had had second thoughts about representing him. That kind of thing happened all the time, didn't it?

At the end of the day, he was here to get the ring back, nothing else. This wasn't research, nor a pleasure trip—far from it. It was a mission.

He would take back his ring and then return to London where he would propose to Vanessa and get on with the rest of his life.

Minutes later, the cab pulled up to a curb near Dublin's Ha'penny Bridge, and Ethan thanked and quickly paid the driver.

He took his case out of the car, looked around for the purple building Rachel had mentioned, and found it easily a little way down by the river.

To the right of the entrance, behind a large plate glass window, was a wicker basket display of every type of freshly baked bread imaginable, alongside a large selection of pastries as well as the cookies she'd promised.

Just by the door, the lunch menu announced a tantalizing selection of Mediterranean dishes, and the wood-paneled interior, colorful leather banquette seating, and soft lighting looked cozy and inviting rather than the harsh monochrome look favored by the majority of modern restaurants.

Strange, but Gillini was almost exactly how Ethan had pictured it. Warm and welcoming.

A bit like Rachel, the thought came, unbidden.

Stop it, he thought, mentally smacking himself on the forehead. He needed to stop thinking of this woman as a friend and instead start treating her and her boyfriend as the foes they were—when it came to the matter at hand at least.

Taking a deep breath, Ethan steeled himself to go inside, willing her to be there. Despite what he'd said before about phoning beforehand, he didn't want to give her or the fiancé too much advance warning, just in case they decided to make themselves scarce.

The front door of the restaurant jingled as he stepped inside, and he immediately realized that the even though it wasn't quite yet lunchtime, the dining room was abuzz with customers.

He was impressed. Rachel obviously did a booming business here. The feel of the place in addition to the smell of fresh baking from the artisan bakery section was enticing, rather old-fashioned and charming. The atmosphere was a mixture of cozy nights by the fireplace and breakfast in bed all wrapped into one, and he realized he could stand there all day in the entryway just breathing in the delicious aromas.

"Hello there. Can I help you?" a woman greeted, and immediately he broke from his daydream. A redhead dressed in jeans with a chef's jacket over her top was looking at him expectantly, and he noticed that the name tag on her shirt read "Terri."

"Hello, yes. I'm here to see Rachel. Is she in?" He sounded nervous, and once again, he mentally berated himself for being so hesitant.

"She's not due back until this afternoon actually. Is there anything I can help you with?" she asked warmly. "I'm co-owner of the bistro."

"Oh." Damn. Ethan had budgeted on Rachel being here, what with it being a busy Saturday. "Well, I suppose I should really have called first. You say she'll be here this afternoon?"

"Yes. She's away catering an event this morning." The woman was watching him with interest. "Can I take a message, maybe get her to give you a call when she arrives back?"

"No need. Perhaps I'll just pop back later." Again, he was banking on the benefit of surprise.

"Well, it shouldn't be more than an hour or so till she gets in." Her gaze dropped to the carry-on luggage Ethan held by his side, and she looked at him speculatively. "In the meantime, you look like you've been on the road. Fancy a bite to eat while you wait?"

He thought about it. He hadn't eaten since breakfast, and the food here really did smell awfully enticing…

"If you have a free table, yes, I'd love that, thank you."

"Not a problem. Just this way." She led him through to a free table near the back of the dining room. "You'll have to forgive me. This is all we've got left just now. Usually after lunch, the rush tapers off," she said, motioning to the crowded room.

"Well, if the food tastes anything like it smells, I can understand why you're so busy," he replied, and Terri smiled.

"Thanks. Now are you sure I can't do anything for you in the meantime? My name is Terri. I'm Rachel's business partner." She held her hand out, and Ethan somehow got the impression that he was being railroaded into an introduction. Well, since he was going to wait around, he supposed it wouldn't matter.

"Nice to meet you, Terri. I'm Ethan."

A flutter of recognition immediately dawned on her face. "Oh," she said. "Yes, Rachel was expecting you."

He was slightly taken aback. "Really? Because I wasn't entirely sure I'd be able to visit."

"I've heard all about you, of course." She smiled broadly. "I think what you did for Gary was wonderful."

"Excuse me?" He looked up, momentarily wrong-footed.

"For helping him out in New York."

"Oh, yes, of course."

"And very nice of you to come by to check up on him too."

"Yes. Actually, would he be here by any chance?"

Terri chuckled. "No, no, Gary doesn't work here. Actually, he doesn't spend a whole lot of time here at all, unless it's to be fed or watered," she added, her tone wry as she fussed over the table setting. "But I'm sure he'd love to see you so he could thank you again and you two could catch up. After all, if it weren't for you, he might not be with us at all."

Ethan noticed something in Terri's voice, something that sounded like sarcasm, but he wasn't sure if it was directed toward him or Gary.

He shifted uncomfortably in his seat. "Well, I haven't met him at all, as it happens."

"Not at all?" she repeated, coming to an abrupt stop.

"Well, no, not officially. He was unconscious when I reached him, and I didn't manage to speak with him at the hospital either."

"You've never even spoken to Gary?" Terri narrowed her expressive green eyes, and for some reason, Ethan felt like he was under a microscope.

"Well, no. As I said, he was unconscious." He wasn't sure where this was going and was reluctant to say too much just in case this woman was in on Knowles's scam and was trying to lead him off the scent. "I tried of course…because my daughter was keen to see if he was okay in the end. She's only eight, you see, and was a little shaken by it all."

"I can imagine." Terri smiled then, and there was definitely something behind it, Ethan was sure. He felt awkward. It certainly seemed like she was fishing for something. Was it possible she knew about the mix-up and was in on the deception?

He wanted to ask her point-blank if she knew about the ring but couldn't realistically divulge such information, not yet and especially not to anyone other than Gary or Rachel.

"So seeing as I'm here on a spot of business this weekend, I thought I'd call on the off chance—"

"Oh, I'm so sorry. Let me get you a menu," Terri said, interrupting him.

All of a sudden, she rushed off, and Ethan watched her go. Near the entrance to the kitchen, he saw her tap an older man who looked to be a chef on the shoulder. She whispered something in his ear, and then both of them turned back to look at him.

Immediately, he felt himself blush and turn away. He had no

idea what was going on here but sorely hoped that Rachel would appear soon so he could do his business and leave.

Seconds later, Terri was back with a menu and also with the man she had been speaking to. "This is Justin, our chef. Justin, this is Ethan, the man responsible for saving Gary's life on Christmas Eve." This time, there was no mistaking that undercurrent to her tone and a subtext that he himself seemed to be missing.

Justin nodded and smiled. "Ah, our famous New York hero. So great to meet you."

By now, Ethan wasn't sure who the butt of the joke was, but he hoped it wasn't him. He nodded briefly at the chef. "Yes, lovely to meet you too, I'm sure."

"So Ethan was just telling me that he and his daughter took care of Gary after the accident. Wasn't that good of him?"

"Very good of him," Justin agreed sagely.

Ethan looked up. Something was definitely amiss here. But what to say or do? Should he admit to these strangers the real reason he was here or just wait until Rachel arrived and speak candidly to her? The problem was that Ethan had no idea which, if either, party would be on his side.

"I'm sorry, but is there any chance I could order some food?" he muttered. "I'm actually quite hungry."

"Of course, of course," Terri soothed. With that, the chef duly headed back toward the kitchen, and Ethan breathed a momentary sigh of relief.

"So what can I get you, Mr. Greene?" she asked, her tone now all sweetness and light. So much so that he wondered if he'd been imagining that interrogation just then.

Feeling idiotic afresh, he looked down the menu, eager to get back on an even keel.

Clearly, this entire sideshow was messing with his head and driving him crazy.

Chapter 28

DAISY WAS WORRIED, ALTHOUGH SHE TRIED TO TELL HERSELF THERE was little reason to be. According to her best friend, Tanya, her dad had a greater chance of being stampeded by a herd of donkeys than he did of being killed in an airplane crash, but still she didn't like the idea of him being so many miles up above the ground like that, and especially not without her.

Once her dad had left for the airport that morning, Vanessa had suggested that after returning from ballet class, they should load up on popcorn and junk food and watch movies on the couch for the rest of the evening. Daisy thought this was a great idea, as normally, she always tried her best to eat healthy food as a good example to her dad.

It would be nice to just gorge on ice cream and chips without having to worry about being a bad influence. As far as she knew, eight-year-olds didn't have to worry about cholesterol or heart problems, not yet anyway.

About halfway through the second *Pirates of the Caribbean*, Vanessa put her hands in the air and yawned. "I wonder how your dad's getting on in Dublin?" she asked casually.

Daisy shrugged and spooned out some ice cream. "Fine, as long as he gets the ring from Rachel—" Too late, she paused, immediately realizing she'd forgotten herself and spoken out of turn.

Vanessa sat up ramrod straight and turned to stare at her. "What did you say?"

Daisy reddened furiously and looked hard at the Ben & Jerry's carton she was eating from. "I mean…as long as he gets to do his *research* for Rachel."

"That's not what you said, Daisy." Vanessa's voice took on an edge that she didn't like. "What's going on here? Rachel…the agent from New York? Why would he be seeing her in Dublin?" She paused slightly. "And what's all this about a *ring*?"

Daisy wouldn't meet her gaze. "Nothing. That's not what I meant. I meant that Dad just has to do loads of research for his book…so he can get it *ready* for Rachel," she mumbled, but inside she was panicking like mad.

Oh no. Her dad would *kill* her!

Although not if his girlfriend did first, and by the way Vanessa was looking at her, she worried this was a real possibility.

Vanessa was silent for a moment before she spoke again. "Daisy, there's something going on here that I don't know about, isn't there?"

Daisy's eyes stayed glued to the TV where Johnny Depp was doing something silly. "No."

"Come on. You can tell me, I promise. Your dad hasn't gone to Ireland to do research like he said. We both know that, don't we?"

"He has, honestly." Daisy's lip trembled. "Look, I don't know why I said that…about Rachel, I mean. I just got confused…because we were talking about Dad's book, and she was talking about it when we met her in New York." She really wished Vanessa would stop going on about it. Why did she have to be so suspicious about what her dad was doing? It wasn't as if they were married or anything.

Yet.

"So this Rachel, the agent from New York..."

"Yes?"

"Was she the one in your drawing—the pretty woman?" Vanessa asked, and Daisy looked at her. Oh no, why did she have to go and put Rachel in her drawing? Now it seemed like Vanessa was suspicious about that too.

Daisy nodded vigorously, trying to make it all look innocent and normal and, more importantly, enough to make Vanessa stop talking and just watch the movie. There was this big fight scene between Johnny and Orlando going on, and she tried her best to concentrate on it.

"But she's definitely an agent from New York—not from Ireland?"

"I think so..." Daisy was deliberately noncommittal as she thought like crazy, trying to remember what her dad had said to Vanessa.

Oh, this was all her dad's fault for not telling Rachel everything that day at the hospital. She was so nice, she would have understood, Daisy was certain of it. And maybe then Vanessa wouldn't be pestering her with all these questions now.

"Honey, what were you and your dad *really* doing in New York?"

"What?" Daisy mumbled, feeling decidedly cornered now.

"All those times you two kept disappearing, where were you really going?"

"Erm…" She was now staring intently into the bottom of the ice cream carton, willing herself not to say another word.

"Daisy, you can tell me. Honestly, it's okay."

"No. My dad said…"

Vanessa went very still all of a sudden. "Your dad said what?"

Daisy's heart pounded in her chest. "My dad said not to tell," she replied in a very small voice. Oh no. Dad was seriously going to *kill* her!

"Not to tell me what?" Vanessa's voice was stern, sort of the way Daisy's piano teacher sounded when she got the notes wrong. "Daisy, look at me. I asked you a question."

Suddenly tears filled her eyes. "I can't!" she cried. "I really can't! It was supposed to be a surprise."

Then Vanessa's face changed, as did her voice. "A surprise?" she repeated, sounding much more like the old Vanessa. "What kind of a surprise, darling? For you, for your dad…or for me, even? And who is Rachel really? How does she come into it? You need to tell me."

But by then, Daisy'd had enough. She tossed the carton of ice cream aside and stood up, tears stinging her eyes. "I don't want to watch movies anymore." She headed toward her bedroom, but Vanessa stopped her.

"I'm sorry, darling. I didn't mean to upset you. I just—"

"Leave me alone," Daisy said, shrugging her off. "I don't feel like talking anymore either."

"Of course, of course. Whatever you want." Vanessa ran a hand through her long hair as Daisy stomped past.

Inside the safety of her bedroom, Daisy fretted about what had happened, and a knot of worry settled into the pit of her stomach. She'd ruined everything now, hadn't she?

She'd said something very stupid, and even though she'd tried to cover up the part about the ring, she knew Vanessa would be even more suspicious and would probably be able to guess.

She stood by the window and looked out across the park in front of their house. Why did that stupid man have to get knocked down in New York? And why did her dad have to help him? If they hadn't done that, then he would have given Vanessa the ring on Christmas morning, and everything would have happened the way it was supposed to.

Instead, everything was a mess. If only she'd taken better care of the Tiffany's bags…

Suddenly Daisy thought of something. She remembered what her mum had said while she used to play with the necklaces and bracelets her mother had collected over the years, about Tiffany's being a magical place.

Daisy had always been fascinated by her mum's jewelry collection and all her lovely clothes and shoes, which she vaguely remembered playing dress-up with when she was small and Mum was still here. She knew her dad had kept some things in storage for her when she was old enough to wear them, and she couldn't wait. Her mum had the loveliest things.

And she thought again about Mum's exact words.

"There's a sprinkle of Tiffany's magic on every piece," she'd told her fondly, and the man Daisy and her dad had spoken to in the store had said something similar.

Which meant that maybe everything from Tiffany's was kind of enchanted—a bit like the enchanted forest in the fairy tales Daisy used to read.

So maybe everything that happened in New York had happened for a reason—sort of like in a fairy tale. Maybe the bags getting mixed up *hadn't* been her fault at all.

Maybe it really was Rachel and not Vanessa who was *supposed* to get the ring.

After all, if the ring fit her finger, then maybe Rachel was the one her dad was supposed to marry—like in *Cinderella*.

Daisy's heart raced with excitement. She would get her dad to find out if the ring fit Rachel, and if it did, then...

Suddenly realizing she was being silly, she shook her head, trying to shake the stupid thoughts away. She was old enough to know that life wasn't quite like her storybooks.

Instead, her dad would go to Dublin, straighten everything out, and come back home with the ring. Then he would ask Vanessa to marry him, she would accept, and they would all be a family, like her dad always wanted.

That was the way it would work out, Daisy told herself, once again feeling a little empty inside.

That was real life.

Chapter 29

"Ethan, hi!" a voice from behind greeted, and Ethan turned his head to see Rachel standing in the entryway of the kitchen, smiling at him. "I just heard you were here. Delighted you had time to come and see us."

"I hope you didn't mind my arriving unannounced. My meeting ended far earlier than expected you see and…" He trailed off, unwilling to get into too many specifics.

"Not at all. It's lovely to see you again. And I hope Terri and Justin have been taking good care of you?"

He looked down at his near-empty plate. The paella was one of the most delicious he'd ever eaten, and the accompanying bread was out of this world. "Yes, they've been great. This is magnificent." He wasn't about to add that her colleagues had also been playing twenty questions upon his arrival. Remembering his manners, he stood up and offered his hand. "So nice to see you again."

But instead Rachel gave a him a little hug, and she smelled like fresh dough and sunshine.

Then she took the seat opposite. "Please, finish your lunch. So how have you been? Happy New Year by the way."

"Same to you. Is Gary here?"

She blushed furiously. "I'm afraid not. He needed to be somewhere else this afternoon, and of course we weren't entirely sure when or even if you'd be coming."

Hell! On second thought, perhaps he should have been more specific instead of trying to catch them unawares. "Of course, I understand."

"He'll be kicking himself though, as I know he really wanted to see you and thank you."

"Oh well, not to worry." Ethan had truly hoped to keep Rachel out of this, but now it seemed he had little choice. He took a deep breath. "I was wondering…" He glanced around the bistro, now a lot quieter since his arrival. "I know you're working, but would you have time for a quick coffee perhaps? There's something I wanted to discuss with you."

Rachel looked so apologetic, he felt like a heel. "Oh, I'd love to, Ethan, but I'm covering Terri's break just now, and then we've got to prep for the evening sitting."

Right then, as if on cue, the aforementioned appeared at the table.

"Was the food okay?" Terri asked him. "Can I get you a coffee or some dessert perhaps?"

"It was delicious. I really couldn't eat any more," he joked lamely, handing her a plate that couldn't be any cleaner if he'd licked it. And Ethan was almost tempted to.

"Yes, I can see that."

"But a coffee would be lovely, thank you." He hoped that given the circumstances, perhaps she might urge Rachel into joining him.

"Such a pity Gary isn't here, isn't it?" Terri said. "Oh, and have you told Ethan about your engagement?" she added, smiling at him. "After all, you played such a large part in the whole thing—rescuing Gary like that. If you hadn't come along when you did, who knows what might've happened?"

But Ethan barely heard her. Instead, he just stared at Rachel's hand.

There it was. His ring, exquisite and sparkling beneath the overhead light just as he remembered it, but on another woman's finger.

Immediately he was reminded of what Daisy had said before and realized that it did indeed fit Rachel to perfection. As if it had been made for her.

Then he quickly shook himself out of it, figuring that Terri had unknowingly given him the perfect opportunity to raise the subject. His heart sped up. All he needed to do was explain the situation, take the ring back, and he could be on his way.

But for some reason, mostly Rachel's happy, radiant expression as she lovingly caressed the diamond, he couldn't get the words out.

"It's…beautiful. Congratulations," he mumbled, the words out before he could stop them, and noticing Terri giving him a speculative glance, he squirmed uncomfortably.

"Thank you. We're so thrilled." Rachel looked at Terri and stood up. "Okay, okay, I'm coming!" she said, laughing. "Ethan, again I'm so sorry. I really wish we had more time to chat but—" Then she stopped short, looking thoughtful. "Actually, what are you doing this evening? I'll be finished here at six, and Gary should be back by then, so if you're free, it might be nice for the three of us to meet up for dinner somewhere. That's if you're not rushing back to London?"

His heart lifted. Bingo. "No, I'm not flying out until tomorrow, and I don't have any plans for tonight as it happens."

"Fantastic! Where are you staying? I'll give Gary a call and arrange somewhere nice close by, and we'll both get the chance to thank you properly. Does that sound okay?"

"Sounds wonderful."

Having quickly filled her in on where he was staying and what cuisine he might like, Ethan sat back and relaxed a little. He felt a lot more optimistic now that he knew he'd be seeing Knowles in person and definitely much better about not having to unburden himself to Rachel and burst her bubble.

Because tonight, when the truth was finally revealed, wasn't it only right that Gary Knowles—and not he—should be the one dealing with the fallout?

Chapter 30

Back in the kitchen, while Rachel was making dinner arrangements, Terri nudged Justin hard on the shoulder. "Did you *see* that?"

He drew back. "Hey, stop the abuse. You know I bruise easily."

She put her hands on the counter and started drumming incessantly. "Well, did you?"

"I sure did. He's cute, isn't he?"

"That's not what I'm talking about," she replied, exasperated, although yes, there was no doubt that Ethan Greene was extremely cute in that open, earnest sort of way. With his soft blue eyes and sculpted masculine jawline, he certainly looked like no professor Terri had ever encountered. "I *knew* it," she said triumphantly.

"They say you always know when you've found the one," Justin teased.

"Could you be serious for just one second? Forget what he looks like. You and I both knew that there was something off-kilter about all this. Any fool could tell that Ethan Greene isn't here merely to inquire after Gary's health. Hell, he'd barely sat down at the table earlier before he started quizzing me about him."

It was also pretty obvious by Greene's jumpy demeanor that there was something else at play here. The problem was that she couldn't quite put her finger on what that was. Yet.

"Okay. Well, yes, I agree with you that there's certainly something fishy about the way he's just turned up out of the blue—"

"*And* you should have seen how Gary reacted the other day when I told him that his 'rescuer' had phoned here looking for him. He didn't look at all happy, considering the guy is supposed to have done him such a big favor."

"So what do you think, Sherlock? Is it that there's more to this story than we've been told?" the chef wondered.

"Or Rachel's been told."

Justin narrowed his eyes. "Well, that wouldn't surprise me in the least, knowing our Gary's ability to…ah…make friends and influence people," he muttered sarcastically. "But what then? Does this Greene guy have some kind of bone to pick with Gary or something?"

Terri shrugged. "It wouldn't be the first time, would it?"

"But didn't he say earlier that he'd never actually met him?"

"You're right." She thought hard. "But something is going on nonetheless. Greene is here for some reason other than to inquire after Gary's health, that much is obvious."

At that moment, Rachel rushed into the kitchen. "I'm so sorry," she began, flustered. "Go ahead and take your break. I'll get cracking here." She grimaced apologetically. "I didn't think he'd just arrive announced like that, and since Gary isn't around…"

"It's not a problem," Terri assured her. "Anyway, I wouldn't blame you for wanting to chat longer. He's gorgeous."

"Isn't he? And such a lovely guy too. I'm so glad all three of us will get a chance to chat properly tonight, after all that's happened." Rachel looked at Justin. "Will I start on the pastry for the eggplant tarts?"

"Good idea."

"What did happen?" Terri asked, fishing. "I know you said Greene gave Gary first aid on the street and all, but for a complete stranger, he seems very interested in Gary's well-being, doesn't he? I mean, to come all the way over from London just to check on him…"

Rachel opened a fresh bag of flour. "Well, it wasn't just that. He was going to be here anyway and… Ah hell." She grasped at the ring. "I keep forgetting to take this off while I'm working."

Justin gasped dramatically. "Yeah. Knuckle-dusters can be *such* a drag."

❦

"So how's everything going?" Vanessa asked when, later, Ethan called to say hello from the comfort of his hotel room.

If he was being honest, he was still rattled from seeing his ring on Rachel's finger earlier, and he hoped that a well-timed call home would ground him and bring him back to reality.

He smiled into the mouthpiece, hoping to sound enthusiastic and hoping that Vanessa wouldn't detect the strain in his voice. "It's going well. I'd forgotten how charming Dublin is actually. We really should visit your parents more often."

"I'm sure we will," she said, sounding uncommonly enthusiastic, given that she was usually rather lukewarm about the idea. "So how's the...ah...research coming along? Has the muse struck yet?"

There was something about the way she said this that put Ethan on alert. Then he realized he was probably just being paranoid. Seemed like the day for it. "Well, I've only just gotten here, but I'm feeling lots of inspiration all the same," he muttered quickly. "How's Daisy?"

"She's great, reading in her room just now. I'll put her on to you in a sec." She sighed. "Did her best to pretend earlier that she wasn't worried about you flying, but I know she couldn't really relax until you sent a text."

Ethan had suspected as much, which was why he'd messaged as soon as the plane had landed to reassure his little worrywart.

"Again, I'm not entirely sure you should entertain this type of behavior from her," she continued, and she'd already made it clear that by trying to counter Daisy's fears, Vanessa felt he was only validating them.

The truth was that he didn't know the best way to approach this kind of thing long term, but how could he not want to set his daughter's mind at ease?

Nevertheless, it was a relief to be able to discuss Daisy's emotional well-being with someone else. As she grew older, things would undoubtedly get trickier, and it could only be good for his daughter to have a strong woman in her life. And Vanessa was certainly that. With her determined, no-nonsense approach and especially given her sharp rise to the top in business, she was a force to be reckoned with.

"I know, but I still don't like to have her worrying."

"No need to be concerned. She really was fine. This afternoon, we had a good girly time watching movies and eating junk food."

He had to smile. Daisy—eating junk food? "That's great. Thanks again for staying with her. You know I really appreciate that."

"Don't be silly. You know I see her as practically my own daughter—the closest thing I'll get to it anyway," she joked in a thinly veiled reference to her inability to have children of her own.

Once again, Ethan had to admire the way she'd come to terms with that too. Apparently it was because of some gynecological problem she'd had in her teens, and it was strange, but the knowledge merely made him even more eager for her to be part of their family. Silly too, when Vanessa was so easygoing about it all, but if felt to him almost as if they could complete each other's missing parts.

"Well, I'm happy you both had a nice day."

"So, speaking of work," Vanessa said, "have you heard any more from Rachel?"

His heart hammered. "Rachel?"

"Yes, the agent you met with in New York. I figured she might have been the one who'd suggested the Irish angle? For the manuscript, I mean." While her tone sounded completely casual, he could hear the italics.

He bit his lip, not sure what to think now. Something had happened in the meantime, he was sure of it. Could Daisy have spilled the beans?

No, he thought, shaking his head. She would never have revealed to Vanessa what was going on—not in a million years. Unless she happened to let something slip by accident…

But of course he couldn't come right out and ask Daisy that on the phone now either, not with Vanessa in earshot.

It was unlikely, and chances were Vanessa was only asking about the manuscript because she was in the publishing business—not to mention genuinely supportive of his ambitions.

"Like I said, I still have quite a bit of work to do to convince her. That's what this weekend is all about really," he continued, pleased that for the first time throughout all this, he wasn't technically lying.

"Well, good luck with it all. I can't wait to hear how it goes," Vanessa said breezily. "What are you up to this evening then?"

"Nothing much. Just planning a little more location scouting. There are some beautiful country estates in the vicinity, and I thought I might check those out."

This notion had come straight from a tourist brochure in front of him in the hotel room, but he thought he should try and at least make his research sound authentic.

There was a tiny pause. "That sounds like a lovely idea. I went to one of those a couple of years back for a wedding, although this was more of a castle than a country estate. Perfect for weddings, those places."

Now she sounded so enthusiastic and much more like herself that Ethan felt stupid for thinking she'd suspected something before.

"So you're thinking an old country estate might be a good setting for the story?" she went on. "I think you're right. It would be absolutely stunning."

"Well, I have a few things in mind, but it's certainly worth checking out," Ethan said, not wanting to commit himself too much. Otherwise, he really would have to visit some random Irish country estate and whatnot.

He sighed heavily, realizing that all the subterfuge was becoming too much for him. He couldn't wait to fly back with the ring in his pocket. This had gone on long enough.

"You sound tired, darling. Don't do much, okay? As it is, you really shouldn't have taken all this upon yourself. You know I'd love to help if you'd let me."

"Of course. Anyway, I just wanted to call and see how you and Daisy were getting on. I'm heading out again soon, but it might be a bit late when I get back so—"

"No problem. I'm sure you have lots to do and plan. Oh, I have to say, I just can't wait to read this book," she gushed happily. "I realize a lot of planning needs to go into it, but believe me, when everything is ready, I know you and I are going to have such a wonderful time reading it together."

Ethan wrinkled his brow. This conversation was definitely borderline surreal.

"Well, I don't want to take anything for granted," he said, chuckling nervously. "This weekend is just to hammer out the idea, get the ball rolling and that. You know how it is."

"Of course. But just keep in mind that I'll be happy with whatever ideas you come up with. Anyway, better put you on to Daisy for a bit. Have a lovely time, and see you tomorrow night."

They said their goodbyes, and having spoken briefly to his

daughter, Ethan hung up, thoroughly confused about the conversation with Vanessa.

If nothing else, at least it had succeeded in briefly putting tonight's confrontation with Knowles out of his head.

In truth, he was absolutely dreading the prospect of dinner. He despised conflict, and there was no doubt that this conversation was going to be…tricky. He just hoped that the guy would be man enough to confess to the mix-up and reassure his fiancée that their engagement wasn't just a spur-of-the-moment thing.

It certainly sounded like that to Ethan, and from what little he knew of Rachel, she truly didn't deserve that. Hell, what woman did?

Taking a shirt and a pair of chinos out of their suit carrier and laying them on the bed, Ethan turned on the shower and commenced preparations for tonight's battle.

Chapter 31

"Gary, no. I can't believe you would do this to me."

Rachel wanted to scream. Having finally gotten Gary on the phone (network reception could be dodgy in the Dublin Mountains) to make dinner plans, she'd discovered that he and Sean had spent much of the afternoon knocking back pints with some "old mate" they'd met in the pub.

"Sorry, babe, but there's nothing I can do," he said contritely "There's no way I can drive back to Dublin tonight. It wouldn't be responsible."

Although she was annoyed, of course he was right. "So you mean to tell me that you and Sean are going to stay the night with this… mate of yours?"

"Yeah, Liam says we can leave the bikes overnight in the parking lot and get a cab back to his place. Then he or the missus will drop us back to collect them in the morning."

"And where does this Liam live?"

"Not far. Only a stone's throw, so it makes sense."

It all sounded so rational and sensible that Rachel really couldn't argue.

Granted, he couldn't have known that she'd arranged to meet with Ethan, but he could have at least called and told her he was planning on pulling an all-nighter.

But that was Gary: impulsive to the last. She supposed she should remember that his unpredictability was one of the things that had made her fall in love with him in the first place. Actually it was probably this very character trait that had led to their engagement.

"Please don't be mad at me, babe. It wasn't as if I planned this, and it's been years since we've seen Liam. We were just having a bite to eat for lunch and couldn't believe it when he walked into the pub. Then one pint led to another, and you know yourself."

"I can imagine." Rachel knew exactly how it had gone. The more pints that went down, the more reminiscing and shenanigans there would be. As was always the case where Gary and the lads were concerned.

Still, she supposed she couldn't be too annoyed. What with the accident and the injuries, he'd had a tough time of it recently, so a Saturday night out with the boys was probably exactly what he needed.

She just wished it didn't leave her in such a pickle.

"Anyway, we didn't have anything on, did we?" he asked, and she figured that it mightn't be the best idea to confess that she'd actually made dinner plans without consulting him. It would make her look just as thoughtless.

Better to just say nothing, and Rachel could call and cancel with Ethan Greene, tell him that something had come up. Although by now, she was sick to the teeth of making excuses to him.

"Not exactly... Oh, it doesn't matter. You're right, of course. I wouldn't want you to drink and drive. Just take it easy on the beer too, okay? You're still on painkillers, remember."

"Yes, Mammy." Gary chuckled, and despite herself, she felt a bubble of irritation. She hated the way he poked fun at her like that in front of his friends. Typical male bravado—mostly harmless but sometimes annoyingly immature. "Hey, I promise I'll make it up to you. Okay, babe?" But the comment was drowned out by more background laughter.

"Okay then. Have a good night, and we'll talk tomorrow. Tell Sean I said hi."

Hanging up the phone, Rachel returned to the kitchen, where Terri was getting ready for the evening rush.

"What's up with you?" her friend asked, noticing her vexed expression.

Rachel harrumphed. "Just Gary…again."

"Oh? Sounds ominous."

"Ah, it's nothing really." She went on to explain about her fiancé's afternoon drinking exploits. She shook her head. "It's my own fault for arranging that dinner without asking him. Problem is, I couldn't get him on the phone before now. You know how bad the reception can be in the back of beyond."

"So it's just going to be you and Blue Eyes tonight then?"

"Hardly. I'm going to phone him now and cancel. There's little point when it's Gary he really wants to see. I'd wager that Ethan's had enough of listening to me apologizing on Gary's behalf." She shook her head. "Anyone would think that somebody somewhere was trying to keep those two apart."

Terri was silent for a moment. "He's such a nice guy and sounded like he was at a loose end tonight. Maybe you should just go along anyway?"

Rachel frowned. "Would it not seem a little…weird to have dinner with him though—without Gary, I mean?"

"Not necessarily. You're the one he knows really. He mentioned he hadn't actually spoken to Gary. Not unless he managed to before the accident."

"Not that I'm aware of. Gary was unconscious afterward, and by the time he woke up, Ethan had gone back to London."

"Well, for what it's worth, I think you should go along," Terri insisted. "You said yourself you owed him one, so why not? And it's not as though he's hard on the eyes either."

"Terri!"

"What?"

"Why would you say something like that? I'm engaged."

"Oh, stop it. You're still human, aren't you? Greene is a hunk and a half, and if I had the opportunity to go out to dinner with a guy like that—"

"Why don't *you* go then?"

"Because none of this has anything to do with me? Anyway, I kind of get the impression that he's spoken for."

"Really? Why do you say that?"

"I'm not sure, just a hunch. Anyway, it would be very last minute to cancel at this stage, not to mention rude—to Ethan and the restaurant you're going to. Where did you book anyway?"

"Venu. It's near his hotel, and he said he quite likes seafood so…"

"Oh, just go. It's Saturday night and your night off too. Greene seems like he could be good company, and you'll have done your duty by saying thanks on Gary's behalf. What harm can it do?"

Rachel thought about it. Maybe Terri was right. Ethan did seem lovely, and she and Gary really were beholden to him.

What harm could it do?

Chapter 32

ETHAN TOOK A DEEP BREATH AS HE OPENED THE DOOR TO THE RESTAURANT. He couldn't understand why he was so nervous. These people had something that belonged to him, something important and personal, not to mention eye-wateringly expensive.

To add insult to injury, he wouldn't even be in this position if he hadn't gone out of his way to help a complete stranger. So much for good karma…

He supposed he was just uneasy about coming face-to-face with Knowles. The guy was the wild card in the entire scenario, whereas Rachel seemed like a rational, normal person who would no doubt be horrified when she found out the truth.

He drew in another deep breath and steeled his nerves. To hell with it. What was he so worried about? It was his ring, and he himself—not Knowles—was the injured party, so to speak. So really, all Ethan had to do was go in there, politely explain the situation, and refuse to leave until everything was resolved to his satisfaction.

Still, there was a side of him that wished he had brought Brian along for company. From what he remembered of Knowles at the time of the accident, he was pretty well built, and Ethan could do with a little brawn on his side if things got messy.

But if it came to it…

As he marched into the dimly lit restaurant, fully intending to get this out of the way from the get-go, he looked around. Rachel had mentioned something about meeting them at the cocktail bar beforehand, but he didn't see them there. Maybe they were already at the table?

As he waited to inquire at the front of the house about the reservation, he heard a voice from behind.

"Ethan, there you are!"

He swallowed hard. There was Rachel, removing her coat to reveal a red dress that could stop traffic.

Her smiling face took on a slightly confused expression, and he realized he was standing there, staring at her with his mouth open.

He quickly tried to compose himself and cleared his throat. "Sorry, I was a little early." His thoughts were moving slowly, taking in every aspect of her appearance. Then the bright flash of the diamond on her hand as she smoothed her hair down once again reminded him of the purpose of this dinner. He was here for the ring.

His ring…Vanessa's ring.

Then he noticed something. "Has your fiancé been delayed?"

Rachel colored, and her gaze wouldn't meet his.

"I'm so sorry, but Gary couldn't make it in the end. Long story…"

Ethan's jaw tightened. What the hell was going on here? The guy was avoiding him on purpose, surely? Why else would he refuse to return his calls and now cry off on this so-called gratitude dinner?

But what Ethan really needed to find out now was whether Rachel knew what was going on and was also in on some plan to keep the ring.

Well, forget that. Lovely as she might be, there was no *way* he was allowing himself to be played any longer. Still, judging by the look on her face, he could see that Rachel was deeply uncomfortable about the fact that she had to make excuses once again.

"Oh...I see."

"I'm so sorry, truly. It was my own fault for making plans without consulting him." She went on to explain about Knowles being marooned in some pub miles away from civilization, and although it sounded an unlikely story, for some reason, he believed her. She was so apologetic and seemed so genuinely embarrassed that he could hardly question it. "It was late by the time I reached him, and I figured it would be rude to call and cancel, so if you don't mind, I guess you're stuck with just me for company." She chuckled apologetically, and despite himself, Ethan found he was not altogether resistant to the notion.

"You really shouldn't have worried about being rude. If it's not convenient, of course we can cancel."

"Honestly, it's fine. We're here now, and between you and me, I'm always glad of an opportunity to check out the competition." She winked, and Ethan had to smile.

"Well, based on what I ate today, this place has a hell of a lot to live up to."

"That's kind of you, thanks. You didn't have any problems finding it, did you?" she asked as they were led to their table. "I figured it was best to go for something close to your hotel."

"No, not at all, and it looks great." There was silence for a moment as they took their seats and Ethan looked around.

It was a nice establishment, nowhere near as cozy or intimate as Gillini, but the menu looked good. Then, reminding himself that his real purpose here was not pleasure but important business of the highest order, he tried to regain focus.

When the waiter had taken their drinks order, he decided he should dive straight in and get to the point. But how to even begin?

"So do you and your fiancé come here a lot?" he mumbled uneasily.

She shook her head. "Gary isn't actually a big fan of restaurants—apart from ours, of course." She smiled sheepishly. "He's actually much more of a pub-grub kind of guy."

"I see. And have you two been together long?" Ethan figured he might as well lead into this by getting some background on these two. That way, if Rachel genuinely didn't know about the mix-up, it might make dropping the bombshell that much easier.

"No, it's all been a bit of a whirlwind really," she replied, explaining that they had only been seeing each other less than a year. "New York was actually our first trip away together."

"And had you two spoken about marriage before he…proposed?" Ethan pushed with an edge to his tone.

Rachel beamed. "Honestly no. It was a complete surprise actually, possibly the last thing I expected."

"Really? Why's that?" Then realizing that he might sound too forward, he added, "It's just I'm in a similar position, hoping to propose myself."

"Oh, how lovely. Congratulations."

"Well, I haven't actually done it yet, but plan to very soon."

Rachel smiled. "Well, for what it's worth, it's such an exciting time, and I'm sure she'll be thrilled. How long have you two been together?"

"A little over a year." She was so approachable and easy to talk to that somehow, Ethan found himself telling her all about Jane's death and how much it had affected him. And before he knew it, they had eaten their starters and were on to the main course by the time he'd finished.

Rachel had tears in her eyes. "She sounds incredible. I'm so sorry for your loss. And poor Daisy, losing her mum so young like that."

"Yes, well, we were very lucky to find Vanessa." Realizing he had spent all this time taking about Jane but had barely mentioned Vanessa by name, he felt guilty. "She'll be a great mum."

Rachel cocked her head to the side. "I'm sorry, and please don't take this the wrong way, but you keep saying what a great mum she'll be. Isn't that a little unfair?"

Ethan put his fork down. "What do you mean?"

"Well, and again forgive me for speaking out of turn, but it sounds like your main rationale for marrying Vanessa is so you and Daisy can be a family again. I can completely appreciate you wanting that for Daisy's sake, but surely you must love her as much as you did Jane?"

Ethan looked at her, realizing that this woman, who was practically a complete stranger, had pretty much hit the nail on the head.

But no, he argued then, it wasn't merely about just being a

family again. Of course he loved Vanessa for herself, and perhaps…
maybe not quite as much Jane, but he honestly didn't think that
was possible.

"I'm so sorry," Rachel gasped, looking horrified. "You barely
know me, and here am I sticking my oar in. Forget I said anything."

"No, it's fine," he replied easily. "It's my own fault for making
it sound that way. I do love Vanessa, very much, and I can't wait to
marry her." He figured this was a good opportunity as any to get the
conversation back on track. "The only problem is—"

"Oh, don't mind me. I suppose I'm just projecting really."

He looked at her, curious. "How so?"

"Well, I sort of have the same hopes for me and Gary, about
being a family, I mean. I lost both of my parents when I was quite
young, and since then, I've always felt a bit lonely…slightly adrift,
I suppose." She went on to tell him how Terri and the staff at the
restaurant were the closest thing to a family she had now. "So now
with Gary, I'm finally going to be part of a proper family or help
build one of my own—if we're lucky enough to have kids, that is."

There was so much longing in her voice that Ethan's heart went
out to her.

"And this," she said, lovingly caressing the ring. "This signifies
the start of all that, the start of everything I've always wanted. It's
just so precious and so incredibly beautiful that I can hardly believe
it's truly mine."

"Actually—"

"Something I can pass down to my children and perhaps on to
their children too, like creating a brand-new tradition. Sicilians are

big on tradition, and since I've never been able to take part in all that, it feels so important, almost essential that I start my own, you know?" Then she laughed self-consciously and shook her head. "Sorry, I don't know why I'm telling you all this. You must think I'm crazy."

And just like that, Ethan realized that there was no way he could shatter this wonderful woman's dreams by telling her the truth.

He just couldn't do it, and it wasn't his place to either. Rachel's fiancé was the one who should be here listening to her pouring her heart out about how much all this meant to her.

Despite his failings, at least Ethan knew his intentions toward Vanessa were honorable, whereas the ass that poor Rachel was marrying...

"It doesn't sound crazy at all, and I'm sure Gary is looking forward to those things just as much as you are."

"Well, honestly, I don't think he really understands any of that...mushy stuff as he calls it." She laughed good-naturedly. "You wouldn't describe Gary as the kind of guy in touch with his feelings. Typical Irish macho male, I suppose."

Again, Ethan felt maddened on Rachel's behalf that she'd ended up with a guy who sounded like some kind of knuckle dragger.

"You should tell him anyway. Let him know how much all this stuff means to you at least."

"Well, first I have to try and wrangle him to set a date!" she said jokingly and pushed her plate away. "Goodness, Ethan, I can't remember the last time I've opened up to someone like this. An English lecturer... Are you sure you're not really a psychologist in disguise?"

He smiled bashfully. "No, definitely just a boring old college professor. And despite what you think, you really should share some of this with Gary. He is the man you're going to spend the rest of your life with after all."

Maybe then the cad would have a crisis of conscience and admit that their engagement was all a sham.

Ethan would certainly be urging him to do so anyway. If ever he got the chance.

He sighed. Sod it, the best option now was to put an end to the pussyfooting around and just get Knowles's number from Rachel.

Then once and for all, he could talk to him straight and call him outright on swiping the ring and trying to pass it off as his own. He'd give him a good ear bashing too about resorting to such skeevy shenanigans behind this wonderful lady's back, yet it wasn't his place to.

Rachel blushed. "I know, and he really is a special guy, although I know a lot of people don't see beyond the bluster. But at the end of the day, he completely swept me off my feet."

Ethan didn't know how to respond to this, so he remained silent.

"It would be so nice if you could meet him before you go," Rachel said.

"I'd very much like to meet him too," he replied, gritting his teeth. "So you two haven't actually made many plans for the wedding then?" he asked, feeling somewhat relieved that the two hadn't set a date yet, especially when everything may well end up having to be canceled.

"Not yet. I've started looking into the arrangements, and Terri and I are going shopping for dresses soon, but Gary thinks it's all a bit of a nuisance."

Of course he does, Ethan grumbled silently, though he couldn't help but feel even more trepidation on Rachel's behalf.

The way she was talking, it really did sound as though this engagement was completely out of the blue. Poor girl, she really did have no idea.

He decided he'd try and tease out the specifics of the proposal. That way, he'd know for sure if marriage had been in the cards or it had been precipitated entirely by the ring's unexpected appearance.

"So you mentioned before that the proposal was somewhat of a surprise."

Her eyes sparkled even brighter than the diamond on her finger. "Honestly, Ethan, I couldn't believe it. When I saw the little blue box, I nearly collapsed. Gary with a diamond from Tiffany's? Surreal."

"I can imagine." Ethan's fists clenched involuntarily. "So he went down on one knee?"

"Not exactly. Actually…" Her gaze dropped to the table, and she hesitated slightly, as if she was about to say something but then decided against it. "No, after he was released from the hospital, we were exchanging Christmas gifts, and he just produced that unmistakable blue box and…well, when I saw what was inside, I nearly lost it."

"I know exactly what you mean," Ethan muttered. "I mean, I can imagine," he clarified quickly, but it seemed she hadn't picked up on anything untoward.

Rachel was still smiling at the memory. "So while it took a bit of prompting—it was so funny, I've never seen him so nervous—he popped the question, and the rest is history."

Based on this, Ethan knew for certain that a proposal had never been in the plan, and from what he could tell, this guy was making a complete fool out of this poor woman. She deserved so much better, and he sorely wished he had the courage to tell her the truth. But he couldn't knowingly crush all her hopes and dreams like that.

No way.

"Ethan? Are you all right?" he heard her ask and immediately snapped back from his reverie.

"Yes, of course. Sorry, I was miles away. Just thinking really…"

"About what?" Rachel took another sip of her wine, and as she did, the diamond glistened yet again in the candlelight.

He swallowed hard and his heart sped up.

"It really is a beautiful ring," he murmured, wishing he could somehow finagle her into handing it to him and he could pretend to drop it or lose it or something…anything? His mind raced as he tried to figure it out.

"Yes, it is," she said, holding up her hand to examine it afresh. "So incredibly elegant. Nothing like I'd expected from Gary, actually." She smiled. "He can be a bit…what's the word?"

"Gaudy?" Ethan prompted, his mouth tightening.

She laughed. "Well, no, I was actually going to say careful—with money, I mean. And I'm pretty certain this must have cost a fortune."

Ethan knew all too well how much it had cost, right down to the very last cent.

"It's such a classic setting and a beautiful design, and Tiffany's of all places." She stared dreamily at her finger. "I really had no idea Gary would even know about these things, you know how something from Tiffany's really is the ultimate romantic gesture?"

"So I've heard," Ethan muttered.

"But anyway." She shook her head. "Besides listening to strange women rambling on about their love life, how has your visit been? I hope the meeting went well. Was it something to do with your work?"

"Yes." The question caught Ethan off guard. "It was fine but… well, I'm actually here researching a book." Now that he'd decided to wait until he could tackle all directly with Knowles, he figured he might as well use this tried-and-tested cover story.

Her eyes widened. "You're writing a book? How fabulous. What's it about?"

Just at that moment, a waiter carrying a basket of bread caught Ethan's eye. "It's about…bread actually," he replied impulsively, his mind racing.

Man, he was an idiot! Why didn't he just stick with the same explanation he'd given Vanessa?

"Erm…a kind of exploration of bread in different cultures throughout the world. Jane also used to joke that I should've found a woman who would bake me bread. I'm researching Ireland now," he babbled. Still, he figured that such uninspiring subject matter would be a godsend all the same. How boring did a book about *bread* sound?

But Rachel's eyes seemed to light up afresh.

"Maybe I can help," she offered, smiling. "Considering the business I'm in, I certainly know a thing or two about that."

Chapter 33

HAVING FINISHED THE LAST OF THE SATURDAY NIGHT RUSH, TERRI said goodbye to Justin and the waitresses and was just about to lock up the bistro and go upstairs when none other than Gary appeared at the doorway.

She frowned, cursing his timing. And what was he doing here anyway? Hadn't Rachel said something about him not being able to drive back tonight because he'd been drinking?

Approaching the door, she could see through the glass that he did indeed look a little worse for wear. "This is a surprise," she said, letting him inside. "I thought Rachel said you were staying in Wicklow?"

He grinned sheepishly. "I was going to, but then I felt bad about letting my baby down. Is she still here?"

"No, she's off tonight. I thought you knew that."

"Oh." He looked puzzled. "I suppose I thought she'd stay on since I wouldn't be around."

Not for the first time, Terri wondered how a smart woman like Rachel had ended up with such a self-obsessed moron. "Nope, definitely not here." For some reason, she felt like making things hard for him and decided not to reveal that Rachel was currently out to dinner with Ethan Greene.

Slightly crestfallen, Gary looked at his watch. "Shite. It's a Saturday night. I don't really fancy just sitting in by myself and watching telly."

"Well, I suppose you should have organized your day better then, shouldn't you?" Terri said pointedly.

"Ah, don't you start. I got enough of an earful from Rachel earlier. And I came back in the end, didn't I?"

"How did you get back? I sincerely hope you didn't drive."

Gary shook his head. "Nah, turns out Liam's missus wasn't as cool about us staying over as he'd thought, what with the new baby and everything. So myself and Sean had to get a taxi back. Cost us a bloody fortune, *and* we have to go back up there in the morning to collect the bikes."

"Really." Terri wasn't particularly interested in the ins and outs of Gary's exploits. "So where's your sidekick then?"

"Ah, he was feeling a bit under the weather, so he went on home. Bad pint, I reckon."

"Right." She jingled the keys pointedly. "Well, much as I'd love to chat all night…"

"Hey, any chance of a late one?" he interjected, and Terri felt like throttling him. As if she had nothing better to do than wait hand and foot on him because he fancied yet another freebie!

Then again…

She'd been wondering all week about this bizarre situation involving Ethan Greene. Now, particularly when Gary's guard was down, perhaps this was the perfect opportunity to do a little digging?

"Oh, go on then," she said, standing back to let him inside. "I've still got a bit of cleaning up to do, so as long as you stay out of my way."

He grinned. "You're a star, Terri. Did I ever tell you that?"

"Yeah, loads of times." Going behind the bar, she took a bottle of beer from the cooler, grabbed a bottle opener, and popped the top. Showtime. "Glass?"

"Nah, I'm grand."

Terri slid the bottle across the granite-topped counter, and he lifted it to his lips, gulping it down as if it was the elixir of life. "Good woman." Still standing, he practically drank the contents in one go, then burped loudly. "After the day I've had, I needed that."

"I can imagine." Terri had to bite her tongue. Instead, she proceeded to sweep the floor. "So how's life with you these days? All excited about the wedding?"

He rested the beer bottle on the bar. "Hey, any chance of another one of these? I can get it myself."

Of course you can, she thought. "Sure, go ahead."

"Thanks, it's been a long old day. And nothing better than beer when it's on the house."

Terri shook her head. She truly couldn't fathom how someone like Gary would spend thousands on a ring when he was so cheap.

"I have to admit, you really threw us all for a loop," she went on, determined to keep him on the subject matter. "Who knew you were so good at keeping secrets?"

"What?" He looked puzzled. "Oh, about the engagement you mean. Well, I suppose I wanted to make sure she was surprised."

"Consider it mission accomplished."

He shrugged. "Still, as far as all the wedding shite goes, that's really Rachel's thing. Besides, she'll have to stump up and play her part now. I've done my bit."

Such a Romeo.

"I know. I mean, that rock must have set you back a fair bit, and Tiffany's too."

"Yep, nothing but the best for my girl. Pretty special having a ring worth at least…um…a grand or so on her finger."

Leave it to Gary to talk about price, Terri thought, prickling at his bad taste, but at the same time, the figure he'd thrown out stopped her short.

A grand, my ass. Not for a diamond that size and certainly not from the likes of Tiffany's? Now Terri knew for sure she was onto him.

Something was way off here.

"Right." She stopped sweeping and leaned against the brush. "You know, I think I might join you. Fancy a shot of something stronger?"

Gary's eyebrows shot up. "Of course."

Putting the brush aside, she took a bottle of whiskey off the shelf and grabbed two shot glasses, pouring them each a generous measure. "Bottoms up." She smiled, throwing it back while trying not to grimace. She hated whiskey, but there was a method to her madness.

Gary threw his back too, and immediately she poured another, noticing him stumble slightly against the bar.

"Sit down at a table and relax," she fussed. "Unless you're in a hurry or anything?"

"Course not." Gary beamed. "Anyway, I wouldn't dream of leaving a lady drinking all by herself on a Saturday night."

Crikey, was he flirting with her now? Terri's stomach churned, and this time, it wasn't because of the whiskey.

"You know, I hadn't really figured you as a one-woman man," she cooed, deciding to play along. "You and Rachel are just so good together. I have to admit I'm a little jealous."

He looked at her, trying unsuccessfully to focus on her face, and Terri tried her utmost to keep her smile steady and her distaste at bay. Now he thought *she* was flirting with him. Stifling a guffaw, she poured him another shot.

"Nice one." Gary now wore a satisfied expression, the combination of flattery and whiskey going straight to his head. He sat forward unsteadily. "You know, I like this side of you, Terri, I really do. You're usually so...I don't know, serious all the time."

"I suppose every now and then, everyone needs to get a little crazy."

He hiccupped, and his words slurred slightly. "Good woman." She poured him another, and he looked at her speculatively, as if about to say something.

"What's wrong?"

"I was wondering..." Gary drank down the whiskey but then seemed to lose his train of thought.

"Yes?"

"Ah, it's nothing really."

"No, go on. You can tell me," she prompted.

"Well, it's just this bloke, Greene, that keeps ringing her… He's starting to annoy me."

Terri paused. "Really? Why? Are you jealous or something?"

"Nah!" He cackled loudly. "Why would I be jealous? Rachel's crazy about me."

"Course she is. But actually, I was wondering about that too. Why *does* he keep ringing her?"

"Dunno. I reckon he took a fancy to her at the hospital when I was out for the count."

"I see." Terri was disappointed. She was hoping for some grand revelation from Gary about Ethan Greene, some explanation as to why he was so adamant about keeping in touch.

Could it be that Ethan had a thing for Rachel that had somehow kicked off in New York? Thinking about it, he did seem quite jittery around her as well as being overly concerned about her fiancé's whereabouts. Was this because he wanted to see Gary, or was he actually afraid of him?

Again, Terri decided to bide her time and wait until the moment was right to reveal to Gary that Rachel was at this very moment out having dinner with the guy.

"So you're worried that Greene might steal Rachel away?"

Gary snorted. "You must be joking! Nah, I just don't like the way he's sniffing around her, that's all."

"I can imagine. I suppose it's funny how these things work sometimes. If Greene hadn't come along when he did, then who knows what might have happened? With the accident, I mean."

"Yeah, who knows?" he slurred, eyes unfocused. "Well, all worked out well for Rachel, that's for sure."

"What do you mean? Of course it worked out well. For both of you surely?"

He blinked. "Well, to be honest, I can't really remember much of it myself, but the one thing I do know is that if that hadn't happened, we wouldn't be engaged."

"What?" Terri sucked in her breath, but he didn't seem to notice. "How so?"

He smiled and motioned her closer. "Can I tell you a secret?"

"Of course. My lips are sealed."

He scratched his head, reminding Terri of a gorilla she'd seen on a recent visit to Dublin Zoo. "I don't know where the bejaysus that ring came from."

"What? What do you mean?"

His eyes were glazed. "Dunno where it came from. Was in my stuff after the accident seemingly."

Terri stopped short. "You mean you can't remember buying it at Tiffany's?"

"Nope. Got something there all right, but it sure as hell wasn't that rock."

Terri's mind was galloping like a racehorse. "Back up there a second. You're telling me you bought something from Tiffany's, but when you got back from the hospital, something else was in the bag?"

"Bang on. Reckon somebody messed up in the shop." He raised his glass. "Hah! Worked out well for me."

"Hold on. You mean that you accidentally ended up with that ring?"

"Yup."

"But, Gary, surely you went back to the store and told them about the mistake." Terri was flabbergasted. "Or explained it to Rachel at least."

"How the hell could I when she was doing cartwheels over it?" He looked at Terri as if she were nuts. "Anyway, the way I see it, finders keepers."

"But…" She was honestly finding it hard to get a handle on this. It wasn't what she'd expected at all, yet it also made sense. Gary *hadn't* intended to propose. "And what did you actually buy?"

He shrugged. "Just some crappy silver bracelet that I thought Rach might like." He grinned again. "Dunno, it was late, and I was rushing back to the hotel, and next thing I know, I'm lying in some hospital bed."

Terri was silent for a minute while she tried to think this through.

"So it was right after you left Tiffany's that you got mown down?" She hadn't known the specifics before, but now that she did, this was starting to make a hell of a lot more sense. The ring—it wasn't meant for Rachel and never had been.

Which had to mean…

Suddenly Terri recalled Ethan Greene's wide-eyed expression earlier when Rachel was showing off her magnificent diamond.

Oh dear.

She tried to picture the scene in her head. Two men shopping on Christmas Eve, both laden down with packages. One gets hit by a cab, the other tries to help out, and amid all the melee, the shopping bags get mixed up.

Terri couldn't believe it. Poor Ethan. He must have had a heart attack when he realized that his staggeringly expensive diamond ring had gone astray and, worse, that he'd ended up with a simple bracelet.

And Rachel. Talk about adding insult to injury! Gary thought so little of her that he was willing to pass off the ring as his own and commit to marriage on a random whim?

She was furious.

"I don't understand. If you knew the ring wasn't yours, how could you have used it to propose to Rachel?"

"What was I supposed to do, Terri? Believe me, I was as shocked as anyone when it popped up, but I could hardly spill the beans to Rach when she was mooning all over it, could I? Besides, it all worked out grand, didn't it? So it might not have been in the cards, to be fair, but what can you do?"

Terri was so disgusted, she thought she might throw up. To think that he could blithely go along with something so despicable…

"Gary," she said, deciding to throw the idea out, as clearly he was too dim to put two and two together. "Did you ever consider that *maybe* the reason Ethan Greene has been hounding you, as you say, is not because he fancies Rachel but because *that ring is his*?"

To his credit, he looked completely bewildered, as if the idea had never even crossed his mind. "Huh? But how could it be? It was in my stuff." But she could see his eyes grow wary at the prospect.

"Yes, but perhaps he'd also been carrying a Tiffany's bag, and they got mixed up?"

Gary shrugged. "Nah. Anyway, not my fault." He was seriously slurring his words now, and Terri figured it was pointless trying to get him to see sense at this stage. She wondered if he would even remember this conversation tomorrow.

Still, whatever Gary's feelings about Ethan, Terri needed to know his true intentions toward her best friend.

"So this whole engagement only came about because the ring turned up out of the blue? You hadn't planned it all along?"

"Nope. I mean, I don't mind going along with it though. Rachel's great, easy on the eyes, good fun, scorcher in the sack," he added, and Terri cringed in disgust. Clearly he'd forgotten whom he was talking to and was an even bigger creep than she realized.

At the same moment, Gary laid his head on the table and closed his eyes, muttering something that sounded like, "I could get used to all this free stuff—beer, diamonds…" and then let out a huge snore.

She waited for a moment, making sure he was out cold before she could contemplate her next move. Her first instinct was to whack him over the head with something, she was so enraged by what she had just learned.

Although she'd suspected all along that something wasn't right, she certainly hadn't anticipated this.

Should she tell Rachel? Break the news to her friend that her so-called fairy-tale engagement was a complete sham and had only come about because Gary had come out the better end of a mistake?

She had to. Although, thinking about it, no doubt Ethan Greene was doing exactly that himself right now.

Trying to imagine that conversation, Terri winced. Why should he have to suffer the consequences when dumbass Gary was the one at fault?

Terri looked again at the love of Rachel's life, drunkenly snoring his head off.

She hoped he had the mother of all hangovers tomorrow morning and would be racked with guilt and shame.

Or would he even remember?

She shook her head. Poor Rachel and all her big dreams about tradition, family, and happily ever after.

Being stuck with an oaf like Gary for a fiancé would surely be the very opposite of a fairy-tale ending.

Chapter 34

GARY COULD HEAR SOMEONE CALLING HIS NAME. HE WAS IN A MURKY place, something cold and hard was pushed against his face, and for the life of him, he couldn't figure out what it was.

"Ah, Ma, give it a rest," he mumbled.

"Gary, wake up."

There, he heard it again. Why couldn't he open his eyes? They seemed glued shut. He was slowly becoming conscious, and the first thing he noticed was the shooting pain in his skull, and it was as if his head was locked in a vise. Why did his head hurt so much? And again, where the hell was he?

"Gary, come on. Wake up." There was an insistent tapping on his shoulder, and blearily, he realized he knew that voice.

Finally, he was able to open one eye, then the other one. There in front of him stood Rachel. His fiancée, he remembered. She didn't look happy though.

"Gary." She shook his shoulder. "What are you doing here?" It was more of a demand than a question.

There was a whiskey bottle in front of him, along with two shot glasses. He appeared to have his head resting on the dark wood of a table and was sitting on a chair. He noticed that not only did his head hurt, but so did every other part of his body. He could only imagine it had to do with the fact that he had slept practically upright all night.

"Hey, babe," he mumbled as he started to slowly pick his head up from the table.

Rachel's nostrils flared and her eyes narrowed. He tried to think of a time when he had last seen her mad and realized he couldn't recall a single moment. Sure, there had been times when she had been stressed out about this and that with work, but her anger had never been directed at *him.*

"What the hell are you doing?" she asked again.

Good question, he thought to himself. What *was* he doing? He tried to think back to the previous evening. He remembered getting back from Wicklow with Sean and then looking for Rachel at the bistro, but she wasn't there.

Terri had been, though, and she'd given him more to drink. More importantly though, Terri had been *nice* to him, invited him in for another beer, and what man would turn down free beer?

Strange because he'd always thought she didn't particularly like him, but last night, had Terri...*flirted* with him? Gary tried desperately to think back.

Yes, there could be something to that. She'd certainly been very friendly anyway. He was missing something though; there was something important he couldn't remember. They had started doing shots of whiskey; he remembered being surprised when she'd pulled the bottle out. They'd done a couple—no—it had been a lot more than a couple. Terri had kept refilling his glass.

And she had kept asking questions.

It kinda sounded as if she was jealous of Rachel, and he hadn't realized this before, but maybe she'd fancied him too.

Then Gary's skin broke out in a cold sweat as, suddenly, the most important part came rushing back to him. He'd told Terri about buying the bracelet and ending up with the ring. He had told her the *whole* bloody story.

Christ.

He wondered if Terri had since told Rachel about the mistake. If she had, it would certainly explain why she seemed so mad at him now.

"Well? Do you plan on answering?"

Gary snapped back to the present, wondering if he had the presence of mind to bluff his way out.

Problem was, he wasn't sure what he was supposed to be explaining: why he was here or why he'd proposed to her with a freebie ring.

"Why are you sleeping on one of my tables?" Rachel entreated, and he breathed a sigh of relief.

"What time is it?" he asked groggily. It was bright outside.

"Past 9:00 a.m. And you still haven't answered my question."

"I came here last night, looking for you."

Something crossed her face very briefly, and it piqued his interest. Was it guilt? If so, he wondered if he could maybe turn this around.

"But you weren't here, so I decided to stay for a while, and I had a drink with Terri. We had a couple of drinks and…"

"Looks like it was a hell of a lot more than a couple," she said, incredulous.

Gary blinked. Now he wasn't sure if she was angry about him drinking with Terri or sleeping at the bistro. He decided to wing it.

"Come on, babe. You don't need to be jealous or anything."

"Oh, please. I'm not jealous. I'm just wondering how you ended up sleeping all night in my restaurant."

Gary shifted gears. "Well, it's not my fault. She got me drunk and then left me high and dry here, so blame her." If he shifted the blame onto Terri, then Rachel could take her anger out on her.

Instead, she rolled her eyes and sighed. "Last time I checked, you're an adult. It's hardly Terri's fault. Didn't you tell me yourself you were drinking all day yesterday? Besides, how could she have possibly moved you? And I can't imagine she'd want to put you up upstairs either." She put her hands on her hips. "Problem is, I need to open up, and I can't have you in here looking or indeed smelling like you do. It wouldn't be good for business. So scoot."

Was she really kicking him out? Couldn't she at least offer him some coffee first? Or maybe a bite to eat while she was at it?

He started to open his mouth to ask these questions, but Rachel held up her hand. "Please, just get a move on. I don't have time for any of this right now. I have too much to do. Go out the back way."

So now she was making him exit through the back, like she was ashamed of him or something? What the hell?

Shaking her head in irritation, Rachel started to clean up around him while Gary sat there, confused and unsure. She had never acted this way around him before; usually she was all over him.

He started to panic, wondering if Terri had in the meantime

told her the truth, but she just wasn't saying anything, expecting him to guess why she was cheesed off, like women often did.

He glanced at her hand for the diamond, but thankfully it was still there. Okay, that wasn't the problem. Nice one. At least he didn't have to face all that shite now too.

Rachel came back over and started making shooing motions. "Come on, come on. What are you waiting for?"

She herded him through the door to the kitchen and then out back. When he reached the exit, he turned around and tried to summon his most charming grin. "Don't I get a goodbye kiss?"

"Gary, you stink. Just go and maybe I'll talk to you later." She pushed him out the door and closed it behind him.

Alone in the back alley, he sniffed his armpits. She was right; he did smell rank. He didn't like this, having Rachel mad at him. Usually, she was so happy to be around him. Should he try to make it up to her? Buy her flowers or something?

Walking around the front of the building, he peered in the window to where she bustled among the tables, getting ready for business. He waited for her to look in his direction, but she didn't; it was as if she was purposely ignoring him.

But if Rachel was this annoyed at finding him passed out on the table, what would she be like if Terri told her about the blasted ring?

Chapter 35

RACHEL COULD SENSE GARY'S GAZE ON HER FROM THE OTHER SIDE of the window.

She knew he was looking in, but she'd already decided that there was no way she was acknowledging him. She felt as if she were holding her breath, waiting for him to leave. She had never spoken to him that way before, had never cajoled or been angry with him. It was a completely new departure.

She felt a little off-kilter today, presumably because she'd walked in to find her errant fiancé passed out after a drunken night.

But regardless of how much she tried to convince herself of that, a little voice in the back of her mind was telling her something else.

She'd felt differently toward Gary today for some reason, and the scary thing was that it might have something to do with last night's dinner with Ethan.

He was so different, so warm and easy to talk to. Last night, they'd stayed on after dinner and talked for ages over coffee.

She still couldn't believe she'd opened up to him like that about her desire for a real family and to create real traditions. She was sure he'd thought she was some kind of loon, but no, actually he seemed to understand perfectly what she meant.

After all, he was hoping for the very same thing with his soon-to-be fiancée.

Despite herself, Rachel couldn't help wondering what his girlfriend was like. No doubt intelligent, stylish, and definitely beautiful, since Ethan himself was incredibly suave and handsome. And wonderfully gentle, with impeccable English manners, insisting after their meal that he saw her safely off in the taxi.

Taking a wet rag, she wiped down the table upon which Gary had been drooling all night.

She sighed and went through to the kitchen to start on making bread and pastries for their breakfast offerings, which immediately reminded her of the subject matter of Ethan's book.

Damn it, no matter what she did this morning, her thoughts kept drifting back to him. What was wrong with her?

For some reason, she felt uneasy. Last night was the first time in a long time that a man had sat down and showed a real interest in her and her life.

Ethan had asked questions and listened patiently to the answers. He wanted to know everything about her life and business, her hopes and dreams even, and for once, she had no problem sharing.

It wasn't as if she didn't share things with Gary; it was just... different.

Their relationship was one of extremes. He made her laugh, even when he was being ridiculous, and normally she loved the fact that she never really knew what he was going to say or do.

But she thought again about what Ethan had said last night about sharing those hopes and dreams with Gary and realized that she had never actually done that.

Probably because he was a man's man and had no real interest in all that kind of malarkey. And for the most part, she understood that.

Still, when she thought about some of the sacrifices she'd made and the little oddities that she'd brushed off—things like Gary's reluctance to eat in some of her favorite restaurants, "too fancy, and they never give you a decent feed," the fact that he rarely noticed or complimented her on her appearance or things she did for him—suddenly seemed to come sharply into focus.

Rachel felt almost surprised by the realization. Was Gary... inconsiderate?

Her head said no, but deep down her heart seemed to argue the opposite. No, he was mostly just clueless, really.

She sighed, deciding to turn some of this sudden reflection back at herself. Maybe the problem wasn't Gary at all. Was she really so shallow that the first time another man paid her some attention, she immediately began picking faults in her partner?

Anyway, and notwithstanding the fact that he was already attached, Ethan wasn't even her type.

In fact, he went completely against the norm. She usually went for the brooding, macho, unpredictable kind, not the decent, uncomplicated type. Dreamy blue eyes notwithstanding.

At that moment, she heard movement and the jangling of keys from outside, signaling Terri's arrival downstairs from her flat.

"Well, good morning," Rachel greeted with a smile. "How are

you feeling today?" Considering the state Gary had been in, she'd been expecting her friend to be just as hungover. However, she looked bright as a button.

Actually, Terri looked slightly…wired.

"Great, actually. Why do you ask?"

Rachel raised an eyebrow. "Well, considering you and my darling fiancé had a late night of it, I figured you'd be the worse for wear."

"Nope, I know how to control myself. I take it his lordship was still here this morning when you arrived?"

She rolled her eyes. "And *I* take it you were forced into a spot of babysitting last night. Sorry about that."

"It's not a problem. I didn't stay on that late." Terri took off her fleece and put on her chef's whites. "How about you? Did you have a nice night?"

"Yes, it was great actually. Ethan is such a nice guy, and we had a lovely time."

"I see." Terri kept looking at her strangely, and Rachel blushed a little, worrying that her earlier thoughts were written all over her face.

"I mean, it was a shame that Gary couldn't be there too but… What was he doing here anyway? I take it he managed to make his way back from Wicklow after all."

"Yeah."

"Again I get the impression he outstayed his welcome."

Terri shrugged. "Well, he was kind of the worse for wear when he arrived, and then after a few more here, he fell asleep, so I couldn't really move him."

Once again, Rachel felt an odd surge of distaste at her fiancé's boorish behavior. "I'm so sorry. I'm sure Gary rolling up at closing time was the last thing you needed."

"It was fine. Actually, we had a chance to talk a little."

"About what?" Gary and Terri rarely "talked."

Again, some kind of look passed over her friend's face, but Rachel wasn't sure what to make of it.

"Nothing really, just this and that. But anyway, tell me more about your night. What did you and that handsome Englishman talk about?"

"He told me about this book he's researching. It's about bread. Can you believe it?" She smiled. "And all about Daisy, his daughter, and of course his fiancée."

Terri stopped halfway to the fridge. "His fiancée. You mean he's engaged too?"

"Not yet. He's planning to propose soon, apparently. Seems you were right about him being attached."

"Right. And was she with him in New York?"

"The girlfriend? I'm not sure. I think so. His daughter was anyway. Actually now that I think of it, remind me to hold back about a dozen cookies or so from today, will you? Preferably the chocolate chip ones. I promised Daisy I'd make her some to thank her for looking after Gary's shopping bags, and Ethan's popping in for them before he leaves."

Terri stopped what she was doing. "The daughter had his bags?"

"That's what he said. Anyway, look at the time. We'd better stop nattering and get cracking."

"Yeah," her friend agreed. "Thanks to that fiancé of yours, last night was a late one."

"You and me both. It was almost one by the time we finished."

Terri's eyes widened. "Wow, the conversation must have been good."

"It was. Like I said, he's great, so easy to talk to, and we just didn't realize the time."

"Because you were so busy…talking."

Despite herself, Rachel colored a little.

"Oh my goodness, you're blushing!"

"I am not."

"You are. What the hell happened last night? What did Greene say to you?"

Rachel shook her head, mortified. "Nothing. It was just a nice night. Hell, Terri, I barely know the guy. Besides, in case you've forgotten, I'm engaged to Gary."

"Who didn't seem to know you were meeting another guy for dinner."

"Honestly, it wasn't like that."

"Hey, it's okay. Don't be so hard on yourself. Ethan seems lovely, and I'm glad you had a good time. And for what it's worth, I didn't say anything to Gary about it either," Terri added meaningfully.

Why was she sounding almost like a coconspirator? Because there was no cover-up or conspiracy. Ethan was a nice guy, but he was attached, as was she. They'd been thrown together by circumstance, and she owed him a debt of gratitude for saving Gary's life in New York.

Last night, they'd had fun, exchanged life stories, and enjoyed one another's company, but that was all there was to it.

End of story.

Chapter 36

TERRI FELT LIKE A CAT ON A HOT TIN ROOF. SHE COULDN'T BELIEVE that this morning, far from crying into her coffee about Gary's deceit, Rachel had actually had a lovely night with Ethan Greene.

She had to smile at the irony, and while of course, she hated the idea of her friend being embarrassed or humiliated, she took some pleasure in the fact that after a nice evening with Ethan, Rachel had the next morning found her errant fiancé passed out, drunk and drooling all over the place.

But what was Ethan up to? He obviously hadn't told Rachel about the mix-up last night, because she was still wearing the ring this morning and evidently had no idea about anything untoward.

After all, he must have realized the mistake pretty soon after it occurred. Terri thought again about the frantic phone calls he'd been making and then his sudden appearance at the bistro yesterday.

Clearly he was here to get the ring back, so why hadn't he?

Especially when the mistake had cost him a lot in more ways than one. According to Rachel, he'd planned a proposal, but of course that would have gone awry.

Poor guy. To think that he'd gone out of his way to help the likes of Gary and then gotten rightly shafted in the process.

She still couldn't believe that Gary hadn't copped to the cause of the mistake and had instead been going around thinking it was some random stroke of luck that he'd ended up with a diamond worth a small fortune.

So why hadn't Ethan confessed all to Rachel? Terri could only imagine how anxious he must be to get it back. She thought again about the quietly contented expression on her friend's face this morning. Could it be possible that the two of them had truly clicked last night at dinner, and as a result, he was afraid to hurt Rachel?

That had to be it. Perhaps Ethan couldn't bring himself to tell her the truth just yet and bring her entire world crashing down. Terri had to admit she understood exactly how that felt.

❧

"Have you heard from Dad today? What time is he coming home?" Daisy asked.

Vanessa's eyebrows automatically shot together, but then she quickly smoothed her expression. After yesterday's discussion, she didn't want to come across as impatient, but she had to admit that she was actually way past that and now full-on agitated.

It was almost midday and Ethan hadn't called since the day before.

"I'm not sure, darling, and no, he hasn't called yet."

Daisy smiled weakly, and Vanessa knew she was still feeling upset that she had let the cat out of the bag. She'd been quiet for most of the day afterward and had since confined herself to her bedroom, barely speaking to her other than briefly over dinner and at breakfast this morning.

"Are you going to tell him I told you about the surprise?"

"Of course not." Vanessa was quick to reassure her. "After all, you didn't actually tell me anything."

Which was the most frustrating part, really. When Daisy had inadvertently revealed something about a *ring*, Vanessa was so curious, she wanted to shake the information out of her.

Based on what Daisy had said, though, she was almost certain his so-called research was merely a cover story for something else—namely some kind of intricate plan to propose? If there was a ring involved, that had to be it, didn't it?

She wasn't quite sure where this Rachel person came into it (perhaps she was a wedding planner?) if at all, but knowing Ethan, chances were he'd gone to Dublin to visit her parents to officially ask them for her hand.

He was such a traditionalist, it was *exactly* the kind of thing he'd do, and it had taken every ounce of restraint in her not to phone her mother in the meantime and find out if he'd been in touch. But she really couldn't risk Ethan knowing that she was onto him or indeed risk falling flat on her face if her suspicions weren't correct.

But then, last night on the phone when he started talking about visiting Irish country estates, she was pretty sure he was researching wedding venues, although she really would have preferred he included her in that.

Still, if all the subterfuge meant that a proposal was imminent, then Vanessa could certainly forgo that much. She'd known from the start that Ethan was perfect marriage material—mature, well respected, and talented. And possibly best of all, with Daisy, they would be a ready-made family.

Then the phone rang and she jumped.

"There, that must be him now," she said to Daisy. With any luck, she would find out all she needed to know very soon.

Vanessa held the device to her ear. "Hi, darling. How are you? How's everything going with the research?"

"Yes, well…I'm doing as much as I can in such a short space of time."

"I can imagine. I really can't wait to hear all about it. It sounds like such an interesting prospect."

"Well, everything's still in the very early stages yet," he replied.

Vanessa stayed silent, feeling somewhat disappointed. Damn, what did *that* mean? She didn't think she could wait much longer; the suspense was killing her. And was it her imagination or did he sound a little…distant?

"Actually," Ethan continued, "it now looks like I may have to rethink the idea altogether."

"Why would you need to do that?" she asked, frowning. "Especially after going to so much trouble. You know, all the way to Dublin and everything."

"Let's just say the idea I had didn't quite go according to plan, so now I think I may need to consider a different one."

What did that mean? If he hadn't arranged to see her parents in advance and then had maybe missed them when he called…

"Really? Why didn't your first idea work?" she inquired.

"Well, I suppose I'm a bit worried that some people might be upset about the outcome."

If by some chance, her father had said or done something stupid, Vanessa would *murder* him.

"Well, there will always be critics, Ethan. You can't please everyone."

"I know."

"So perhaps you should care less about readers and more that you—or even *I*—are happy with the outcome?"

"As I said, it's early days and I'm not sure I'm ready."

Damn. Now Vanessa's thoughts were all over the place. What the hell was he trying to say?

"So where does that leave us in the meantime?" she asked, momentarily forgetting that they were supposed to be speaking in code.

Although of course Ethan couldn't know that.

"What do you mean?" he asked.

She deliberately lightened her tone. "Well, I should hope you're going to let me read it sometime."

"Of course. It's just still a bit messy at the moment, that's all."

"I see." Vanessa's heart sank. Could Daisy have misread the situation? Or had she completely misread it herself?

She turned to look at Ethan's daughter, who was sitting quietly at the breakfast bar.

"Well, we're looking forward to seeing you soon. When are you due back?"

"My flight's this evening at seven. Are you and Daisy having a nice time?"

"We're having a lovely time," she said. "Do you want to talk to her?" She was rather hoping Ethan might confess to Daisy what was going on and then she in turn might be able to enlighten her further.

"Yes, please."

"Hi, Dad. Yes, we're having a great time... No, not really."

At this, Vanessa could see the guilty shadow that crossed Daisy's face and realized that Ethan must be asking something about the secret they were keeping. She clenched her hands into fists. How could she get it out of Daisy?

"Yeah, I miss you too. See you soon, Dad."

With that, Daisy handed Vanessa back the phone.

"We can come to Heathrow later and collect you."

"No, it's fine. No need to go to any trouble. I can get the train."

"Well, as long as you're sure..."

"I am. I'd better go. I have quite a lot to get through today. A few more options to explore."

"Of course. Well, enjoy the rest of the trip, and if there's anything I can help with...any research I can do, let me know."

"Ah, no, after today, I should have it all under control," he said, sounding uncomfortable.

"Good to know. See you soon."

But as Vanessa disconnected, she wondered how much longer she would be able to stand the suspense.

Chapter 37

ETHAN KNEW THAT HE SHOULD HAVE BITTEN THE BULLET AND TAKEN the ring back last night, but he just couldn't do it.

He was too soft…or too bloody stupid, more like. By rights, he should be on a plane back to London by now. Instead, he was heading back to Gillini for one last-ditch attempt at getting the job done.

"Ethan, hello again!" Before he could ponder his predicament any further, he was greeted with Rachel's beaming smile.

All thought of getting the ring back suddenly left his mind as he stood there stupidly staring at her, and he felt a spasm of something go through his stomach. He couldn't put his finger on what it was exactly, but he knew it was no longer just about the ring.

The truth was, he was still struck by Rachel's comment last night about wanting to marry Vanessa so that he and Daisy could be a family again. Was there something to it? Was that the real reason he was so keen to make her his wife?

For her part, at least Rachel understood the importance of family in her own life following the loss of her parents.

But that didn't necessarily mean it was good enough reason for either of them to be committing. And Ethan figured that they each had far more in common than he realized.

"Sleep well last night?" she asked, and he willed himself to snap out of it.

"Yes, very well actually."

"So what are you up to today? More research for your book?"

He nodded uncomfortably at the mention of his pathetic cover story.

Earlier that morning at the hotel, he'd passed an hour googling any practical knowledge that he should have if he were indeed writing a book about the history of bread in other cultures.

He now felt that he could not only list hundreds of different types of bread across the world but also had a working knowledge of symbolism, rituals, and ingredients. Just in case anyone started asking questions.

"Well, as I said last night, if you need my help in that regard, don't hesitate to ask."

He smiled. "Thanks, that's very kind of you. I'll certainly keep it in mind."

There was a slight uncomfortable moment as the two stood there in the middle of the bistro staring at one another.

"Oh!" Rachel exclaimed as if remembering. "You must be hungry. Here, let me get you a table."

"Thanks, but no. I had a huge breakfast at the hotel earlier." He looked hesitant. "Ah, I just wanted to pop in to thank you for a lovely evening. It was really good of you to spend your Saturday night babysitting me."

"Not at all. I had a lovely time."

"Me too. But I just wondered…about your fiancé…could I possibly have a contact number for Gary? I'd really like to talk to him today if I could."

Was it his imagination, or did a shadow cross her face at the mention of Knowles?

"Ethan, again, I really have to apologize on his behalf. I don't know what's gotten into him lately, and it's just not good enough that you should have to chase him. When are you going back to London? I'll make sure he calls you today. If not, it'll definitely be this evening." She pursed her lips. "Let's just say Gary is a little… under the weather at the moment."

"I see. But I'd quite like to be able to get in touch with him myself, just in case it slips his mind again."

Damn it, couldn't she just hand over the blasted number? Having a go-between was becoming tedious—irrespective of how much he enjoyed talking to her, it wasn't getting him anywhere.

"Believe me, I'll make sure that doesn't happen, but here." Rachel walked over to the bar area and grabbed a notebook. "This is his mobile number," she said, writing down a sequence of digits, and Ethan wanted to punch the air.

Finally, he'd be able to sort this man-to-man.

"Thank you." He put the slip of paper carefully into his wallet, as if it were made of gold. "And best of luck to you both with the wedding plans."

He went to shake her hand, but again to his surprise, she stepped forward and engulfed him in a warm hug. Ethan felt almost dizzy as he breathed in the scent of her hair.

"Well, it was so lovely to see you again. And please do keep in touch. You have my number too, and like I said, if you ever need to know anything about bread…"

He smiled. "I know exactly who to ask." He looked at his watch, suddenly reluctant to leave. "I suppose I'd better get a move on. Lots to do today."

"I know what you mean. Weekends can get a bit crazy around here." She smiled and ran a hand through her hair, and again he saw the diamond sparkle in the sunlight.

As Ethan turned to leave, the thought struck him that having seen how perfectly it suited Rachel, he was finding it increasingly difficult to picture it on Vanessa.

Chapter 38

GARY FELT HIS PHONE VIBRATE IN HIS RIDING JACKET. HE SMILED TO himself, pleased that he was such a connoisseur of bikes that he could distinguish between the vibrations coming off the riding machine and those of the device in his pocket. Actually, he was pleased that his brain could distinguish anything at all this afternoon, given that he was nursing such an almighty hangover.

Probably Sean ringing him back about meeting up for a cure. Gary reckoned a pint was the only way he'd be able to relieve the ache in his bones and the persistent twinges in his ribs.

Sleeping upright in the bistro last night didn't help, and while he'd tried his best to sleep off the worst of the aftereffects earlier, he figured the only thing for it now was a spin on the bike, followed by another afternoon in the pub.

Rachel was annoyed anyway, so he might as well be hung for a sheep as a lamb. And after him going out of his way to come back early from Wicklow last night to see her.

Sometimes you just couldn't win—especially with women.

Although Terri had been nice enough to him last night, what with the free booze and good company. She blew hot and cold sometimes, Terri, but she was all right at the back of it all. Gary smiled, figuring she must have always had a bit of a thing for him, but because he was with Rachel, he'd never really noticed.

He brought his bike to a halt, spraying gravel as he stopped. Still sitting on the saddle, he reached into his pocket and brought the phone out. He didn't recognize the number but decided to answer it anyway.

"Yo."

"Is that Gary Knowles?" The voice was male with an English accent that sounded posh.

Shite, Gary thought, realizing.

"Yup," he replied.

"Well, nice to talk to you finally. It's Ethan Greene here."

"Right. Em, hello." He tried to sound nonchalant, but the truth was his nerves were in bits. Especially if, as Terri tried to point out last night, the piece of luck that had landed in his lap (or at least in that Tiffany's bag) wasn't luck at all.

Well, if something had indeed gone amiss, it was an innocent mistake and had nothing to do with Gary, him being unconscious and all.

"I'm not sure if you remember, but our paths crossed in New York," Greene went on, not sounding particularly friendly. "I've been trying to get in touch with you a number of times since, but it seems you're a very hard man to pin down."

"Right, yes. I think Rachel might have mentioned something."

"Let's not beat around the bush here. You have something of mine, and I want it back."

Gary's eyes narrowed defensively. He didn't like this guy's tone. Who did he think he was, ringing up out of the blue and making demands? "I don't know what you're talking about."

"Oh, I think you know very well what I'm talking about. The diamond ring that is currently in the possession of your girlfriend? You and I both know that you didn't buy it yourself."

"Like I said, I don't know what you're—"

"We can do this the easy way or the hard way. The ring is mine, and I want it back. I'm also more than happy to give you back your own Tiffany's purchase—a silver charm bracelet, I believe?"

"Dunno what you're on about." Gary knew better than to admit anything up front. "Thanks for looking after me after the accident and everything, but as far as this stuff goes, it's all news to me."

There was no way he could turn around and ask Rachel for the ring back now, not when she thought the sun shone out of his backside for giving it to her.

No, what was done was done, and how was he supposed to know that the stupid ring belonged to someone else? Surely it was Greene's own fault for not looking after his stuff?

Gary was annoyed now. It was bad enough that he'd been put in the awkward position of having to propose unprepared because of this bloody ring, so for this guy to just turn around and expect him to hand it back after all, that was a bit rich.

Anyway, for all he knew, any stranger could ring up and claim the ring was his.

"Look, I don't have time for this," he said in an attempt to get the guy off his back. "Dunno what you're spouting off about, to be honest."

"Fine, then you leave me little choice but to go to the police."

"Grand. Do what you like." Gary didn't know what else to say. Anyway, what could the cops do? He'd committed no crime, and actually if you thought about it properly, he'd also been the victim here, considering that the appearance of this ring had led to him being engaged without having the chance to think properly about it.

So the last thing he wanted to do was have to fork out a bleedin' fortune for another fancy diamond just because some randomer had taken the notion to blame him for losing one.

"You're seriously refusing to give it back?" Greene said, and Gary knew that he'd been calling his bluff about the cops.

"Look, mate, I'm sorry for your troubles, but I really haven't a clue what you want from me. I don't know you from Adam, and here you are ringing me up and accusing me of all sorts—"

"You stole my engagement ring, for crying out loud!"

"Now hold on a moment," Gary said, his hackles rising. He'd had just about enough of this. "I didn't steal anything. If you've lost something, then I'm sorry, but as I said, it's nothing to do with me—"

"I saw the ring on your girlfriend's finger just now. There's no question that it's mine!"

Gary stopped short. What the hell? How could Greene have seen it on Rachel's finger? Unless he was actually in—

"And quite frankly, I cannot understand what such a lovely woman is doing with someone like yourself. Over dinner last night, she told me all about your so-called proposal and how you had it all planned. Planned my foot."

Gary was incredulous. Right. That was enough. First the guy

accuses of him of stealing, and then he has the audacity to sneak around with his fiancée?

Rachel hadn't said a word about going out to dinner with anyone last night, and especially not this guy.

Was this his true game at the back of it all? Was all this talk about a ring a mere front for him to get into Rachel's pants? He wouldn't put it past him.

"Right, Greene," he said, his tone steely. "I'll tell you one thing. I don't take kindly to strange men sniffing around my girlfriend. So if you know what's good for you, you stay away from her."

"For goodness' sake, all I want is my property back," Greene said, backing down immediately, much to Gary's satisfaction.

"Well, good luck with that," Gary said, hanging up on him.

Stupid prat obviously didn't know who the hell he was dealing with, and if he thought he could just roll up in Dublin and use some cock-and-bull story to try and swipe his woman from him, he had another think coming.

Gary put the phone back in his inside pocket and revved up the bike again.

He needed to talk to Sean about this, get his take on it.

Granted the ring had appeared out of the blue, but that didn't mean anything. He was only sorry that he'd admitted as much to Terri and hoped she wouldn't go blabbing to Rachel.

After all, the ring did belong to him—once it landed in his bags anyway. And although the proposal hadn't been as well planned as everyone thought, he had asked Rachel to marry him—and in front of half the country on New Year's Eve.

So surely she couldn't get too upset about a technicality?

With any luck, he was worrying for nothing. Terri had been pretty drunk herself last night, so maybe she wouldn't even remember. But in the meantime, just in case she did blab, he supposed he'd better start thinking about his own version of events.

Gary zoomed down the road in the direction of Sean's place.

He shouldn't waste time worrying about that plonker.

Rachel would believe him any day over some crackpot toff from London. He knew that much.

Chapter 39

Terri was surprised to see Gary at the bistro again that evening, and even more so when after speaking briefly to Rachel, he came into the kitchen and asked if he could have a private word with *her*.

"What's up?" she asked, drying her floury hands on a nearby tea towel. He looked preoccupied and uncomfortable, a notable change from his usual cocky demeanor.

"I…ah…just wanted to talk to you about last night," he began, his tone cautious.

"Last night. What about it?"

"Well, I had a few in me, and I might have said some things…"

"I'm not sure what you mean," she said, feigning innocence. Was he worried she might tell Rachel about their so-called flirting? Or did the concern stem from elsewhere, namely the sorry truth?

"Well, as I said, last night is a bit fuzzy, but you know the way we were talking about the engagement stuff and all?"

Aha! So he *was* worried, she realized with some satisfaction. Maybe she'd misjudged him, and he was about to come clean after all.

"Yes, you might have mentioned something about it all being a bit of surprise for both of you."

"Yeah. It's just that…" Then he looked at her as if trying to figure out something. "Did Rachel mention to you where she was last night?"

"After work, you mean? As far as I know, she went out to dinner."

"Any idea who with?"

Terri was all innocence. "Well, actually, now that you say it, I think it was with that guy who saved you, Ethan Greene."

There was a strange look on his face. "Don't believe everything you hear, Terri. That guy didn't save me."

"Of course he did."

Gary shook his head. "Dunno. I think he's a bit of a player, this fella, making up stories to try and get into Rachel's pants."

Terri couldn't believe what she was hearing. Was Gary seriously trying to justify keeping the ring and now trying to accuse Ethan of moving in on Rachel?

"Think about it. If this Greene guy was so anxious to speak to me, then why did he go behind my back and ask her out to dinner?"

"Because you weren't here, and Rachel thought you were staying overnight in Wicklow. Anyway, he didn't ask her. She asked him, to thank him for helping you out."

He rubbed a hand across his stubbly jaw. "I don't know. This fella seems a little too cute for my liking, and if he thinks I'm going to fall for that sorry story he fed me earlier…"

"So you have spoken to him then." Terri was relieved that the two had at least been in contact. It meant that Gary would now have no choice but to be up front. Granted, Rachel would be hurt and feel very deceived, but the truth needed to come out sooner rather than later. "I'm glad. The sooner Rachel knows about this, the—"

Gary looked at her. "Rachel doesn't need to know anything."

"But…but we both know that the ring isn't yours," Terri replied, wide-eyed. "You must give it back to Ethan."

"Nope. It's Rachel's now, and none of us wants her to get hurt, do we?" He looked at her closely, and she realized that behind his Neanderthal bluster was a calculating mind.

This worried her even more.

Even worse, he was calling her bluff, daring Terri to admit what she knew to Rachel when they both knew how much it would hurt her.

By the looks of things, Gary was even planning to suggest that Ethan was using it all as a cover story to get closer to Rachel. Perhaps convinced of that himself.

Either way, it looked like Ethan wasn't going to get the ring back without a fight.

Just then, Rachel arrived back in the kitchen. "Hi. What are you doing hiding away in here?" she said, sidling up to Gary.

"Just thanking Terri for keeping me company last night," he said, putting an arm around her, and Terri was perturbed at how easily he could lie. "Anyway, I'd better go and let you ladies do some work."

"Are you sure you don't want to throw on an apron and give us a hand? I've got some fresh dough that needs making," Rachel teased him, going to the storeroom.

"Nah, best to leave all that stuff to the experts," he joked. Giving her a peck on the cheek, he eyed Terri briefly as if to challenge her.

Her heart sinking, Terri knew that realistically, even if she wanted to tell Rachel the truth, she didn't have a leg to stand on. It seemed so unlikely and fantastical that she ran the risk of coming across as jealous or spiteful.

What made it harder was that Gary was willing and, it seemed, well able to cover his tracks, and as Justin had pointed out, by saying something, Terri ran the risk of ruining not only their friendship but their business relationship too.

So what was she going to do?

Rachel came back out of the storeroom. "Making more already?" she said, noticing that Terri was kneading out fresh dough. "Yours must be doing a bomb today."

She and Rachel had an unofficial competition going on in the artisan bakery. Today, the olive bread was lagging behind.

"Doesn't it always?" she teased, hoping her despondency didn't show in her tone.

"I think we're looking low on cookies too, and... Oh, blast it," Rachel added, her face falling. She wiped her hands and fished around in the pockets of her apron for her phone.

"What's wrong?"

"I don't know how many times I promised Ethan I'd make some for his daughter. I should have given them to him earlier, but I completely forgot. Maybe he can pop back and collect them now?"

Terri watched as Rachel waited for the call to be answered.

Then Rachel rolled her eyes. "No answer. I'll just leave a message and hope he gets it before he leaves for the airport."

Terri idly wondered why Ethan hadn't taken the call. Although, given Gary's response to his plight, he was perhaps down at a police station trying to make a complaint, or worse, she thought grimacing, in the River Liffey.

"If he calls back later, will you make sure he gets them if I'm not here?"

"Of course." Terri now wondered if the guy would be back with the cops, given Gary's recent stonewalling.

Yet she knew he wouldn't make a scene, for Rachel's sake at least.

Her friend was breaking up pieces of fat for puff pastry. "Damn, I keep forgetting to take this off," she said, catching the ring as it was just about to slide into the mixture. She laughed lightly. "If I'm not more careful, one of these days, someone'll end up choking on it."

Chapter 40

ETHAN WAS SO ANGRY, HE THOUGHT HE MIGHT BURST. THE GALL OF
the man to deny outright that the ring was his when he had to know
full well he had come by it in dodgy circumstances!

Enough was enough. There was nothing else for it but to take
this whole thing straight to the police now. But the problem was,
which police? The incident had happened in New York, so why
would the Irish or indeed the British police be interested? And even
if they were, what proof could Ethan offer them other than a non-
specific transaction on a credit card statement? He had the Tiffany
Diamond Certificate also, but this served more as a warranty for
stone quality and wouldn't necessarily do as definitive proof that
the diamond was his.

He wondered then if he might be able to claim the loss back on
his credit card insurance altogether. There would be visual proof (as
well as witnesses) to his buying the ring in the store, and he supposed
he could ring Tiffany's and ask them to send him security footage of
Gary Knowles buying the silver bracelet.

Ethan was annoyed he hadn't thought of this before now, but
stupidly, he'd thought he was dealing with reasonable, rational

people, not a thug with no morals who thought nothing of pocketing such a valuable item!

And of course, he'd been somewhat blindsided by Rachel too, hadn't he?

Well, no more. He'd tiptoed around people long enough, and since Gary had no compunction about deceiving her, Ethan couldn't realistically be responsible for her feelings either.

He was actually only too delighted to have been offered another excuse to return to the bistro by Rachel herself after her message about collecting cookies for Daisy.

This afternoon, he'd go back, then tell her straight out exactly the kind of man her fiancé really was.

And this time, *nothing* was going to stop him.

❧

"She's not here," Terri told him when he arrived.

His flight was due to leave at seven, and he figured he'd have ample time to pop back and set the record straight to Rachel before heading to the airport.

"She's catering another event tonight."

He ran a hand through his hair. "I don't believe this!"

"And I know why you are," Terri added pointedly.

Ethan's face grew wary. "What do you mean?"

"I know that your trip this weekend has nothing whatsoever to do with researching a book about bread."

"I really have no idea what you are talking about."

Terri smiled and shook her head. "Sweet, but that whole big blue eyes thing isn't going to work on me. I know about the accident in New York, and I know about the mix-up with the engagement ring. I know you bought an expensive diamond from Tiffany's but that your girlfriend ended up with a silver charm bracelet."

His face went white. "How could you possibly—"

"And I also know that you've been trying to tell Rachel the truth but for some reason have come up with this cock-and-bull story about researching a book."

He was about to argue but couldn't find the words.

"A book about the history of bread? Sounds tantalizing," Terri drawled in amusement. "Anyway, I know all this because I got Gary drunk last night, and as they say in the movies, he sang like a canary."

Ethan's head shot up. "He admitted to stealing the ring?"

"Not exactly. Take it from me, Gary isn't the sharpest tool in the box. In fact, he's so stupid that the thought the ring might have been someone else's never even crossed his mind."

He looked at Terri. "Where on earth did he think it came from?"

She rolled her eyes. "From the great ring fairy in the sky? Who knows?" Then Terri looked at him closely. "I'm also guessing that you haven't said anything to Rachel for another, slightly more personal reason?" she suggested gently, and his cheeks flared pink.

He lowered his gaze "I have no idea what you—"

"Don't be embarrassed. I think it's wonderful that you two got on so well."

He cleared his throat. "Look, the only reason I came here was to get back what's rightfully mine but..."

"But you've gotten a little more than you expected?"

Ethan paused, unsure what to say. "Not that it's any of my concern, but I still can't believe she would agree to marry this guy," he muttered.

"You and me both. I was never Gary's number one fan, and I must admit the engagement threw me a little, but not for long." She shook her head. "Like you, I just don't know how to break it to Rachel without hurting her. Anyway," Terri continued, taking a white cardboard box from beneath the counter. "She asked me to give you these. Cookies for your daughter, she said?"

"Thanks." Ethan absently tucked them under his arm.

"And this is for you," she added, handing him a parcel with Gillini's logo emblazoned upon it. "Some more of that bread you liked so much at lunch yesterday."

"Thanks, but that really won't be necessary." In truth, Ethan didn't want anything to remind him of this godforsaken place.

"I suspect Rachel would really like you to have it, considering your research and all," Terri insisted, pressing it into his hands.

There was something in her voice that caused him to look at her more closely, but then he wondered if he might be imagining it. God knows his head was all over the place this weekend.

Her green eyes bored into his. "Please, I insist. It won't stay fresh for long. Maybe have some on the flight back even?"

"Thanks." He took the parcel, out of politeness and so that he could get out of this blasted place and back to London. First thing tomorrow, he would talk to the credit card company and indeed his lawyers to see what other options he could explore.

Terri smiled and patted his hand. "Try not to worry, okay? Things have a way of working themselves out in the end."

Chapter 41

"Welcome back!" Later that evening, Vanessa hugged him warmly upon his return. Ethan was so exhausted by the weekend's events that he felt almost relieved to be back despite not achieving what he'd set out to do.

Daisy stood in the background, obviously waiting for a moment alone to find out how everything had gone.

He lifted her into his arms and hugged her tightly until she squealed. "I missed you, buttercup," he said before whispering into her ear that he'd tell all later. "And you too, darling," he said, kissing Vanessa briefly.

"I wasn't sure whether you'd eaten on the plane, so I made a light supper," she said.

Actually he was starving. He didn't fancy any of the options they had on the flight service and had (stupidly in retrospect) packed the food in his checked luggage.

Then remembering the cookies were for Daisy, he opened his case and withdrew the box.

"Especially for you," he said, winking at her. Then remembering he couldn't make mention of Rachel, he mumbled something about picking them up at the airport.

"Yay, thanks, Dad."

But immediately realizing that now it looked like he hadn't sought out a similar treat for Vanessa, he meekly picked up the bread. "And this is for you. Well, for us really. There was a lovely bistro with an in-house artisan bakery near the hotel, and I thought you might like it."

"Bread?" She looked suitably underwhelmed.

"Yes. It smelled so delicious, I couldn't resist." He shrugged, realizing that making up excuses and sounding like an idiot seemed par for the course these days.

"Lovely. Well, I suppose it'll do nicely with supper then. Shall we eat?"

Ethan nodded and followed her into the kitchen. He tried to avoid Daisy's still-probing gaze, too weary to try and get the message across that his visit to Dublin had been a complete and utter waste of time.

Vanessa had laid on a very nice spread of olives, cheese, and Parma ham, and he set to it with gusto, pleading hunger as a good excuse not to talk about his trip.

Making up more tall tales was the last thing he wanted to do, given that the entire thing had been such a disaster.

Taking the bread out of its Gillini paper packaging, Vanessa sniffed it approvingly. "You're right. This does smell delicious." She tore a large piece from one side. "Daisy, would you like some?"

"No thanks." She seemed put out that her father was keeping her in the dark, but Ethan didn't have the energy for explanations just then. He didn't have the energy for anything at all. In truth, what he needed now was a good night's sleep and a recharge of his batteries for—

"Ow!" Vanessa cried out, and he saw her put a hand to her mouth. "What the hell? I almost broke a tooth."

Ethan watched wordlessly as she extracted something solid from her mouth.

"Goodness, I could have choked on something this size," she said disapprovingly.

"What is it?" Daisy asked, and upon closer inspection, they saw that Vanessa was holding up something small wrapped in greaseproof paper.

Something that looked an awful lot like…

"Oh my God."

Ethan's heart skipped a beat as, having unwrapped the paper, Vanessa's eyes widened, and she held up a diamond ring—*the* diamond ring.

His jaw dropped, and he suddenly remembered Terri's earlier insistence that he take the bread and her cryptic assertion that everything would turn out okay.

"How did you… Is this what…?" Vanessa's eyes bugged out, and she was grinning from ear to ear as Daisy looked on in amazement. "I can't believe this!"

Although he too was knocked for a loop, he automatically felt a huge weight lift from his shoulders.

Terri… How had she done it? She must have somehow purloined the ring from Rachel, possibly because she knew he was getting nowhere with Gary.

And she needed a way for the truth to come out to do right by her friend.

Thank heavens.

Vanessa was still staring at the ring, a look of complete and utter delight on her face.

"Ethan, is this what I think it is?" she said, beaming at him. "Forgive me, but it's not a...joke or anything, is it?"

He forced himself out of his reverie. "No, darling. It's exactly what you think it is," he reassured her, wondering why his tone sounded so leaden when this was what he'd wanted all along.

It was just all so unexpected.

"Oh my. I don't know what to say. What a perfectly amazing surprise."

He could see Daisy watching him carefully, as if she sensed that he was just as surprised as Vanessa.

The whole scenario felt almost like a replay of that Christmas morning in New York.

"So," he said, turning to her and clearing his throat. "I suppose I haven't actually asked the all-important question yet. Vanessa, will you marry me?"

She stared at the ring, and her eyes glistened with tears. "Of course I will!" she cried, jumping up to embrace him. "Oh, Ethan, this is just the most wonderful surprise!"

And as he held her in his arms, Ethan wondered why the moment felt so surreal, and so....anticlimactic almost.

Nothing was different. But everything had changed.

Then taking the ring, he slipped it onto the third finger of her left hand, where it should have been from the start.

"Oh," she said, giggling a little when the ring failed to glide smoothly into place like it was supposed to. "Seems a little tight."

She wedged it more firmly onto her finger, but still it wedged firmly above the knuckle. "Doesn't matter. I can always get it resized," she assured him blithely, but Ethan was baffled.

His mind thought back to last night, when the band seemed to fit Rachel's finger perfectly, a rather strange coincidence given that Tiffany's had sized it especially for Vanessa.

Once again, his gaze met Daisy's, and he saw that she was watching the scene with interest. He suspected she was thinking the same thing.

How could it be that the ring didn't fit Vanessa but was somehow perfect on Rachel?

Chapter 42

RACHEL WAS PERPLEXED. HOW COULD SHE HAVE LOST IT? AND where? She distinctly remembered taking it off on yesterday morning before she went to work. Or had she removed it *at* work?

Maybe she'd taken it off when she returned home after dinner with Ethan on Saturday night. She might have been a little tipsy but not so much that she wouldn't remember taking the ring off.

And if she had, then where else would she have put it other than on the nightstand?

She couldn't be sure, she admitted, panicking as she checked down the side of the bed and the floor beneath to try and locate it.

After that, she went out into the living room and began turning over all the cushions on her sofa, but to no avail.

She'd first noticed it wasn't on her finger at the anniversary event they'd catered for last night. The happy couple had been married for forty years, and during the speeches, Rachel instinctively imagined her and Gary's forthcoming anniversaries, remembered looking down at her engagement finger, only to find that her precious ring wasn't there. She hadn't been able to rest until she returned home to find it.

But since there was no sign, she decided now that she must have removed it at work, and it was probably in the kitchen. Surely Justin or Terri had spotted it lying around, hidden under a tea towel or a bag of flour or something, and put it somewhere else for safekeeping?

Rachel took a deep breath and tried to calm herself. That had to be it, she thought, feeling better already. Goodness knows what she'd do if she had to tell Gary she'd misplaced it. He'd go ballistic.

She'd check with the others today, but first she needed to make an appointment with the bridal store to coincide with her day off next week.

She couldn't wait and still couldn't quite believe that all this—the New York proposal, huge Tiffany diamond, fairy-tale stuff, really—was truly happening. This time last year, she didn't even know Gary, and look at her now, running a successful business and planning the wedding of the year. It was everything she'd ever wanted—or at least it would be again, Rachel thought, worriedly caressing her engagement finger, once she'd located her ring.

Looking around her little mews house, she wondered what she and Gary would do about their living situation.

They'd be moving in together obviously, but where? They hadn't yet discussed these practicalities. No doubt they'd start looking for a house in the future, but what to do in the meantime? His place was too far out of town for her, and her own little one-bedroom place would never be big enough for the two of them.

Not to mention Gary's beloved bike.

Already he was talking about buying another once the money

from the accident came through, and she groaned inwardly, having visions of their future home being strewn with engine parts.

Rachel was of two minds about the lawsuit; once Gary was okay, she didn't think there was anything to be gained from suing the taxi company, but of course she wasn't the one who'd ended up with broken ribs and a concussion.

Thank goodness he'd had health insurance though. Who knew what would have happened if he'd had to pay out a fortune for the hospital bills? Her precious ring may well have been making its way straight back to Tiffany's before she'd even gotten a chance to see it.

But once the idea of legal action had entered his mind, Gary couldn't be dissuaded, and apparently his solicitor had readily agreed to take a case on his behalf.

Rachel couldn't help but feel sorry for the poor taxi driver, and she hoped the lawsuit wouldn't get him into trouble with his employers, or worse, cause him to lose his job. Ethan had mentioned that the man seemed incredibly remorseful at the time, and Rachel really couldn't see the point in punishing him even further, but there was no reasoning with Gary.

"Are you mad?" he'd argued when she'd suggested it might be best to just move on and forget about it. "The fool almost killed me! Anyway, these guys have insurance for this kind of thing."

She also wished he would spend less time on pursuing a case against the person who'd hurt him and more on showing gratitude to the one who'd helped, thinking again of Ethan.

She wasn't sure if the two men had since been in touch over the weekend. It was so embarrassing having to make excuses for him, especially when Ethan had gone out of his way to follow up on everything afterward. He was such a gentleman and a kindhearted old soul, considering everything he'd been through.

She couldn't imagine what it would be like to experience the sorrow of losing the person you knew was "the one."

And despite not knowing Ethan's soon-to-be fiancée, she couldn't help but feel a little sorry for her. It must be difficult having to live in the shadow of a past love, particularly one who obviously still weighed heavily on his mind.

She shook her head. There she was, worrying about complete strangers and trying to imagine what they were or weren't feeling. How stupid was she? Especially when it was highly unlikely she'd ever come across Ethan Greene—never mind his girlfriend—ever again.

⤳◈⤶

"It was you, wasn't it?" The voice on the other end of the line said without preamble.

"Ethan, hi."

"Why? I'm massively grateful of course, but why did you help me?"

Terri sighed. Already she was having second thoughts about intervening, especially now that Rachel had realized the ring was missing and was frantic about it.

But she couldn't just stand by and watch her friend be made a fool of. And since Ethan was too bloody nice to spill the beans, something had to be done.

So on Sunday afternoon, when Rachel's ring had almost

slipped off and she'd subsequently removed it and placed it on the windowsill, Terri had seized the opportunity. When her friend had gone out front to replace some stock, Terri had slipped it in the dough she was making and then later passed the loaf on to Ethan.

But she realized now, she wasn't really thinking at all. If she had, she should have considered Rachel's feelings and how upset she'd be once she realized the ring was gone.

"Because you might never have gotten it back from Gary," Terri told Ethan now. "And you certainly wouldn't have taken it back from Rachel."

"Still, it was exceptionally decent of you, especially when you don't even know me."

She knew enough to know he was a good person though. His reluctance to hurt Rachel demonstrated that.

When Terri told him as much, he gave a soft laugh. "Too much of a wimpy old sod, you mean."

"Doesn't matter. Your intentions were good, and once I got the truth out of Gary, I knew I couldn't let him get away with it."

"But what will happen now? I take it Gary's confessed everything?"

"As far as I know, he doesn't know it's missing yet." He would soon though, she realized, biting her lip.

"Poor Rachel. She'll be so upset, I'm sure."

"I know." But it was for the best. Terri was sure of it. "At least it's not something you need to worry about anymore."

"Thank you again, truly, although I must admit, I do wish you'd told me you'd put it in the bread," he said, a slight twinge in his voice that Terri thought sounded like regret.

She frowned. "Well, I couldn't say it out straight, but I thought I did, in so many words. Remember I told you to eat it on your flight back?" She chuckled. "I just hope you didn't break a tooth or anything."

"Actually…" Ethan went on to tell her about how Vanessa had been the one to find it. "It rather caught us both by surprise."

"Wow, that ring really does seem to have a mind of its own. So I guess congratulations are in order. And all's well that ends well."

Chapter 43

FOR ETHAN, THE FOLLOWING WEEK WENT BY IN A DAZE. HE STILL couldn't believe that after all the worry, all the hassle of going to Dublin and trying to get the ring back, he'd had it returned to him just like that.

And although he was hugely grateful to Terri for intervening, in truth he'd rather she'd told him up front what she was doing. That way, he could have fished it out himself and decided what to do with it after that.

But what was there to decide? The ring was meant for Vanessa after all.

Still, what must poor Rachel be thinking? She must be going out of her mind, wondering where it was and how she could have lost it. Especially when she already had such an attachment to it.

While Ethan knew that what Rachel was and wasn't feeling was none of his business, still, he couldn't help but feel somewhat invested, never mind responsible.

He thought again about Vanessa's delighted reaction to his "surprise proposal."

"Well, I knew you had a great imagination, but even I'm taken aback at this level of elaboration," she had laughed after the rather awkward moment when the ring didn't fit. "So this whole going to Dublin for 'research' was just a big ruse to throw me off?"

"Sorry, yes," Ethan agreed, still trying to get over the shock of it all himself.

She laughed lightly. "So what did Mum and Dad say?"

"I'm sorry…what?"

"Mum and Dad. What did they say when you told them what you were planning?" She set down her fork. "That's the real reason you went, yes? To officially ask Dad for my hand?" When his expression revealed his surprise, she raised an eyebrow. "Oh, I honestly thought… Why did you go then?"

"For the ring of course!" Daisy piped up, and Ethan looked at her aghast. "We tried to get it in New York, but they didn't have the special one he wanted for you, did they, Dad?"

He nodded wordlessly, at this point resigned to just going with the flow.

"So *that's* why you two kept disappearing all the time!" Vanessa seemed even more delighted. "I had no idea you had such specific taste. But you couldn't get it at Tiffany's on Old Bond Street?"

"No, not that particular setting… Though I'm sorry, of course I should have asked your parents—"

"Don't be silly. It's fine! It was the only reason I could pinpoint for that sudden jaunt to Dublin, and it's not as though you didn't put a huge deal of thought into all this in any case." She indicated the sourdough and then reached across the countertop for the wrapper. "Gillini," she read out loud from the sticker on the front. "Do they do this kind of thing on request?" she added, picking up the ring again. "Specialized proposals, I mean. How did you hear about them?"

"Just saw something online a while back," he mumbled, not wanting to get into any specifics.

"It was a brilliant idea, Dad," Daisy chimed in. She met Ethan's eye, and a smile of understanding passed between them. "See, I told you he had a great imagination," she said to Vanessa.

That night, Ethan had slept better than he had in weeks. The ring was back in his possession, he and Vanessa were back on track, and all was once again right with the world.

Until his new fiancée dropped another bombshell.

"Don't get me wrong. The way the proposal happened was sooo romantic and really original," Vanessa had said over breakfast the following morning. "But forgive me. I must admit I'm also rather partial to tradition. What about the little blue box? It would be so nice to have it so I can keep it safe when not wearing it, and silly perhaps, but I'd quite like the whole Tiffany's kit and caboodle."

"I'm sure it's in my luggage somewhere..." Ethan had fudged, knocking back his early morning coffee.

Bugger Tiffany's and their blasted little blue box! Given the circumstances, he was lucky to have gotten anything back at all. But now his stomach lurched as he realized another visit to the store beckoned.

At this stage, it felt like he should be buying shares in the place.

He'd head down to Old Bond Street after his last lecture today and try and pick up something small and inexpensive, something for Daisy even? Then he could give the packaging to Vanessa so she could have her precious paraphernalia.

Sometimes he didn't understand women at all.

"Don't worry about it for now. I just thought I'd mention it in case you'd decided to throw it away or something."

Now he wanted to kick himself, wishing that he'd thought of saying he'd done exactly that.

At this rate, Ethan would be happy if he never saw a little blue box again in his life.

Chapter 44

Gary was in the middle a job when he got a call from his solicitor.

"Frank, what's up?" he said, positioning the phone under his chin.

He hoped it was information about the lawsuit. Frank Donnelly was a viper by reputation, and Gary suspected he would go all out to ensure he got a big payout.

Well, it was no more than he deserved. He'd missed nearly two weeks' work because of that accident, *and* he'd had to shell out for those extra nights in the New York hotel as well as the flights home.

Okay, so Rachel had actually taken care of that, but since they were engaged, it was practically the same thing. She was the one who'd been talking about opening a joint account to keep track of the wedding expenses, something that put the fear of God into Gary in case she'd figure out how broke he was.

He couldn't for the life of him understand why she didn't approve of him going after the cab company, calling it "bad karma" and all that crap. Wasn't it bad karma that he'd been hit in the first place?

"Just a bit of an update on the cab thing," Frank replied, and Gary straightened up in anticipation.

"Oh?"

"Good news and bad news. From our point of view, the CCTV footage looks good." Gary recalled that his solicitor had requested footage of the area along Fifth Avenue from the relevant New York authorities, which would hopefully be able to show the incident in its entirety. "Looks straightforward enough and easy to see you on the side of the road trying to hail a cab. Then out of nowhere—bang, you're on the ground."

Yep, that was exactly the way it had happened. From what little recollection Gary had of it anyway.

"So what's the bad news?"

"Seems the taxi company have a witness—a passenger in the cab. This guy reckons that *you* the one were at fault."

"What the hell?" Gary fumed. "How could I have been at fault? I was only walking down the street, minding my own bloody business."

"Their witness is saying you were distracted when you stepped out onto the road. The way he sees it, the driver couldn't have avoided you."

"Frank, it all happened so fast, it's hard to remember exactly how things went," he told him quickly.

"Of course. Especially with the concussion and everything. That's what I told the New York suits. Sure, how are you supposed to know what happened? All you remember is waking up in hospital."

"Exactly." Gary was pleased Frank seemed to understand completely.

"All right. I've requested a copy of the so-called witness report, and when I get that, pop into the office here and we can have a chat. Then we can take it from there."

"Sounds good. Cheers."

"And even if it does look like you were caught unawares, we should be able to nail the guy for speeding or reckless driving, something like that."

"Perfect." Witness or not, Gary was confident that Frank would interpret the situation in some way that would turn this to his advantage. Although if the issue of fault wasn't as clear-cut as he'd thought, then maybe the payout wouldn't be as lucrative.

Well, whatever it was, it would be better than a kick in the arse, and he was sure he'd get the price of a new bike out of it at least.

Gary grinned. The one good thing about Rachel being against all this meant that she wouldn't be looking to get her hands on the money to spend on this wedding. Already he had it up to his neck in quotes for hotels and flowers, and she was already shopping for dresses that would no doubt cost half the national debt of a small country.

That was the problem with highfalutin engagement rings, Gary thought and grimaced as he returned to work. They set the bar for the rest of the circus.

Chapter 45

As she sat in the bridal studio and watched the delight on Rachel's face as she tried on wedding dresses, Terri sorely wished she'd minded her own business.

This was supposed to be one of the happiest times in her best friend's life, and if she thought about it properly, she'd been just as deceitful as Gary in hiding the truth from Rachel.

The poor thing had been distraught when she'd confessed to Terri and Justin that her beloved ring had gone astray.

"I can't remember if I took it off here or at home. You know the way it's always getting in the way while I'm baking."

Terri still felt sick when she thought of how she'd lied bald-faced to her best friend.

"Can't remember the last time I saw it on you. Are you sure you didn't leave it at home?"

Rachel had shaken her head and with obvious distress confessed she couldn't remember the last time she'd had it on. "Gary will kill me," she gasped. "How am I supposed to tell him I can't find it?"

"I'm sure he'll understand," Terri soothed, privately hoping that when Gary realized her anguish about losing the ring, he would finally come clean. That had been her ultimate intention in purloining it and returning it to its rightful owner.

How could she realistically tell her friend that her dream engagement was all a lie? And that the wedding she was so excited about was a complete and utter sham? So there was no point in feeling guilty at this point; what was done was done, and she just had to pray that all worked out in the end.

Gary would surely confess all once he knew how distraught Rachel was.

But it had been almost a week now, and still nothing had changed.

As it was, Terri hated having to go through this whole wedding charade, not least because of her own deceit. So much for being a loyal bridesmaid.

Her friend was currently standing in a slinky mermaid-style gown that looked like it was literally made for her curves. Rachel was holding her hair up and examining herself in the mirror. "What do you think of this one?" she asked.

While under normal circumstances, Terri would suggest she buy it straightaway, instead she grimaced and shook her head. "I'm not sure... Do you think it might be hard to walk around in all day?"

Rachel walked a couple of steps and then turned around. "No, it's fine actually."

Terri wrinkled her nose. "I dunno. I'm still not sure if it's really you."

"You've said that for every single one I've tried today," her friend said testily, and again Terri felt like a heel. But what could she do? How could she allow Rachel to spend money on a dress knowing deep down that the entire wedding preparations were the result of a lie?

"Maybe, but you know I won't let you settle for second best," Terri said, even though Rachel would be oblivious as to her true meaning. But the comment also seemed to annoy the sales assistant, and the atmosphere in the bridal studio grew tense.

Rachel turned around to let the woman unzip her, and they waited in silence as she put the dress back on its hanger and got out the next one.

It was a strapless princess gown made of ivory silk. It had very little detail, just yards and yards of the luscious material. Rachel stepped into the dress, and once it was all zipped up, she stood up onto a small riser to examine herself in a three-way mirror.

"Oh my goodness. This one is beautiful," she gasped, staring at her reflection.

Terri had to admit, it was. There was no way anyone could find fault with that dress.

"Ah, I almost forgot the finishing touch." The saleswoman rushed forward with a simple ivory veil, which had the smallest amount of lace running around the edges. Rachel fastened her dark hair into a loose bun on top of her head, letting the saleswoman slide the comb of the veil over the top of it. The result was spectacular.

"This is the one. I know it," Rachel whispered.

Again Terri felt racked with guilt for putting her through this. What if Rachel really was over the moon about marrying Gary— irrespective of how the proposal had come about?

Rachel continued to stare at her reflection. "I know it's cheesy, but this is the type of dress I've always pictured myself in. It's not too fussy or fashionable—more sort of...timeless, isn't it? The kind of dress that could be passed down through generations."

Oh Christ. Terri knew how much this sentimental stuff mattered to Rachel, and she also knew that if she was looking for tradition, Gary Knowles was the last person she should be marrying.

The guy's notion of tradition was drinking the same pint in the same pub every Saturday night. Terri pursed her lips together, not sure how to respond.

"Isn't it wonderful?" Rachel urged. "Do you think Gary will like it?"

Terri waited for a moment and then decided to ask the question. "Are you absolutely sure about this?" She looked meaningfully at the sales assistant, who caught the look and reacted appropriately.

"I'll give you both a minute."

Rachel turned to look at Terri. "Sure about what?"

"About marrying Gary."

Her friend colored. "Why wouldn't I be?"

"I don't know. It just all seems to have happened very quickly, doesn't it? I mean, you two haven't been seeing one another all that long, and then in New York, he just proposes out of the blue?"

Rachel paused ever so slightly, and there was a strange look on her face that Terri couldn't pinpoint. Was it hurt, or could it be doubt?

Rachel turned back to the mirror and squared her shoulders. "Look, I know you don't particularly like him. You've made that perfectly clear. And that's fine. You don't have to, but the truth is I'm committed to the idea."

Terri sat up straight. "Committed to the idea? What the hell does that mean?"

"It means…it means that yes, of course I love him. Okay, so he might seem a little…brash at times, but at the back of it all, I know he's a good guy. And I know that he loves me. He wouldn't have asked me to marry him or bought me that amazing ring if he truly didn't want me to be his wife."

Terri took a deep breath, desperate to blurt out the whole sorry truth so that her friend would finally be able to see the light. But looking at Rachel's face, again she knew she couldn't do it.

"Maybe you should take that dress," she said finally.

"Do you really think so?"

"Yes, it's lovely. It was made for you. Wait there, and I'll go get the sales assistant."

When Terri found the woman, she offered up an apology. "Sorry about that," she said, smiling. "We just needed a minute to chat about it, but I think we're ready now."

"Marvelous." The saleswoman started to walk back to the fitting room to take Rachel's measurements. "Has your friend decided what she wants?"

Terri sighed despondently. "Well, she seems to think so, and I guess that's all that matters."

Chapter 46

RACHEL WAS TRULY GOING OUT OF HER MIND. IT WAS OVER A WEEK since she'd lost her engagement ring, and she'd long since run out of places to search.

She'd turned every room in the house upside down, checked the pockets in all her clothes, and gone over every nook and cranny in the restaurant. The only explanation she could realistically come up with at this point was that it had fallen down the sink drain when she was washing her hands or been swept into the bin at work with a pile of garbage.

At this stage, though, what had happened to it didn't seem to matter nearly as much as what she was going to do about it.

Gary didn't appear to have noticed anything amiss just yet, although he had commented on its absence during a recent visit to the bistro. She'd quickly made up an excuse about not wearing it at work in case she lost it, which was the truth of sorts.

"I just don't know how I'm going to tell him," she confessed to Terri now. They were in the kitchen getting ready for the lunchtime trade.

Her friend shrugged. "It's not as though you lost it on purpose. These things happen. I'm sure Gary will understand."

Rachel looked at her. While Terri had been sympathetic initially, Rachel also got the feeling she wasn't taking the ring's disappearance seriously enough. Didn't she know how much it meant to her or, more importantly, how much Gary had spent on it?

"I really don't think he will," she replied, somewhat testier than she'd intended. "When I think of how much he must have paid for it…it makes me sick to my stomach."

"Well, maybe it didn't cost as much as you think," Terri ventured. "Anyway, the ring or indeed the price isn't the important thing. It's the sentiment behind it, isn't it? I'm sure Gary gets that."

But the comment got Rachel thinking. Maybe it wasn't so expensive that she could replace it herself without Gary realizing?

Before confessing to him that she'd lost the ring, she'd first see if she could try and replace it. That way, he'd be none the wiser. Okay, so it would be an unexpected expense on top of all the others they were facing this year, but wasn't it her own fault for not taking good enough care of it?

There was a small Tiffany & Co. concession store in Brown Thomas on Grafton Street, and she could pop down there after the lunchtime rush and see if she could find a replacement, or at least a reasonable alternative.

And not that it mattered, but she was also slightly curious as to exactly how much Gary *had* spent on the ring.

Which would no doubt correlate exactly with how bad Rachel would feel about having lost it.

"Can I help you with anything?" the smiling Tiffany's assistant asked as Rachel perused the display later that afternoon. Her eyes eagerly took in the glass case and the stunning jewelry laid out. Rings, bracelets, and earrings that colored the dreams of women around the world, jewels so beautiful that they were really only a fantasy to most.

How lucky was she to have been gifted something so precious, and how idiotic to have lost it!

Her heart sank afresh.

"I'm looking for a diamond ring," she told the assistant. "It's a style from your Fifth Avenue store, but I don't think I see it here."

"Because of our size, we can only carry a select range here, but all jewelry is available to order. Maybe you'll recognize it from our catalogue?" The woman reached under the counter and brought out a copy of Tiffany's famed Blue Book. Rachel felt an automatic shiver of delight at the instantly recognizable robin's-egg blue on the elegant catalogue's cover. "Was it three-stone or solitaire? Or perhaps a diamond band?"

"Solitaire," Rachel told her, and her breath caught a little at the ensemble of diamond rings of every shape, setting, and design. The photographs were so vivid and the jewels looked so real, she almost expected them to sparkle on the page as they did in real life.

The woman turned to the solitaire section, and Rachel immediately recognized her own platinum marquise design. "That's the one," she said, pointing to it.

"Classic marquise," the assistant clarified with a smile. "Yes, that's a very popular one for us—gorgeous."

Looking at the image afresh, Rachel felt sick to her stomach to think she had truly lost something so beautiful. But perhaps with luck, she might be able to recover the situation.

"But you definitely don't have this one in stock at the moment?" she ventured.

The assistant looked rueful. "I'm afraid not. We'd be happy to order it for you and can have it in-store and ready for collection by the end of the week if you'd like. Though we do require a deposit for special orders. Two thousand for this one."

"Two thousand?" Rachel's heart lifted and her face broke into a huge smile.

It wasn't as though she had that amount of money lying around in loose change, but really, the ring was nowhere *near* as expensive as she'd imagined. Yes, replacing it would mean sacrificing the majority of her share of the income from Gillini for the next few months, but it would be worth it. She shook her head, amazed afresh that Gary had managed to choose a ring that looked like it cost an absolute fortune but in reality was actually rather reasonable.

"For the deposit, yes," the assistant continued, taking out an order book. "I can take it today if you'd like. Or maybe you'd prefer to wait for your fiancé—let him be the one to injure the credit card," she joked easily.

Now Rachel felt nauseous. "Two thousand…for the *deposit?*" she repeated in a whisper, all thoughts of replacing the ring suddenly going right out the window.

"Yes, ten percent of the overall price is standard."

Her head grew light and she began to see stars in front of her eyes. It didn't take a genius to work out that if two thousand was ten percent of the overall price, then Gary had spent the sum of…twenty thousand—*twenty thousand dollars*—on the ring.

And she had lost it.

Oh Christ…oh Christ…oh Christ. Her head spinning, Rachel held on to the edge of the glass display case. She was so dizzy, she was sure her legs would give way beneath her.

"Are you okay?" the woman asked, seemingly unaware that she'd as good as cut the legs from beneath her latest customer.

"I'm fine," Rachel managed. She tried to compose herself as best she could. "Um…actually, I think you're right. Probably best to wait for my fiancé to do the honors."

The woman chuckled. "Wise decision. Pop in anytime you like, both of you. We'd be delighted to look after you, and of course we provide a glass of bubbly to all our happy couples to get the celebrations going. Would be a shame to miss out on that," she added with a wink.

"Yes…a shame." Desperate to get out of there before she embarrassed herself by crumpling in a heap on the ground, Rachel bade the Tiffany's sales assistant a quick goodbye. Then she stumbled her way through the store and back out onto Grafton Street as fast as her woozy legs would carry her.

Twenty thousand…the ring had cost all that money, and she'd gone and lost it. What was she going to do? And why had Gary spent so much? She felt inexplicably angry at him.

As it was, she'd have *died* if she'd known she was walking around with something that valuable on her. And to think that she'd been wearing that ring while blithely kneading dough and getting it covered in flour and eggs and all sorts...

It was *way* too much to spend on her—way too much to spend on anyone or indeed anything that didn't at the very least have four wheels or a roof on it.

There was no *way* she could tell him she'd lost it now; Rachel knew that for certain. Especially when cognizant too that times were tough in the building trade and for a while suspecting that Gary was just barely keeping the business afloat.

He was way too proud to admit it of course, but Rachel wasn't stupid, and reading between the lines, she'd figured things were bad when he was so eager to return from New York so quickly in order to get back on the job.

She sighed, everything suddenly becoming a hell of a lot clearer. No wonder he'd been so reluctant to participate in her enthusiasm for the wedding preparations when no doubt all he could think about was how much more they'd need to shell out for the big day.

But what had possessed him to spend so much on the ring? He knew she wasn't one of those high-maintenance types who expected the best of everything, and really this was worlds apart from the perfume he'd given her for her birthday.

And to think that he'd never said a word, never even let on that he'd flashed so much cash, which was unusual actually. Much as she loved him, Gary did have a tendency to brag.

She looked blankly around at people rushing past on the street, trying to figure out what to do. Maybe she could try and replace the ring with a cheaper substitute so that Gary wouldn't notice the difference?

But it was Tiffany's, for crying out loud. Of course he'd notice.

And dishonesty was hardly the best start to a marriage.

Rachel's head spun, not knowing what she should do now. Was there a chance she'd gotten it wrong back there and picked out a ring she only *thought* looked like hers?

Though in all honesty, there was no mistaking it. She knew deep down that the solitaire she'd lost was indeed the one with a twenty-grand price tag. It was just so hard to believe or even imagine Gary spending so much money on a single item.

"I had no idea you could even spend that big on a credit card," she said afterward to Terri and Justin, who both seemed just as shocked upon hearing how much her engagement ring had cost. At least that was how she presumed Gary had paid for it, since he couldn't realistically have taken that much in cash with him on their trip.

"Are you...sure?" Terri asked, looking decidedly shell-shocked, and Rachel was somewhat gratified to think that at least *now* she'd understand why she was so frantic about losing it. "Christ, that's a hell of a lot to spend on a rock."

"I know. What should I do? Gary will hit the roof when I tell him I've lost it. He might even call off the wedding." She bit her lip in an effort to quell impending tears.

Terri put a comforting hand on her arm. "Ah, no, I'm sure he wouldn't do that."

"What about insurance?" Justin suggested.

"No good. I didn't have a chance to get it insured," Rachel replied mournfully.

"Well, what about Gary's credit card insurance? I know my Visa has some kind of purchase protection included. Maybe his does too?"

"Yes, that's a possibility," Terri murmured quietly.

"It is," Rachel said, heartened. "How would I find out about that, Justin?"

"You'll need to get your hands on Gary's statement," he told her. "There's a monthly fee, so if that's listed on the statement and he bought the ring with the same card, there's a good chance it's covered." He draped an arm around her shoulder. "So maybe you're worrying for nothing, sweetheart."

Rachel wanted to hug him. Justin was right; if the ring was automatically covered by credit card insurance, then chances were Gary couldn't be too upset, since it could be replaced.

"Yes, I'm sure you're worrying for nothing," Terri soothed.

"Course, now you'll have to find some way of getting the statement without alerting Gary," Justin pointed out. "And I don't know about you, but I know for sure that Bernard would leave me if he knew how much I rack up every month." He grinned. "Or maybe he'd be proud. Who knows?"

"Well, we'll need to share stuff like that soon enough," Rachel replied, wondering how she might go about purloining a statement without alerting Gary as to what she was up to.

And notwithstanding the insurance, there was a second advantage too. On the off chance that she'd been mistaken about the ring in question today at the store, she could check the Tiffany's transaction to ascertain for certain if her future husband had indeed spent the best part of a year's salary on it.

Yes, a quick peek at Gary's credit card bill should draw a line under all this one way or another.

Chapter 47

VANESSA WAS WALKING ON AIR. THERE WAS SO MUCH TO DO, SO much to plan, and she was itching to get started.

Not to mention so much to celebrate, which she, Ethan, and Daisy would be doing in spades. Her mum and dad were over the moon about the engagement, and she was really looking forward to going home and showing off her magnificent Tiffany diamond.

She glanced down at her newly resized ring, still finding it hard to believe that he had actually proposed. She was delighted she'd gotten to the bottom of his and Daisy's little secret and that there was a reasonable explanation as to why he'd been acting so strangely in New York.

After that trip, she'd felt that something wasn't right, that perhaps Ethan had gone off into one of his dreary funks about Jane. In truth and despite her best attempts to hide it, Vanessa couldn't help but always feel threatened by Jane's memory, and for this reason, she was never entirely sure of Ethan's feelings for her or if there was a serious future for them.

She knew that she'd never replace the love of his life, but now that she was certain he was committed, she would try her utmost to be a good stepmother to Daisy and a good wife to him.

At least it didn't include the prospect of other children, and Vanessa was relieved that this had been headed off at the pass from the outset, as the truth was she had no real desire to procreate and no interest in all the hassles and inconveniences that went hand in hand with kids.

A ready-made family would do just fine. Yes, he was absolutely the right man for her, the perfect person with whom to share the rest of her life, and she was pleased he'd finally come to realize that too.

And to think that he'd gone to such great lengths, first in New York and then to Dublin, just for this specific ring!

But Ethan was like that, very exacting and, despite his mild temperament, hugely determined when he set his mind to something.

There was also another reason Vanessa was looking forward to their visit to Dublin. If she was getting married at home, she was going to do it in style. Especially since all her publishing friends and colleagues would be attending, and maybe even some from New York too.

Now that Ethan had popped the question, she was determined to get the wedding plans afoot. There was little point in waiting around.

She was already thinking August—it was traditionally a quieter time in publishing, and of course he'd be on summer break from the university and Daisy from school.

The forthcoming visit to her folks would be the perfect opportunity to scout out locations and florists, caterers, and all that. But nothing wrong with getting started in the meantime.

Picking up the telephone, Vanessa smoothed out a piece of paper she'd brought to the office and dialed the number.

A friendly male voice replied. "Gillini Bistro. Justin speaking. How can I help you?"

"Oh, hello. I understand you have a catering service?"

"That's correct, yes."

"As well as a sideline in quirky wedding proposals, apparently," she added, laughing lightly.

"I'm sorry?"

Vanessa went on to explain about the ring hidden in the bread. "It was such a lovely idea, although a little precarious all the same. I did almost break a tooth."

"I see." The guy didn't seem to know what she was talking about, but that hardly mattered.

"My fiancé was raving about your food, and I must admit what little I tasted was indeed impressive," she went on. "And since your company has already played such an integral part in our plans, I'd like to get a sample menu and catering quote for our wedding. We don't have an exact date just yet, but it should be sometime later this summer, possibly August?"

There was a brief pause on the other end. "Of course. Can you give me your details? Terri, our catering manager, isn't here just at the moment, but if you'd like to leave your number, I'll get her to call you back."

"Thank you, that would be wonderful." Already Vanessa was impressed with this level of professionalism. Living in London, she was expecting it to be difficult to organize the wedding from afar, so good recommendations were everything. And what better recommendation than the establishment that had been directly involved in the proposal?

"I'll be visiting Dublin shortly, so perhaps my fiancé and I could pop in for a chat."

"We'd be delighted to have you. Can I take your name?"

"Oh yes, of course. It's Vanessa Fox. And my fiancé is Ethan Greene," she added before giving him her number. She couldn't help it; she just adored using the word *fiancé*.

She was just about to set down the handset when her internal line buzzed.

"Brian Freeman for you," her assistant told her. "Line three."

Vanessa hesitated for a bit, her finger hovering over the connect button, before eventually making a decision. "Tell him I'm in a meeting."

❧

"Someone's been naughty," Justin said to Terri. "Or should I say stupid?"

It was late afternoon, and she'd just arrived for the evening shift. "What are you talking about?" she asked, frowning as she tied an apron around her waist.

"I got an interesting call today from a lady who seemed very appreciative of our part in her fiancé's wedding proposal."

"What? Did someone pop the question here?" she replied easily.

"No, not here." Justin put his hands on his hips. "It was the strangest thing. Apparently *somebody* baked a Tiffany diamond ring into a loaf of our sourdough."

Terri's mouth dropped open. "The *fiancée* called here?" Then realizing she'd unintentionally landed herself in it, she reddened furiously. Finally she met his gaze. "Something had to be done."

"Oh my God, Terri, what did you think you were doing?" he exclaimed disbelievingly. "You had no right to take—or should I say steal—Rachel's ring!"

She reddened. "It's not her ring," she replied half-heartedly, but the words sounded weak, and she knew it.

"Still, it wasn't your place to interfere."

She folded her hands across her chest. "I don't know about you, but I couldn't stand by and watch her mooning over that diamond for a minute longer."

"So you just decided to steal it and give it away to some stranger with a sob story?"

"It wasn't stealing, and Ethan isn't a stranger. Look, the guy was just too nice to take it back from Rachel, and since Gary had no intention of coming clean, I had to do something."

"But you've seen Rachel moping around this week. She's devastated over the missing ring and terrified of telling Gary."

"I know. But this will surely bring everything out in the wash."

"Well, something is going to come out in the wash soon, that's for sure," Justin said, sighing grimly.

"What do you mean?"

"That woman I spoke to, Greene's girlfriend, she was asking about catering for their wedding. I told her you'd call her back."

"What? Oh Christ." There were so many unpleasant scenarios that Terri couldn't get a handle on them. "Why on earth would she want *us* to cater for a wedding in London?"

"Because apparently the soon-to-be Mrs. Greene is one of our own, so the wedding will be taking place in her old stomping ground."

"Here in Dublin? You've got to be kidding me."

"Nope."

"Oh man." Terri broke out in a cold sweat. Surely Ethan wouldn't want them to cater for his wedding though? She looked at Justin. "You're right. I know I was wrong to take matters into my own hands," she admitted, shamefaced. "But it's done now. Gary was never going to own up, and I just couldn't stand by and watch Rachel get sucked in by his lies. He's an ass, Justin. We both know that."

"Hmm, ass or not, it looks like you've landed us all in the middle of it now," Justin said solemnly. "Because if that girl rocks up here wearing Rachel's precious ring, there's gonna be one hell of a shitstorm."

Chapter 48

RACHEL WAS LOOKING THROUGH GARY'S CREDIT CARD STATEMENT for January. Having puzzled for a while about the best way to get her hands on it, she quickly realized that a perfectly good excuse was staring her right in the face.

They were in the process of setting up a joint account for the wedding expenses, and the bank had requested ID documentation and proof of address for them both.

"Bank statements, utility bills, passport copy, you know yourself," she reminded him.

"Well, I can get you a bank statement, but I'm not sure about the utility bill," he'd replied reluctantly. "Out of sight, out of mind."

"What about a credit card bill, then? I'm sure that would also do as proof of address," she said, trying to make her voice sound casual, but luckily he didn't notice anything untoward.

Now in the privacy of her living room, Rachel took the opportunity to look through the Visa bill for the insurance charge Justin had mentioned.

If it was there, then she would tell Gary straight out that she had lost the ring. If it wasn't…well, then Rachel didn't know what she'd do.

She ran her gaze through a list of the most recent transactions, easily pinpointing the U.S. dollar purchases. One from Saks, a couple from Bergdorf Goodman, and ah…there it was: Tiffany & Co.

Rachel looked across the page to check the corresponding charge and blinked.

How could that be? She frowned and looked again at the figure, perplexed. Not that it mattered, but she didn't think it was actually possible to spend so little in the store, unless it was for a souvenir or some such.

Then, recalling her own recent conversation at Tiffany's about the deposit, it hit her. Of course, he had probably ordered and paid for the ring in advance, so perhaps the transaction she was looking at was the balance remaining, or even a gift wrap service?

But assuming that he'd paid for it in increments with the credit card, did that mean the insurance might still cover it?

She flicked through the pages, but to her dismay, there was no mention of the purchase protection insurance Justin had mentioned.

Rachel gulped and looked again at her bare ring finger. It was now weeks since she'd last seen it, and having searched every nook and cranny she could think of (not to mention avoiding Gary's questions), it seemed unlikely it was going to turn up at this stage.

She sighed. There was nothing else for it; she had to bite the bullet and confess that the ring had disappeared.

She bit her lip.

Whether the admission caused her fiancé to disappear too remained to be seen.

⁓෧⁓

Daisy had a dilemma. There was something very important she needed to talk to her dad about, but she didn't think she could do it now.

Although she was pleased that he'd gotten the ring back, the truth was she'd been very concerned since.

Why didn't it fit Vanessa, particularly when it was made especially for her?

"I'm sure they just made a mistake with the sizing," her dad had said when he and Daisy spoke about it afterward and he'd explained how another nice woman in Dublin had helped him get it back. "Anyway, what does it matter? All that matters is we've got it back and we've done what we set out to do."

But it mattered to Daisy, because it didn't feel right.

According to her dad, the ring had fit Rachel. He'd told her so when she asked him about it again on his return.

And because her dad had gone to so much trouble to get the ring back and seemed relieved that everything was resolved, Daisy thought she'd better wait a while before mentioning her thoughts.

Mum had been a big believer in fate and that the universe was supposed to always make things right. So had the universe made sure that she and her dad were in the right place the day that man got knocked down in New York?

Maybe even her mum had made sure that everything had gone astray so that the ring would find its way to the right person?

Up until this morning, Daisy had believed that, but now she wondered what the universe was trying to do when it had led her to find the box hidden deep in the garbage can.

Vanessa was all moved in to their house now, but she still didn't understand how things were done, like how there was one bin for normal garbage and a different one for recycling.

Recycling to help save the earth was important to Daisy in the same way it had been important to her mum.

While it had been hard enough trying to persuade her dad to stick to the rules, it was even tougher trying to teach them to a new addition, and Daisy was frustrated at yet again having to separate recyclable stuff out.

This morning, while Vanessa was in the shower and her dad was out for a jog, Daisy had taken the trouble to fish out a plastic bag and pink-and-white box that it contained.

And when she realized what the words on the box meant, her dilemma began. She'd read enough medical brochures and health information to know what a pregnancy test was.

Did this mean she might be getting a baby brother or sister? It was something she'd have liked but figured was impossible given the circumstances.

Now that her dad and Vanessa were engaged, they'd obviously decided to get started on being a family right away. She knew how much her dad wanted that too.

And in all honesty, Daisy thought she would like a brother or sister. Being an only child was lonely sometimes, and she'd felt even more alone since her dad had started going out with Vanessa. He didn't read to her as much, and they didn't get to spend a whole lot of time together, just the two of them.

So maybe a new baby would be good news.

But one thing was for sure. Now Daisy knew about that, she

couldn't possibly confess to her dad her worries that the ring might have gone astray for a reason.

Not if she, Dad, and Vanessa were about to become a proper family in every way.

Chapter 49

GARY CRANKED UP HIS BIKE AND SET OFF TOWARD RACHEL'S, ANTICI-
pating yet another bombardment of wedding stuff.

He just wasn't in the mood, not after the day he'd had. Earlier this afternoon, he'd been to his solicitor's office to check out the CCTV and witness report from the accident, and things weren't looking good.

Seems there'd been a couple of passengers in the cab at the time, and the witness was adamant that the driver couldn't have avoided hitting him and had described in detail how the whole thing had played out.

Nosy bastard. Gary couldn't understand how some stranger could have such perfect memory of the incident when he himself could barely remember what he'd had for breakfast. Especially when immediately after he was hit, the same passengers apparently just hopped out and left him to fend for himself.

The footage had also shown that guy Greene and his kid breaking their way through the crowds to help him just outside the Tiffany's store, bags in hand.

If that was the case, Gary kind of felt bad now for basically telling the guy to go and stuff it. But what else was he supposed to do, when at that stage, Rachel was doing cartwheels over that ring? He could hardly go and take it back off her based on some stranger's likely story, could he?

So he figured the best thing to do was keep his mouth shut until he was forced to do otherwise.

He just wished that that so-called witness had done the same. According to his solicitor, the cab passenger's account of events had been clear, concise, and unfortunately quite damaging for their case.

Gary was livid. So much for his brand-new bike! Still, at least he'd gotten something out of it, he thought now when Rachel opened her front door.

Despite his stupid drunken blabbering, Terri had kept her mouth shut so far, evidently understanding that it was important not to upset the applecart.

But when his fiancée appeared with a peculiar look on her face, he wondered if that was still the case. Shit, had Terri finally spilled the beans?

His worries were allayed somewhat when Rachel put her arms around him and hugged him tightly. "Thanks for coming over."

"No problemo. What's up?"

Her voice was soft. "There's no easy way to say this." She shook her head and tears filled her eyes.

Gary's heart dropped into his stomach. Shit—was she breaking up with him, calling off the wedding, maybe? "No easy way to say... what?" he repeated, stammering a little.

She looked down at her left hand, and with a start, he realized she wasn't wearing her engagement ring. *Shite.*

"I lost it."

"Rachel, I can explain—" Gary began, but the two of them spoke at exactly the same time, and he honestly thought he'd misheard. "What?"

She looked up at him through lowered eyelashes. "I've mislaid it somehow. I'm so sorry. I didn't want to tell you it was missing until I was sure, but I've searched high and low for the last couple of weeks and—"

"Hold on," Gary interjected, flabbergasted but also slightly relieved that it was *she* who was apologizing. Still, alarm bells were going off in his head. "It's been missing for a couple of weeks?"

Around the same time as Greene's appearance.

Rachel nodded. "I'm so sorry. I know I should have said something, but I honestly thought it would turn up, that maybe I'd taken it off and left it somewhere at the bistro, but there's been no sign. Believe me, I've left no stone unturned. All I can say is that it just seems to have vanished into thin air."

"Vanished." Gary's mind was racing so fast, he couldn't do anything other than repeat random words.

She reached for him, misinterpreting his reaction for annoyance or anger. And the truth was he *was* annoyed, but not for the reason she suspected.

No, he was downright fit to be tied because he was certain that there was something else at play here.

And absolutely positive that Greene was at the center of it. No wonder he hadn't heard anything since.

Rachel was crying openly now. "I'm so sorry. I've been going out of my mind. I haven't been able to sleep or eat thinking about it and how much it cost."

Gary could only imagine how bad she felt and mentally urged himself to try and make her feel better. But this posed a bit of a dilemma. He couldn't very well throw his arms around her and tell her it was okay, not if he was supposed to have spent a couple of grand on a diamond, could he?

Yet at the same time, he didn't have the heart to pretend to be angry. Instead, he continued to stare at the floor in the manner of someone who was trying to get a handle on such news. "I have to say this was the last thing I expected," he said truthfully, and she nodded.

"I know, and I hate myself for not taking better care of it. I should have guarded it with my life, especially knowing how much you paid for it and how hard you must have worked to afford it."

Christ, now he felt like a right heel.

"Look, don't worry about that. It's only money."

"Only money?" She laughed through her tears. "Oh, you really are the most wonderful man. Thank you for trying to make me feel better when we both know that ring cost enough to bankrupt most."

"Erm…yeah."

She bit her lip. "I know this might be a long shot, but was it insured by any chance? Justin thought that maybe your credit card insurance might cover it, but I wasn't sure."

"Hold on, Justin knows about this?" Which meant Terri did too of course.

"I had to check if they'd come across it at work. I would have told you first, only I couldn't bring myself to admit that I'd gone and done something so stupid." She burst into tears then, and Gary wasn't sure what to do.

"Ah, look, it's okay. I'm sure it'll turn up," he said, encircling her in his arms and patting her gently on the back.

"Little chance of that at this stage," she sniffed. "I know I should have been more careful. Really, I shouldn't have been wearing it to work at all." She sniffed.

"It does sound like you lost it at work," he agreed as things began to click into place. This was way too coincidental for his liking.

"I don't know… I just can't say for sure. Hey, I promise I'll make it up to you, honestly. I went about getting a replacement but…" Her face fell. "I just couldn't afford it."

"Don't worry about it," he replied, feeling like a right fraud. He wished she wouldn't keep going on and on about how much the bloody thing had cost. "I know it wasn't your fault."

For once, Gary was telling the truth. Given the circumstances, he was pretty sure that however the ring had "suddenly" gone astray, it was through no fault of Rachel's.

Chapter 50

"I'm really glad Gary was okay about it," Terri said into the mouthpiece. "See, I told you he'd understand… Yes, he really is one in a million." She rolled her eyes across the kitchen at Justin. "But no need to come in today anyway. I insist. At least now that it's all out in the open, you should relax and take a breather."

Having convinced Rachel that a busy Saturday at the bistro was the last thing she needed after the stress she'd been under recently, Terri hung up the phone. "Seems he was fine about it," she told Justin sardonically. "There's a surprise."

He shook his head. "Wasn't she the tiniest bit suspicious about that even? She loses a rock that cost a small fortune, and tightwad Gary doesn't even raise an eyebrow?"

"I guess not. Anyway, she's taking the day off. I told her to use it as a good excuse to spend some time making it up to him." The words had tasted bitter in her mouth, but Terri knew she had to try and keep Rachel away, today of all days.

Because today the newly engaged Ethan Greene and his fiancée were due to make an appearance for lunch.

When Justin had initially told her about the fiancée's catering inquiry, she'd thought about getting in touch with Ethan to ask him what the hell he was playing at.

But then she realized that it was unlikely he would have been party to such a thing, and in any case, she didn't have a contact number for him.

Rachel would of course, but what reasonable excuse would Terri have for asking for it without arousing suspicion?

As far as her friend was concerned, Terri had only met Ethan briefly, that day he first appeared looking for her and Gary, and while she considered concocting some random story about how he'd left something behind, she knew it wouldn't ring true.

So when she returned Vanessa Fox's call and subsequently arranged a reservation, her next priority was making sure that Rachel was nowhere near the vicinity.

Notwithstanding the fact that it would be coincidental for Ethan to choose Gillini as his wedding caterers, his fiancée wearing an identical ring to the one Rachel had lost around the time of his last visit was a bridge too far.

And not for the first time, Terri wondered if that blasted ring truly did have a mind of its own.

❧

Ethan could have counted on one hand the number of times he'd been to Dublin in his lifetime, yet here he was in the place for the second time in the space of two months.

He was still reeling a little.

Much to his surprise, Vanessa was powering ahead with the wedding plans and had even gone so far as setting a date.

He wasn't sure why, but for some reason, this made him feel uncomfortable. "What's the rush?" he'd asked, although he didn't know why he'd expected anything less of his supremely organized fiancée. In life as in work, she didn't wait around.

"I've never believed in long engagements. Either we're getting married or we aren't. Don't worry," she added with a playful laugh. "I'll take care of everything. You just need to turn up on the day."

And it seemed the day in question would be this coming summer, August apparently. It all felt like a bit of a whirlwind, but then again, he'd barely had time to pause for breath since Christmas.

Now, having visited her parents the night before, he was just about ready to climb the walls of the country estate Vanessa was considering as a venue.

"What's wrong, Dad?" Daisy asked, taking his hand as they walked among the landscaped grounds, and he quickly rearranged his expression into what he hoped was less anxious.

As always, his daughter was just too perceptive for her own good.

"Nothing, darling. Just lots to think about for the wedding. What do you think of this place?" he asked, indicating the estate's perfectly manicured gardens.

She shrugged. "It's okay, I suppose."

"Just okay?"

Daisy seemed to hesitate. "I don't know, it's sort of…posh, isn't it?" she whispered, and Ethan couldn't help but smile. Once again, she had hit the nail on the head.

"Are you looking forward to the big day?" he asked. He still hadn't been able to tease out her feelings about the wedding taking place so soon. "I know it might seem fast but—"

"That's okay, Dad. I think I know why," she replied ominously, but Ethan didn't have the opportunity to query this any further before Vanessa, who'd been chatting to the estate's event manager, came rushing over.

"Isn't it perfect?" she gushed. "I just adore these grounds, and if the weather is kind, we can arrange for a garden party on the terrace upon arrival—sort of like a grander version of afternoon tea. I'm thinking perhaps macarons and champagne? Remind me to suggest this to the caterers this afternoon, won't you?" She smiled at Daisy. "Does that sound good to you?"

She looked dubious. "I think most people would still be hungry. Maybe dinner might be best," she suggested, her tone perfectly serious, and Ethan had to smile.

Out of the mouths of babes…

"Well, of course, we're going to have that too, silly!" Vanessa joked, and Ethan noticed that Daisy seemed hurt by the dismissal. His fiancée looked at her watch. "In fact, since it's almost midday, we really should be heading back to the city soon. I hope everyone's hungry. I've made us a lunch reservation at the caterer's. They have a restaurant." She winked at Ethan. "I think you might be familiar with it."

"How so?" he replied, genuinely baffled by this.

"Gillini. I thought it would be fitting, considering?" his fiancée said, smiling. "And I for one can't wait to see what all the fuss is about."

Chapter 51

"HELLO, WELCOME." TERRI GREETED THEM WARMLY, AND MUCH TO his relief, Ethan noticed that she seemed to be going out of her way not to make eye contact with him while she fussed over Vanessa.

Inwardly, he relaxed a little, guessing that today's visit wasn't news—to her at least. When his fiancée had dropped her bombshell about coming here for lunch, he'd almost had a heart attack and tried to put her off by feigning a headache and insisting he wasn't hungry.

But since it was supposed to be wedding-related, he couldn't be too insistent either. Plus there really was no dissuading Vanessa about anything once she set her mind to it. Still, the very prospect of returning to Gillini of all places—to say nothing of using them as wedding caterer—filled him with doom.

"And you must be Daisy. Hi." Terri gave her a little wave before finally looking at Ethan. "Mr. Greene, so nice to see you again. So pleased our proposal surprise worked out well for you guys." With that, she gave a surreptitious wink, and his blood pressure subsided.

Perhaps it was going to be okay after all. Terri clearly had it all under control. *Thank goodness.*

"Thank you, yes indeed. Nice to be back."

"Well, I have a lovely table set up for you all here," Terri sang, leading them toward the rear of the restaurant. As she continued her merry chatter to Vanessa about the tasting menu and catering samples, he kept a cautious eye out for Rachel.

"I must apologize, we're pretty short-staffed today," Terri mentioned then as if reading his mind. "My colleague Rachel is off today, so forgive me in advance if things are a little slow."

"I see." Vanessa looked slightly miffed, but Ethan immediately deduced that the information was for his benefit, so as to put his mind fully at ease, and he had to thank Terri yet again for saving his bacon.

"But in any case," she continued, smiling winningly, "I'm sure you'd all much rather eat in peace, and perhaps when you've finished sampling the menu, we can discuss all in more detail?"

"That would be wonderful, thank you," he replied.

"Great. First, let me grab you some drinks, and then I'll have our chef bring out the first platter."

"Um…do you need any help?" Ethan asked, and Vanessa shot him a look.

"Thank you for offering, Ethan, but really, I have it all under control," Terri said, and once again, he caught the subtext.

"That's great to know. I—I mean we," he corrected, forgetting himself, "appreciate that. Don't we, Vanessa?"

His fiancée looked at him as if he were stone mad. "Well, I'd certainly appreciate a drink if it isn't too much trouble."

"Of course." Terri leaped into action. "I'll be right back."

"Is it just me or does she seem a bit…odd?" his fiancée said, wrinkling her nose.

"I think she's nice," Daisy piped up. "I really like her eyes."

"Hmm, she seems a bit too overfamiliar for my liking." Vanessa turned to look at Ethan. "Did you notice she called you by your first name just now? A bit much, I thought."

"Wasn't the personal touch the very reason you're considering them as wedding caterer?"

"Perhaps, but decorum is important too." Vanessa picked up the sample menu. "Still, I must admit the food really does sound delicious." She sat forward and glanced around. "Shame about the surroundings. It's a little bit…twee, isn't it?"

"I actually rather like it as it happens," Ethan said testily. "It's warm and cozy, and more importantly, it doesn't feel like you're eating in a science lab." A thinly disguised barb at Vanessa's preference for minimalist London hotspots, which to him felt rather sterile.

"Smells delicious too," Daisy agreed. "I'm sooo hungry."

"Well, we're just in time then," Terri chuckled, followed by Justin, who was carrying a platter of savory goodies. "Now this is a broad selection of options, so I'll leave you three to dig in. Then, when you're ready, we'll bring out some mains samples. Sound okay?"

Already Ethan's mouth was watering, and he worried that if Vanessa did choose Gillini for the wedding, it meant there could be no avoiding Rachel forever.

While they ate, Vanessa verbally rated every morsel she put into her mouth while Ethan tuned out and wondered again how Rachel had reacted when she realized her precious ring had disappeared. He knew that he wouldn't be able to relax properly until he found out.

He spotted Terri across the room chatting to customers at a table near the bar and, vaguely recalling the restroom facilities were situated in that area, figured this was a good opportunity to get her alone.

"Back in a moment." Excusing himself, he stood up and tried to catch her eye as he approached. She seemed to sense his gaze and very quickly finished up and proceeded to a small alcove by the entrance to the bathrooms. He followed, conscious that while the area afforded them some privacy, it would still be all too easy for Vanessa or Daisy to spot him.

"I'm so sorry about this," he began without preamble. "I had no idea Vanessa was going to arrange this, but thank goodness she spoke to you on the phone. I can only imagine how awkward it would've been if Rachel—"

"How much trouble it would've caused, you mean," Terri interjected shortly. "Seriously, what the hell were you thinking coming back here?"

"I couldn't help it. It was all arranged without my knowledge. Believe me, I had no intention of coming within a million miles of the place again, and sorry," he added quickly. "Don't get me wrong. I'm incredibly grateful that you helped me sort it all out before, but what about Rachel?"

"What about her?"

"Well, she isn't here—on a Saturday. I take it that's also your doing?"

"Of course. I couldn't risk her seeing that ring on another woman's finger. Rachel can be a bit innocent, but any fool would be able to put two and two together."

He frowned. "Knowles still hasn't told her the truth, I take it."

"You take it right." She shook her head. "I know I did you a favor, but really, Ethan, if I'd known how upset she'd be, I'm not so sure I'd have intervened."

"For goodness' sake, how is he still getting away with putting her through this?" He clenched his fists.

Terri looked at him curiously. "I thought you said it wasn't any of your concern."

"It isn't, but I can't bear to think that the guy is still stringing her along. She's far too good for him."

"I know, but at this stage, it's out of our hands."

"Greene!"

They both started at the sound of the voice and turned to see a tall, broad-chested man Ethan vaguely recognized headed toward them, a thunderous look on his face.

"Shit...speak of the devil," Terri muttered, and to his dismay, Ethan realized that all attempts at controlling this situation had suddenly gone right out the window.

"Mr. Knowles, I presume?" As his nemesis stood in front of him, Ethan tried to remind himself that he had nothing to worry about, since Gary Knowles was and had always been in the wrong.

But when the guy had a good twenty pounds on him, this was... difficult.

"I knew it. I bloody *knew* you were behind this," Knowles boomed, and Terri grabbed each and pulled them into a doorway out of sight of other customers.

"Gary, what the hell are you playing at?" she hissed. "This isn't your crappy local."

"You should have thought of that before you helped Mr. Do-Gooder here steal Rachel's ring," he growled.

Ethan was flabbergasted. "*Rachel's* ring?" he retorted hotly. "For goodness' sake, you know damn well that it was never Rachel's or indeed yours!"

Knowles took a threatening step toward him. "Where is it? What did you do with it? I'm warning you, Greene. You make sure she gets it back right now or I'll—"

"Ethan? What's going on?" Vanessa interjected with a white-faced Daisy by her side. "Who is this man?"

Knowles remained standing there, a satisfied smirk on his face as if he realized that this was an awkward moment in more ways than one.

"Don't worry, darling. It's a long story," Ethan replied, putting a soothing hand on Vanessa's arm. "You two head back to the table, and I'll explain all later," he added with a tight smile. The last thing he wanted was for Daisy to be upset, so he prayed Vanessa would take the hint.

"No, I want to know what's going on *right now*," she insisted forcibly.

"Hey, Daisy, would you like to come into the kitchen and say hi to Justin, our chef? I know he'd love to meet you," Terri interjected, swiftly taking the girl's hand and turning her away from the spectacle.

"Good idea, buttercup," her dad reassured with a small wink while Daisy reluctantly followed Terri through to the kitchen.

"Well?" Vanessa looked from one man to the other. Then she frowned at Knowles. "Excuse me, why are you staring at me like that?"

Ethan noticed that he was indeed staring at her with a perplexed look on his face.

"Hey, I know you," Knowles said, his eyes narrowing.

"What? What are you talking about? I've never seen you before in my life. Ethan, are you going to tell me what the hell is happening here?" she beseeched impatiently.

"Hold on. I *do* know you." Knowles continued to stare with confused recognition.

"I really don't see how—" She glanced disparagingly at the man as if he were a particularly annoying fly she wanted to swat and refocused her attention on Ethan.

"Bloody hell," Knowles said finally. "It's you."

"Excuse me?"

"It *is* you. The bird in the taxi—in New York."

"I'm sure I don't know what you mean," Vanessa replied shortly, but Ethan noticed a low blush creep across her face.

"No, no, I'm right. I know I am. I'd swear to it," Knowles insisted. "I twigged you from the CCTV footage I saw only yesterday. You and that fella were in the taxi that ran me over."

Ethan was now seriously perplexed. "Knowles, what on earth are you talking about? How could Vanessa possibly have been…" But the rest of the question trailed off when he noticed that she was looking exceedingly uncomfortable.

What the hell?

"Nonsense. You've clearly mistaken me for someone else, but regardless, why are you two arguing?" she asked again, her voice a low hush. "And how do you know this man, Ethan?"

"You were with the guy...the blabbermouth witness. What was his name again?" Knowles was adamant. "Freeman, that's it."

Suddenly the mood shifted.

Brian?

Wrong-footed, Ethan turned to look at Vanessa, who by now was looking decidedly unnerved. Clearly, there was something to Knowles's take, and Ethan's mind raced as he struggled to figure it out.

"Brian? He was in New York while we were there at Christmas?" he said, addressing Vanessa. "What were you and Brian doing in a taxi? You never said anything about seeing..." All too quickly, Ethan realized that his best friend, in return, had also failed to mention anything about seeing Vanessa in New York or indeed being in the city at the same time as them. Let alone at the scene of the accident that preceded all Ethan's problems in the first place.

He was caught completely unawares. How had the tables suddenly been turned? Instead of demanding an explanation, now Vanessa was the one under scrutiny.

Was it possible that she and Brian had been in the cab that knocked Knowles over? And if they were, why on earth hide it?

Then an uneasy feeling came over him, and just like that, he understood. "Oh," he whispered. "You...and Brian?"

One look at her shamefaced expression told him everything.

"It's not how it seems, Ethan," she began, her voice pleading, and his stomach dropped into his shoes.

"Nice try, babe, but Freeman's already hung you out to dry," Knowles said, relishing the discomfort. "It's on record that the cab picked you two up from some hotel uptown."

Vanessa didn't even look at him. "We were having a business meeting," she explained weakly, but Ethan was by now an expert in lame excuses.

"Really? A business meeting—on Christmas Eve?"

Suddenly, Ethan recalled Brian's rather odd reaction when he'd told him about his planned proposal going awry. Now in retrospect, it made sense.

He couldn't believe he'd been betrayed in such a way, and by two people he cared for and trusted. Clearly it didn't work both ways.

"We didn't … He doesn't… Ethan, things are different now. You and I are engaged, whereas before I…I was never sure how you… if you really…" Her gaze dropped to the floor. "Brian and I…we'd known each other for a while, and it was sort of ongoing before you and I met. We bumped into each other a lot socially, and it gradually became a…I don't know, a kind of arrangement of sorts." She shook her head, unable to explain it, and Ethan couldn't believe that he'd been made such of fool of. "Truly, Ethan, it meant nothing, and it's over now. As soon as you proposed, I told him we were done."

He wanted to be sick. To think that he'd trusted Brian, confided all his doubts and worries, and all along, his so-called friend had been sleeping with her behind his back. Man, he was an idiot.

"Yeah, you two lovebirds can sort it out in your own time, but speaking of engagements…" Knowles interjected, and if Ethan had any inclination to punch the guy before, he seriously wanted to now. "I take it your missus won't be needing that anymore." He indicated the ring, and Vanessa looked at it, puzzled.

"I still don't know who the hell you are, but what I do know is this is absolutely none of your business," she said through clenched teeth. "Haven't you caused enough trouble?"

"I want an explanation," Ethan said, ignoring Knowles. "If you and Brian were in the cab that day, why didn't you mention it? You knew I was involved in the aftermath of that accident—I told you all about it—so why hide it, apart from the obvious?"

"Yeah, and why didn't you stay and try and help out instead of taking off like a rocket?" Knowles queried. "I could have died, you know. The police call it 'fleeing the scene,' which I suppose is why your boyfriend finally came to his senses about making a statement." He grunted. "Fat lot of good it did me."

Ethan tried to pretend Knowles wasn't there. "Vanessa, I asked you a question."

She sniffed and looked away, refusing to meet his gaze, but he could tell from her demeanor that she knew the game was up. "Brian was heading downtown, and I had an errand to run, so we shared a cab back from...our meeting," she began, her hazel eyes shining with tears as she spoke. "When we reached Fifth Avenue, I spotted you and Daisy on the street outside Tiffany's. I started to panic, worried that you might see us, even though it was unlikely, but..." She shook her head. "Brian tried to calm me down, and we started arguing, and then—"

"I knew it!" Knowles proclaimed. "I knew that gobshite driver wasn't paying attention! Walked out in front of him, my foot! Tell lover boy thanks very much. His lies fucked up my lawsuit."

Ethan couldn't believe it. "So you were actually there when it happened? What about when you saw Daisy and I trying to help? Did you just...sneak away hoping we wouldn't notice?"

Obviously, he hadn't noticed though. Why would he, when at the time, his only concern was for the injured Knowles?

He remembered the cab driver mentioning something about his fare abandoning him, but the last thing Ethan would've expected was Vanessa to be in cab, let alone contribute to the very accident that…

And right then, he wondered if up there somewhere that day, darling Jane was having a word in the ear of her beloved universe.

"So about this ring," Knowles continued.

Just then, Terri reappeared with a perturbed Daisy in tow. "Might I remind you all that this is a restaurant and I have customers to serve." Her voice was hard. "If you want to continue this, then please do so elsewhere."

Daisy stared at Vanessa's stricken face. "What's wrong?" she asked, and Ethan could sense her anxiety levels rising.

"It's nothing, darling," he soothed, reaching down to put an arm around her. "Why don't we do as Terri says and go back to our table? Did you have fun meeting the chef?" He was trying desperately to keep his voice light, while inside, he wanted to put a fist through the wall.

"Ethan, I—" Vanessa began, but he held up his hand.

"Now is not the time."

There must have been enough in his voice to warn her not to push it, as instead of continuing to argue, she quietly relented. "I'm sorry," she sobbed, turning on her heel and heading straight for the ladies' room.

He and Daisy made their way back toward their table, his legs weak, while vaguely aware of Knowles following.

"Dad? What's going on? Why is that man here? And why is Vanessa crying?" Daisy looked at Ethan for reassurance.

"It's okay. She's just…upset."

"Is it the baby?" Daisy asked, and right at that moment, Ethan was glad that he'd just sat down.

He stared at his daughter. "What?"

Terri raised an eyebrow. "Gary, now that you're here, you might as well make yourself useful," she urged, nudging him. "I've got some tables that need clearing."

"To hell with that." But something in her tone must have given Knowles pause, as he hesitated for a brief moment before reluctantly moving away, leaving Ethan and Daisy alone.

Ethan looked at his daughter. "Honey, what are you talking about? What's all this about a baby?"

Daisy looked around hesitantly, as if trying to locate Vanessa.

"We just had a little argument," he said by way of explanation. "I think she'll be gone awhile."

His daughter sighed and looked down at the table, where the platter of wedding nibbles had long since gone cold. "Please don't be mad," she said, looking guiltily up at him through her long eyelashes.

"What? Why would I be mad at you?" At this point, Ethan had no idea what was coming. What was all this about a *baby*?

"Okay." Daisy sighed again. "Well then, I think I'd better tell you everything."

Chapter 52

AFTER PRYING GARY AWAY FROM ETHAN AND WHATEVER DRAMA HE was having now, Terri strong-armed him into helping her clear tables by promising that she'd tell him what she knew.

Evidently he wasn't completely dumb, and once Rachel had revealed the ring was missing, he must have put it all together.

"Come on, Terri. You can't fool me. I saw the ring on Greene's missus. A bit coincidental that it just 'disappeared' the last time he was here? The very same time he came crying to me with some sorry story? And what is he doing back here anyway? Trying to rub Rachel's nose in it?"

She put her hands on her hips. "How many times do I have say it before it gets into your thick skull? The ring isn't yours. It never was—you admitted as much to me yourself."

Justin came rushing into the kitchen, but they both ignored him.

"As far as I'm concerned, it *is* Rachel's, and regardless of how we ended up with it, she adored that ring," Gary retorted. "But I wonder what she'll think when I tell her that her so-called best friend conspired to steal it from her. It was you, wasn't it? You and Greene in it together. I wonder what Rachel will think when she realizes she can't trust her own friend. What do you think about that? How is she going to feel?"

At that moment, the door from the dining room swung open.

"How am I going to feel about what?"

They all turned to face the doorway where Rachel stood, a perplexed expression on her face.

⚬~⚬

"What's up?" Rachel urged, laughing lightly. "Everyone's gone very quiet all of a sudden."

She quickly noticed that they had all become deathly silent upon her entry.

And what was Gary doing here? He looked worked up too; she recognized that vexed expression, and it seemed as though he and Terri were having a spat of some kind. Justin too had dropped whatever he was doing upon her arrival and had rushed into the kitchen ahead of her.

"Well? How am I going to feel about what?" she repeated, and a shiver of unease ran down her spine. Neither would meet her gaze. "What's going on? And am I seeing things, or was that Ethan out there? I'm almost certain I spotted him on my way in."

Terri smiled, but Rachel could tell it was forced. "Yes, he's here with his fiancée. They were thinking of hiring us to cater their wedding and are trying the tasting menu."

"Oh, so he did pop the question." Rachel smiled, unsure how to feel. "That's nice. I must go out and say hello."

But her words were automatic, because deep down she knew

that there was something not quite right about Ethan's presence here either. He lived in London, so why on earth would he want Gillini to cater for his wedding?

Gary spoke then. "Funny you should mention him," he said scathingly, and Terri shot him a look.

"Well, you've certainly no excuse not to catch up this time." Rachel tried to keep her voice light, but every bone in her body was telling her there was something awry.

"Oh, I've caught up with him all right," her fiancé replied.

"So what were you lot talking about?" she asked again. "I thought I heard my name being mentioned."

"Nothing, really," Terri told her. "We were all just chatting about the…wedding."

"Oh." *Of course*, Rachel thought, relaxing a little. Terri was her bridesmaid after all, so perhaps she was planning something that needed Gary's approval? And she'd walked in right in the middle of it. Whatever it was, she was sure she'd find out in time.

"What are you doing here anyway?" she asked Gary. "I thought you said you had something on with Sean."

"I did, and I just popped in for a sandwich on the way."

That wasn't especially unusual, but Rachel knew it annoyed Terri that he took advantage of free food because of their relationship. So that could have been what they were arguing about.

"How come you're here, boss?" Justin asked. "I thought you were taking the day off."

"I was bored." She laughed. "Can't keep away. Anyway, might as well give a hand while I'm here," she said, looking at the pile of dirty plates on a nearby countertop. "But first, I might pop out and say hi to Ethan."

"Ah, better leave it for the moment." Terri grimaced. "Last thing I heard, he and the girlfriend were having a bit of a...discussion," she said.

"Oh?"

"Yeah. Seems the missus had a bit on the side that Mr. High -and-Mighty didn't know about," Gary added snidely, and Rachel wondered how he could possibly be party to this.

"Okay. Well, I'll go and get changed, and maybe I'll get the chance to say hello before they leave."

"And I'll go back out and check on tables—" Terri began, but she stopped in her tracks when there came a soft knock on the restaurant's connecting door.

They all turned to see a young girl peek wide-eyed inside.

"Daisy, hi!" Rachel smiled, recognizing her immediately.

"It's okay. *I'll* check on tables," Terri said, giving the girl a light pat on the head as she passed while Gary just stood there, looking uncomfortable.

"Everything okay, sweetheart?" Rachel asked, going straight to her, but it was clear that the opposite was the case. She bent down in front of Daisy and took her hand.

The child's bottom lip trembled. "I'm so glad I found you. Vanessa came back from the bathroom, and now she and Dad are fighting. I think I really messed everything up."

"Oh, honey, I'm sure it's probably just a silly disagreement. Adults do that sometimes. Please don't think it's your fault." Rachel gently tucked a lock of Daisy's blond hair behind her ear.

"No, it is all my fault. I told him everything." Daisy began fiddling with the hem of her dress. "I told him what I thought about the ring."

"What ring, honey?" Rachel asked, coming closer.

The little girl's eyes were filled with tears. She hiccupped loudly. "The Tiffany's ring was supposed to fit Vanessa, but it didn't. Mum always said that she and Dad were a perfect fit, that when you found the right person, everything fit. But the ring doesn't."

Rachel pulled her into a hug. "I understand why you might think that, honey, but I suspect your mum might have meant something other than jewelry."

But wait. Vanessa had a Tiffany's ring too?

"My mum also said that Tiffany's was magical, so maybe the ring didn't fit Vanessa because she's not the right person for my dad." Daisy looked up mournfully, tears in her eyes. "I know she's been keeping secrets from him. That's why they're fighting now."

Rachel struggled to keep up with what was going on. "Adults often fight, sweetheart, even when they love each other," she soothed, wondering what on earth was going on with Ethan and his girlfriend. Especially if he'd just proposed.

"It fit you, though." Daisy sniffed, looking closely at her.

Rachel frowned. "What?"

"The ring, the one you got by mistake. Dad said that it fit you."

Rachel wasn't sure where all this had come from, but Daisy sure seemed like one very confused little girl. "Honey, what makes you think that? How would I possibly…"

Gary stepped forward. "Um, Rach?"

Rachel shrugged him off, a knot of unease growing in her

stomach. There was something very off about what Daisy had said, about this entire situation actually.

"Something happened in New York, something really weird," Gary continued. "I was going to tell you but—"

Right then, Ethan himself came rushing through the door, followed by Terri.

"Daisy!" he gasped, going to his daughter and engulfing her in his arms. "What were you thinking slipping away like that without telling me? I was so afraid you'd—oh, Rachel, hi."

He stopped short, reddening a little, and somehow she knew instinctively that his multiple appearances here had nothing to do with concern for Gary after his accident.

Nothing at all.

"Where's Vanessa?" Daisy asked.

"She went back to her mum's house, buttercup." Ethan looked embarrassed. "I'll tell you all about it later."

"I told Rachel about the ring," his daughter cried, and she saw Ethan cast a wary glance toward Gary.

"Daisy, I'm just going on a break now. Fancy sharing a nice big hot chocolate with me—with marshmallows?" Terri suggested brightly, and the young girl looked at her father for permission.

"It's okay, honey. Go with Terri. I'm just going to have a little chat with Rachel."

Daisy beamed. "Great, Dad! Don't forget what I told you, okay?" she said, casting a conspiratorial glance at Rachel as they exited.

The problem was that Rachel seemed to be only one who wasn't in on the conspiracy. Everyone—even the absent Justin—all seemed clearly privy to what was becoming more and more baffling by the second.

There was a momentary silence as Rachel looked back and forth between Gary and Ethan, unsure what to think. "Okay," she said finally. "What am I missing?"

Chapter 53

"Quite a lot, babe," Gary began, looking disdainfully at Ethan. "So, Professor, tell us again how your 'research' went. Rachel told me all about your bullshit cover story."

"Oh, for goodness' sake."

"I'm sorry to tell you that this guy and your so-called best friend have been lying and plotting against you," Rachel's fiancé said solemnly.

Rachel looked at Ethan. "What is he talking about?" she asked, and she noticed that he looked tired and defeated. Those lively blue eyes now looked flat and dulled.

"You're a good one to talk about lies," he said to Gary.

"Oh yeah? Tell us all about your book, Greene," Gary replied with a sneer. "The one you told her all about at your cozy dinner."

She looked at him blankly. "What does Ethan's book have to do with anything?"

"There is no bloody book, Rach. It was just a big lie, another excuse to try and get in your pants."

"Oh, for heaven's sake!" Ethan glared angrily at him. "How about you tell her why I was forced to come up with a cover story in the first place?"

Gary shrugged. "Hell if I know. Because you were trying to manipulate her? And anyway, if you were so sure, then why couldn't you just come out with it from the start?"

"Because I didn't want to hurt her, that's why. Although you seem to have no problem with it, and you're supposed to be her fiancé."

Rachel's head was spinning. "There's no book?" she said to Ethan, who nodded grimly. "And if you didn't come here for research, then why did you? Clearly it's something to do with Gary's accident, although Terri's right. In retrospect, your concern for his well-being did seem over the top."

Obviously there *was* more to Ethan than met the eye, which disappointed her. So his apparent interest in her—her hopes and dreams—was merely part of some ruse? Now she felt stupid and utterly naive to think that maybe they had a connection of sorts. When she'd spied him and Daisy on the way in, her heart had unexpectedly lightened, something Rachel couldn't quite explain, since she barely knew them, really. But sitting here in her restaurant, the two of them just looked so…right.

"I had a completely legitimate reason," Ethan pleaded, and to his credit, he looked shamefaced. "But when it came down it, I just couldn't tell you. It's stupid…I can't explain it."

"Couldn't tell me *what,* for crying out loud?"

"About the ring."

By now, Rachel was completely bewildered. "My ring—the one I lost?" She looked at Gary.

"I bought it for Vanessa," Ethan said gently.

"But how would a ring that you bought for your girlfriend end up with—"

Then suddenly Rachel remembered something he had said way back at the hospital about how he'd lost something at the scene of the accident…and then Gary's half-hearted and, if she thought about it now, rather low-key proposal when they exchanged gifts…

And just like that, coupled with Daisy's comment about Ethan's girlfriend's ring also being from Tiffany's, all the pieces finally fell into place.

"Oh my God," she gasped, turning to Gary, feeling sick. "It wasn't yours. The ring, the Tiffany's bag, it didn't belong to you at all, did it?"

"There's nothing to say it belonged to *him* either," Gary began, but she put a hand up to stop him.

"I'm so sorry, Rachel," Ethan insisted, his face pained. "There was a mix-up when Daisy and I helped him after the accident, but I didn't discover it until the next day, when Vanessa went to open her gift and she got yours instead."

She tasted bile in her mouth. "I can't believe that you proposed to me with a ring that you didn't buy," she said to Gary, tears filling her eyes. "One that was meant for someone else. What kind of person would steal—"

"Hold on. I didn't steal anything."

"What do you call laying claim to something that is not rightfully yours?" Ethan interjected hotly, and the two men glared at each other.

"What was in mine?" she asked then, her tone robotic. "You said that you discovered the mistake when your girlfriend opened her gift," she said to Ethan before turning to Gary again, who was staring at his feet. "What was I supposed to get?" she repeated forcefully, knowing deep down that while it was something from Tiffany's, it certainly wasn't a diamond ring.

There was a long, tension-filled silence until eventually Gary spoke. "A charm bracelet," he admitted, putting her out of her misery.

A charm bracelet.

Rachel's heart plunged to the depths of her stomach. She wanted to die of embarrassment.

Obviously he'd been just as surprised as she was by the engagement ring. Which could only mean one thing—he had never intended to propose in the first place.

And not only that, but they all knew, she realized now, mortified.

Ethan, Gary, Terri, possibly even Justin. They had seen her dancing around like a loon about her so-called fairy-tale engagement, yet none of them had bothered to enlighten her.

And this, possibly more than anything else, hurt the most.

"A charm bracelet," she repeated stonily, and in a quick flash of insight, she recalled the Tiffany's transaction on Gary's credit card, which in retrospect made perfect sense.

Ethan was telling the truth; this was no bad dream, no embarrassing nightmare from which she'd wake up and feel silly.

She looked at Gary with disdain. "You proposed to me with a ring that belonged to someone else?" she said, her voice barely a whisper. "How could you? How could anyone stoop so low?"

He was reluctant to meet her gaze. "What was I supposed to do,

Rach? You were over the moon about that ring and the proposal, and I knew if I said something that you would—"

"Of course you should have said something! Instead, you chose to make a complete fool of me by going along with this huge charade!" She wanted to die of mortification, all the plans she'd been making, not only for the wedding but for the rest of their lives.

She'd been such a fool.

"I didn't know what to do. It caught me by surprise too," he said quietly, seemingly unable to offer any other explanation.

"And you." Now she turned her attentions to Ethan. "You knew the whole time, and you lied bald-faced right from the beginning. All this nonsense about being concerned for Gary and researching some book. Christ, you must all think I'm a complete idiot."

"Rachel, no, of course not," Ethan replied, looking horrified. "I didn't want to upset you. None of us did. And to be frank, it wasn't my place to say anything." Again he stared accusingly at Gary. "I was just considering your feelings."

"Why would any of you think that leading me on this…*farce* is considering my feelings!" she exploded. "What kind of imbecile do you think I am?" Much to her annoyance, she began to sob and saw Ethan move to comfort her. "No," she cried, stepping back. Tears stained her cheeks. "Don't touch me. Don't any of you come near me."

Then she thought of something else. "Where is the ring now?" she asked, realizing that its sudden disappearance no longer seemed so inexplicable. "Oh," she said then, answering her own question. But then she remembered little Daisy's comment earlier about the ring not being the right fit for Ethan's girlfriend.

"So what happened? Did you have a crisis of conscience or something?" she asked Gary. Yet why did he act so surprised yesterday when she admitted that it had been lost?

Christ, had he been up front with her about *anything*?

"As far as I was concerned, the ring was yours now, and there's no way I was handing it over just because some—"

"It was me," Terri injected then, and Rachel turned to look at her, unaware that she'd since crept back in. "I helped Ethan get it back that time he was here. I knew that Gary wasn't prepared to own up, and I couldn't let you—"

Gary took a step forward. "Hey, there's no proof that it was ever even—"

"Save it, Gary," Rachel spat. This was all becoming more hurtful by the second. To think that all along, the people she cared most about were plotting and planning behind her back, and in the most patronizing ways. "Don't say another word to me, any of you. Stop trying to make excuses for your actions. You are all liars. All three of you."

Ethan reacted as if he had been slapped. "Rachel…" he began.

"I'm glad you got your ring back," she told him jadedly, "and that it's finally on the right person's finger." She gave a withering glance at Gary. "No thanks to you."

With that, Rachel walked out of the kitchen, straight through the dining room of her beloved restaurant, and didn't look back.

Chapter 54

THE FOLLOWING EVENING, ETHAN LANDED AT HEATHROW, HIS heart heavy. He walked through the airport as if in a trance, Daisy at his side.

He thought again about Vanessa and Brian and wanted to take his so-called friend and tear him limb from limb. Talk about betrayal. But of course, that wasn't the only secret Vanessa had been carrying, something that much to his humiliation, he'd discovered from Daisy.

During all that hullabaloo at the bistro, when his daughter had mentioned something about a baby and explained about what she'd found, Ethan hadn't known what to think. So when Vanessa had returned to the table and Daisy in turn muttered something about going off to the ladies' room, he knew it was the first thing he had to ask, even before discussing Brian.

Her eyes were still red-rimmed from crying and her face pale, but when he broached the question, her skin turned so white, it was almost translucent.

"What do you mean?" she asked, looking rather like she had when Gary had accused of her of being in the taxi in New York.

Like a rabbit caught in headlights.

"It's a simple question." His voice was hard. "Why was there a pregnancy test in our garbage?"

"What?" She looked at him, her eyes unsure. "How did you—"

"Is there something else I should know, Vanessa?" he demanded.

She shook her head, her eyes downcast and her face defeated. "No. I thought there might be. With the U.S. time lag, I thought I might've missed a pill, but—"

"Contraception? I was under the impression that you couldn't have children."

But Ethan realized now that this too had been a smoke screen.

In fact, when he thought about how Vanessa was so professionally dogged about getting what she wanted, he wondered why it had never crossed his mind that she might do the same in her personal life.

She had played him all along, played on his gullibility.

"Why, Vanessa? Why did you agree to marry me, knowing that our relationship was built on lies?"

"I don't honestly know," she replied, tears in her eyes. "I did—do—want to marry you. I never wanted to go through the whole childbirth thing, and I suppose I thought that with Daisy, we were a ready-made family. I wouldn't need to be a mum as such, and nobody would expect me to replace Jane. Not that I could have anyway," she added, her tone bitter.

"How dare you?" Ethan said, his tone hardening.

Whatever he'd thought before about Daisy's crazy notion about the ring not fitting, perhaps she'd been onto something all the same.

Vanessa stood up to leave. She took the ring off and placed it on the table. "I'm sorry. For what it's worth, I do love you and Daisy. But you were never truly going to let me in."

Now, Ethan thought about what she'd said and wondered if there was any truth in it. *She loved him with too clear a vision to fear his cloudiness.*

Obviously not enough.

Meanwhile, they'd gone their separate ways, Vanessa back to her parents' and he and Daisy to a nearby hotel, and he spent the following day cheering his daughter up by taking her around the sights before getting a Sunday evening flight back to Heathrow.

Maybe there had been signs for a while that things weren't right, and all this business with the ring had helped him realize it.

As Jane would no doubt have said, everything happened for a reason.

He spent the rest of the journey so deep in thought that he didn't even realize the taxi had come to a stop in front of their town house.

"Mate? This the place?" the driver asked.

Daisy nudged him. "Dad, we're here."

Ethan snapped to attention, surprised. He paid the driver and grabbed their bags, then trundled up the steps slowly and extracted his key from his pocket.

Clearly after what had happened, Vanessa must have taken the next available flight back. It hadn't taken her long to remove the few boxes she had brought with her when she moved in. In retrospect, her keeping her old apartment and all her furniture should probably have been the first indication that this arrangement wouldn't be forever.

"She's gone," Daisy said unnecessarily.

"I know, poppet," he confirmed. "Looks like it's just you and me again."

"I'm sorry, Dad," she said through a large sob. "It's all my fault for losing the ring, isn't it?" Suddenly she began to cry openly, and Ethan's heart melted. She took so much on herself.

He pulled his daughter close and led her toward the sofa. "Of course none of this is your fault. These things just happen sometimes, and it's nobody's fault."

Daisy buried her head on his shoulder. "I'm sorry for not taking better care of it," she mumbled through her tears.

"Honey, it doesn't matter. The ring has nothing to do with this." But of course, that wasn't strictly true, was it?

"Are you mad at me?"

"No, darling. Of course I'm not mad."

"But you and Vanessa aren't going to get married now?"

"No, we're not. And that test you found? There was no baby. It was only a way to check if there might be one."

She nodded thoughtfully. "I think I might have liked a brother or sister."

"I know, poppet." Ethan sighed. "I would have liked that for you too."

"Vanessa's not coming back." It was more of a statement than a question.

"No. But it's okay. You and me, we're a team. You know that. We only need each other, don't we?"

❧

"Who is it?"

"It's me. Please, I need to talk to you."

"Leave me alone. I don't want to talk."

"Okay, fine, but maybe you'd like to eat?" Terri tried to keep her voice light, but inside, her nerves were in tatters. If Rachel didn't respond to this—their mutual joke—then their friendship was well and truly over. "I've brought some of my famous sourdough."

It seemed as if several minutes passed until finally the door opened just a fraction. From what little Terri could see of her, Rachel's face looked drawn and she had her hair pulled back.

"Well, I am hungry," she said, and Terri saw some of the old sparkle behind the facade.

"Thought you might be." Terri handed her the loaf. "I really need to talk to you. Please."

"Then talk."

"Can't I come in?"

"Nope."

Although Terri had always known that this whole thing was going to end badly, she hadn't truly anticipated how much Rachel would suffer. But looking at it all from her point of view, the people she loved and who were supposed to love her back had betrayed her.

"I'm so sorry. I know I should have told you the truth. But honestly, I didn't know what to do. You were so happy about the engagement."

"Exactly. I was so happy. And you knew it was all a lie. Why let me go on thinking that I was in some kind of fairy tale and Gary was my Prince Charming? To think that he was basically railroaded into a proposal..." Her hurt and embarrassment were plain to see. "Everyone knew the truth except me. Imagine how I feel. Manipulated. Lied to. Now I see what all this was... I wasn't allowed to make up my own mind. Everything was manufactured by you, Gary, even Ethan, pretending at that dinner that he was interested in my blathering on about my hopes and dreams. None of it was real."

Terri hung her head. "You're right and I'm sorry. Even now, I'm not sure why I didn't tell you straight out, but please believe me when I tell you that the last thing any of us wanted was to hurt you."

"But why treat me like a child? I really hate the way everyone does that all the time. I'm a grown woman, not some toddler who needs protecting."

"I know, but I suppose I've always thought that you're too quick to see the best in people, whereas I'm—"

"A complete cynic who's suspicious of everyone's motives?"

Terri looked down at her shoes. "You're right. Maybe I am too quick to think the worst. But I wasn't wrong about this, was I? And I just couldn't stand by and let Gary get away with it. You deserve so much better. And," she added softly, "I think you need to realize that too. Someone like him was all wrong for you, Rach. I don't know. I always got the sense that Gary just...never fit."

Something changed in Rachel's expression then, but the look was gone almost as soon as it had appeared, and then she promptly changed the subject. "How's everything at work?" she asked, her neutral tone still not giving much away.

"Fine. Justin is holding the fort at the moment." Terri paused, realizing they were treading on dangerous ground here.

What if Rachel had decided she wanted out of Gillini, that because of Terri's deception, she was prepared to give up the business they'd so carefully built up? Or worse, that she wanted Terri out?

"We're looking forward to having you back though," she added delicately. "The place isn't the same without you."

"Hmm, just as long as our customers aren't choking on stuff in their food," Rachel replied archly, and Terri sighed an inward relief at the brief glimmer of humor in her tone. "So are going to share this with me or what?" her friend added, moving aside at the doorway, indicating that Terri should come in.

"I'd love to." Terri stepped past her, and the two proceeded to Rachel's tiny living room. She turned to face her. "Again, I'm so sorry. Swiping the ring the way I did was especially stupid, I know that. But Gary was adamant he wasn't going to own up, and I felt so bad for Ethan. For what it's worth, I know he truly did care about your feelings."

"Maybe, but he lied too," Rachel said, and Terri could tell that she was truly disappointed by this. "You're right. Maybe I do trust too easily."

"Hey, don't ever change either." Terri rested a hand on her friend's shoulder. "While a cynic like me tends to bring a dreamer down to earth, believe me, it's so much more rewarding to have someone whose head's in the clouds to take you by the hand on occasion and show you that view."

A lump came to her throat as she realized this was exactly what

Rachel had been doing for *her* all these years. The world was always so much brighter when seen through her eyes.

"Thank you for saying that." Rachel pulled her into a warm embrace, and Terri knew then that her wonderful friend was going to be okay.

"So has Gary been in touch?" she asked.

"He's been trying but I don't want to hear his excuses." Rachel's tone was hard afresh, but Terri could hear some regret behind it too. "I know he carried on like some big-time property tycoon, but we both know he's just a man with a van," she added archly, and Terri chuckled, realizing that perhaps Rachel wasn't quite as gullible as they'd all thought. "Dunno. I suppose I've always found that a little endearing in a way. He must have thought all his Christmases had come at once when I opened up that box."

"Are you going to forgive him?" Terri bloody hoped not.

"No, I don't think there's any going back from finding out he'd never intended to propose at all. And that he didn't want the same things I did."

"Perhaps he genuinely didn't know where the ring had come from at the start and was worried that Ethan was chasing you?"

"No, Ethan was just chasing his twenty-grand investment." Rachel gave a wan smile. "I feel so bad for little Daisy though. She seemed to think that the whole thing was fated somehow. Sweet."

Terri nodded.

"I remember him saying something before about her mother being a bit airy-fairy," Rachel continued. "And then when things went south, she must have taken what she'd said about Tiffany's to heart."

"That fiancée really got a bum deal, didn't she?" Terri gave an ironic chuckle. "Her future stepdaughter thinking you're Cinderella and she's the ugly stepsister. Though it seems she *was* actually a villain of sorts," she added, explaining what she'd overheard at the restaurant.

"That's terrible. Poor Ethan," Rachel said. "Still, if nothing else, at least he found his glass slipper."

Chapter 55

It had been one hell of a month, Ethan thought. But now at least, life had gotten back to that normal comfortable rhythm he was used to.

No surprises, no drama.

For Daisy's sake, he tried to appear okay. Every now and then, though, he caught her staring at him with a peculiar look on her face, keenly aware of what he was doing and his moods.

He tried not to think about Vanessa and the fool she'd made of him.

Clearly she'd tipped Brian off, and Ethan had been avoiding calls from his so-called friend ever since. He wasn't interested in excuses and explanations, and while he was hurt by their betrayal, he was also taken aback by how little it actually bothered him.

If he truly did love Vanessa, if he really felt deep down in his heart that she was the right person for him, then by rights, he should be inconsolable.

But he wasn't. Instead, he felt almost…numbed by recent events. The mix-up with the ring, the complications in trying to get it back, it was all such a big mess, there was no rhyme or reason to it.

However, he knew he needed to be strong for his girl now and stop mooning over what might have been.

It was the end of a long week, and he was wrapping up his duties at the university. He left campus and took a cab to Daisy's friend Tanya's house. Now that Vanessa was out of the picture, she often went there after school until Ethan finished his lectures.

He knocked on the door, and Tanya's mother answered. "Oh, hello, Ethan. Come inside. The girls are playing upstairs."

Ethan knew the routine. Once Daisy came down to collect her things, Janice would try and insist they stay for dinner. Although it was never said, he knew the other girl's mum was convinced he was a clueless bachelor who couldn't possibly understand his daughter, let alone cook her a good meal.

Sure enough, as soon as the girls thundered into the room, Janice looked at him. "Tell me that you two will stay for dinner. We have plenty."

"Thank you again, but Daisy and I have things to do tonight."

He had planned a fun evening for the two of them. He was going to cook her favorite meal or eat junk food and stay up late to watch a movie, whatever she liked.

Janice smiled and nodded. "Perhaps another night?" she suggested, and Ethan idly wondered if the woman had taken some kind of shine to him now that he was once again unattached.

He hoped not. More hassle of that kind was the last thing he needed.

"So how was your day?" Daisy asked as they walked home.

He reached for her hand. "It was pretty good. The best part, though, is that it's Friday and I get to spend tonight with my special girl."

"And who's your special girl?" she asked, looking sideways at him.

"I don't know. Let me think for a minute," he joked, figuring she was teasing. Then he looked down and saw that her expression was solemn. "You are of course," he insisted, starting to tickle her. "Who else?"

She sighed. "I wish I knew."

Ethan regarded her thoughtfully, worried that this was yet another phase she was going through.

Since the incident in Dublin, Daisy had seemed dissatisfied. He didn't think she was missing Vanessa or anything, more that she was disappointed in him for some reason.

"So what movie do you fancy watching tonight?" he asked, deciding to change the subject.

Daisy looked up at him as if he hadn't spoken. "Are you upset about Vanessa?" she asked.

Ethan looked at her. "Of course I was at first. You know that," he admitted. "But ultimately, I realized we weren't right for each other."

She furrowed her brow, clearly thinking hard. "So who is right for you, Dad?"

He grinned. "You are, buttercup. You know that. You're the only lady in my life, and I'm happy to keep it that way."

"What about New York, though?" Daisy insisted again. "What about the Tiffany's magic Mum talked about?"

"Sweetheart…"

"And if you say you're happy just being my dad, then why are you so sad all the time?"

Ethan was slightly taken aback by her perceptiveness. "What makes you think I'm sad?"

She rolled her eyes. "Dad, I am not an idiot."

Perhaps she was right. Lately, he was indeed down in the dumps.

The ache of Jane's absence seemed to have returned, this time stronger than ever, and as each day wore on, he wondered how long it would be until these feelings faded and got lost to time.

How long would it be until he was truly happy again?

He didn't know, and he wondered if he would still be thinking about Jane when he was ninety years old, wrinkled and alone.

And he sorely wished that if—as Daisy insisted—his beloved had been intervening from above to set things right, he understood what she was trying to say.

Back at the town house, while Daisy was in the shower, he set about making dinner. He gathered together all the ingredients for her favorite, chili con carne, but it was a light meal on its own, and Ethan knew he'd need some kind of accompaniment. Either that or he would end up gorging himself on chocolate and ice cream later, and he knew that wouldn't go down well with Daisy.

He opened the freezer and rummaged around the back of it for the frozen garlic bread he kept for situations just like this. Then he paused, spotting the purple wrapping he was almost too familiar with by now. A bread loaf from Gillini. He hadn't put it there, so he deduced it must have been Daisy who'd brought it back from Dublin that time.

Taking it out, Ethan couldn't help but think that bread seemed determined to haunt him.

Just when he thought he'd left all that behind, the place had reared its head again.

Still, however it had ended up here, there was no denying that it was amazing, and it would go nicely with tonight's meal.

As he took Rachel's olive bread out of its wrapper, the words struck him.

A woman to bake you bread...

Ethan raised his gaze skyward.

"Thank you," he whispered with a smile. "*Now* I get it."

Chapter 56

It was a crazy Sunday lunchtime, and Rachel sorely wished she hadn't so readily agreed to swap shifts today.

But she had little else to occupy her these days. Her and Gary's disastrous romance was very definitely finished.

Like Terri said, she deserved better, and despite his pleas, she was unwilling to let him off the hook for his deception. Especially as it seemed this wasn't the only secret Gary had been keeping from her. He'd admitted how his business had practically gone bankrupt, how the debts kept building up, and perhaps most embarrassing of all, that he was back living with his mother and had been for some time.

Which completely explained Mary Knowles's shock and annoyance when faced with Rachel's lavish diamond on the night of the engagement party, she recalled wryly.

So by all accounts, that ring brought Gary about as much luck as it did her.

But for some reason, she found herself thinking more and more about Ethan and that dinner they'd shared before everything went sideways.

She felt a bit guilty about being so hard on him that day it all came out for being less than forthcoming with the truth when he was merely trying to spare her feelings. Pretty touching considering what was at stake.

And while she'd first believed that perhaps she'd made yet another character-judgment error, pouring her heart out to another man who truly couldn't care less, Rachel recalled that it wasn't all one-sided either. Ethan had opened up to her too about his own—and as it turned out equally ill-fated—relationship.

So much for the famous Tiffany's magic.

Then there was Daisy, a little girl so serious and literal that Rachel could understand why he was so keen to give her some stability. The poor thing was terrified of losing her father, understandable given what had happened to her mum.

She hoped they were both doing okay.

Just then Jen, one of the waitresses, rushed through to the kitchen from out front, a hassled expression on her face.

"Rachel, I'm really sorry, but there's this customer at the bakery counter giving me grief."

She frowned. "What's the problem?"

"Well, he's complaining about the olive bread." Jen shook her head wearily. "Says it's stale."

"What? I made that batch myself this morning."

"I know and I told him that, but I think he's just stuck up." Jen grinned. "Cute though."

Rachel made a face. Cute he might be, but that was no excuse for being rude to her staff.

"He's insisting on talking to a manager. Do you mind?"

"Oh man." She could feel the beginnings of a serious migraine. She wiped her hands on her apron, repositioned any flyaway hair under her cap, and, happy that she looked confident and in control, prepared to face the music. "At the bakery counter, you said?"

Jen nodded apologetically. "Yep."

Putting on her best managerial smile, Rachel went out front and headed directly for the bakery counter.

But realizing who was standing at it, she stopped short.

"Ethan!" she gasped, eyes wide. "What are you doing here? And Daisy too. Lovely to see you both, but I think there's some mistake." She looked back toward the kitchen uncertainly. "I mean my colleague said…"

He looked at her, his handsome face unreadable. "Yes. As I explained, I'm just not happy about this bread."

Rachel was taken aback by his solemn tone, but she noticed that Daisy wouldn't look at her and was trying not to smile. "Well, I'm very sorry about that," she replied, wondering why he was being so formal. "What seems to be the problem?"

This felt surreal. After all that had happened, why were Ethan and Daisy back in Dublin at all, let alone complaining about her bread?

"It's not fresh," he said.

"Of course it's fresh," she replied defensively.

Daisy started to giggle, and Rachel felt as though she was the butt of yet another joke.

"Ask her, Dad!" the young girl blurted and then looked quickly at her father as if she'd said something out of turn.

Ask her what?

"Well," Ethan began, and now there was a smile in his voice. "I was wondering if there was any chance you might make a fresh batch."

"I don't understand."

"Perhaps just for me?" he added meaningfully, and her heart skipped a beat as she thought she realized what he was referring to.

She gulped.

"You want...*me* to bake bread...for you," she repeated, her voice robotic as she tried to figure out if this was real or if she was imagining things.

"Yes, and for Daisy too. If you'd like to, that is." His voice was gentle, and she raised her gaze to look at him. His blue eyes were soft and hopeful. "I know my being in London might be a problem, but I'm sure we'll find ways to keep it fresh."

Nothing was making sense anymore. Yet still Rachel knew in her heart what he was saying, knew exactly what he was asking.

A woman who would bake him bread...

She stared back at Ethan holding Daisy's hand, not sure where this was headed, but whatever it was, she already knew it felt right. She'd known it that night over dinner and had sensed it again when she'd seen them both reappear in the bistro that day before everything went crazy.

Tiffany's magic? Rachel didn't think so. This felt a lot more like the helping hand of good old Sicilian family tradition.

She looked at them both in turn and smiled. "I'd be happy to bake you two all the bread you want. But I must warn you," she added lightly, "no hidden surprises. What you see is what you get."

"And everything we need," Ethan replied, reaching for her hand, while little Daisy completed the circle.

When you found the right person, everything fit.

Reading Group Guide

1. What are Ethan's reasons for marrying Vanessa? What do you think should be the biggest deciding factor when choosing to marry someone?

2. How would you characterize Gary Knowles? Why did Rachel gift him the trip to New York?

3. Why doesn't Ethan immediately explain the jewelry mix-up to Vanessa when she opens the wrong gift? What do you think her reaction would have been if he had admitted that he meant to give her an engagement ring?

4. Daisy's anxieties often manifest in fear of junk food or other things that her mother deemed "unhealthy." What is she actually afraid of, and why does she fixate on food?

5. Why does Gary decide to go through with the proposal after Rachel surprises him by unwrapping the ring? If Rachel could read his mind in that moment, how do you think she would feel?

6. Thanks to Jane, Daisy believes firmly in fate and thinks the ring was always meant for Rachel. How much do you believe in fate?

7. Gary, Ethan, and Terri all lie to Rachel with the intent of sparing her feelings at some point throughout the story. How was Rachel ultimately affected? Which lie hurt her the most?

8. Ethan decides that Gary is not a wholehearted villain but just a man who got carried away. What does this opinion reveal about Ethan as a character? Have you ever been in a situation that seemed to spiral totally out of your control?

A Conversation
with the Author

What was the initial inspiration for *Something from Tiffany's*?

During a visit to New York, I was in Tiffany's Fifth Avenue store when a man from the Diamond Floor got in to the elevator carrying the same little blue bag that I and everyone else had. I immediately thought about the chaos it might cause if a Tiffany's bag containing a diamond ring got mixed up with something considerably less significant (and expensive!) and realized this could be the basis for a fun story.

Some of the themes in the story tie to the idea of fate versus free will. What made you want to explore those ideas?

Although I'm a pragmatist at heart, the dreamer in me also loves the notion that the universe can (and often does!) throw up surprises, so fate versus free will is a common theme in many of my novels including *Something from Tiffany's*.

I suspect most of us like to think that we're in control of our own destiny, but it's comforting to feel that maybe we're part of something bigger too. And that sometimes the stars align in our favor and something works out (or doesn't!) simply because it was meant to be.

This book was originally published ten years ago. Were there parts that you updated from the original version? What made you decide to make those updates?

Within those ten years, life's moved at an incredibly fast pace, so upon rereading the novel with fresh eyes, I was immediately mindful that there were certain elements (primarily technology-related) that might jar modern readers. iPods and landline telephones are pretty much consigned to the past now, social media and app usage is far more commonplace, etc. So I felt it best to remove/amend some of the more dated references, and I also freshened up some of the dialogue and character interactions, while keeping the heart of the story intact.

Talk to us a little about the setting for this book and why you decided to make New York such a central part of the story as an author who lives in Ireland.

I adore the city and am inspired by it every time I visit, so much so that I've set five books there! Manhattan is a hive of energy and a melting pot of people from all over in comparison to Ireland, which is so tiny you practically know everyone!

NYC just teems with energy; it's impossible not to feel inspired everywhere you go. With so many gorgeous locations too, it also feels like one giant movie set, and when I write about it, I try to bottle up all that energy and use it to transport readers there so that they can experience it also.

The Tiffany's brand is so central to the story here, and yet none of your characters are extremely wealthy or overly extravagant (beyond Gary and his motorbike). What were you hoping to convey to readers about value, excess, and privilege when it comes to objects of perceived worth?

Tiffany & Co. continues to capture the imagination and has done a remarkable job of making such a luxurious brand feel almost accessible for so many, primarily because of the famed little blue box. There's an almost mystical allure attached to that and the Fifth Avenue store, thanks to a certain Ms. Hepburn.

In this story, while the ring is of course expensive, it's not so much the cost but the sentiment surrounding it that's most important. Some of the characters even remark that the ring has a mind of its own and is destined to end up with the right person. It's the magical element (akin to Cinderella's glass slipper!) and personal significance—as opposed to the monetary value—attached to a Tiffany's purchase, that I hoped to explore. For me, that little blue box is of course also the ultimate symbol for that all-important fairy-tale ending.

About the Author

Melissa Hill is a *USA Today* and international bestselling author living in County Wicklow, Ireland.

Her warm contemporary novels of family, friendship, and romance are regular chart-toppers worldwide and have been translated into twenty-six languages.

A Hollywood adaptation of her international bestseller *Something from Tiffany's* by Reese Witherspoon's production company Hello Sunshine and Amazon Studios is coming as a major motion picture for release in 2022.

Many of her novels and stories, including *A Gift to Remember* and *The Charm Bracelet* have also been adapted for screen, with multiple other titles in development for movies and TV.

For more info, visit her website melissahill.info or get in touch via social media at facebook.com/melissahillbooks and instagram.com/melissahillbooks.